Splatoon™

VOL. 10

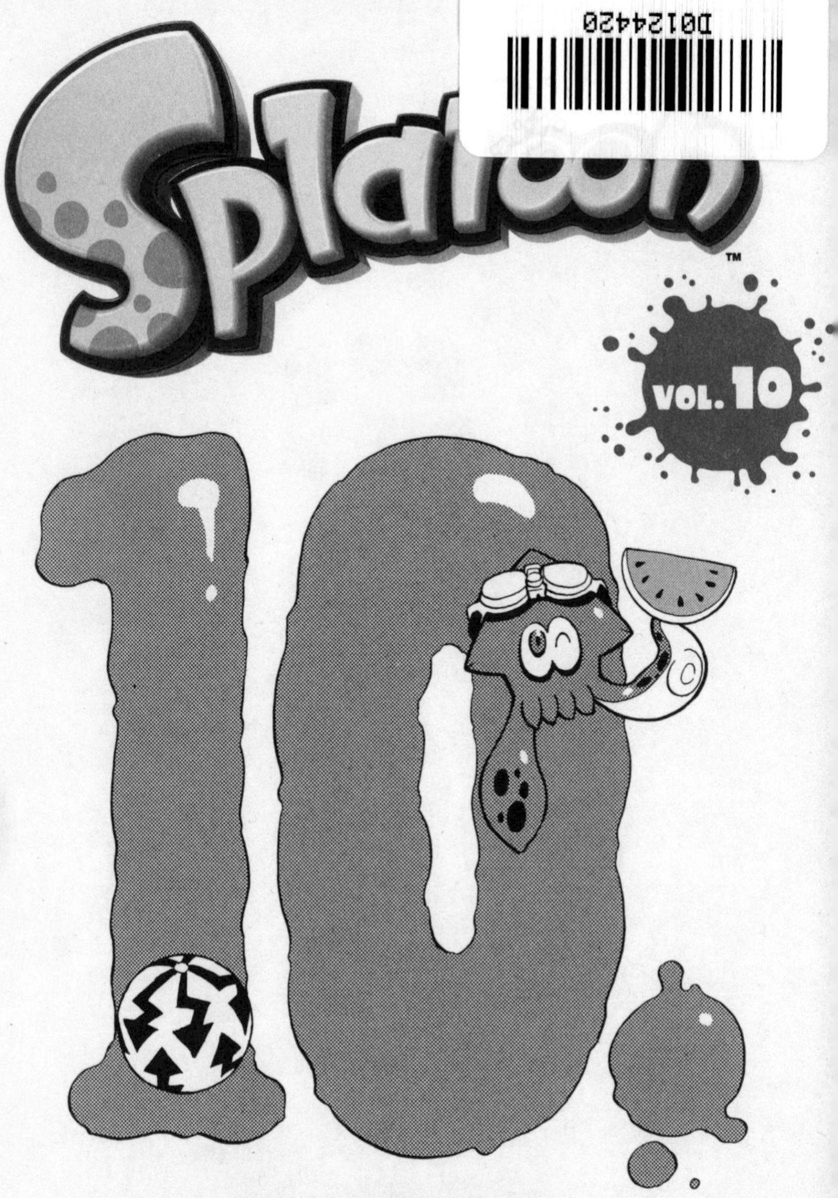

STORY AND ART BY

Sankichi Hinodeya

CONTENTS

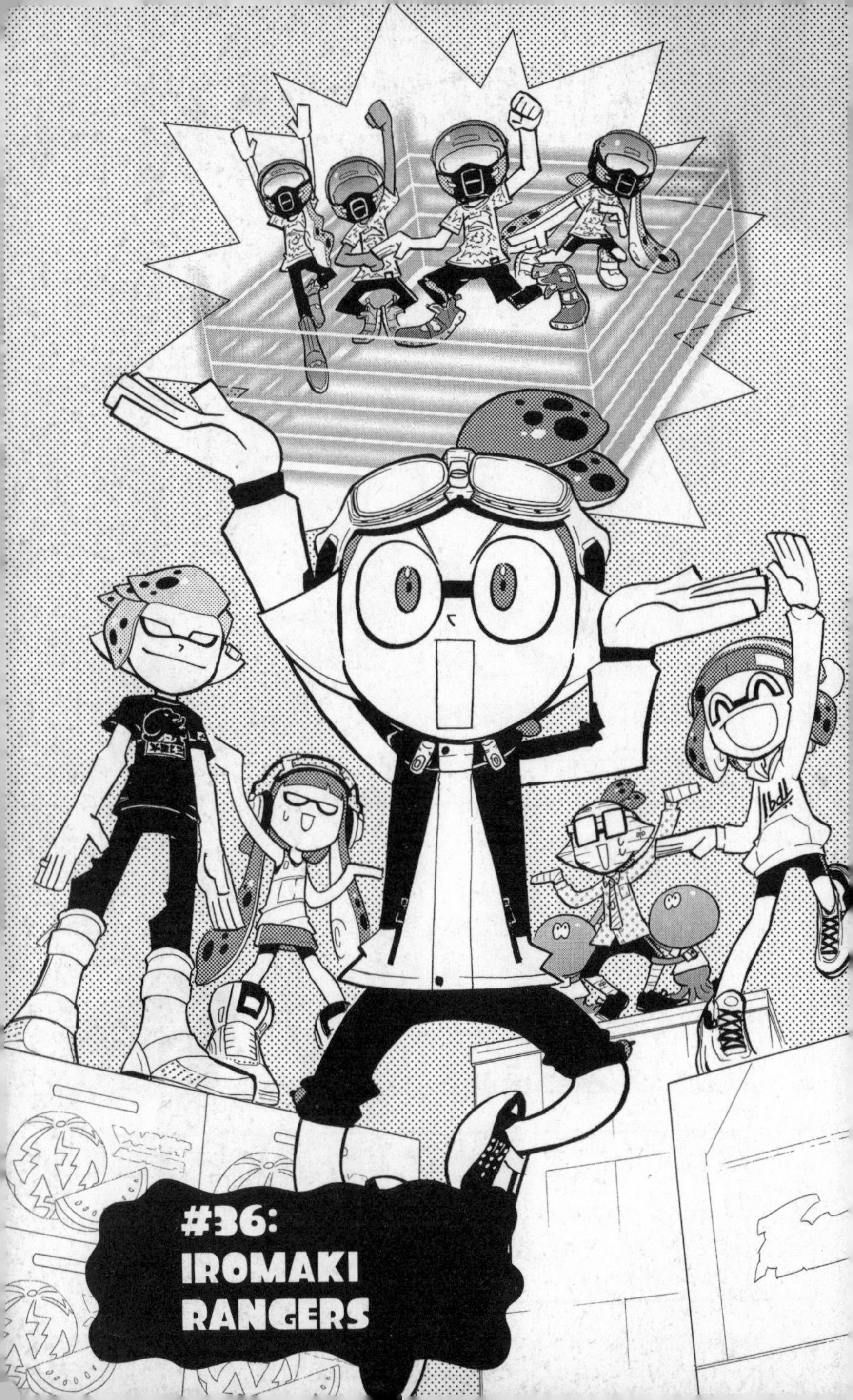
#36:
IROMAKI
RANGERS

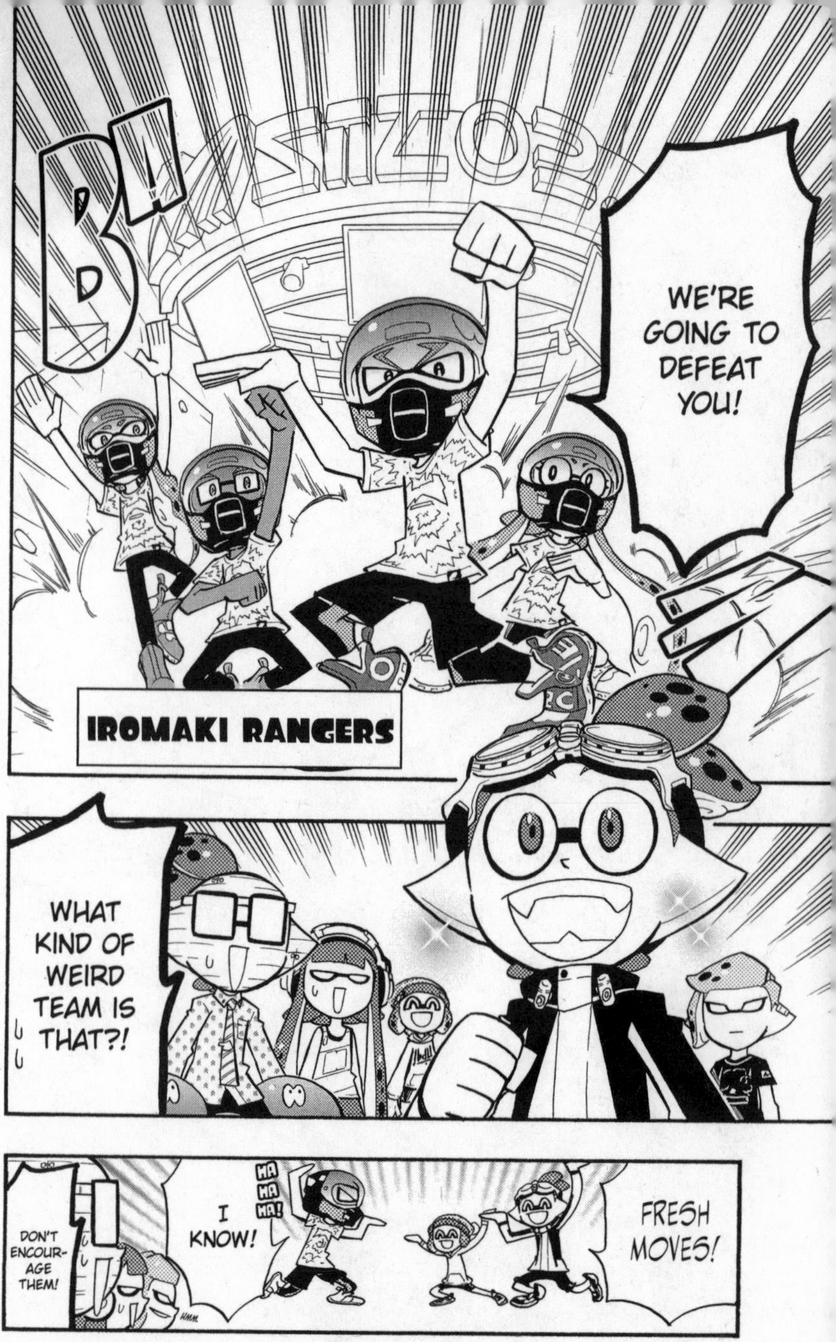
WE'RE GOING TO DEFEAT YOU!
IROMAKI RANGERS
WHAT KIND OF WEIRD TEAM IS THAT?!
FRESH MOVES!
HA HA HA!
I KNOW!
DON'T ENCOURAGE THEM!
HMM

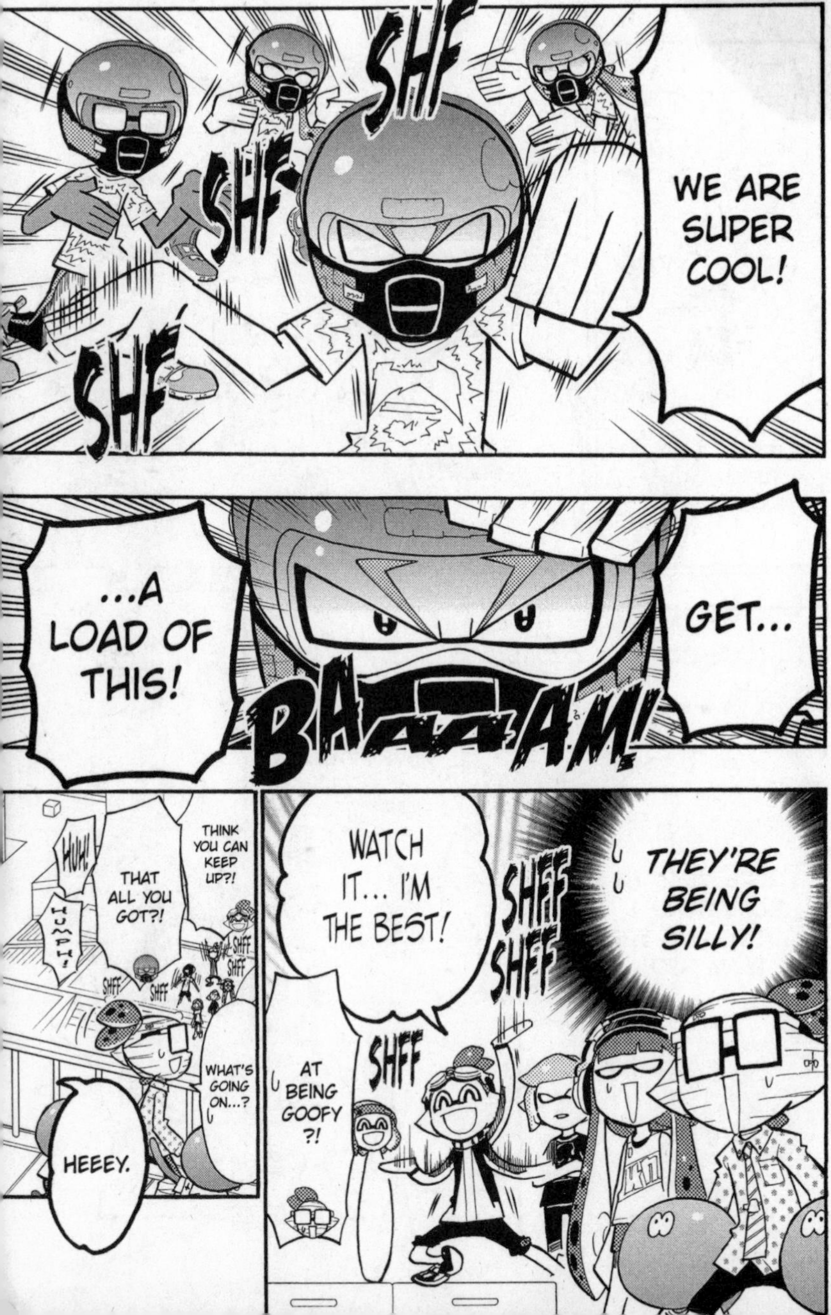
SHF
SHF
SHF
WE ARE SUPER COOL!
GET...
BAAAAM!
...A LOAD OF THIS!
THEY'RE BEING SILLY!
SHFF SHFF
WATCH IT... I'M THE BEST!
SHFF
AT BEING GOOFY?!
THINK YOU CAN KEEP UP?!
HUH!
THAT ALL YOU GOT?!
HUMPH!
SHFF
SHFF
SHFF
SHFF
WHAT'S GOING ON...?
HEEEY.

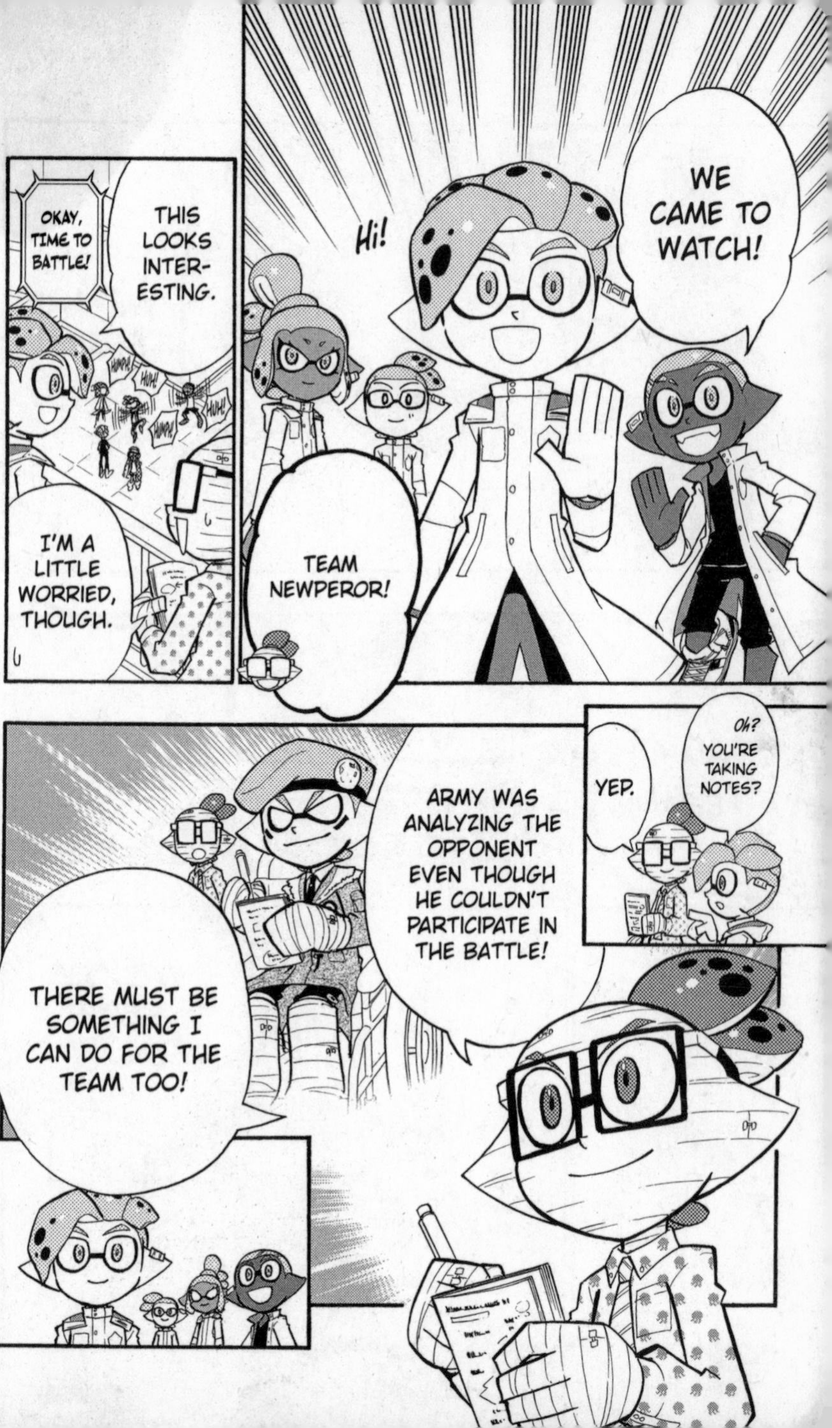
WE CAME TO WATCH!
Hi!
TEAM NEWPEROR!
THIS LOOKS INTER-ESTING.
OKAY, TIME TO BATTLE!
HUMPH!
HUH!
HUH!
HUMPH!
I'M A LITTLE WORRIED, THOUGH.
Oh? YOU'RE TAKING NOTES?
YEP.
ARMY WAS ANALYZING THE OPPONENT EVEN THOUGH HE COULDN'T PARTICIPATE IN THE BATTLE!
THERE MUST BE SOMETHING I CAN DO FOR THE TEAM TOO!

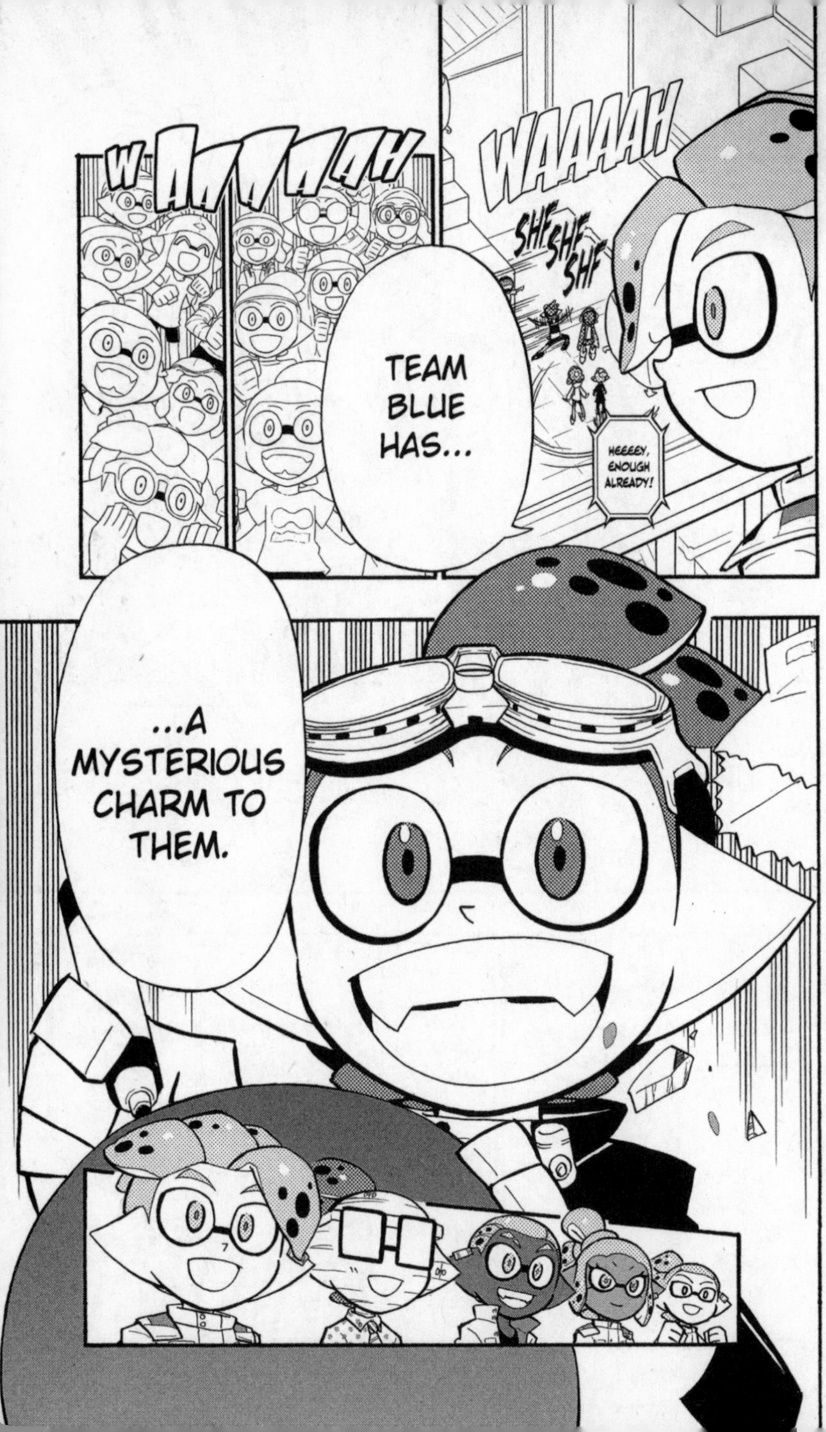
WAAAAH
SHF SHF SHF
HEEEEY, ENOUGH ALREADY!
TEAM BLUE HAS...
WAAAAAAH
...A MYSTERIOUS CHARM TO THEM.

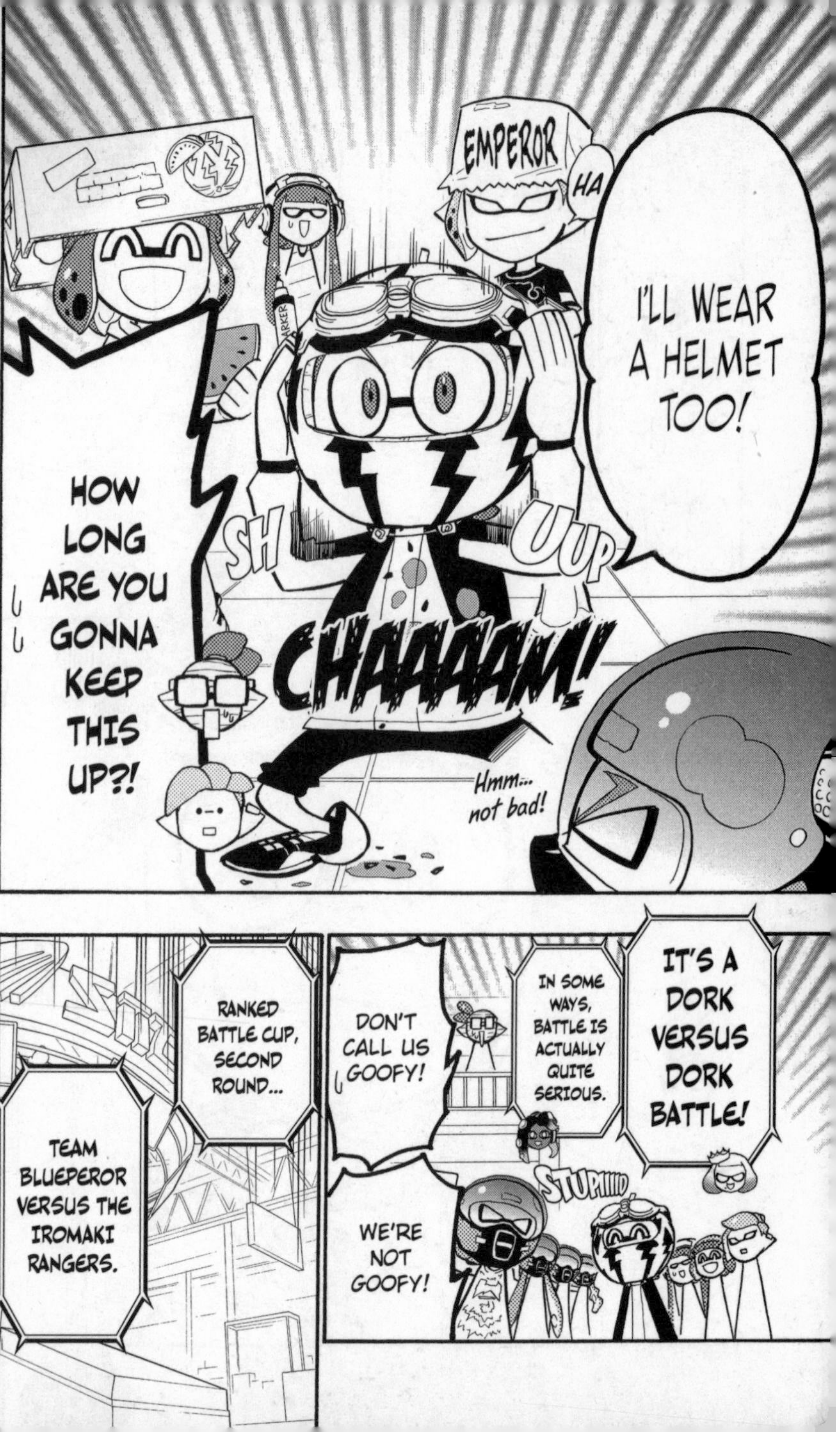
EMPEROR
HA
I'LL WEAR A HELMET TOO!
SHUUP
CHAAAAM!
Hmm... not bad!
HOW LONG ARE YOU GONNA KEEP THIS UP?!
IT'S A DORK VERSUS DORK BATTLE!
IN SOME WAYS, BATTLE IS ACTUALLY QUITE SERIOUS.
DON'T CALL US GOOFY!
STUPIIIID
WE'RE NOT GOOFY!
RANKED BATTLE CUP, SECOND ROUND...
TEAM BLUEPEROR VERSUS THE IROMAKI RANGERS.

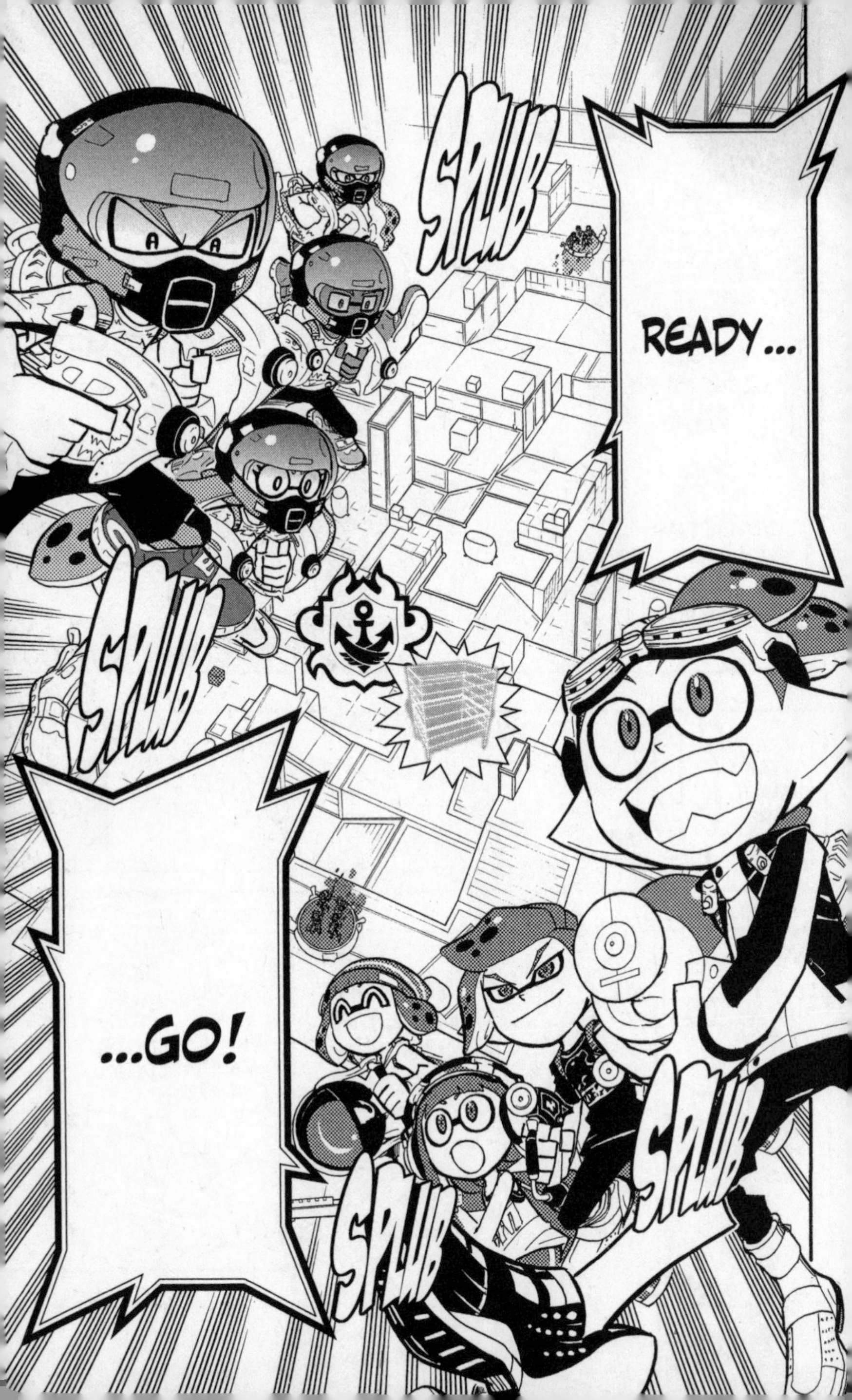
READY...
SPLUB
SPLUB
SPLUB
SPLUB
...GO!

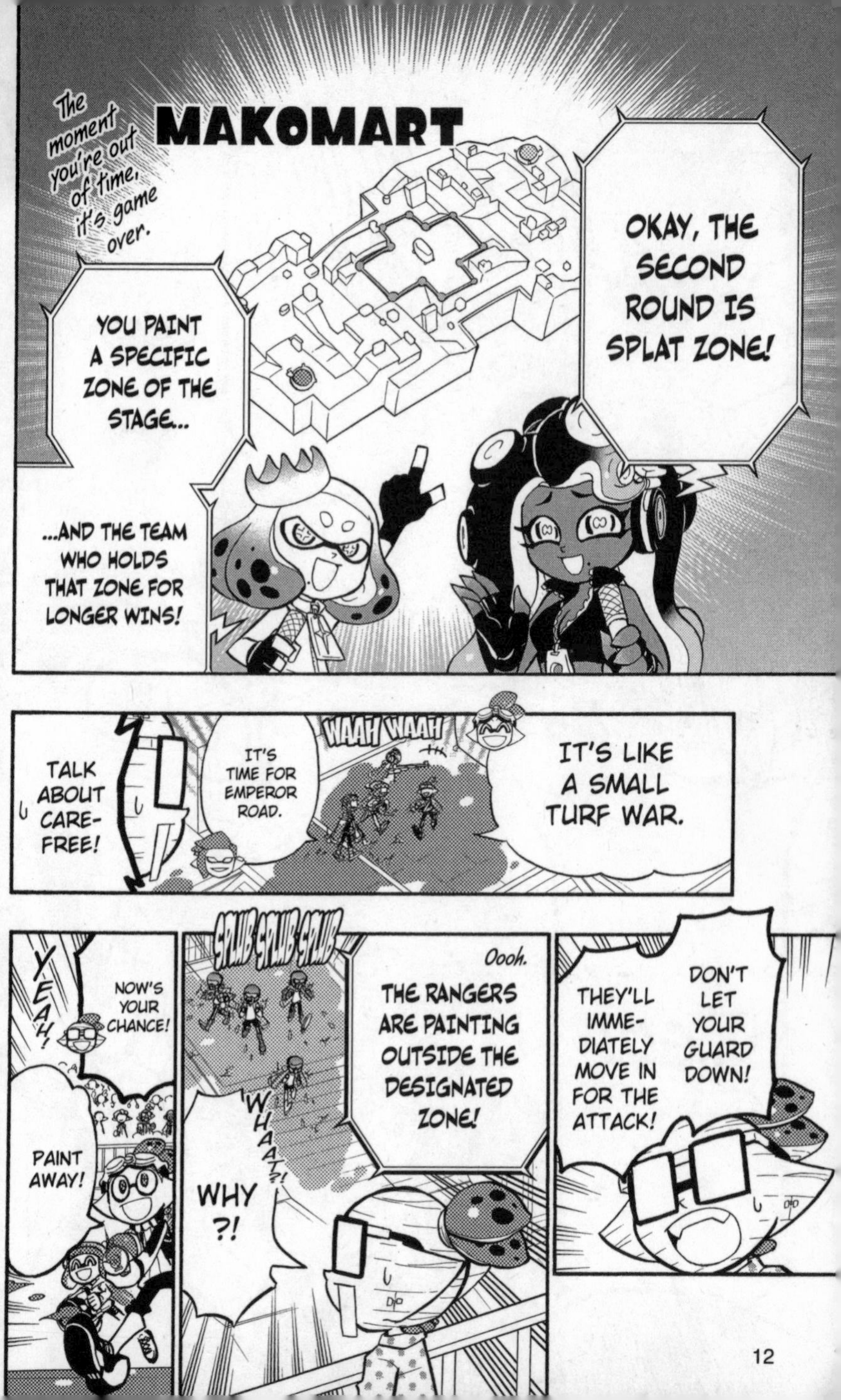
OKAY, THE SECOND ROUND IS SPLAT ZONE!
MAKOMART
The moment you're out of time, it's game over.
YOU PAINT A SPECIFIC ZONE OF THE STAGE...
...AND THE TEAM WHO HOLDS THAT ZONE FOR LONGER WINS!
IT'S LIKE A SMALL TURF WAR.
WAAH WAAH
IT'S TIME FOR EMPEROR ROAD.
TALK ABOUT CARE-FREE!
DON'T LET YOUR GUARD DOWN!
THEY'LL IMME-DIATELY MOVE IN FOR THE ATTACK!
Oooh.
THE RANGERS ARE PAINTING OUTSIDE THE DESIGNATED ZONE!
SPLUB SPLUB SPLUB
WHAAAT?!
WHY?!
NOW'S YOUR CHANCE!
YEAH!
PAINT AWAY!

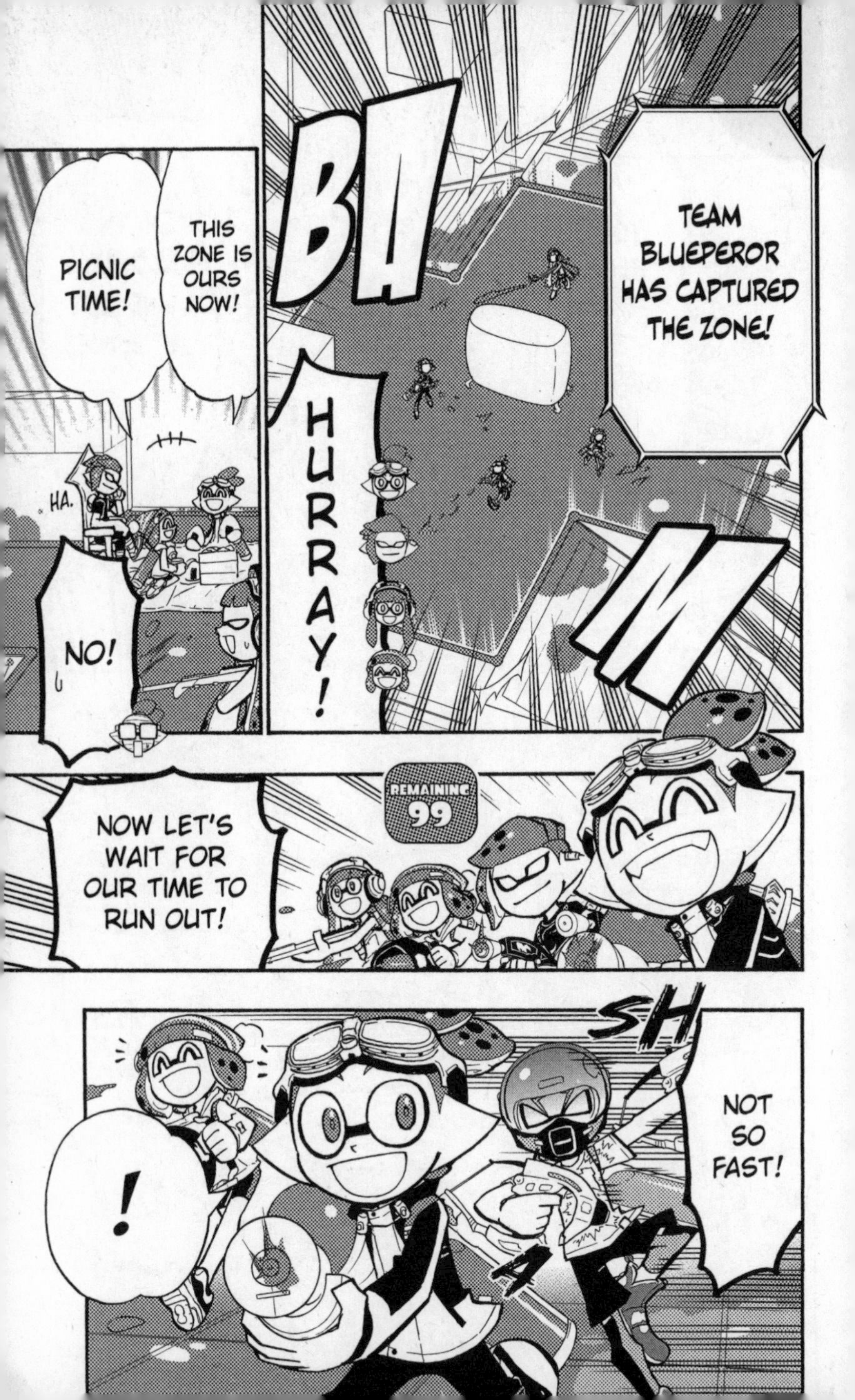

TEAM BLUEPEROR HAS CAPTURED THE ZONE!
BA
M
HURRAY!
THIS ZONE IS OURS NOW!
PICNIC TIME!
HA.
NO!
REMAINING
99
NOW LET'S WAIT FOR OUR TIME TO RUN OUT!
SH
NOT SO FAST!
!

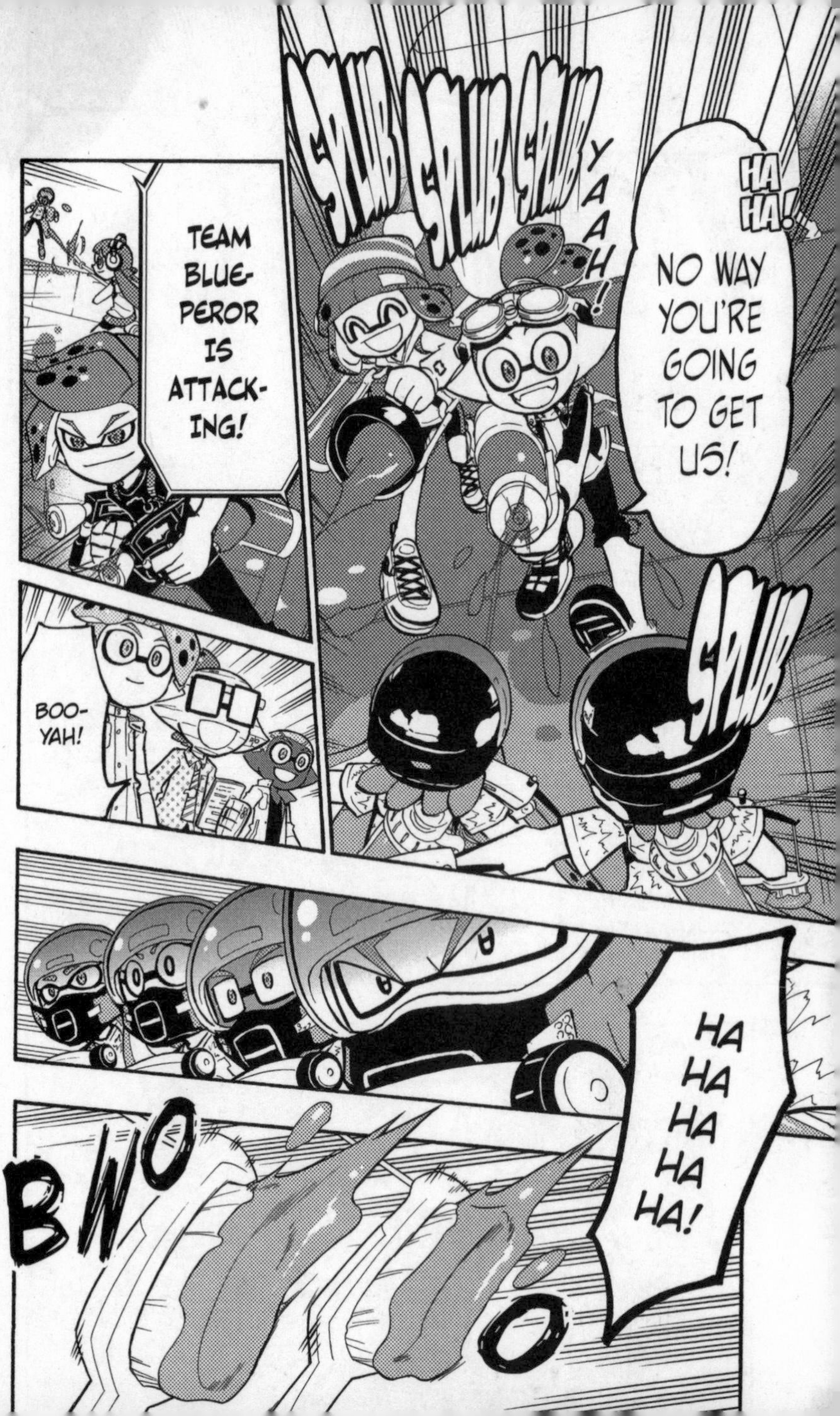
HA HA!
NO WAY YOU'RE GOING TO GET US!
YAAAH!
SPLUB SPLUB SPLUB
SPLUB
TEAM BLUE-PEROR IS ATTACKING!
BOO-YAH!
HA HA HA HA HA HA!
BWOOO

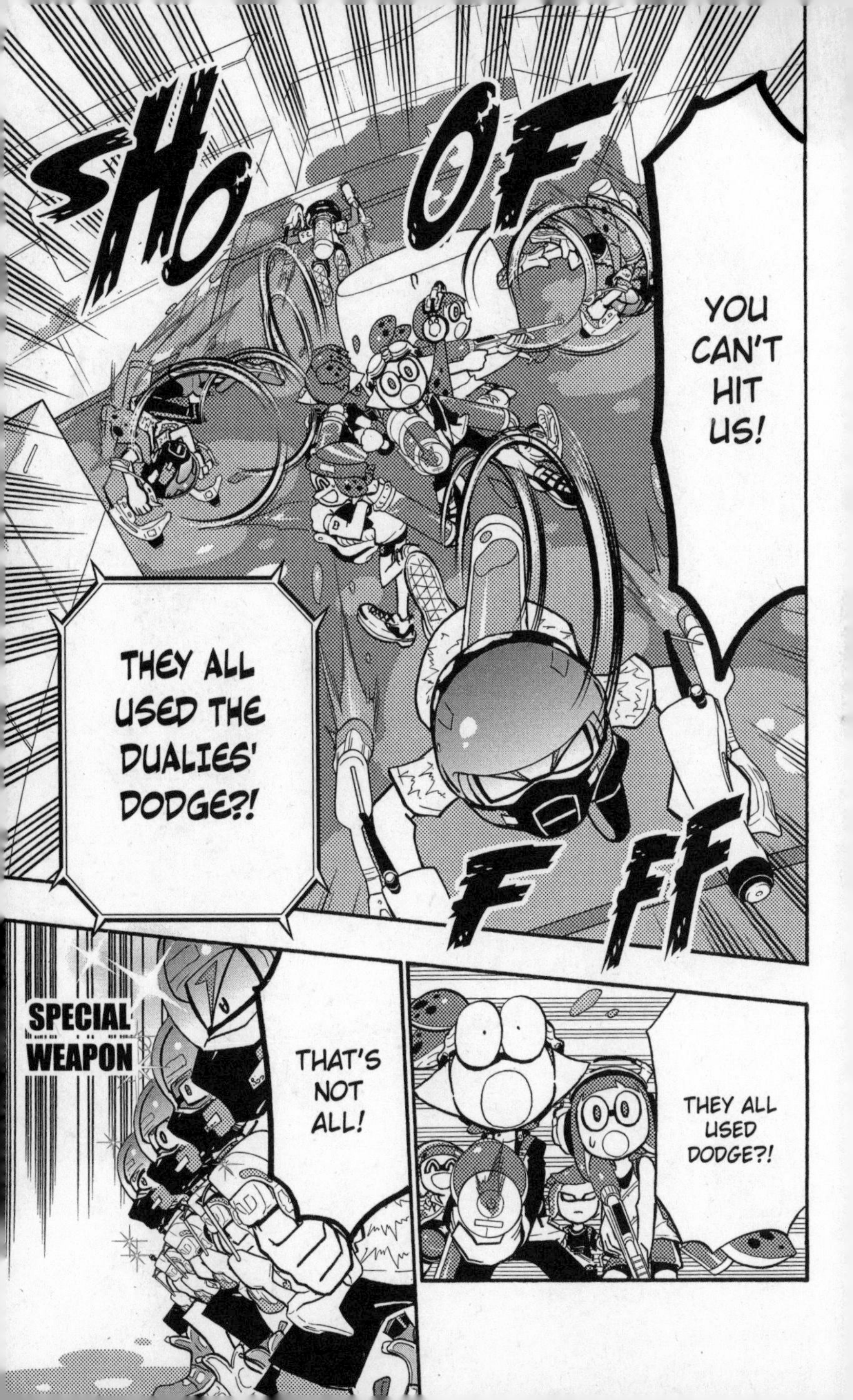
SHOOF
YOU CAN'T HIT US!
THEY ALL USED THE DUALIES' DODGE?!
FFF
THEY ALL USED DODGE?!
THAT'S NOT ALL!
SPECIAL WEAPON

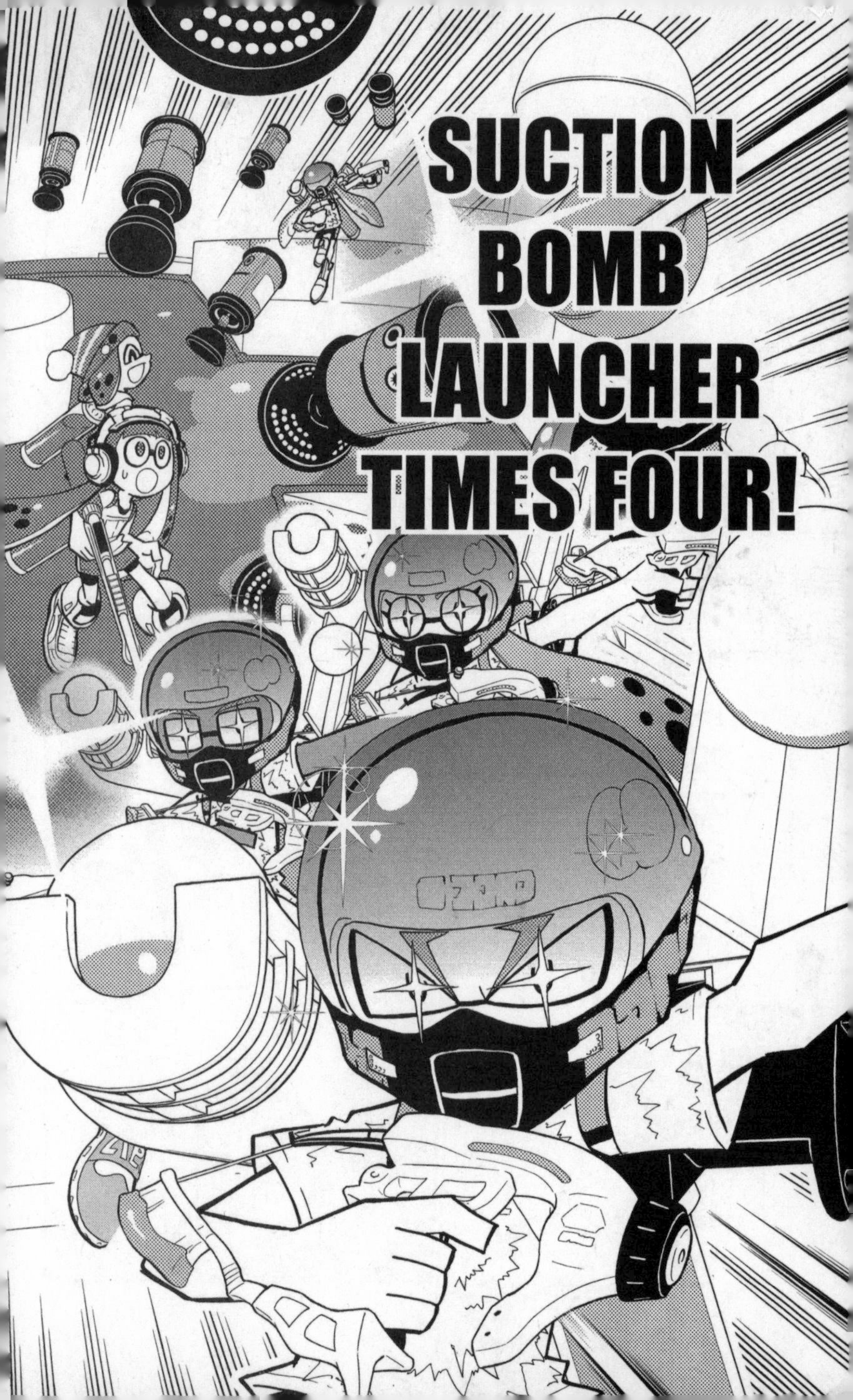
SUCTION BOMB LAUNCHER TIMES FOUR!

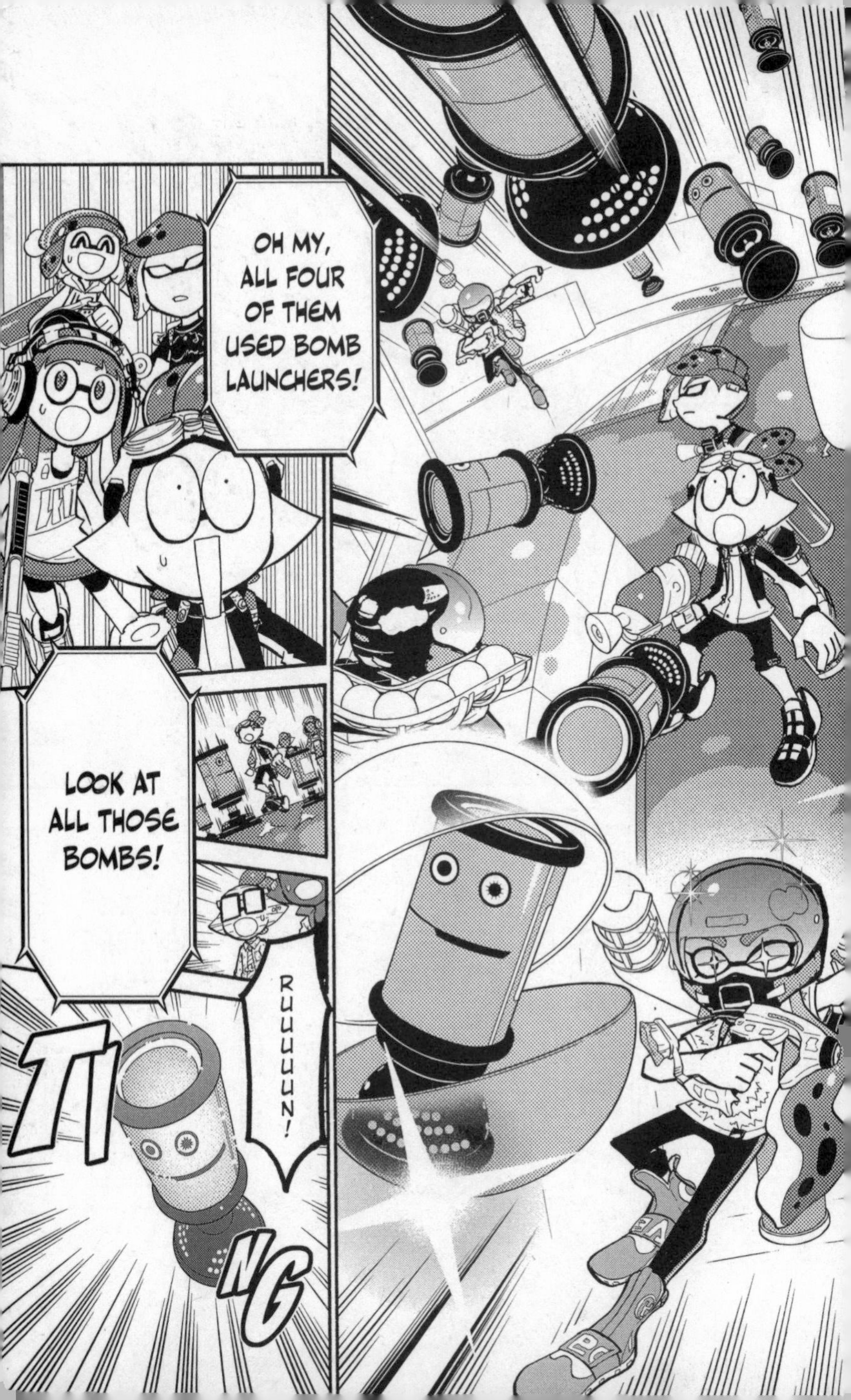
OH MY, ALL FOUR OF THEM USED BOMB LAUNCHERS!
LOOK AT ALL THOSE BOMBS!
RUUUUUN!
TING

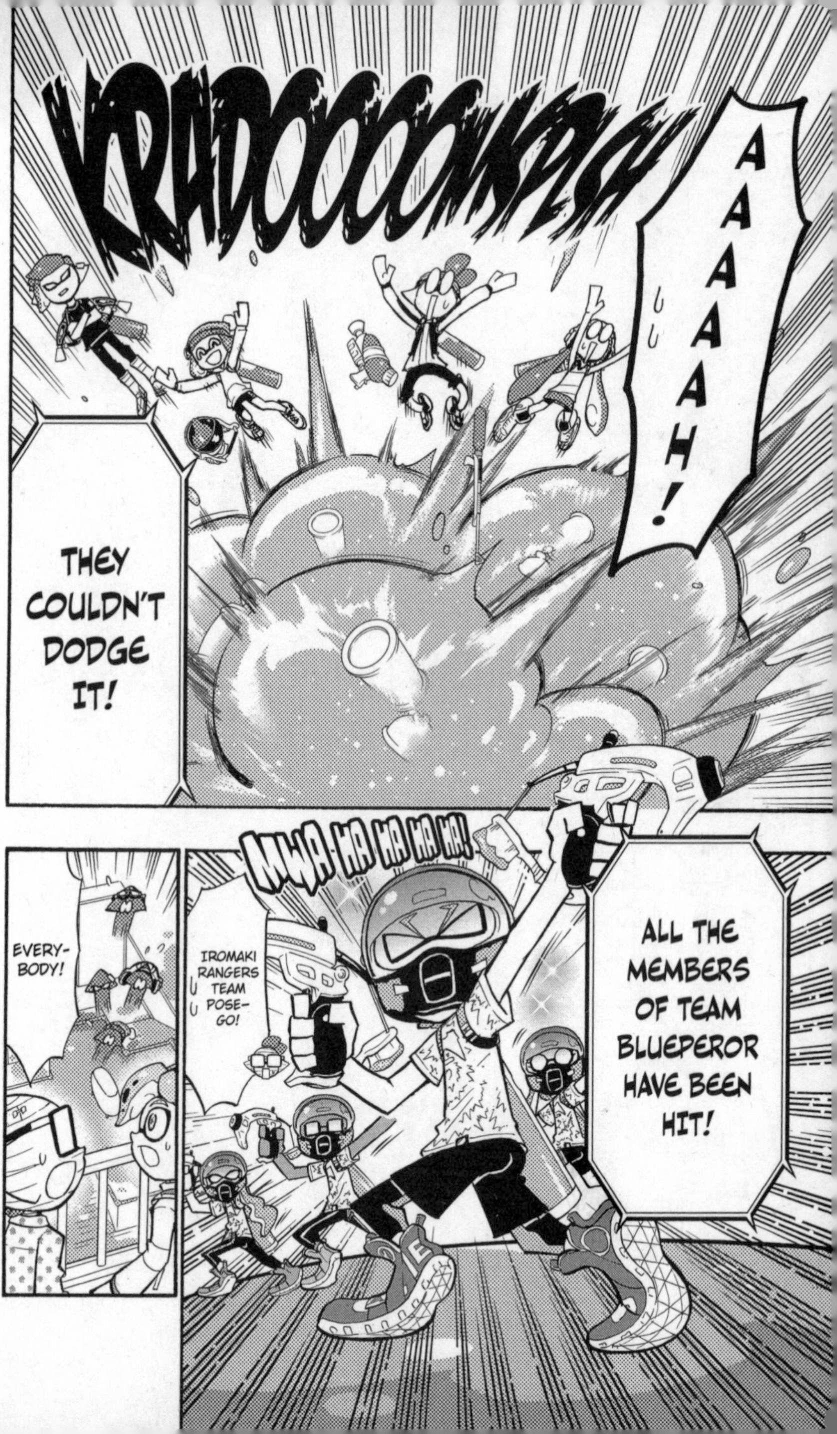
KRADOOOOMSPA
AAAAAAH!
THEY COULDN'T DODGE IT!
ALL THE MEMBERS OF TEAM BLUEPEROR HAVE BEEN HIT!
MWA-HA HA HA HA!
IROMAKI RANGERS TEAM POSE-GO!
EVERY-BODY!

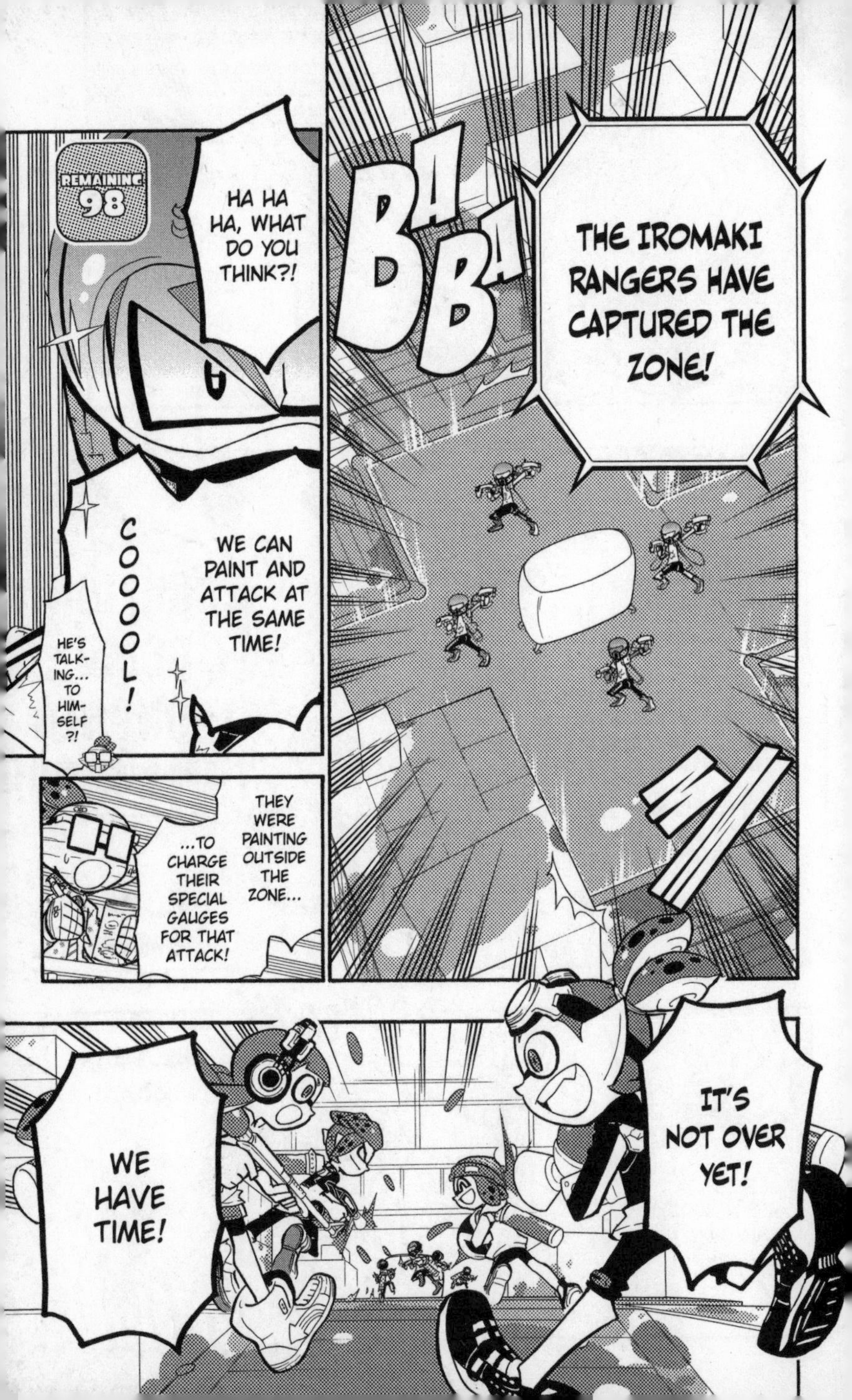
BABA
THE IROMAKI RANGERS HAVE CAPTURED THE ZONE!
HA HA HA, WHAT DO YOU THINK?!
REMAINING 98
WE CAN PAINT AND ATTACK AT THE SAME TIME!
COOOOOL!
HE'S TALKING... TO HIMSELF?!
THEY WERE PAINTING OUTSIDE THE ZONE...
...TO CHARGE THEIR SPECIAL GAUGES FOR THAT ATTACK!
IT'S NOT OVER YET!
WE HAVE TIME!

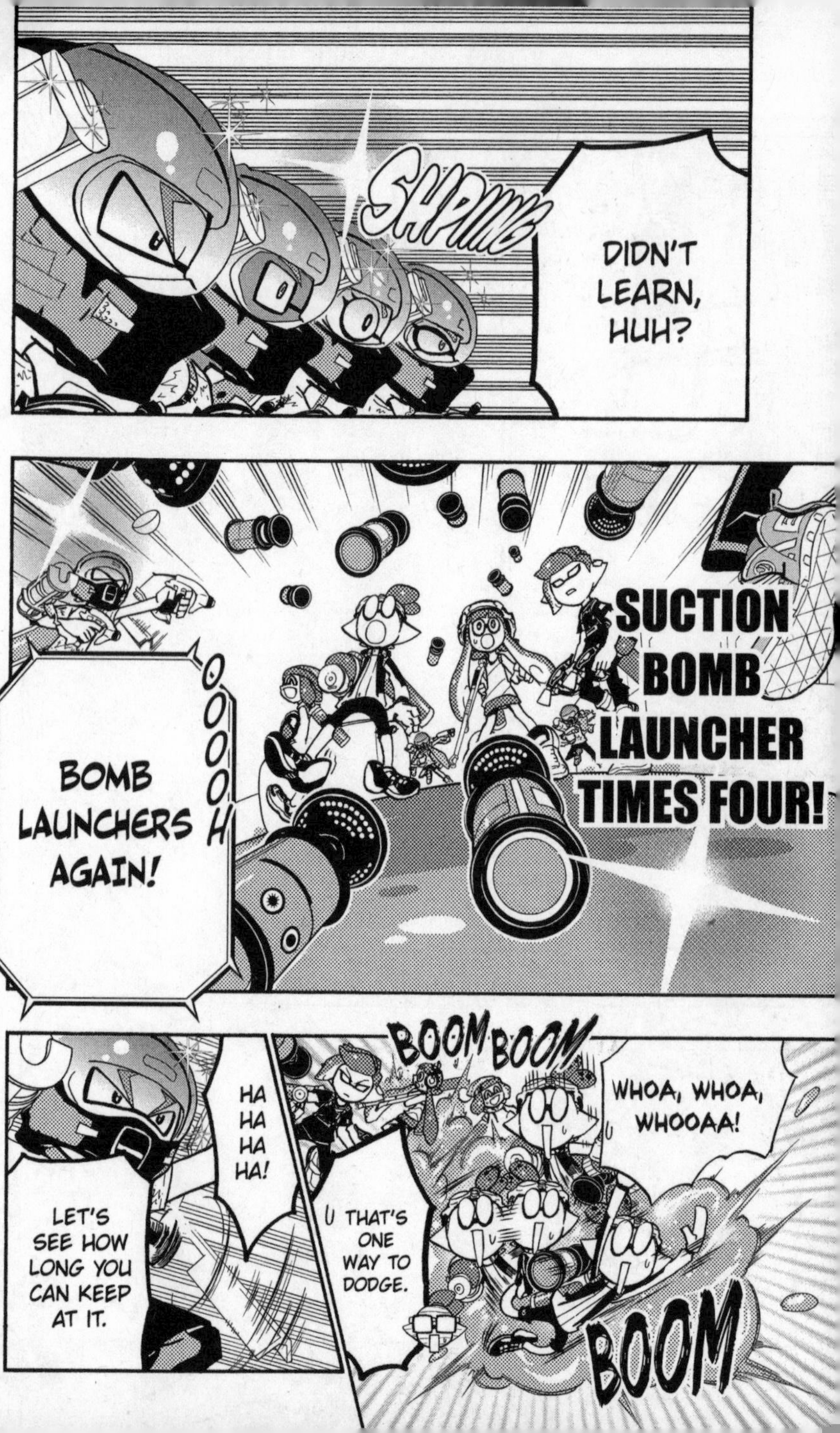
DIDN'T LEARN, HUH?
SHPING
SUCTION BOMB LAUNCHER TIMES FOUR!
BOMB LAUNCHERS AGAIN!
HOOOOOO
BOOM BOOM
WHOA, WHOA, WHOOAA!
HA HA HA HA!
THAT'S ONE WAY TO DODGE.
BOOM
LET'S SEE HOW LONG YOU CAN KEEP AT IT.

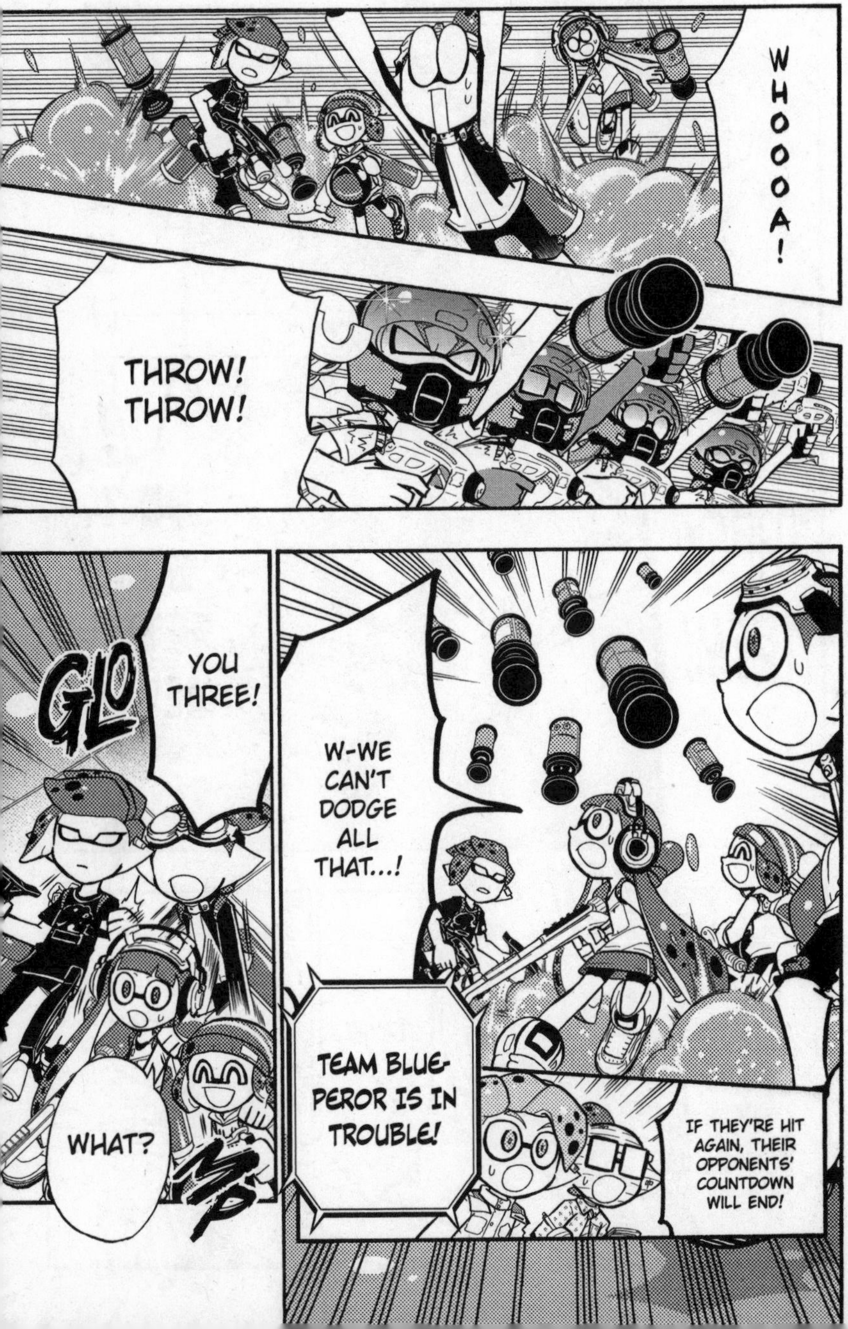
WHOOOA!
THROW! THROW!
W-WE CAN'T DODGE ALL THAT...!
TEAM BLUE-PEROR IS IN TROUBLE!
IF THEY'RE HIT AGAIN, THEIR OPPONENTS' COUNTDOWN WILL END!
YOU THREE!
GLO
WHAT?
MP

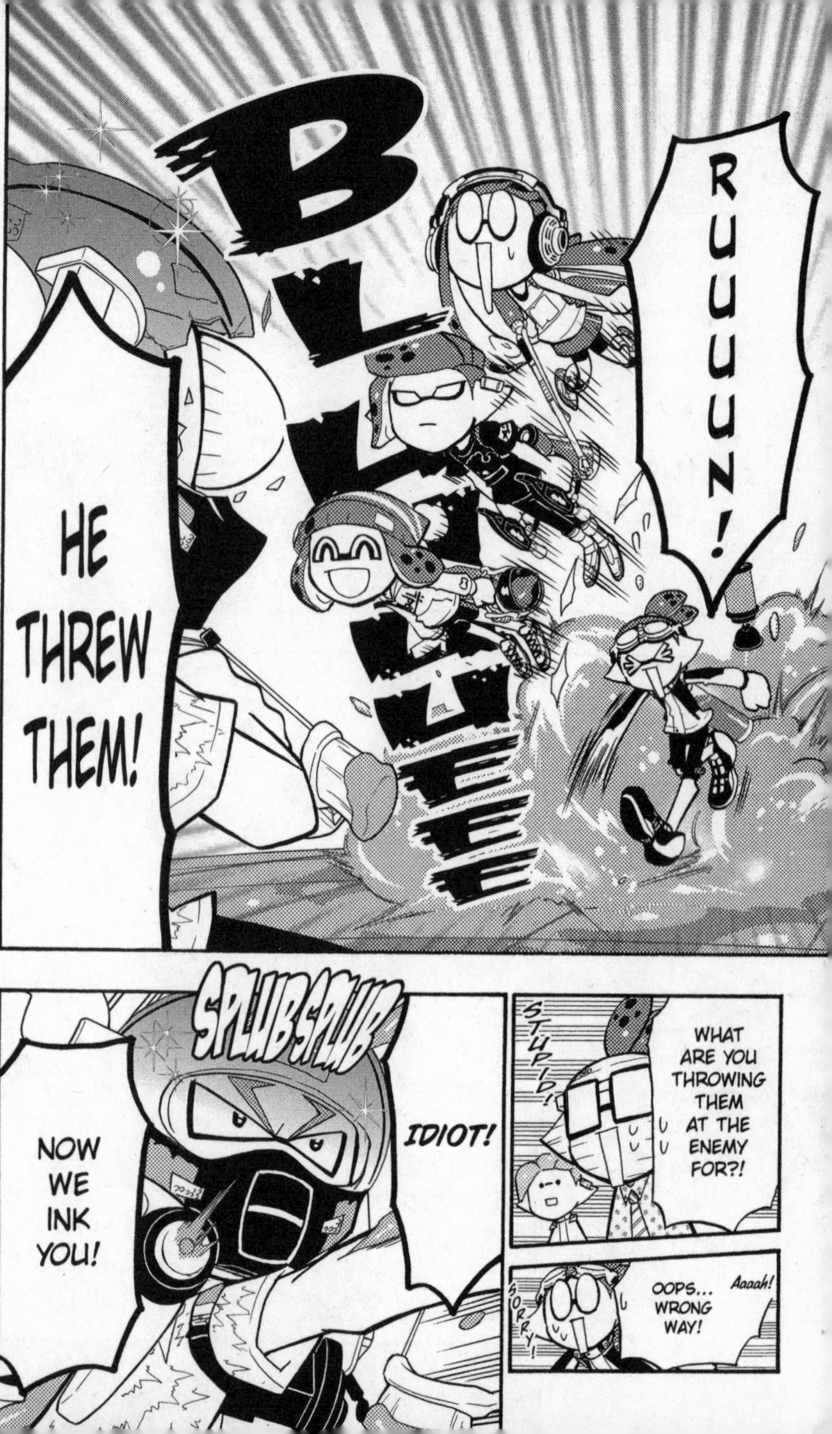

RUUUUN!
HE THREW THEM!
WHAT ARE YOU THROWING THEM AT THE ENEMY FOR?!
STUPID!
Aaaah!
OOPS... WRONG WAY!
SORRY!
SPLUB SPLUB
IDIOT!
NOW WE INK YOU!

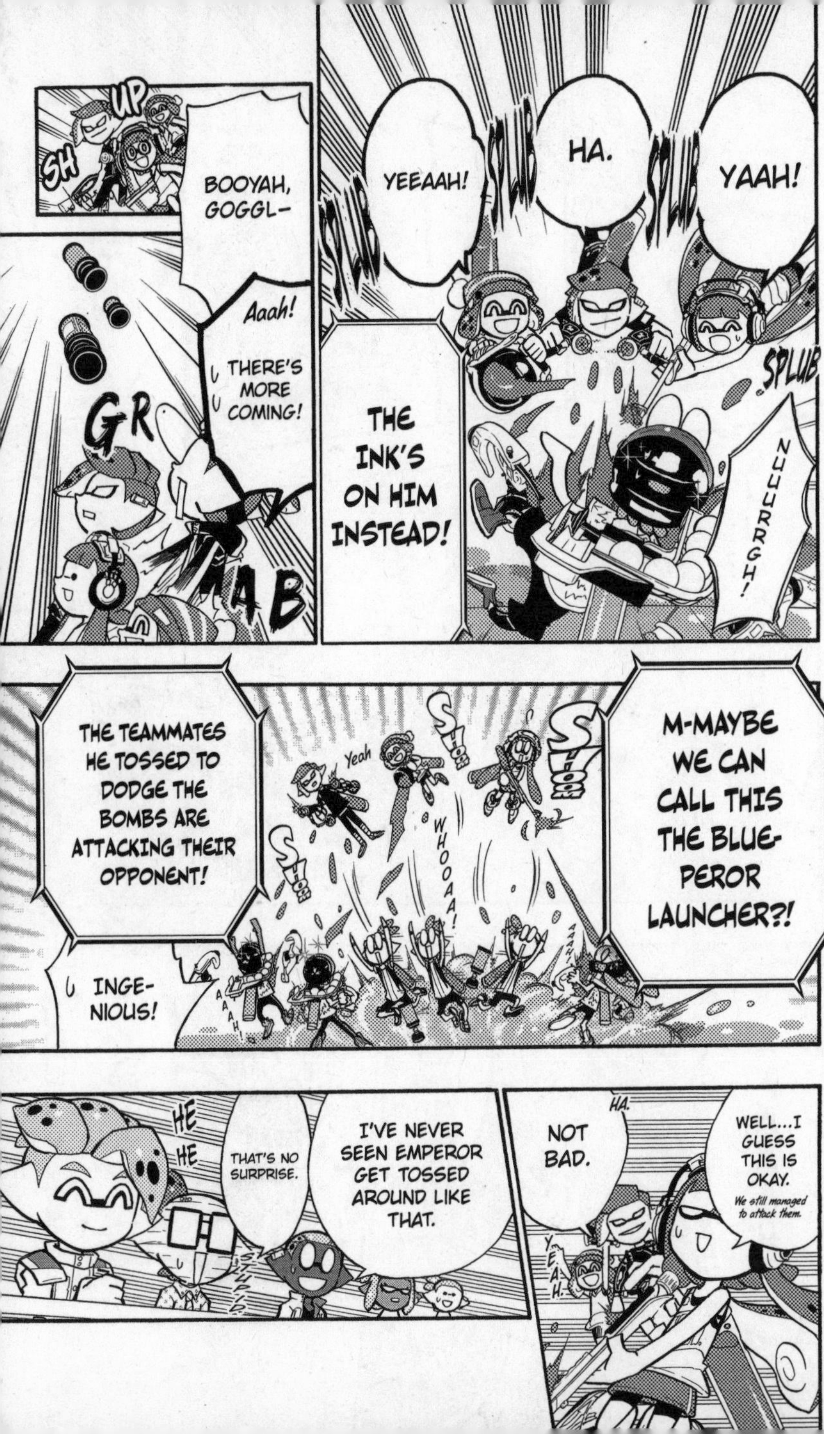
YAAH!
SPLUB
HA.
SPLUB
YEEAAH!
SPLUB
SPLUB
NUUURRGH!
THE INK'S ON HIM INSTEAD!
SHUP
BOOYAH, GOGGL-
Aaah!
THERE'S MORE COMING!
GRAB
M-MAYBE WE CAN CALL THIS THE BLUE-PEROR LAUNCHER?!
SHOOM
Yeah
SHOOM
WHOOAAA!
SHOOM
AAAH!
THE TEAMMATES HE TOSSED TO DODGE THE BOMBS ARE ATTACKING THEIR OPPONENT!
AAAAH!
INGE-NIOUS!
WELL...I GUESS THIS IS OKAY.
We still managed to attack them.
HA.
NOT BAD.
YEAH.
I'VE NEVER SEEN EMPEROR GET TOSSED AROUND LIKE THAT.
THAT'S NO SURPRISE.
STUPID.
HE HE

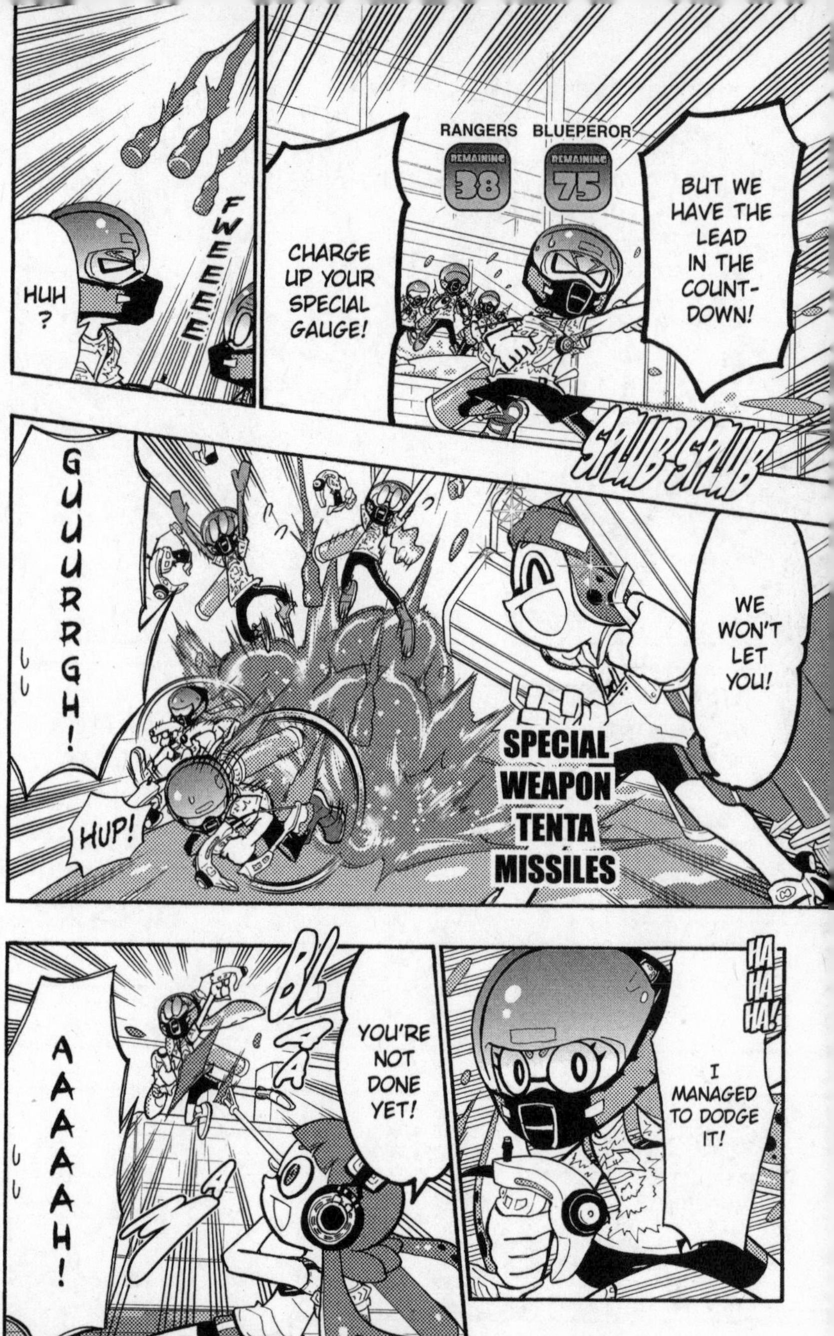
RANGERS
REMAINING 38
BLUEPEROR
REMAINING 75
BUT WE HAVE THE LEAD IN THE COUNT-DOWN!
CHARGE UP YOUR SPECIAL GAUGE!
SPLUB SPLUB
FWEEEEE
HUH?
WE WON'T LET YOU!
SPECIAL WEAPON TENTA MISSILES
GUUURRRGH!
HUP!
HA HA HA!
I MANAGED TO DODGE IT!
YOU'RE NOT DONE YET!
BLAAA
AAAAAH!

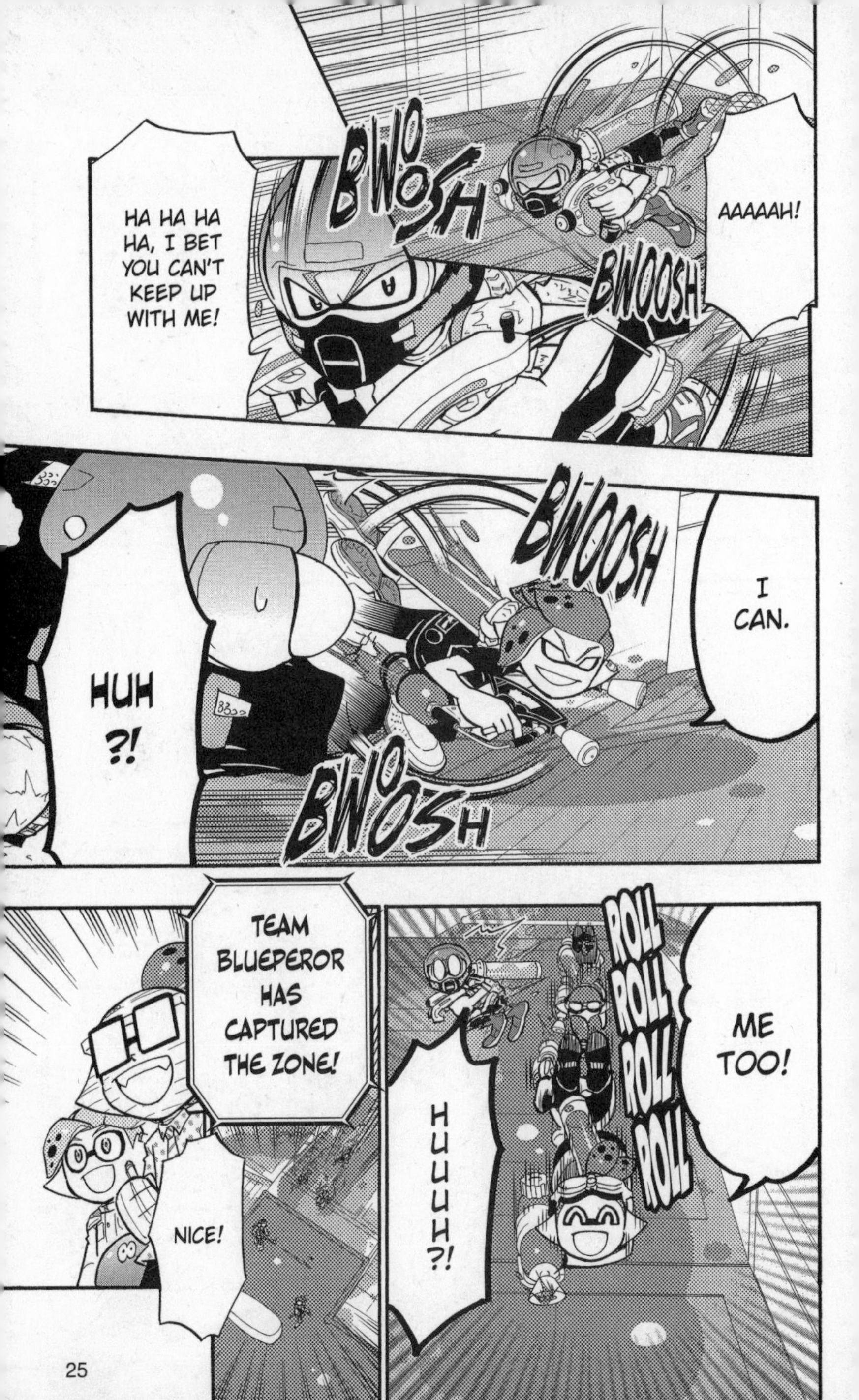
AAAAAH!
BWOOSH
BWOOSH
HA HA HA HA, I BET YOU CAN'T KEEP UP WITH ME!
I CAN.
BWOOSH
BWOOSH
HUH ?!
ME TOO!
ROLL ROLL ROLL ROLL
HUUUUH?!
TEAM BLUEPEROR HAS CAPTURED THE ZONE!
NICE!

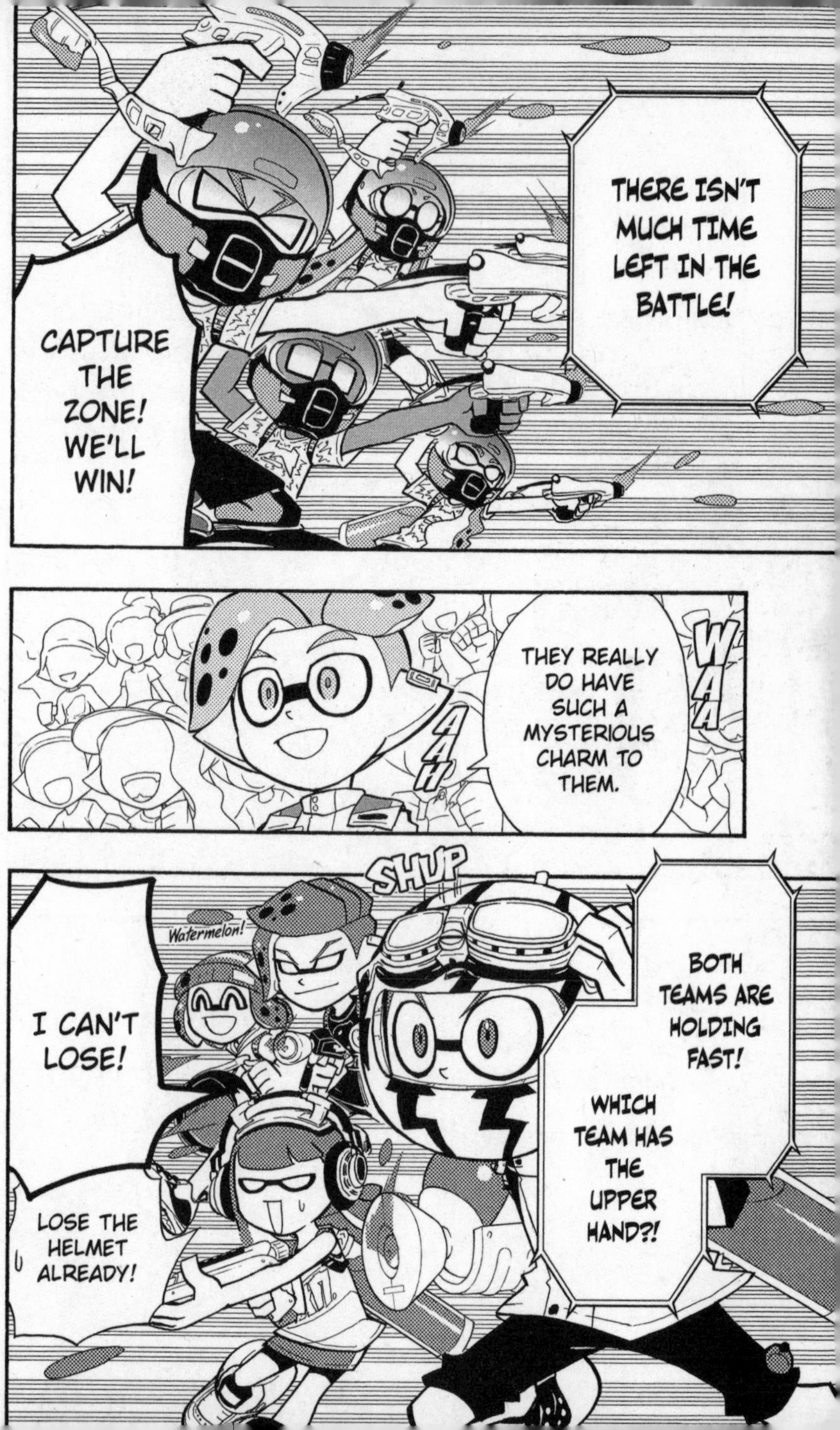
THERE ISN'T MUCH TIME LEFT IN THE BATTLE!
CAPTURE THE ZONE! WE'LL WIN!
WAA
THEY REALLY DO HAVE SUCH A MYSTERIOUS CHARM TO THEM.
AAH
SHUP
BOTH TEAMS ARE HOLDING FAST!
WHICH TEAM HAS THE UPPER HAND?!
Watermelon!
I CAN'T LOSE!
LOSE THE HELMET ALREADY!

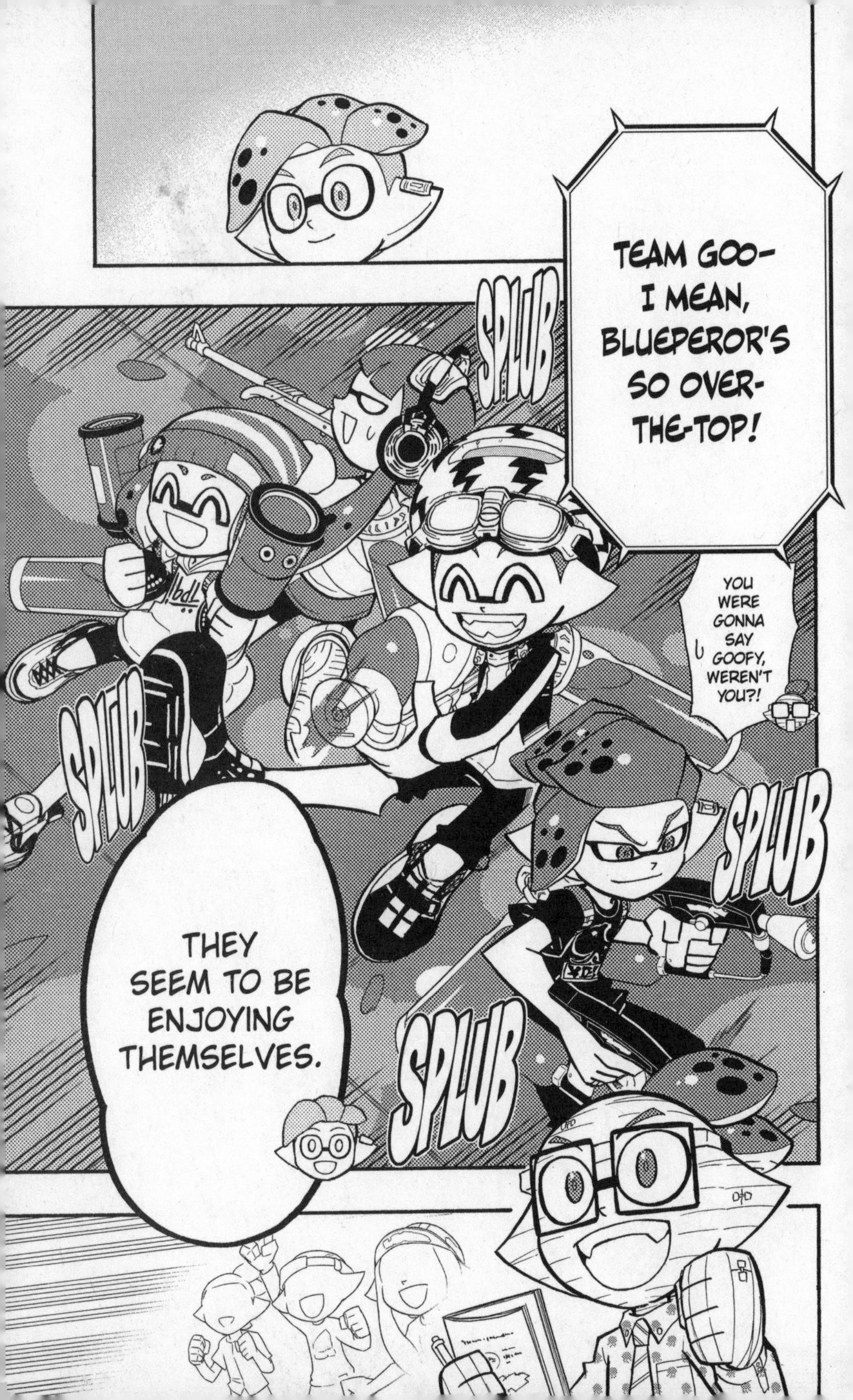
TEAM GOO— I MEAN, BLUEPEROR'S SO OVER-THE-TOP!
SPLUB
YOU WERE GONNA SAY GOOFY, WEREN'T YOU?!
SPLUB
SPLUB
THEY SEEM TO BE ENJOYING THEMSELVES.
SPLUB

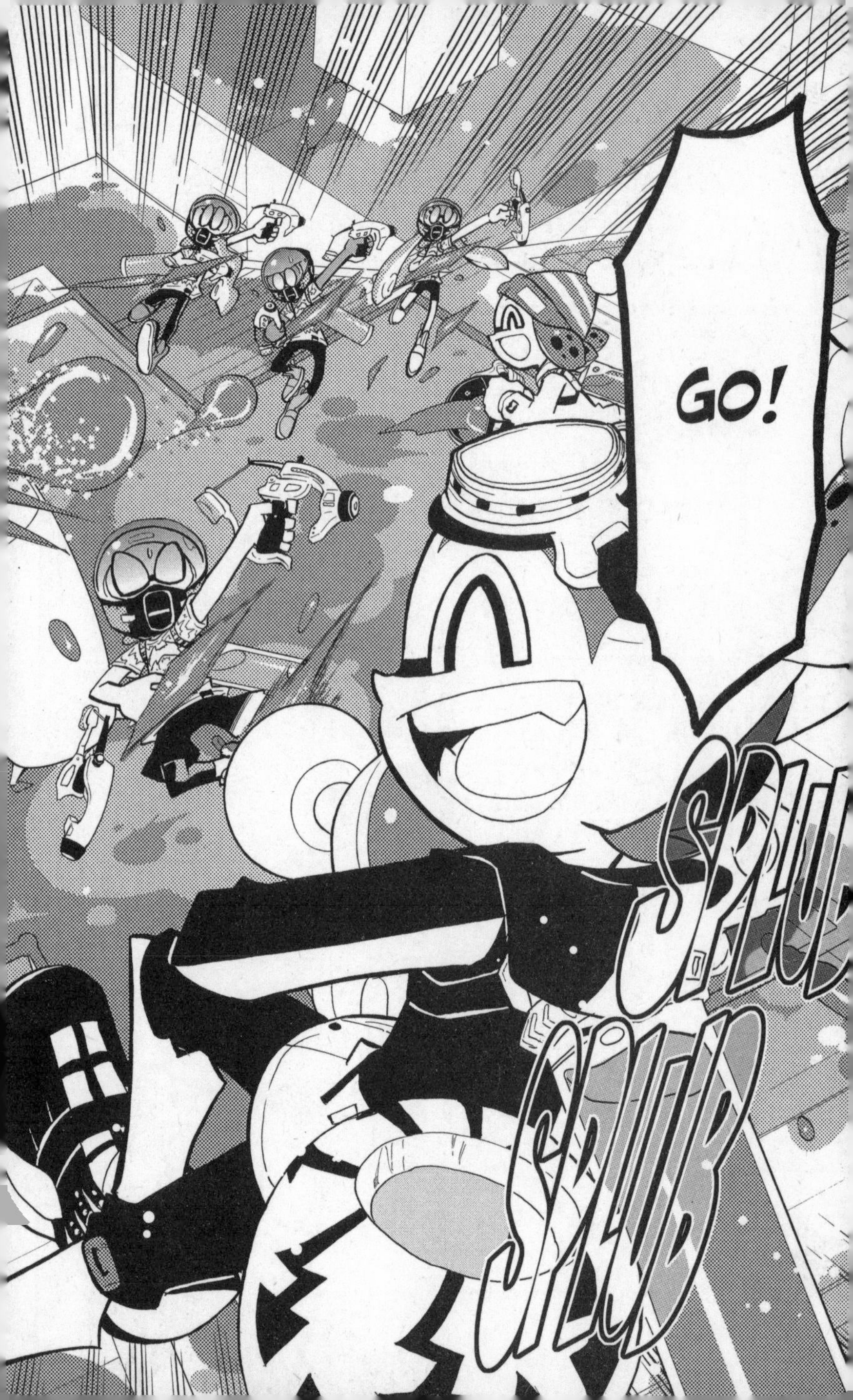
GO!
SPLUB
SPLUB

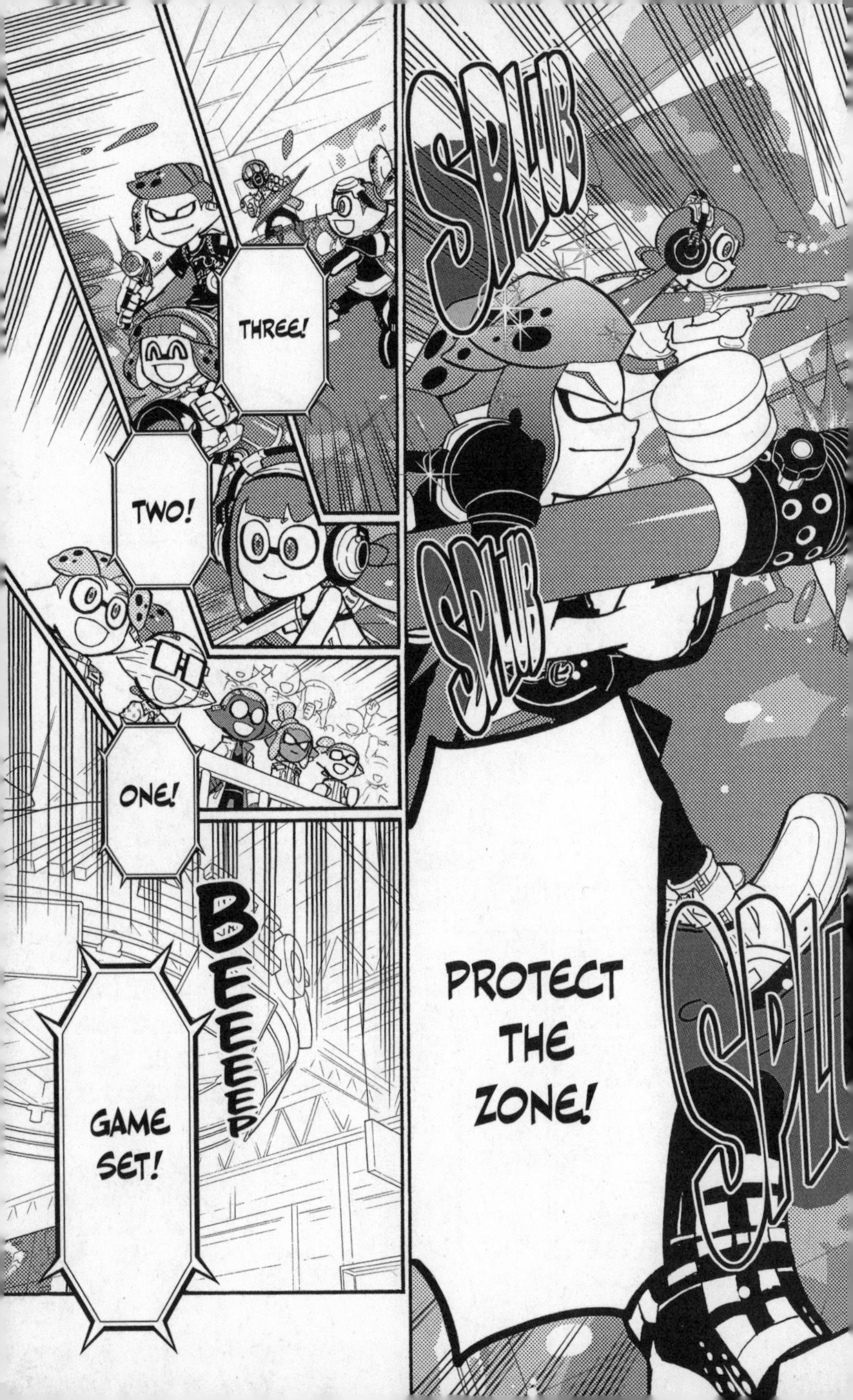

SPLUB
SPLUB
SPLU
PROTECT THE ZONE!
THREE!
TWO!
ONE!
BEEEEEP
GAME SET!

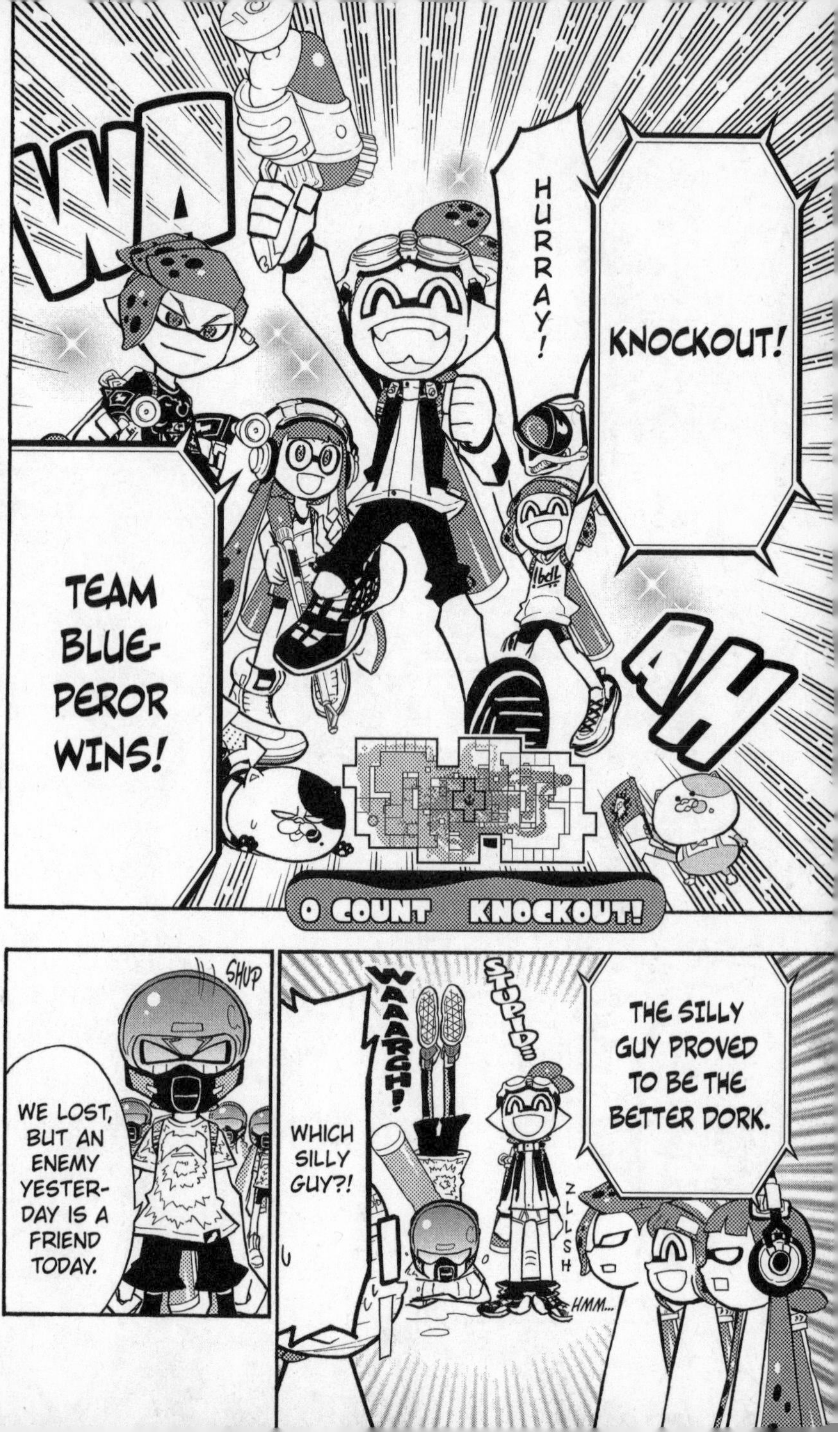
KNOCKOUT!
HURRAY!
WA
AH
TEAM BLUE-PEROR WINS!
0 COUNT KNOCKOUT!
THE SILLY GUY PROVED TO BE THE BETTER DORK.
STUPID!
WAAAARGH!
WHICH SILLY GUY?!
ZLLLSH
HMM...
SHUP
WE LOST, BUT AN ENEMY YESTER-DAY IS A FRIEND TODAY.

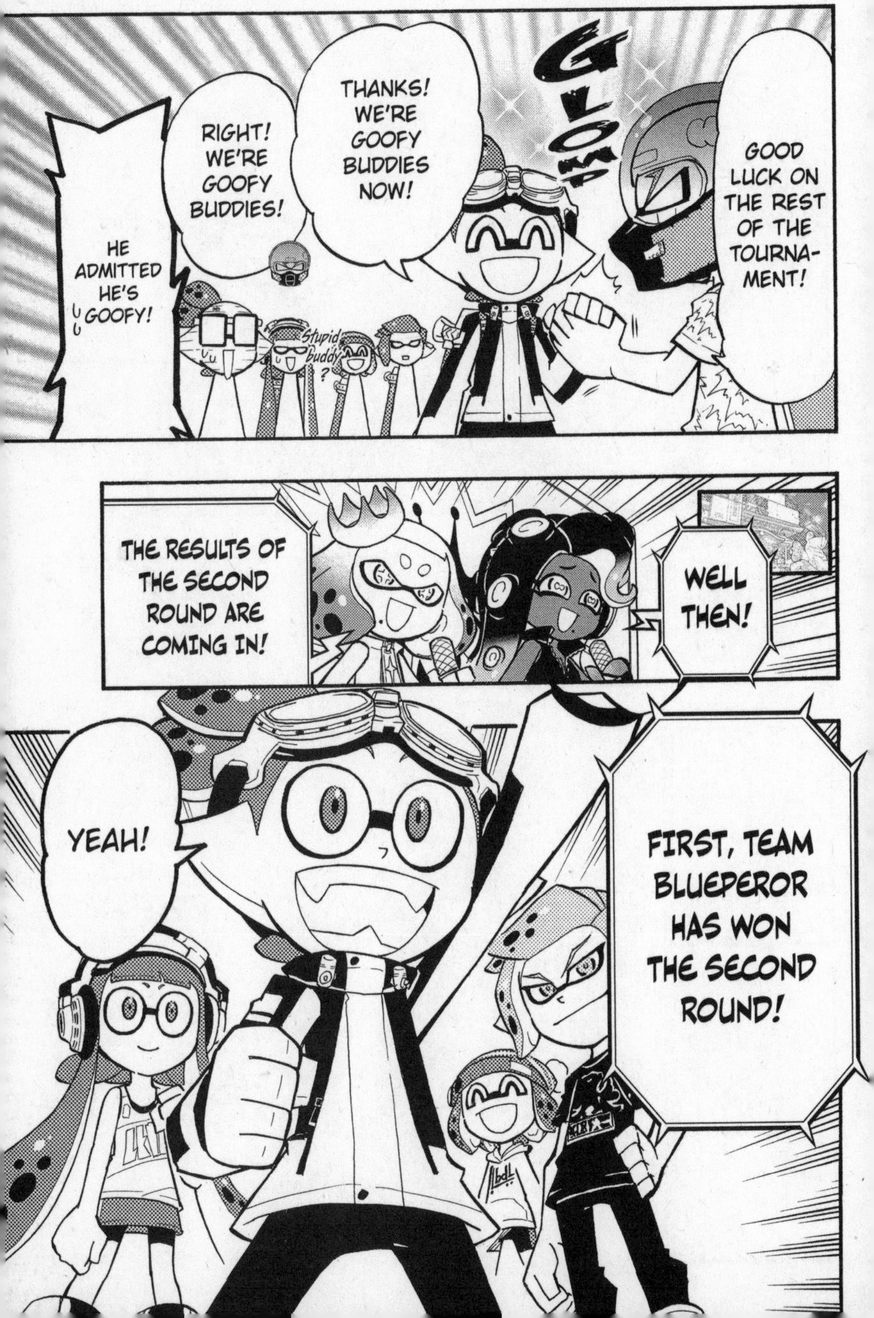
GLOMP
GOOD LUCK ON THE REST OF THE TOURNA-MENT!
THANKS! WE'RE GOOFY BUDDIES NOW!
RIGHT! WE'RE GOOFY BUDDIES!
HE ADMITTED HE'S GOOFY!
Stupid buddy?
WELL THEN!
THE RESULTS OF THE SECOND ROUND ARE COMING IN!
FIRST, TEAM BLUEPEROR HAS WON THE SECOND ROUND!
YEAH!

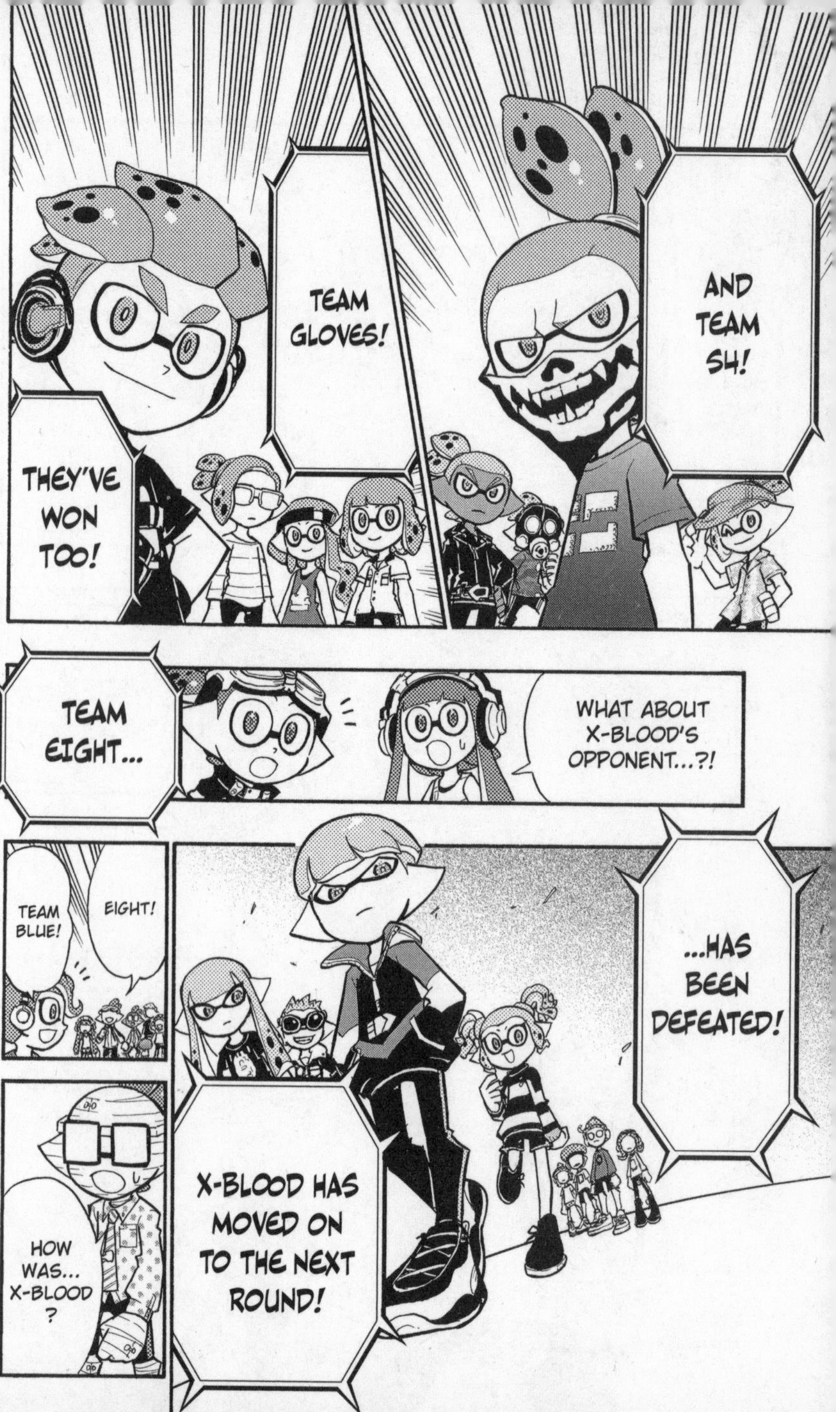
AND TEAM S4!
TEAM GLOVES!
THEY'VE WON TOO!
WHAT ABOUT X-BLOOD'S OPPONENT...?!
TEAM EIGHT...
...HAS BEEN DEFEATED!
X-BLOOD HAS MOVED ON TO THE NEXT ROUND!
EIGHT!
TEAM BLUE!
HOW WAS... X-BLOOD ?

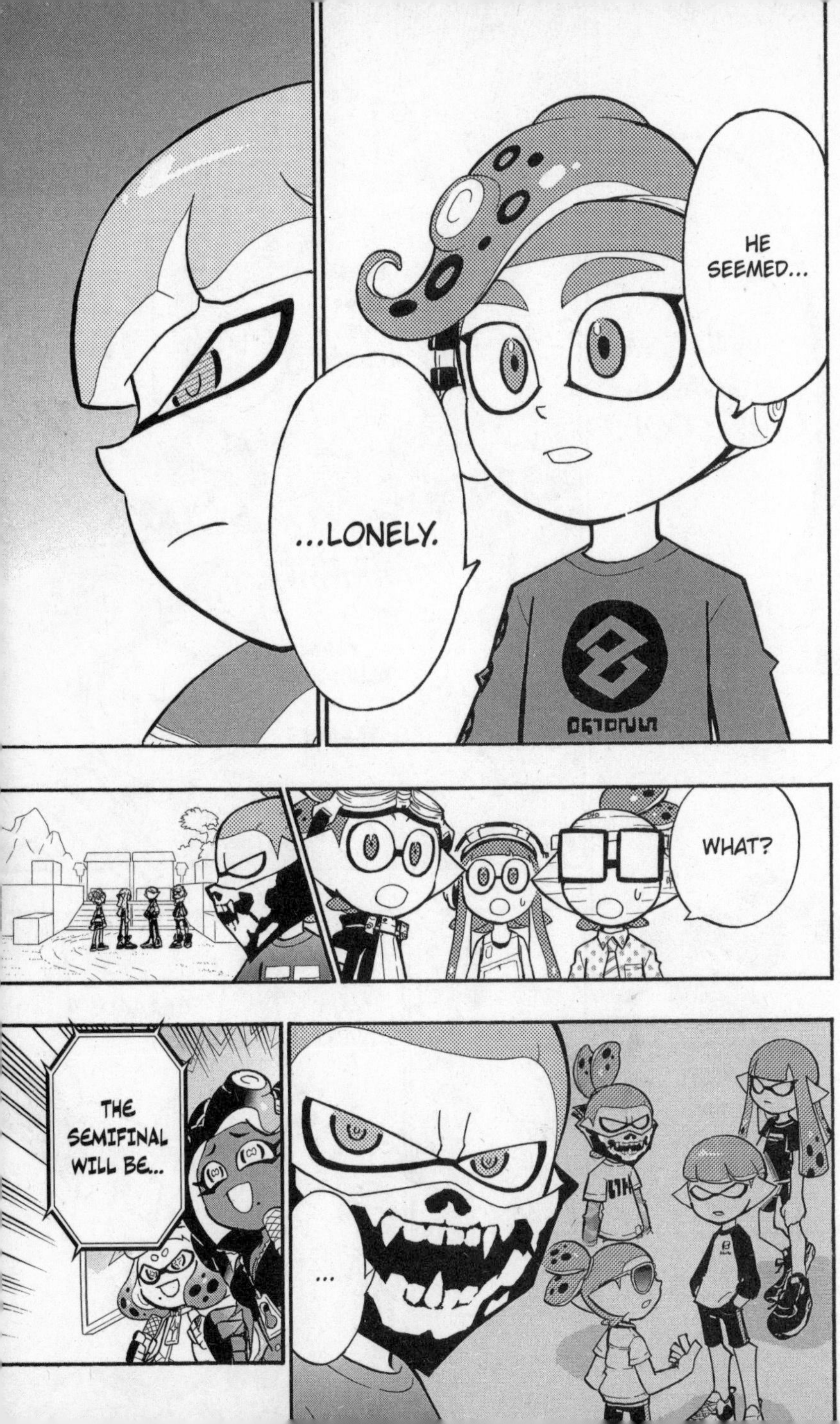
HE SEEMED...
...LONELY.
WHAT?
...
THE SEMIFINAL WILL BE...

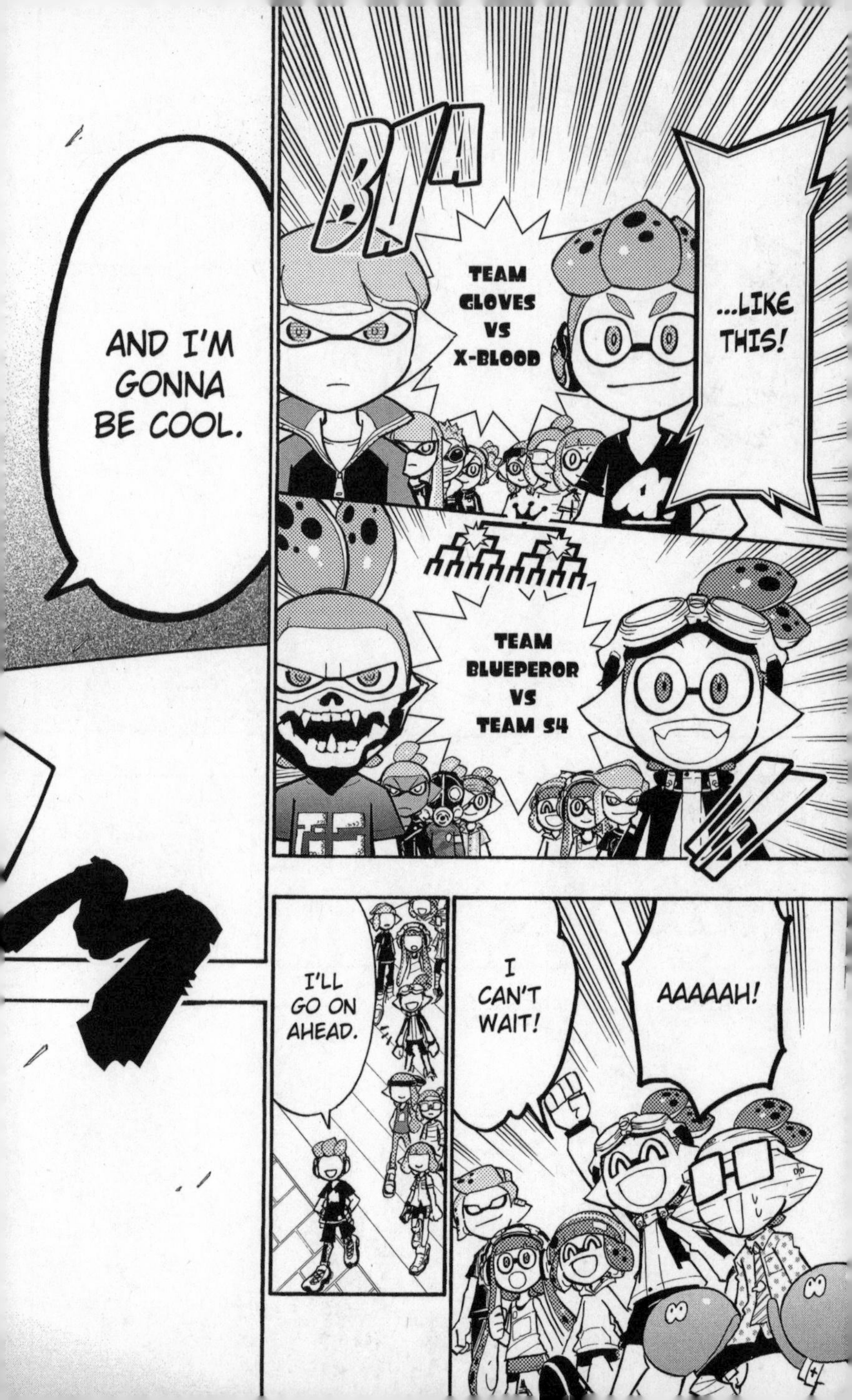
AND I'M GONNA BE COOL.
...LIKE THIS!
BAA
TEAM GLOVES VS X-BLOOD
TEAM BLUEPEROR VS TEAM S4
AAAAAH!
I CAN'T WAIT!
I'LL GO ON AHEAD.

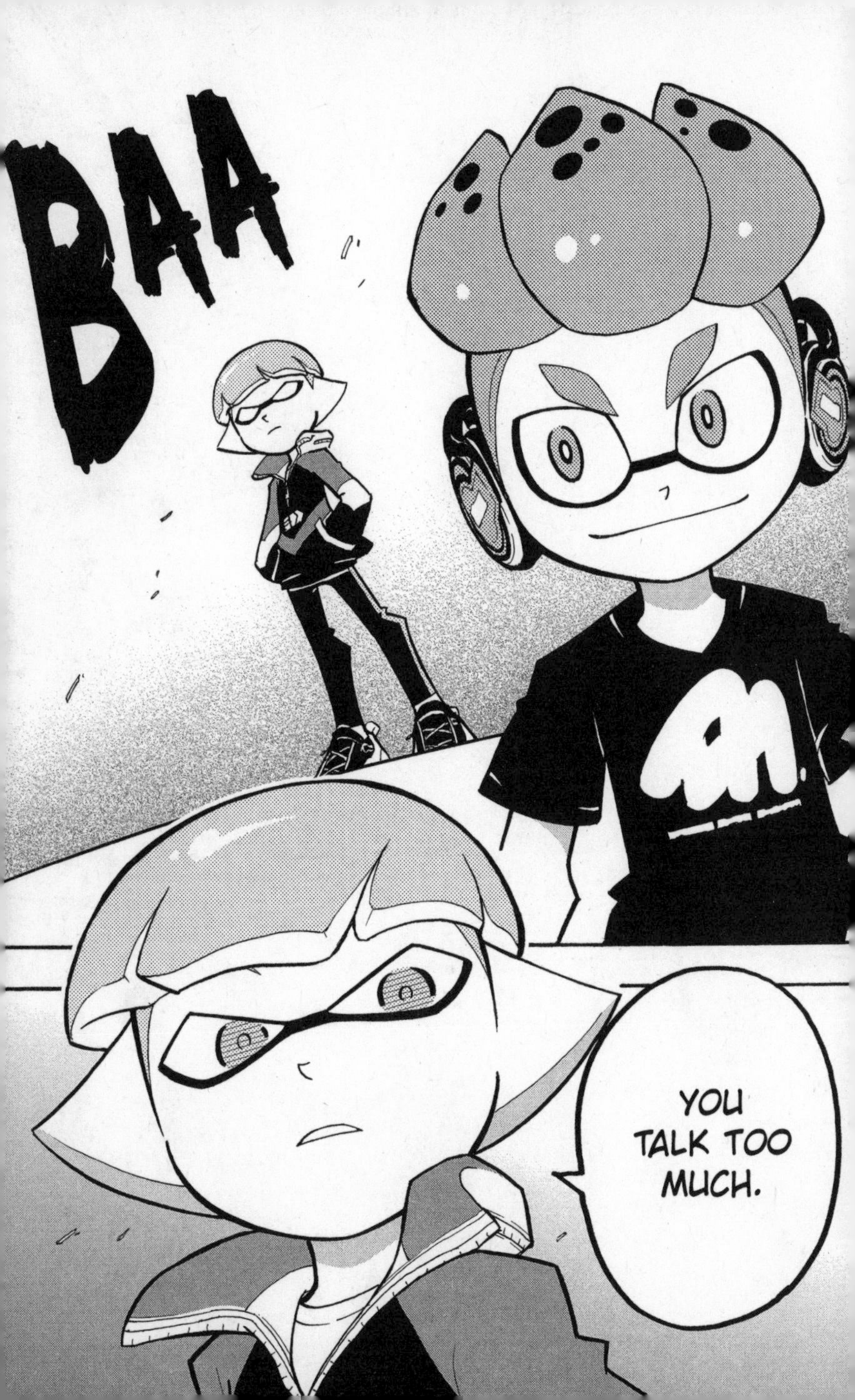
BAA
YOU TALK TOO MUCH.

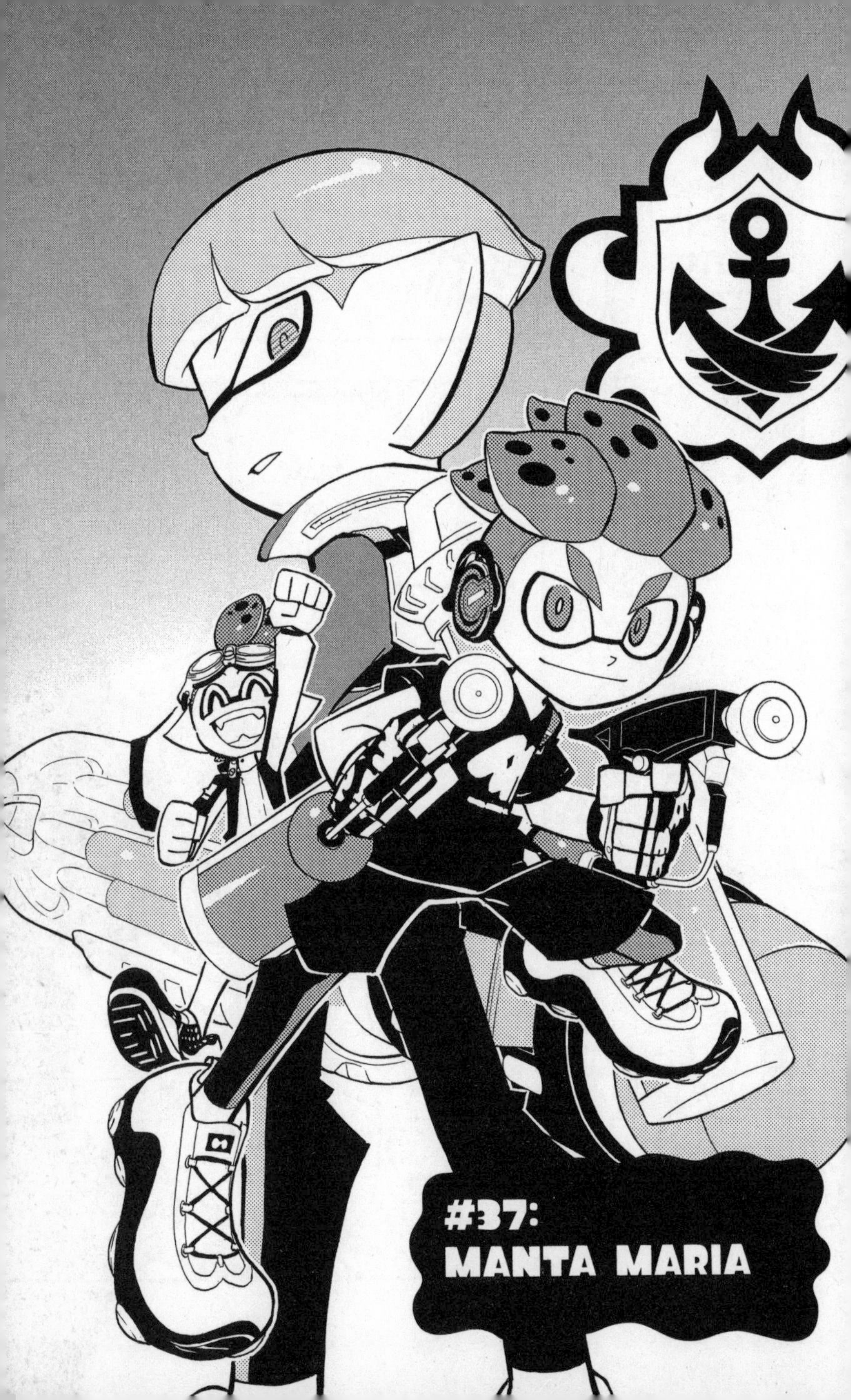
#37:
MANTA MARIA

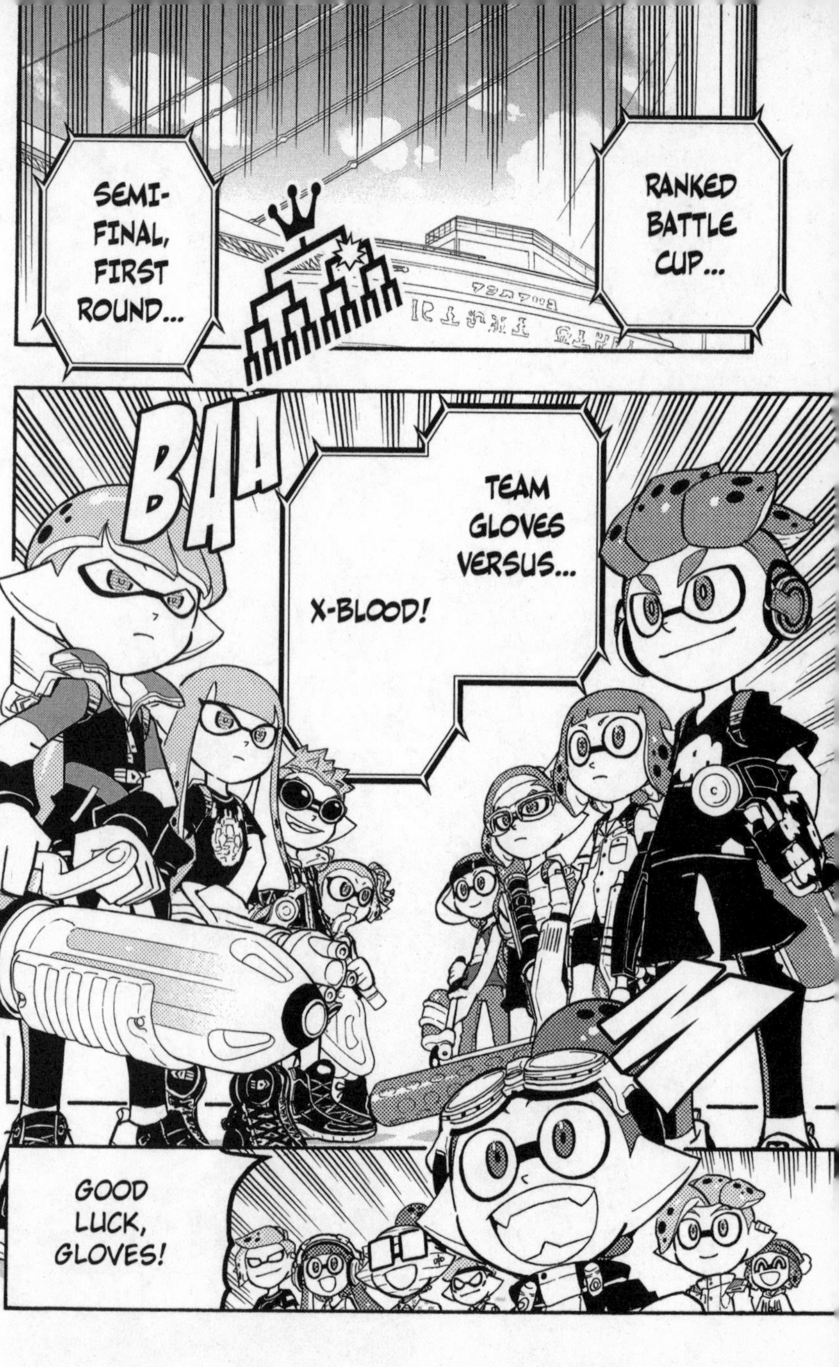
RANKED BATTLE CUP...
SEMI-FINAL, FIRST ROUND...
TEAM GLOVES VERSUS...
X-BLOOD!
BA
GOOD LUCK, GLOVES!

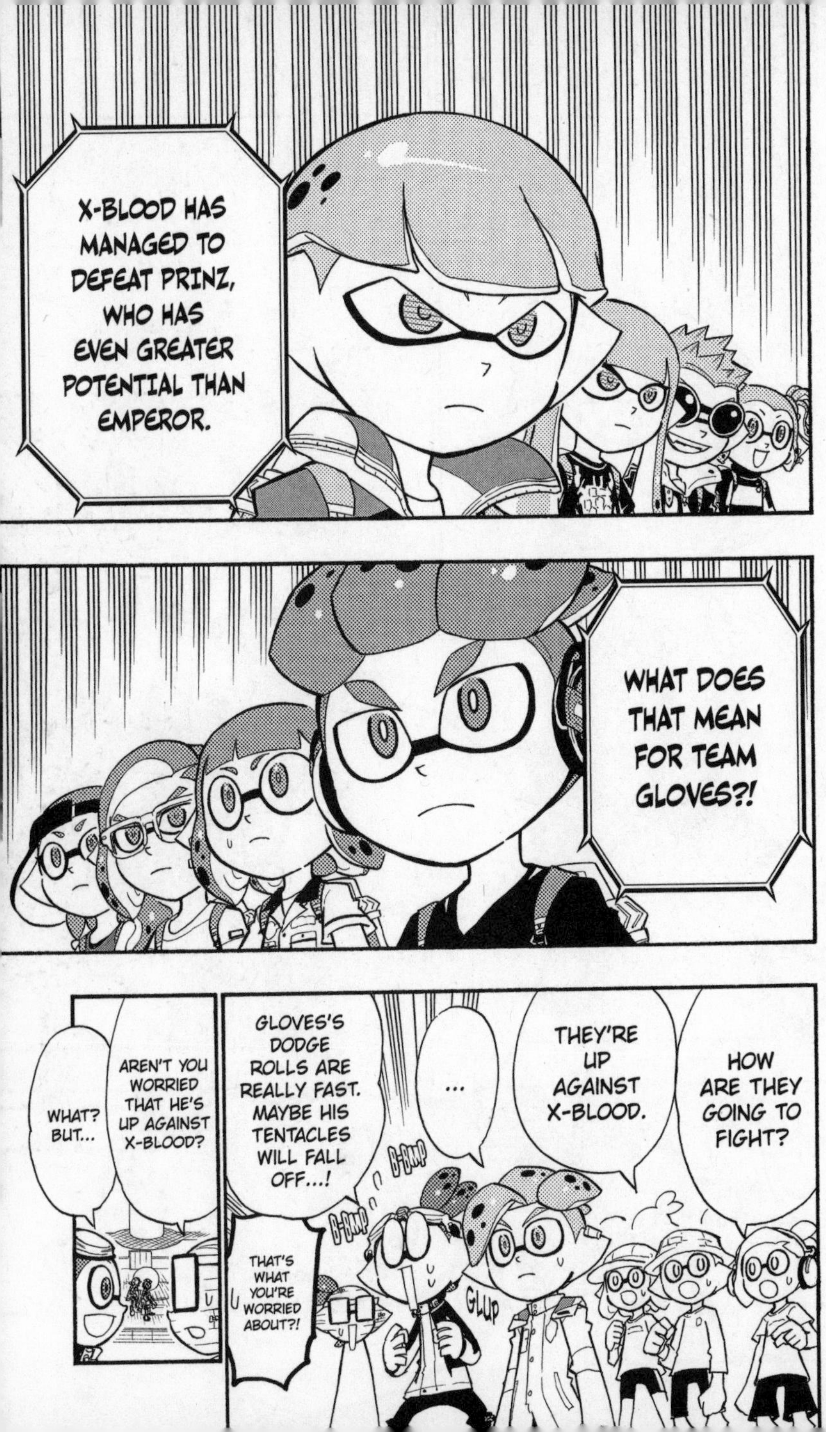
X-BLOOD HAS MANAGED TO DEFEAT PRINZ, WHO HAS EVEN GREATER POTENTIAL THAN EMPEROR.
WHAT DOES THAT MEAN FOR TEAM GLOVES?!
HOW ARE THEY GOING TO FIGHT?
THEY'RE UP AGAINST X-BLOOD.
...
GLOVES'S DODGE ROLLS ARE REALLY FAST. MAYBE HIS TENTACLES WILL FALL OFF...!
B-BMP
B-BMP
GLUP
THAT'S WHAT YOU'RE WORRIED ABOUT?!
AREN'T YOU WORRIED THAT HE'S UP AGAINST X-BLOOD?
WHAT? BUT...

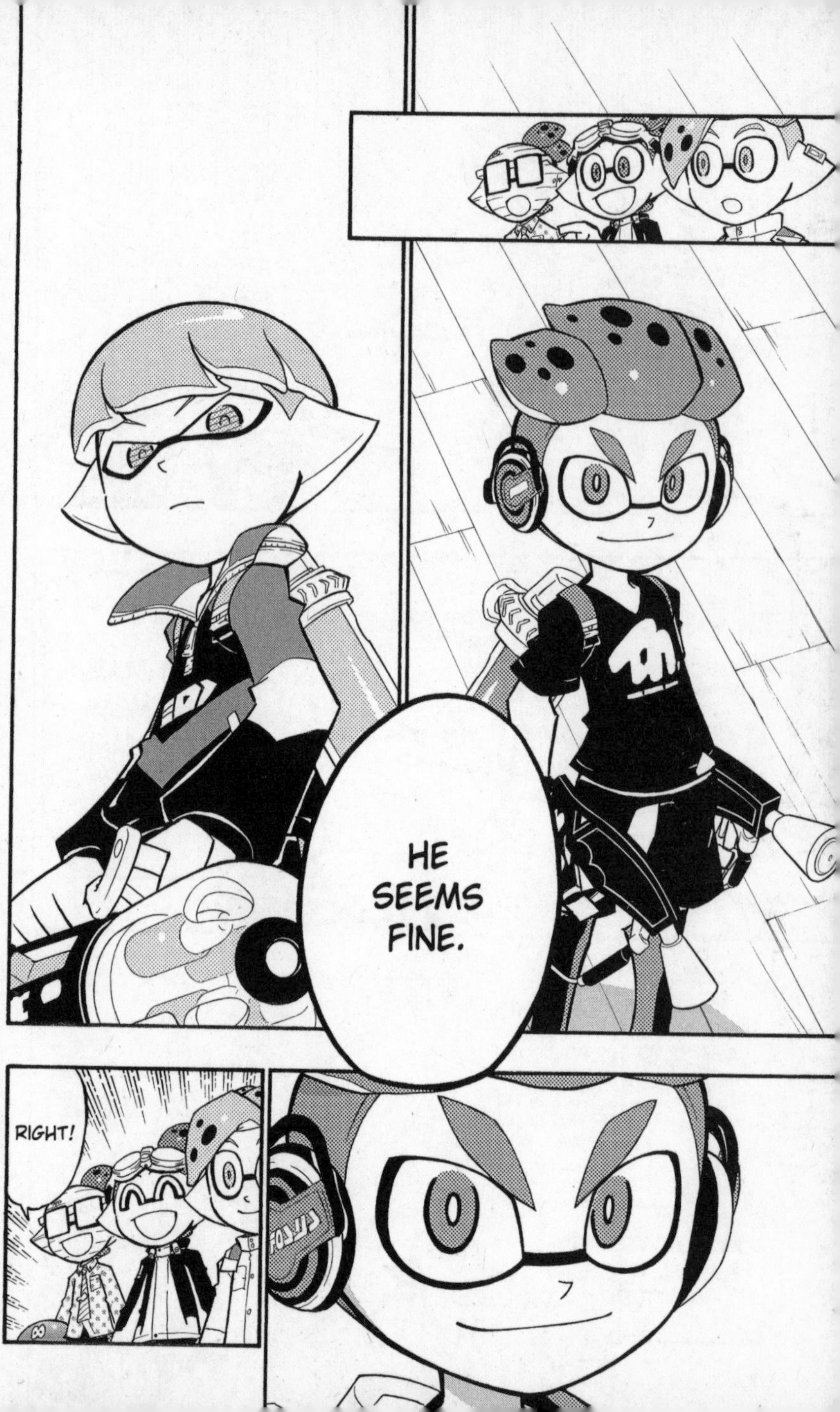
HE SEEMS FINE.
RIGHT!

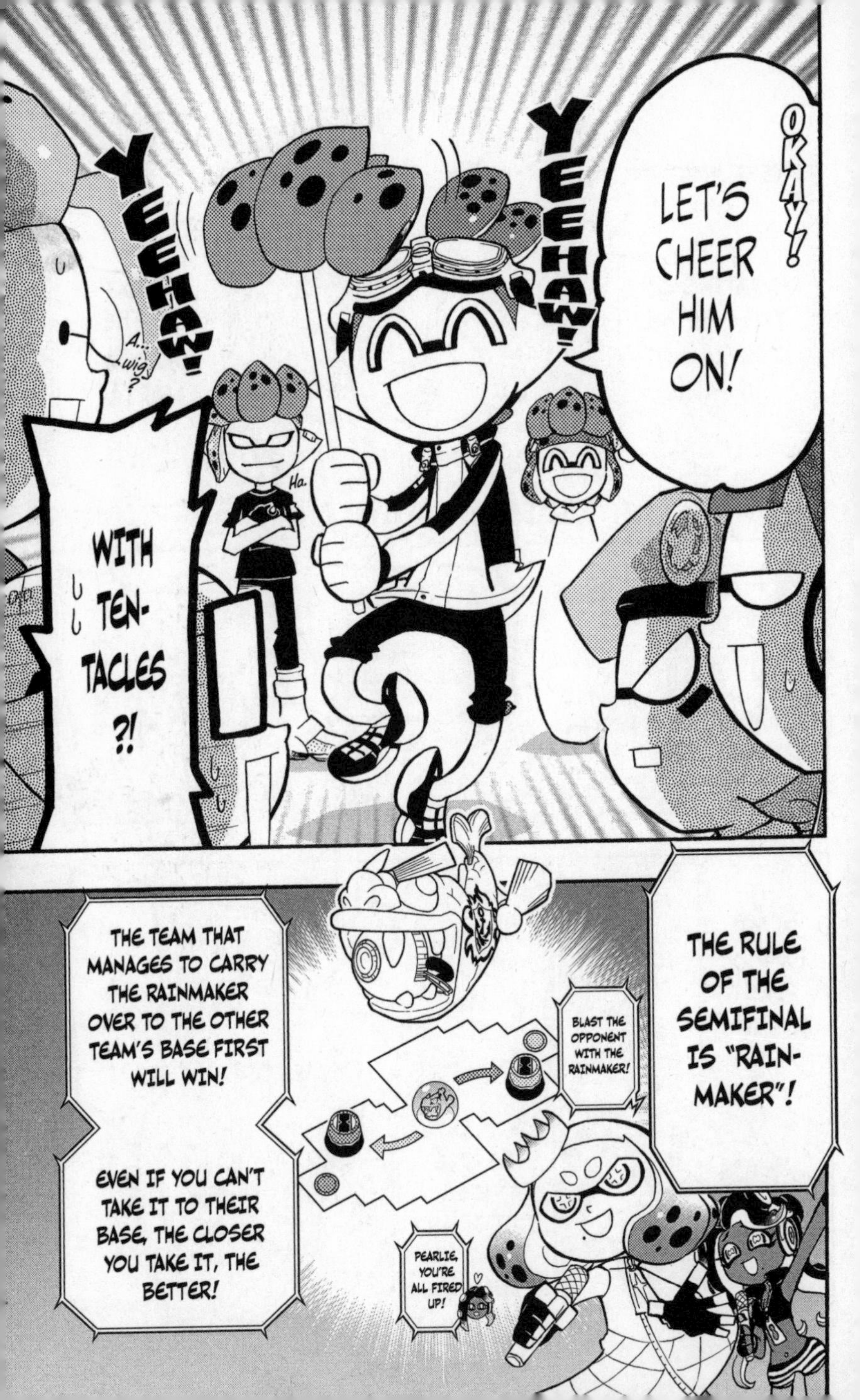
OKAY! LET'S CHEER HIM ON!
YEEHAW!
YEEHAW!
A... wig?
Ha.
WITH TEN-TACLES?!
THE RULE OF THE SEMIFINAL IS "RAIN-MAKER"!
BLAST THE OPPONENT WITH THE RAINMAKER!
THE TEAM THAT MANAGES TO CARRY THE RAINMAKER OVER TO THE OTHER TEAM'S BASE FIRST WILL WIN!
PEARLIE, YOU'RE ALL FIRED UP!
EVEN IF YOU CAN'T TAKE IT TO THEIR BASE, THE CLOSER YOU TAKE IT, THE BETTER!

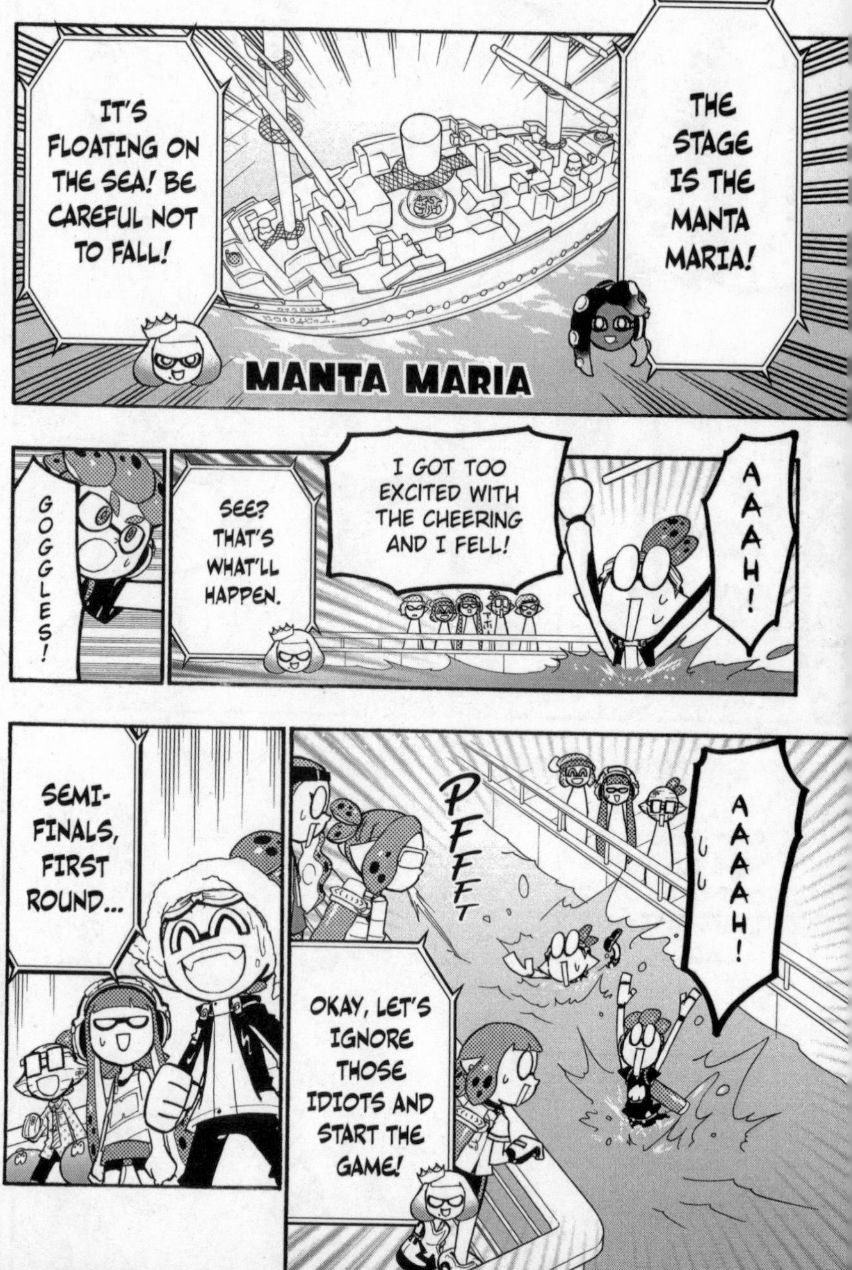
THE STAGE IS THE MANTA MARIA!
IT'S FLOATING ON THE SEA! BE CAREFUL NOT TO FALL!
MANTA MARIA
AAAH!
I GOT TOO EXCITED WITH THE CHEERING AND I FELL!
SEE? THAT'S WHAT'LL HAPPEN.
GOGGLES!
AAAAAH!
PFFFT
OKAY, LET'S IGNORE THOSE IDIOTS AND START THE GAME!
SEMI-FINALS, FIRST ROUND...

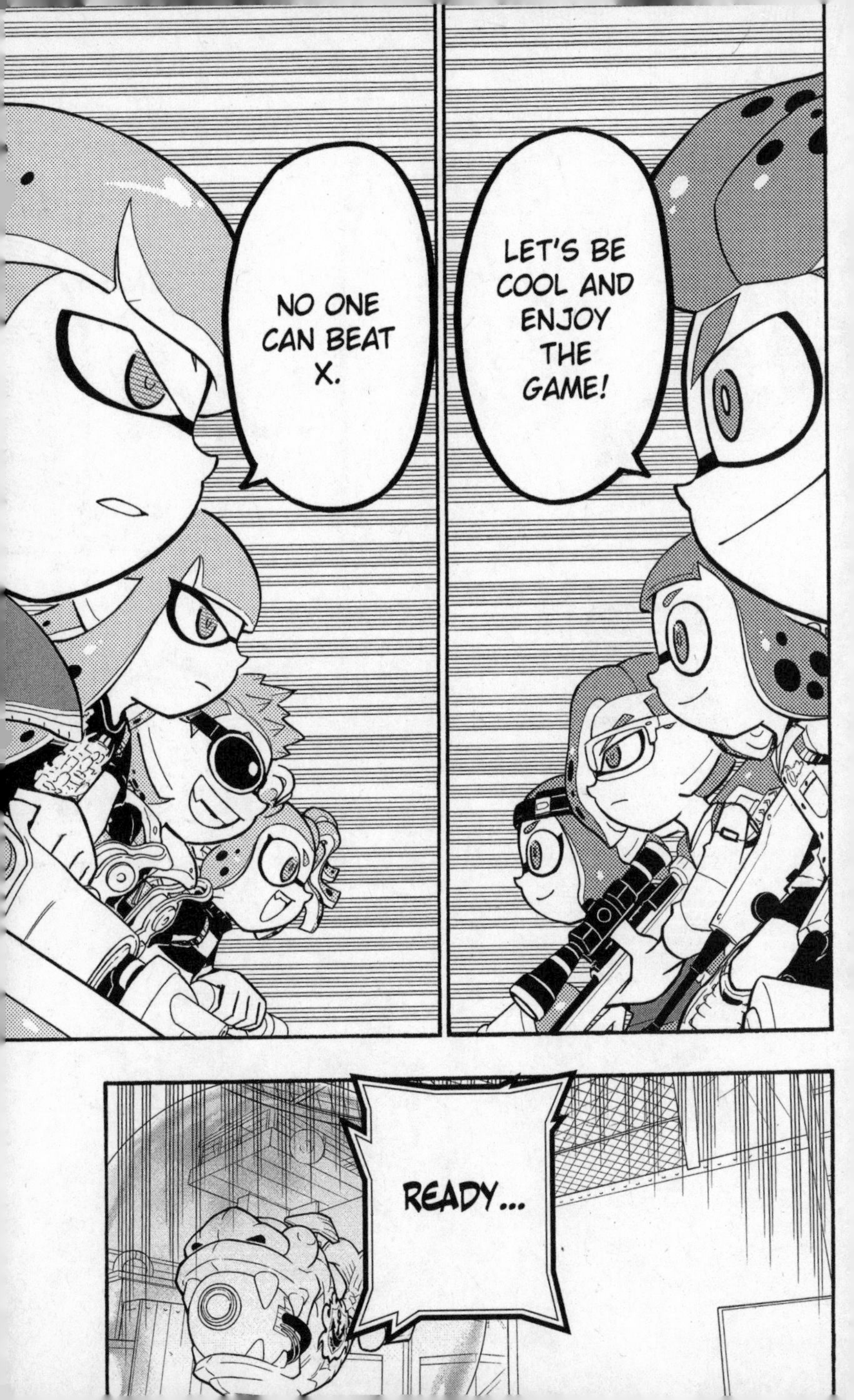
LET'S BE COOL AND ENJOY THE GAME!
NO ONE CAN BEAT X.
READY...

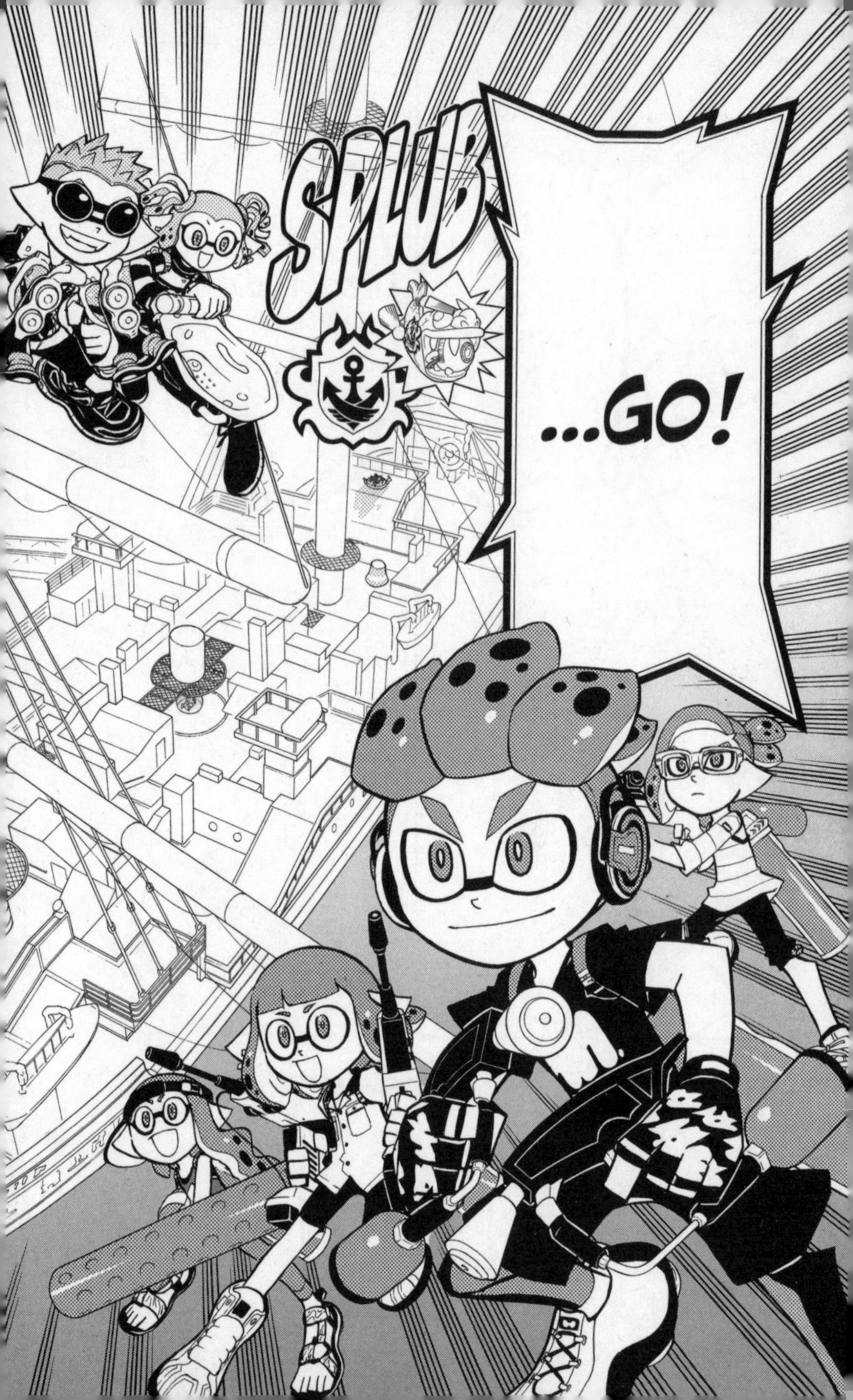
...GO!
SPLUB

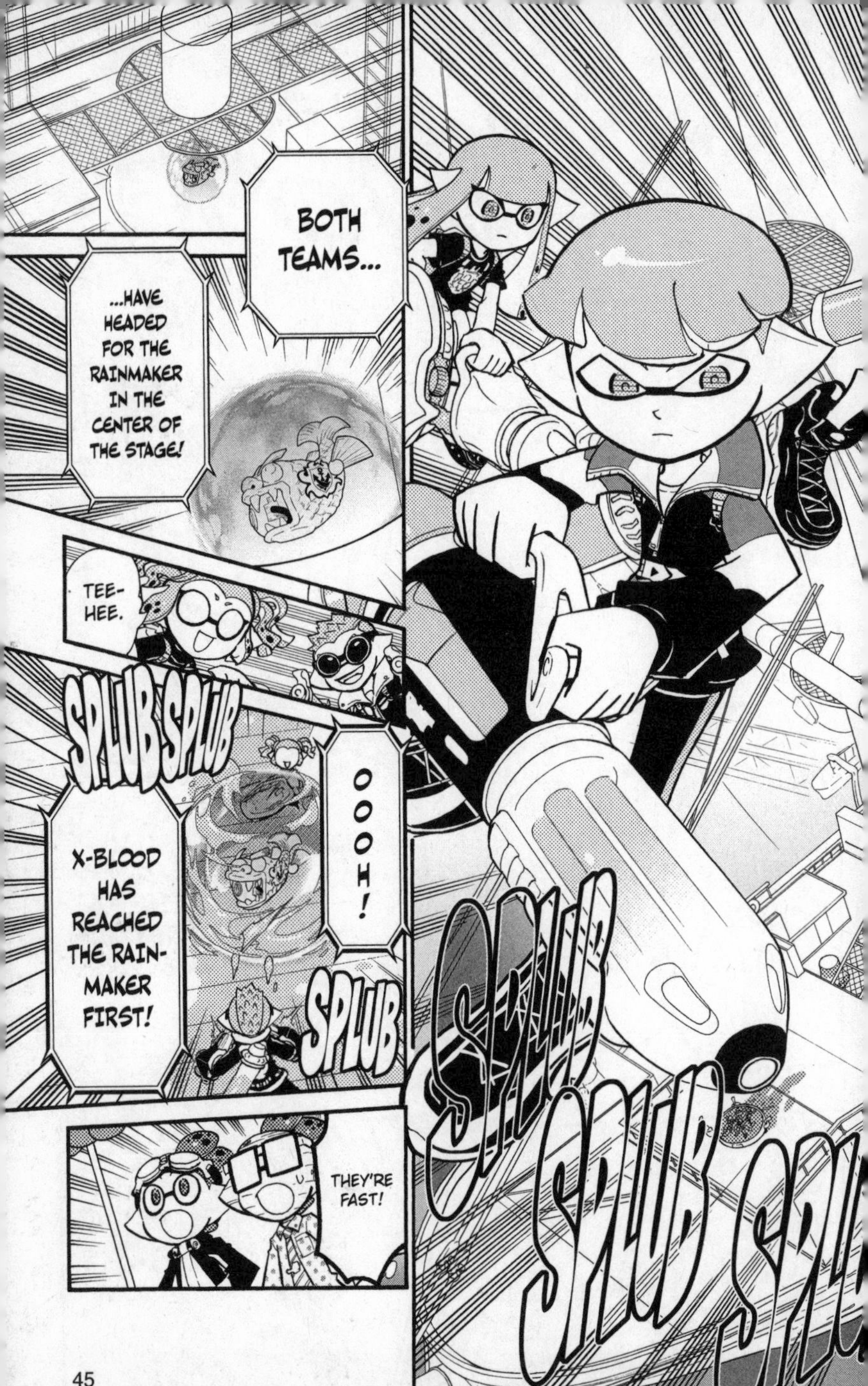
SPLUB
SPLUB
BOTH TEAMS...
...HAVE HEADED FOR THE RAINMAKER IN THE CENTER OF THE STAGE!
TEE-HEE.
SPLUB SPLUB
OOOOH!
X-BLOOD HAS REACHED THE RAIN-MAKER FIRST!
SPLUB
THEY'RE FAST!

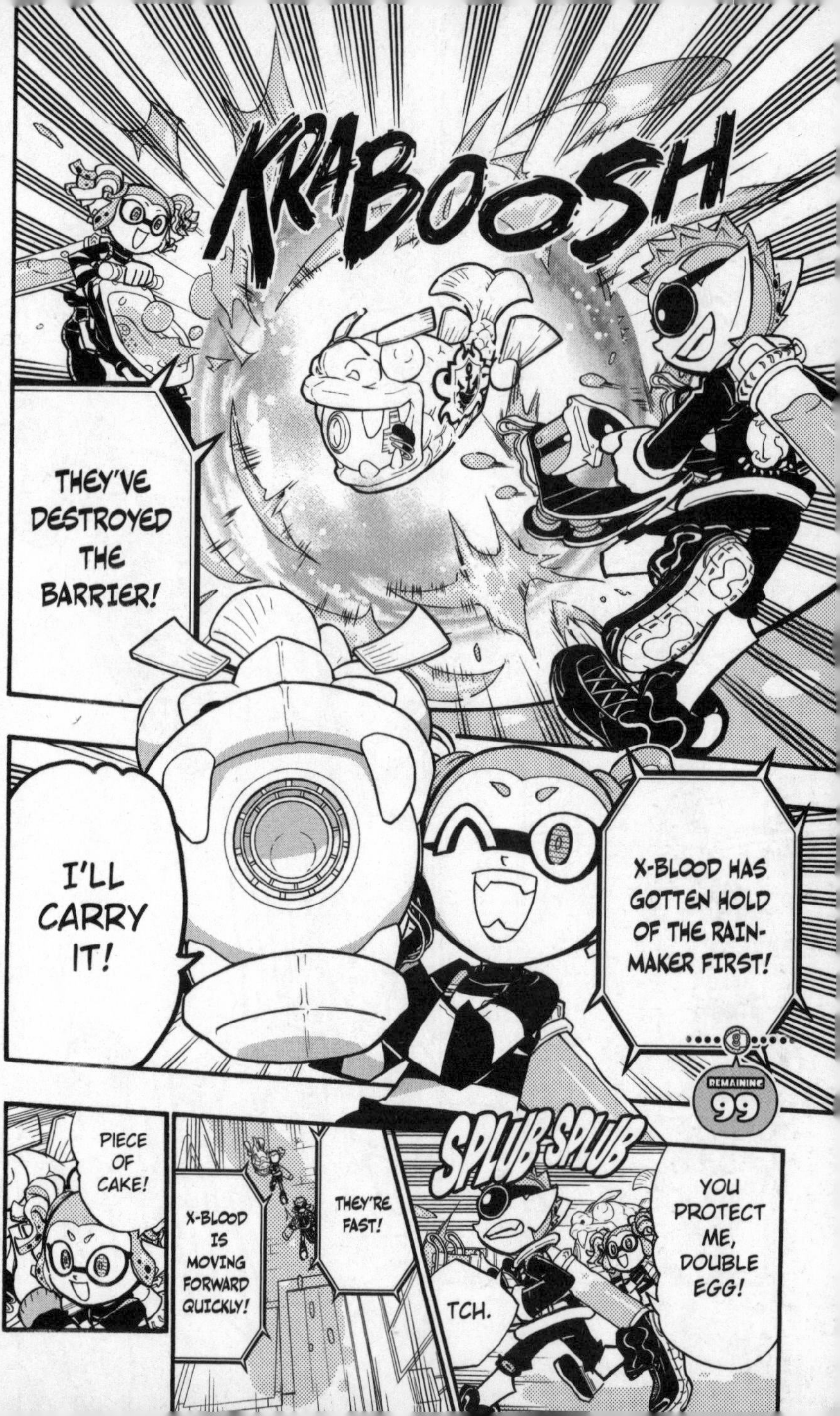
KRABOOSH
THEY'VE DESTROYED THE BARRIER!
X-BLOOD HAS GOTTEN HOLD OF THE RAIN-MAKER FIRST!
I'LL CARRY IT!
REMAINING
99
SPLUB-SPLUB
YOU PROTECT ME, DOUBLE EGG!
TCH.
THEY'RE FAST!
X-BLOOD IS MOVING FORWARD QUICKLY!
PIECE OF CAKE!

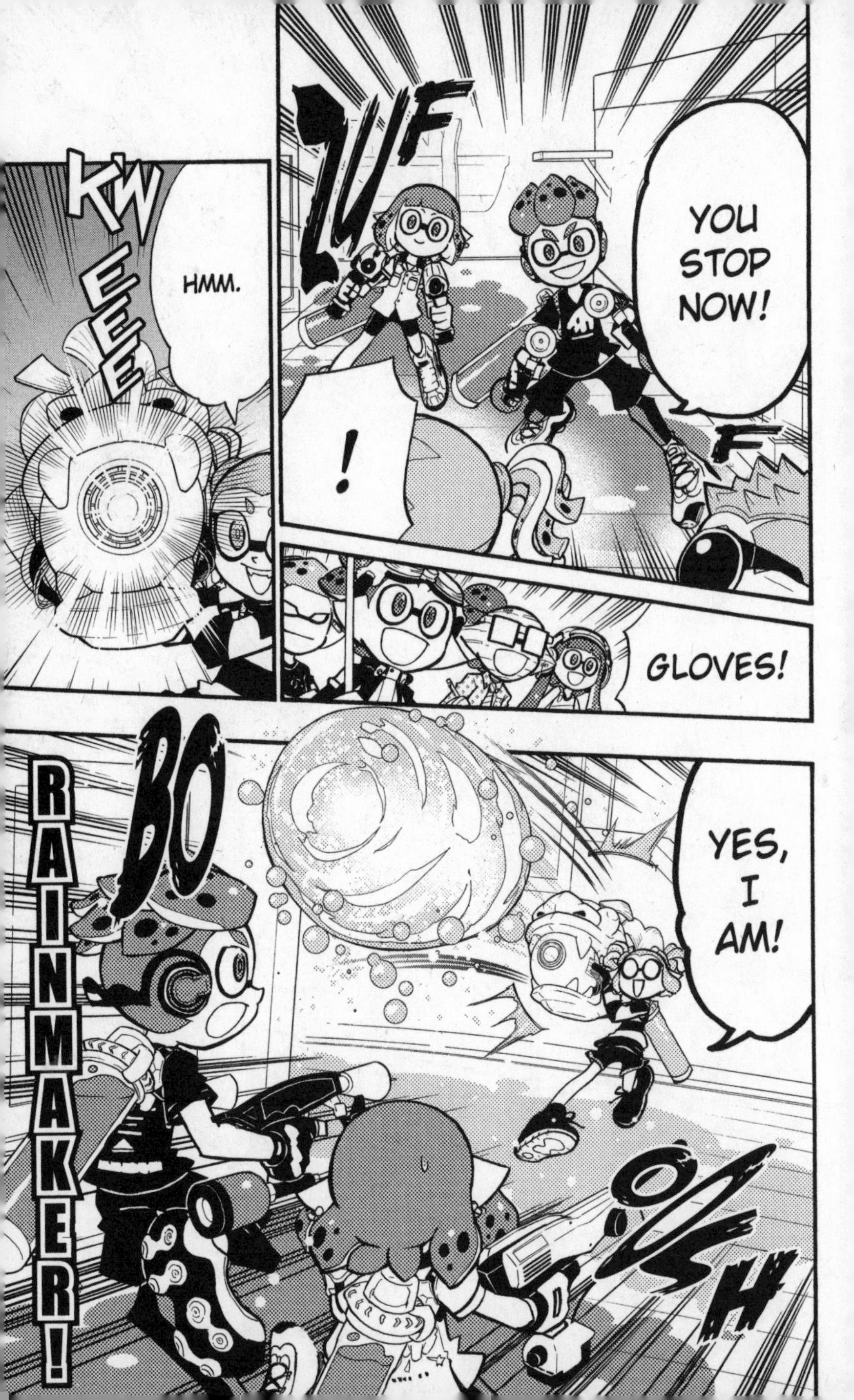
ZUF
YOU STOP NOW!
F
!
GLOVES!
K'WEEE
HMM.
YES, I AM!
BO
RAINMAKER!

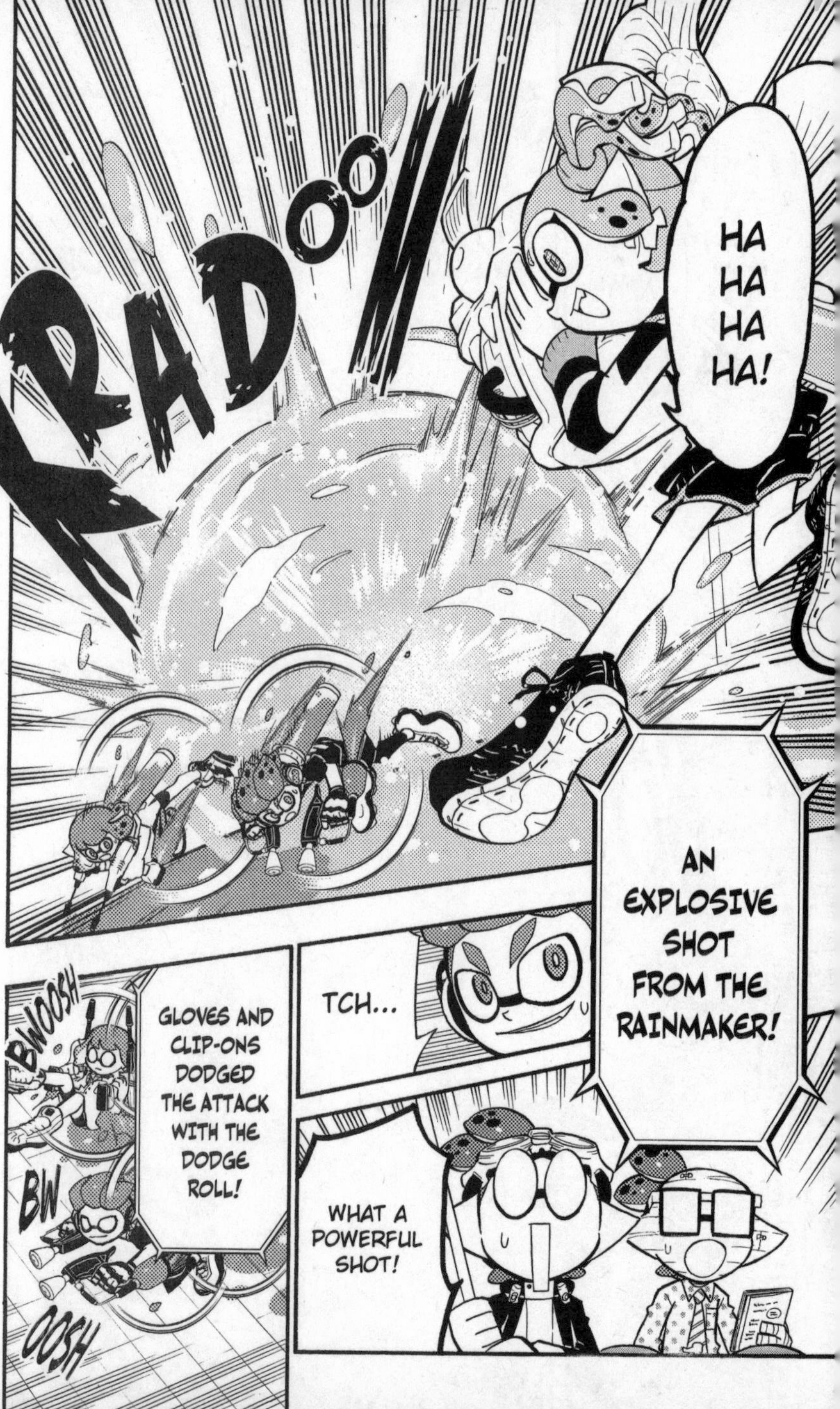
KRADOOM
HA HA HA HA!
AN EXPLOSIVE SHOT FROM THE RAINMAKER!
TCH...
WHAT A POWERFUL SHOT!
GLOVES AND CLIP-ONS DODGED THE ATTACK WITH THE DODGE ROLL!
BWOOSH
BW
OOSH

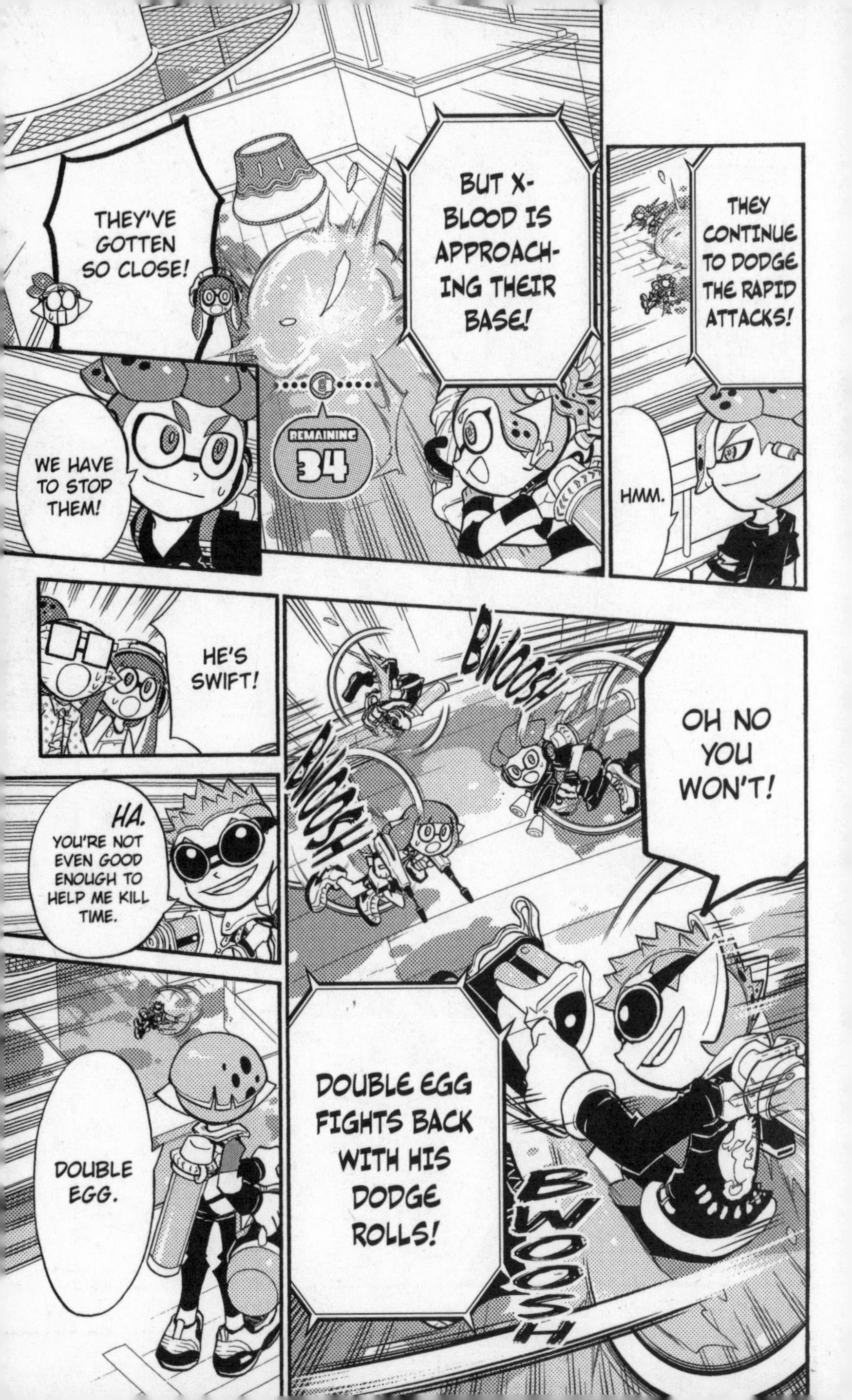
THEY CONTINUE TO DODGE THE RAPID ATTACKS!
HMM.
BUT X-BLOOD IS APPROACHING THEIR BASE!
REMAINING 34
THEY'VE GOTTEN SO CLOSE!
WE HAVE TO STOP THEM!
OH NO YOU WON'T!
BWOOSH
BWOOSH
DOUBLE EGG FIGHTS BACK WITH HIS DODGE ROLLS!
BWOOSH
HE'S SWIFT!
HA.
YOU'RE NOT EVEN GOOD ENOUGH TO HELP ME KILL TIME.
DOUBLE EGG.

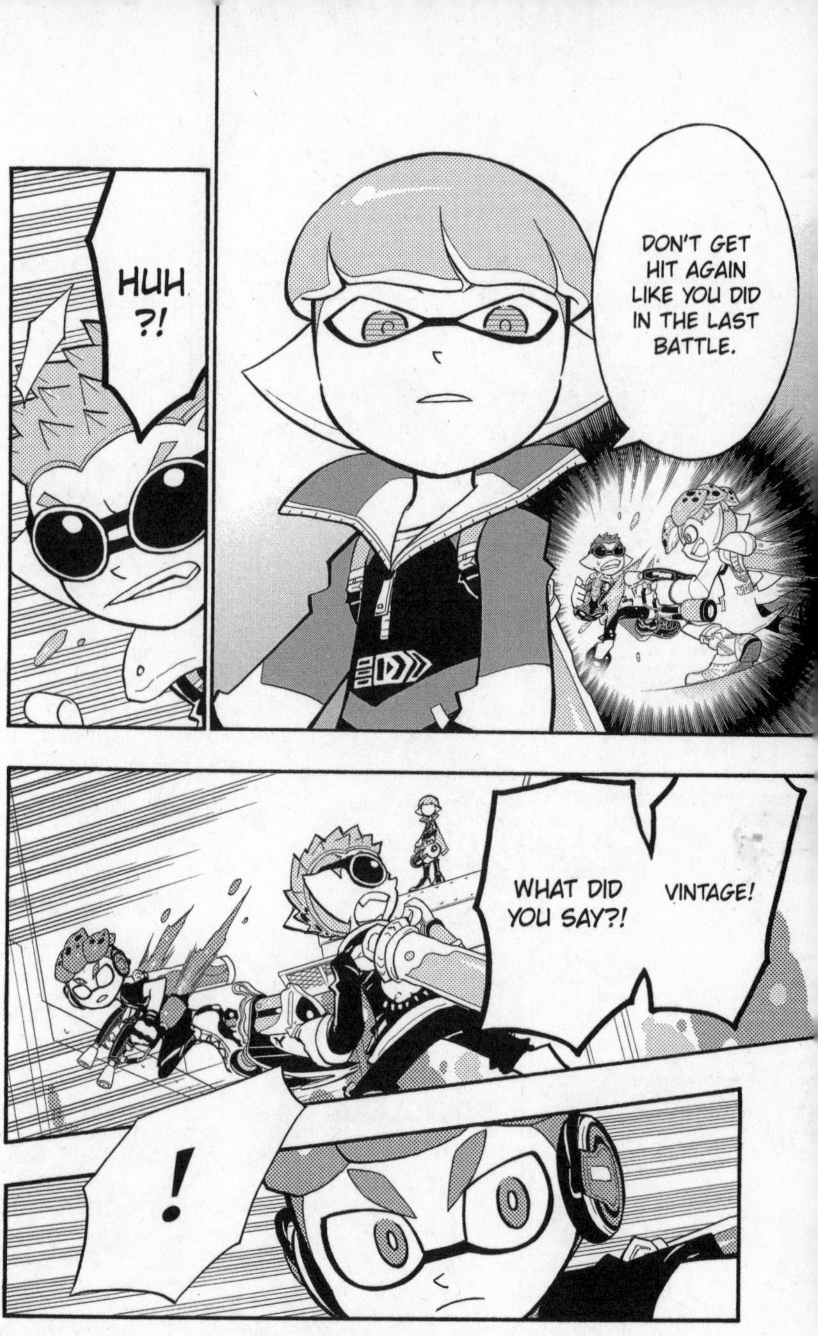
DON'T GET HIT AGAIN LIKE YOU DID IN THE LAST BATTLE.
HUH ?!
WHAT DID YOU SAY?! VINTAGE!
!

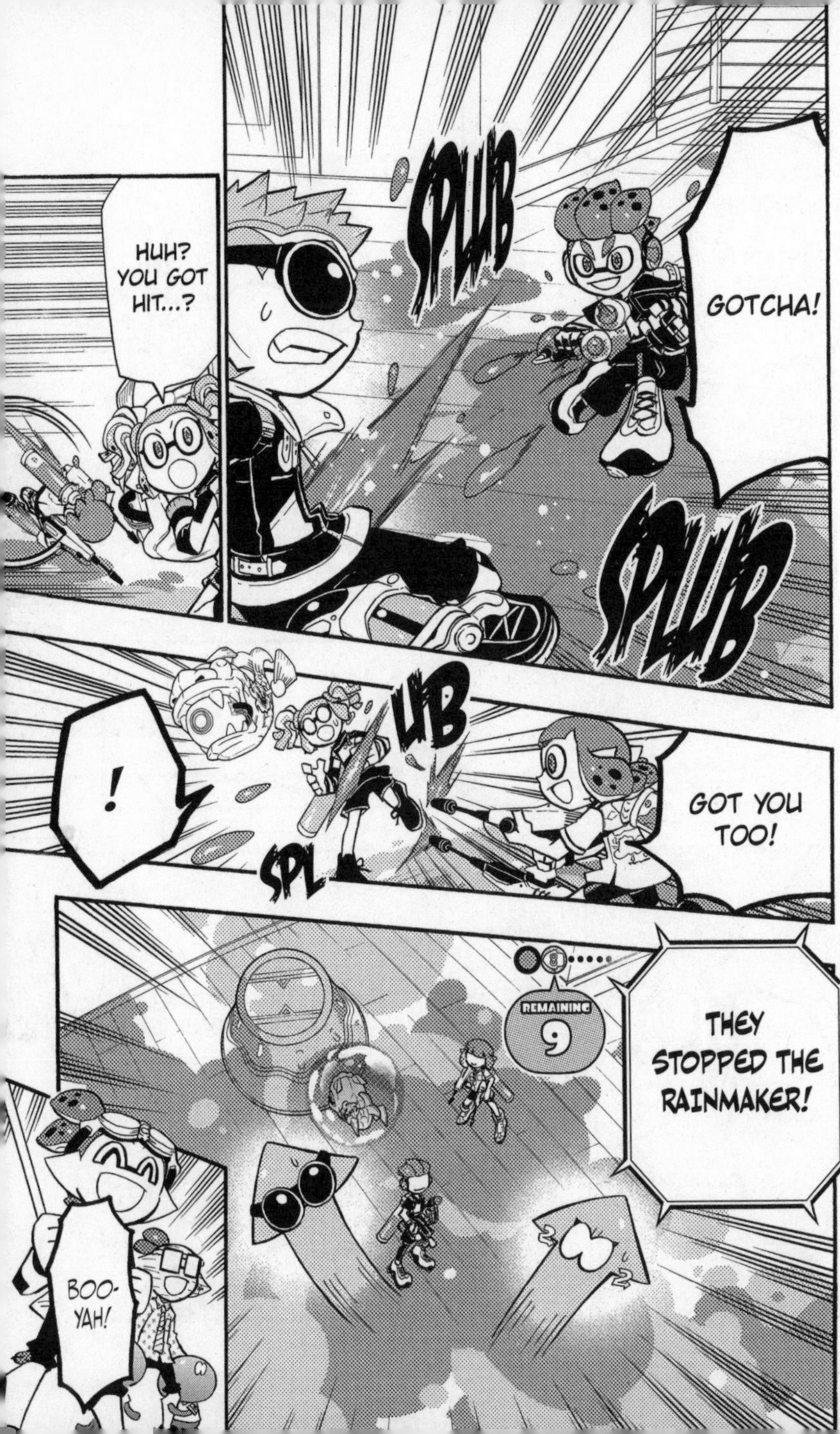
SPLUB
GOTCHA!
SPLUB
HUH? YOU GOT HIT...?
GOT YOU TOO!
UB
SPL
!
REMAINING 9
THEY STOPPED THE RAINMAKER!
BOO-YAH!

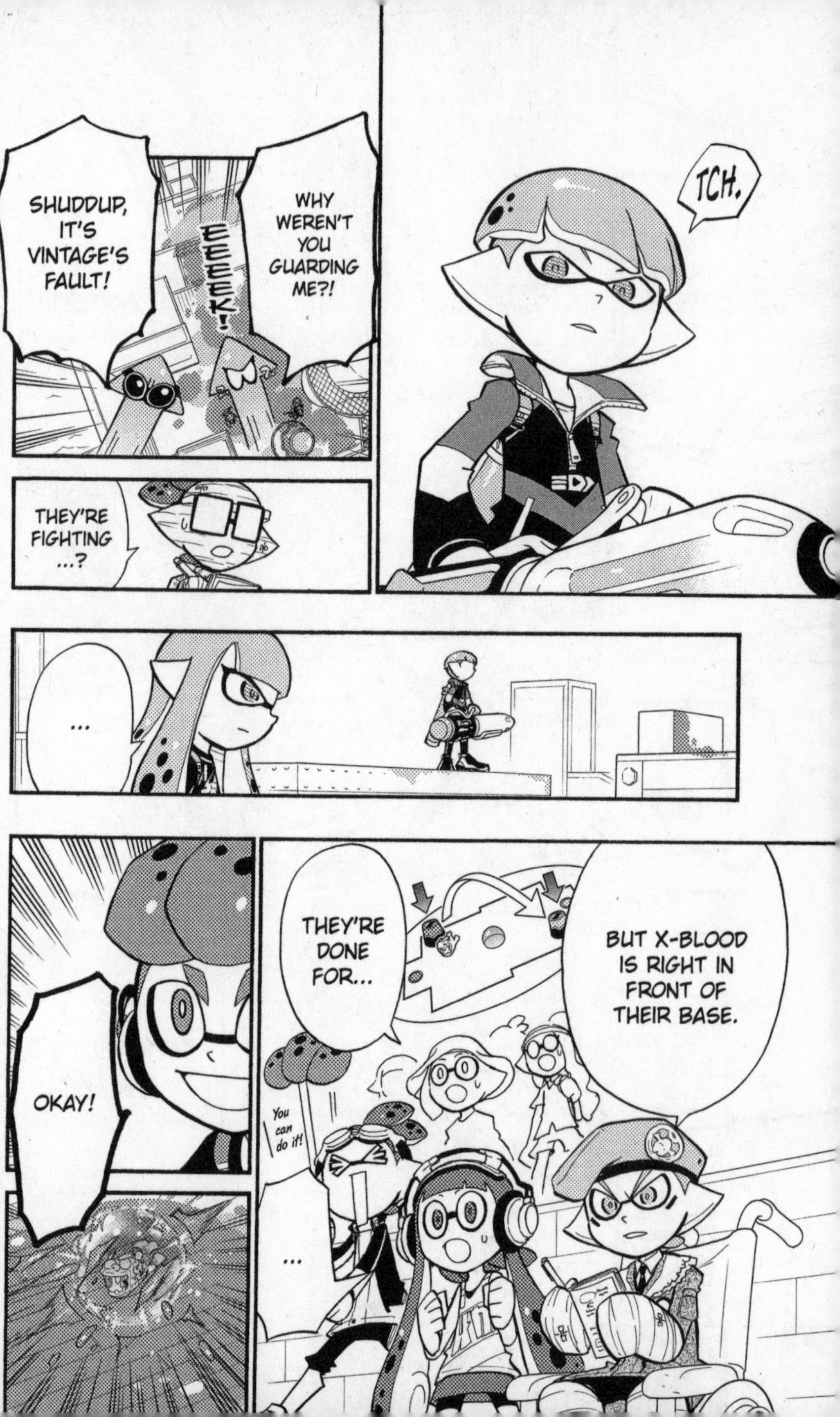
TCH.
WHY WEREN'T YOU GUARDING ME?!
EEEEK!
SHUDDUP, IT'S VINTAGE'S FAULT!
THEY'RE FIGHTING ...?
...
BUT X-BLOOD IS RIGHT IN FRONT OF THEIR BASE.
THEY'RE DONE FOR...
You can do it!
...
OKAY!

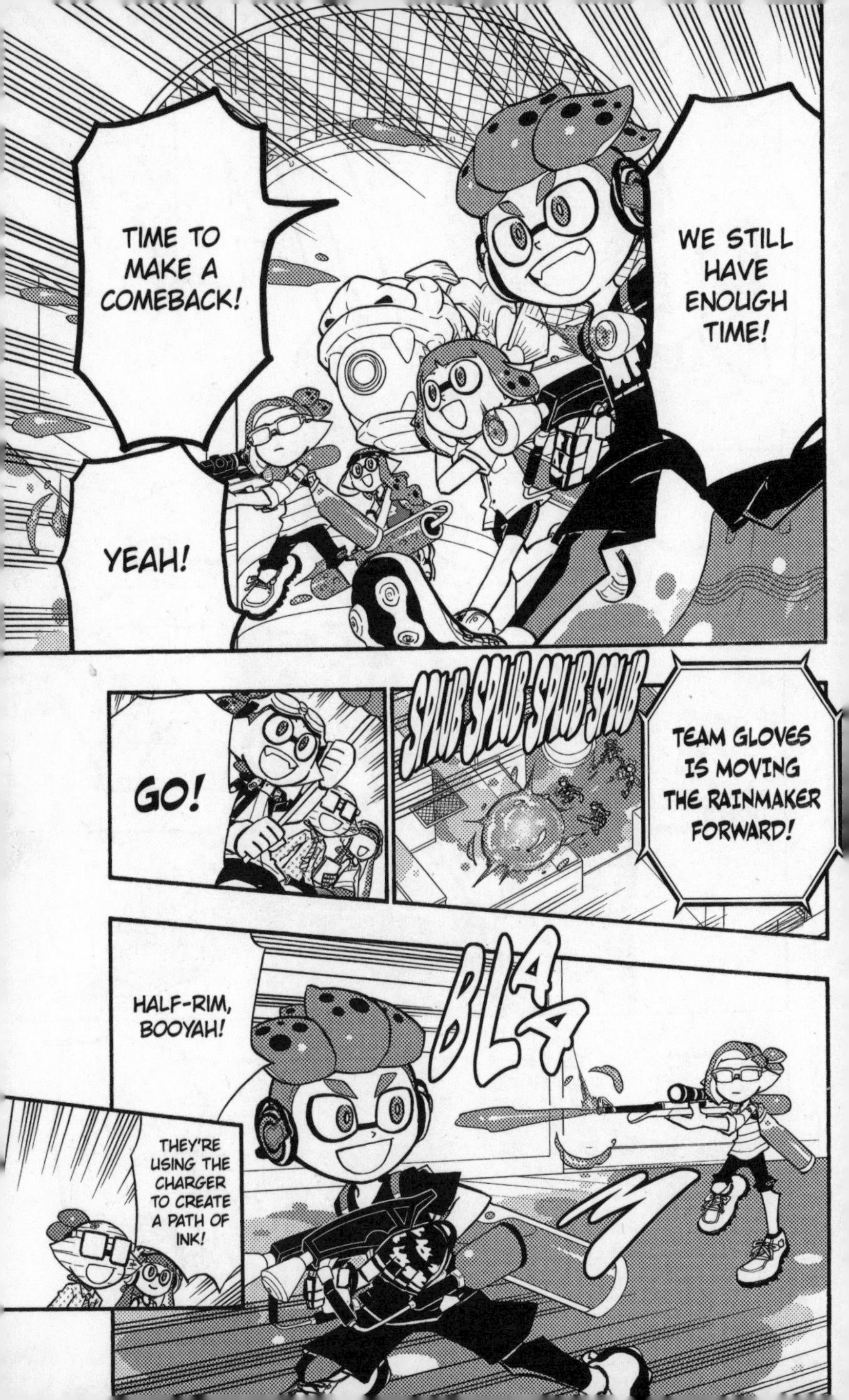
WE STILL HAVE ENOUGH TIME!
TIME TO MAKE A COMEBACK!
YEAH!
TEAM GLOVES IS MOVING THE RAINMAKER FORWARD!
SPLUB SPLUB SPLUB SPLUB
GO!
BLA
HALF-RIM, BOOYAH!
THEY'RE USING THE CHARGER TO CREATE A PATH OF INK!

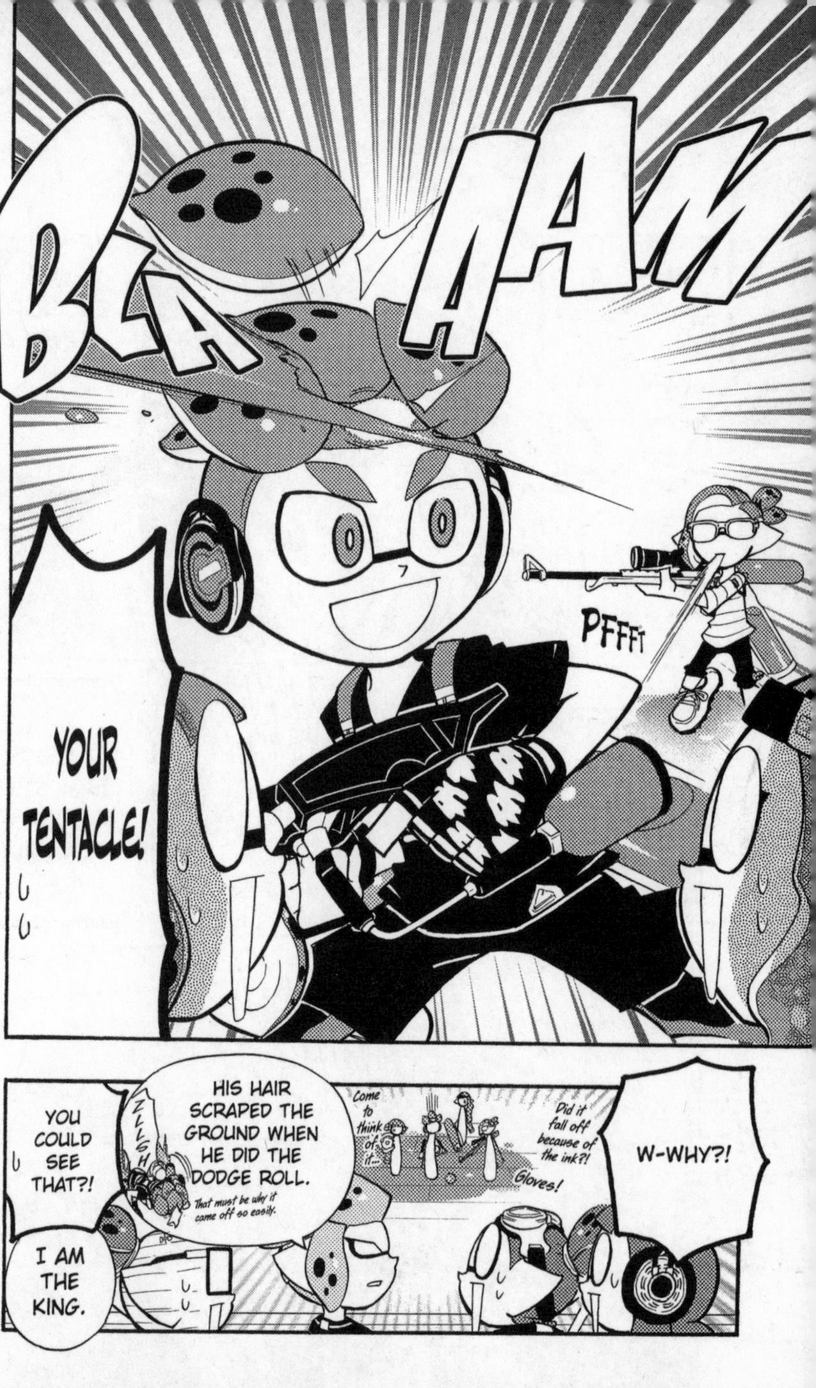
BLAAAM
PFFFT
YOUR TENTACLE!
W-WHY?!
Did it fall off because of the ink?!
Gloves!
Come to think of it...
HIS HAIR SCRAPED THE GROUND WHEN HE DID THE DODGE ROLL.
That must be why it came off so easily.
ZLLGH
YOU COULD SEE THAT?!
I AM THE KING.

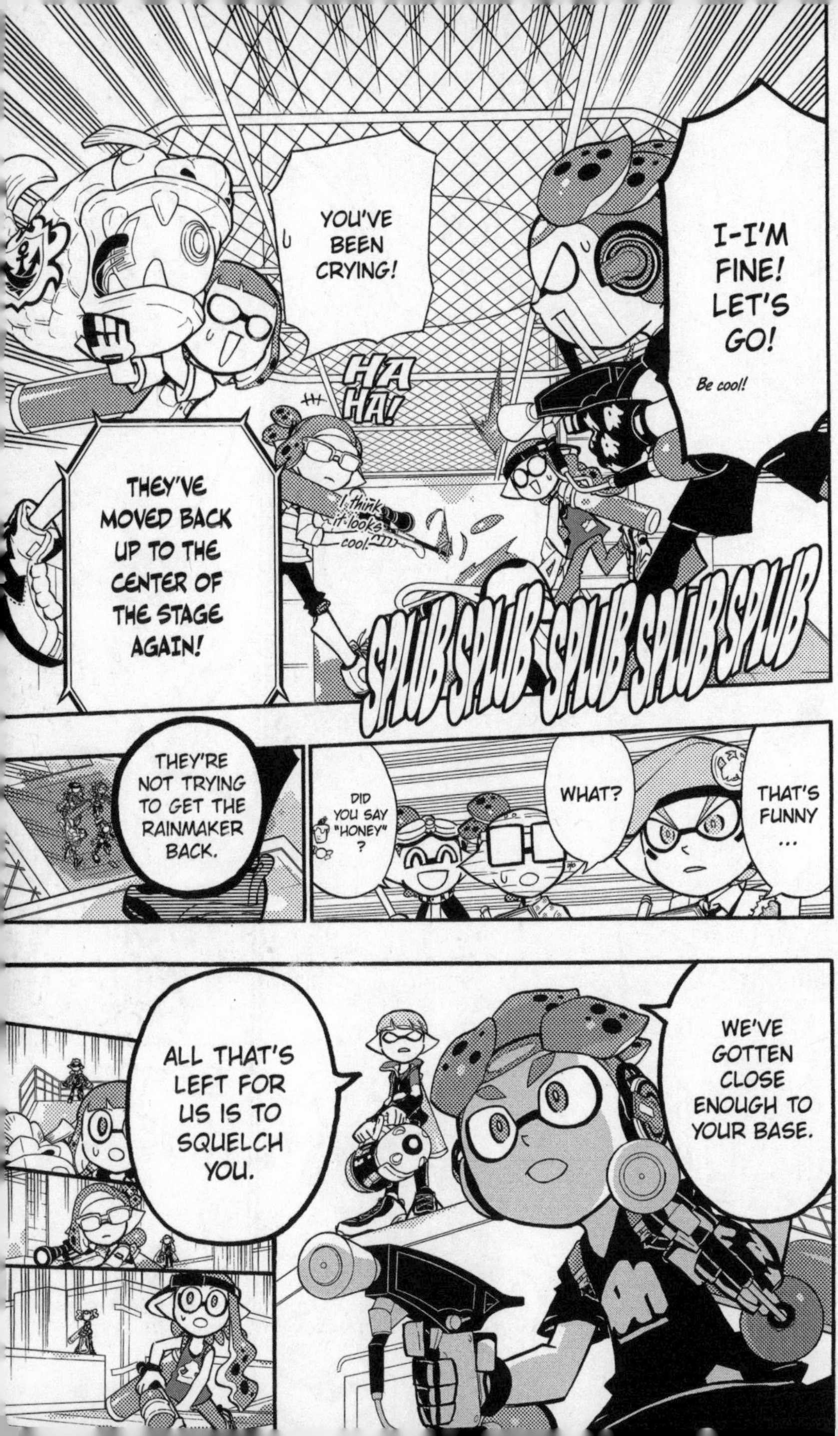
I-I'M FINE! LET'S GO!
Be cool!
YOU'VE BEEN CRYING!
HA HA!
I think it looks cool.
SPLUB SPLUB SPLUB SPLUB SPLUB
THEY'VE MOVED BACK UP TO THE CENTER OF THE STAGE AGAIN!
THAT'S FUNNY ...
WHAT?
DID YOU SAY "HONEY"?
THEY'RE NOT TRYING TO GET THE RAINMAKER BACK.
WE'VE GOTTEN CLOSE ENOUGH TO YOUR BASE.
ALL THAT'S LEFT FOR US IS TO SQUELCH YOU.

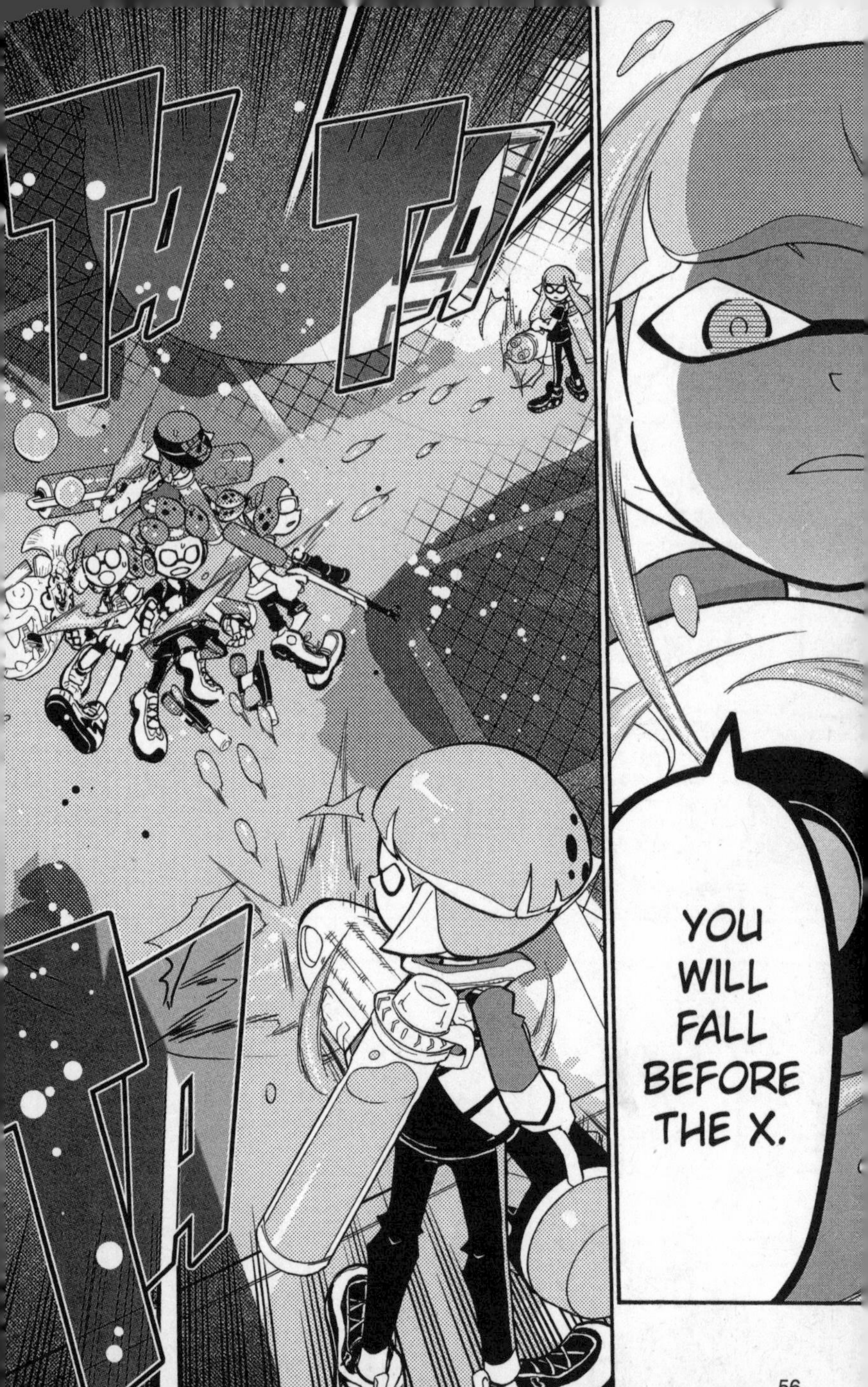
YOU WILL FALL BEFORE THE X.

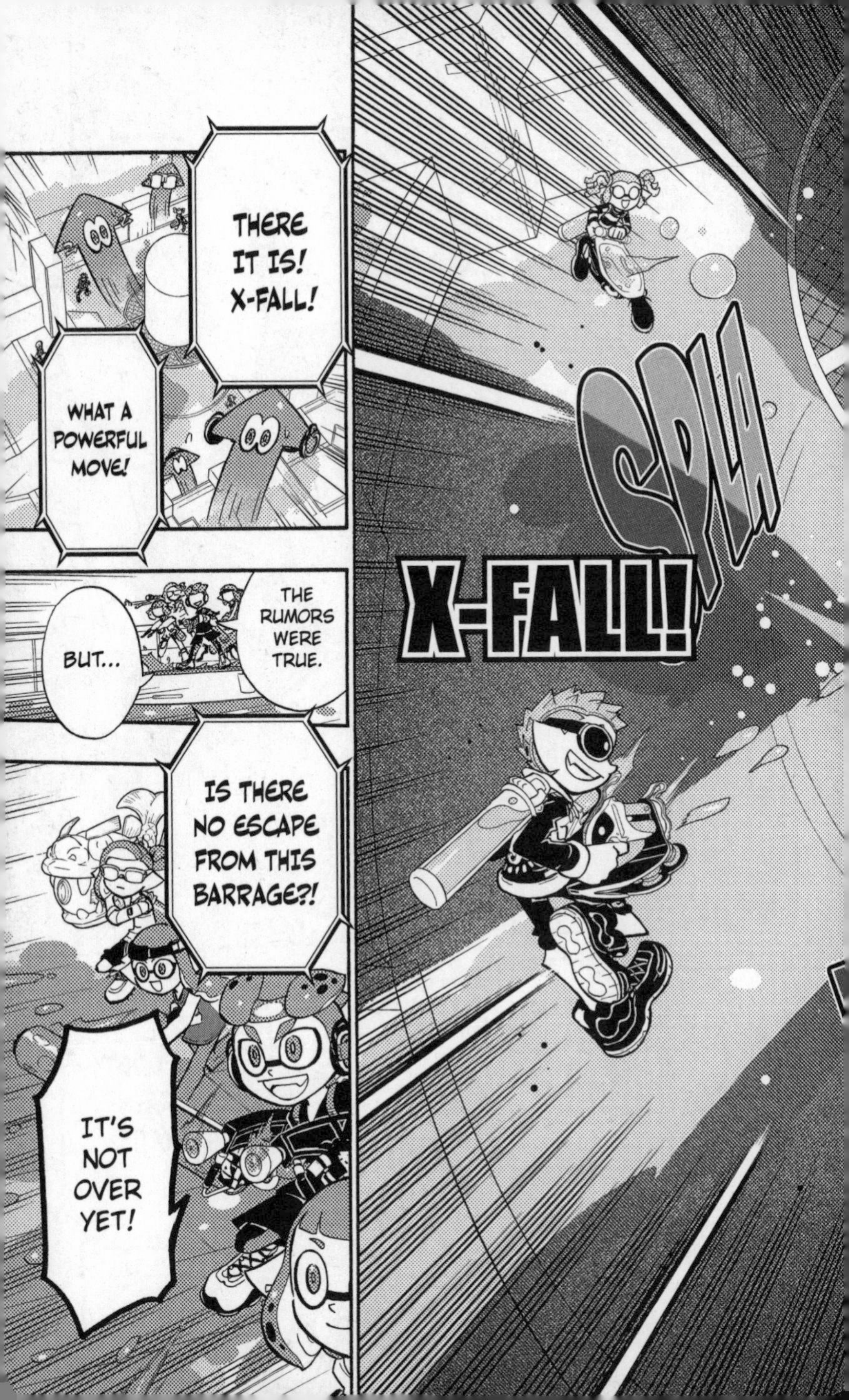
SPLA
X-FALL!
THERE IT IS! X-FALL!
WHAT A POWERFUL MOVE!
THE RUMORS WERE TRUE.
BUT...
IS THERE NO ESCAPE FROM THIS BARRAGE?!
IT'S NOT OVER YET!

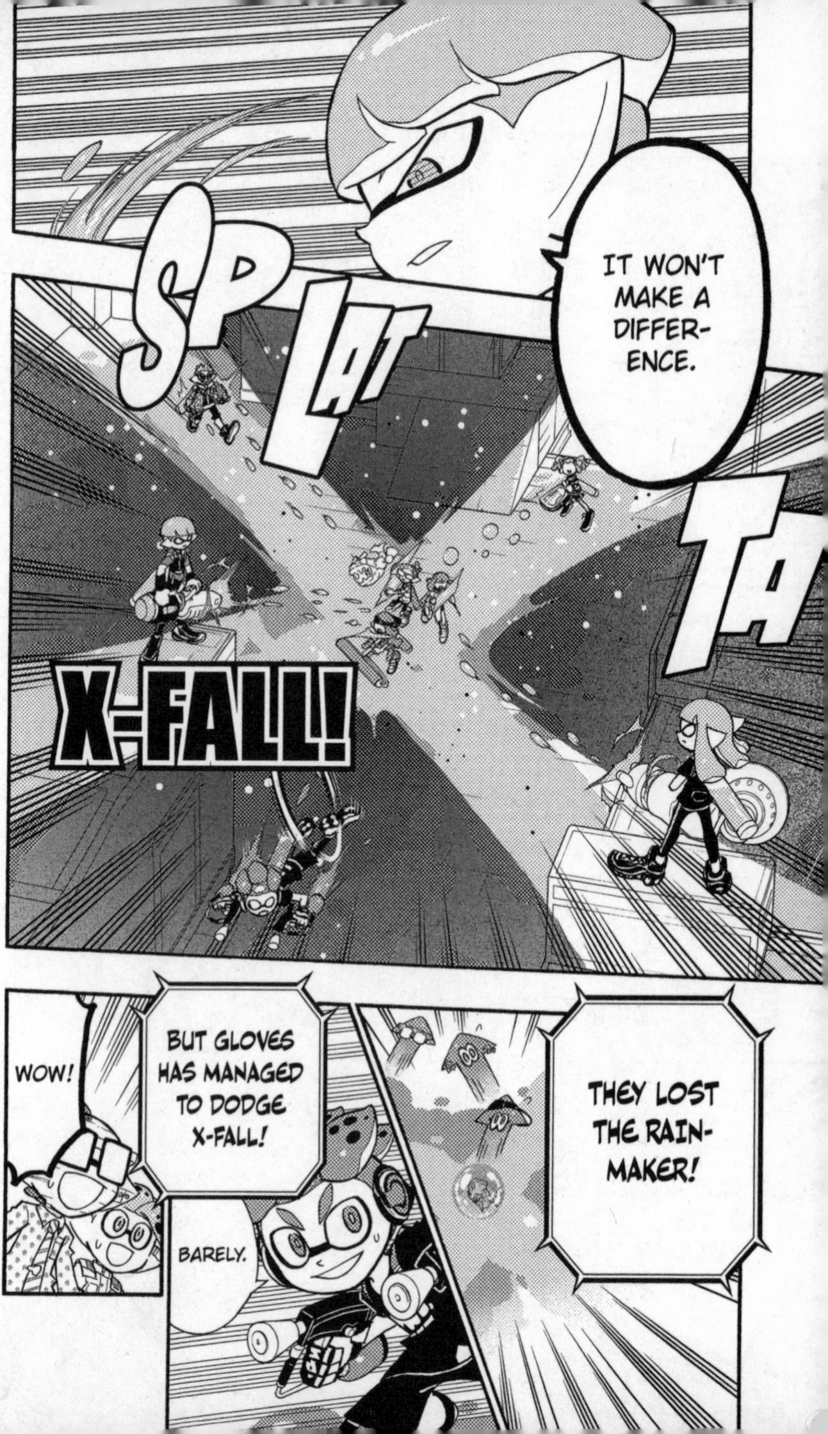
IT WON'T MAKE A DIFFERENCE.
SPLAT
TA
X-FALL!
THEY LOST THE RAIN-MAKER!
BUT GLOVES HAS MANAGED TO DODGE X-FALL!
WOW!
BARELY.

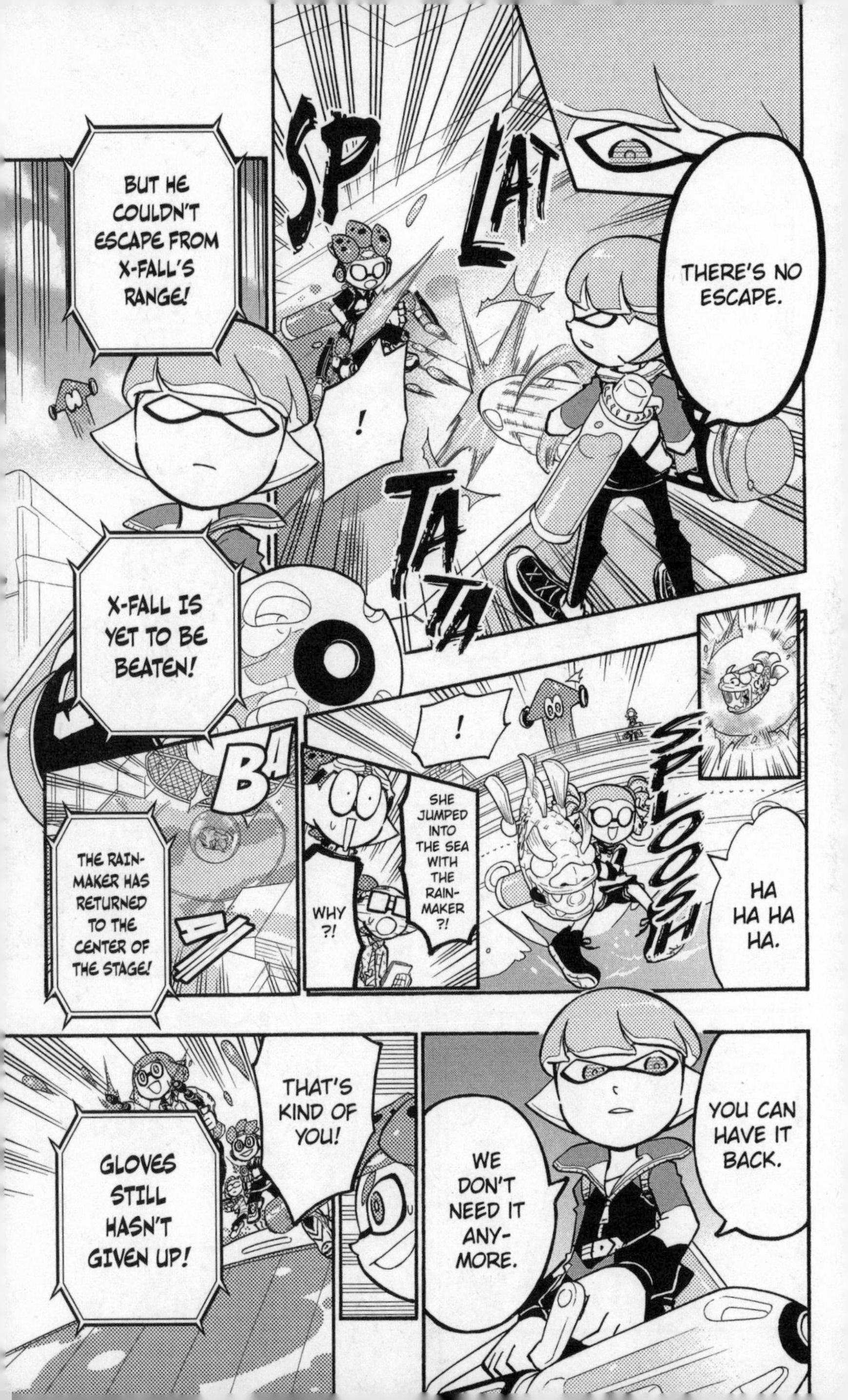
SPLAT
THERE'S NO ESCAPE.
BUT HE COULDN'T ESCAPE FROM X-FALL'S RANGE!
!
TA TA
X-FALL IS YET TO BE BEATEN!
SPLOOSH
HA HA HA HA.
!
SHE JUMPED INTO THE SEA WITH THE RAIN-MAKER ?!
WHY ?!
BA
THE RAIN-MAKER HAS RETURNED TO THE CENTER OF THE STAGE!
YOU CAN HAVE IT BACK.
WE DON'T NEED IT ANY-MORE.
THAT'S KIND OF YOU!
GLOVES STILL HASN'T GIVEN UP!

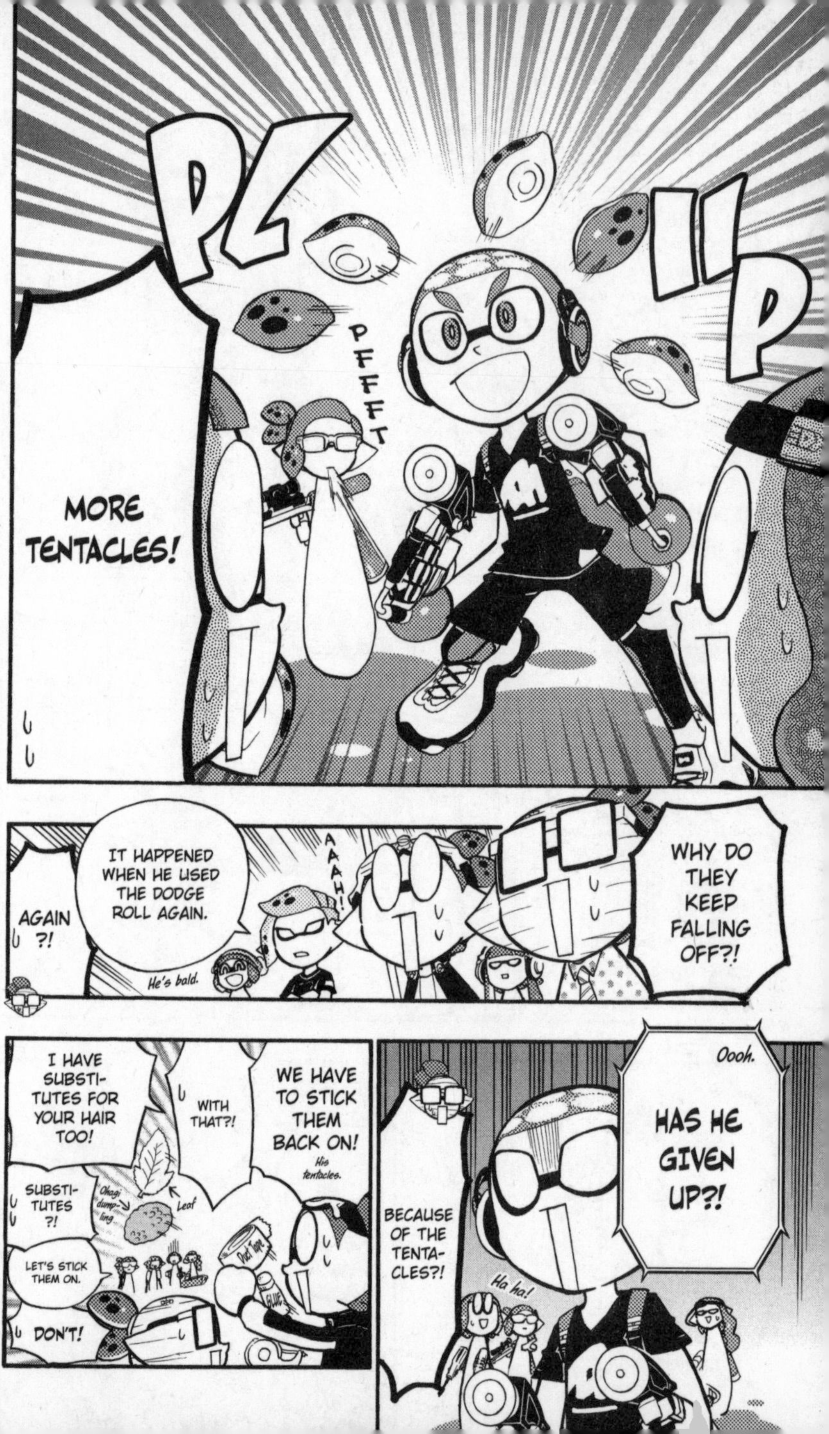

PLLIP
PFFFT
MORE TENTACLES!
WHY DO THEY KEEP FALLING OFF?!
AAAH!
IT HAPPENED WHEN HE USED THE DODGE ROLL AGAIN.
AGAIN ?!
He's bald.
Oooh.
HAS HE GIVEN UP?!
BECAUSE OF THE TENTACLES?!
Ha ha!
WE HAVE TO STICK THEM BACK ON!
His tentacles.
WITH THAT?!
I HAVE SUBSTITUTES FOR YOUR HAIR TOO!
Leaf
Ohagi dumpling
SUBSTITUTES ?!
Duct Tape
GLUE
LET'S STICK THEM ON.
DON'T!

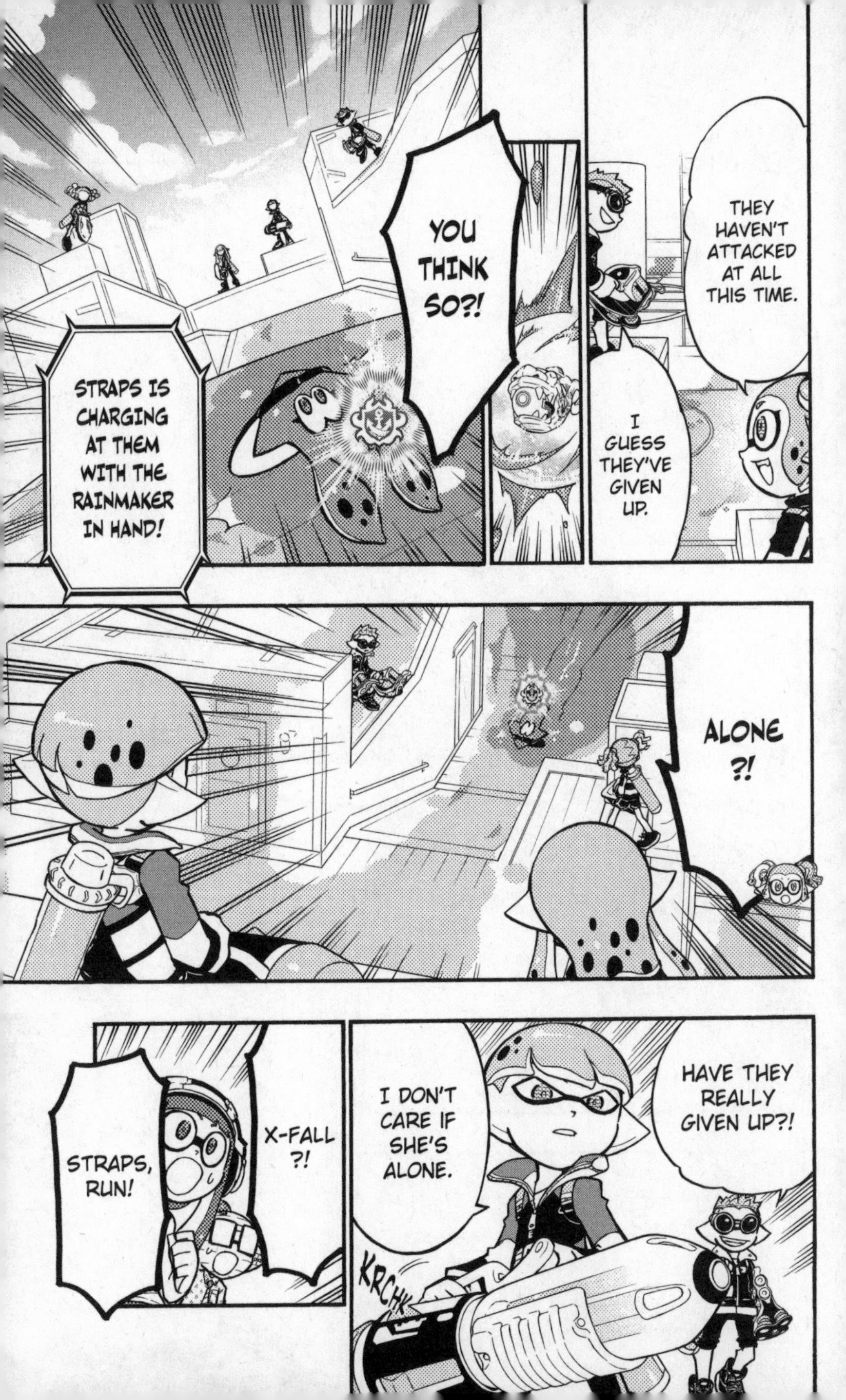
THEY HAVEN'T ATTACKED AT ALL THIS TIME.
I GUESS THEY'VE GIVEN UP.
YOU THINK SO?!
STRAPS IS CHARGING AT THEM WITH THE RAINMAKER IN HAND!
ALONE ?!
HAVE THEY REALLY GIVEN UP?!
I DON'T CARE IF SHE'S ALONE.
KRCHK
X-FALL ?!
STRAPS, RUN!

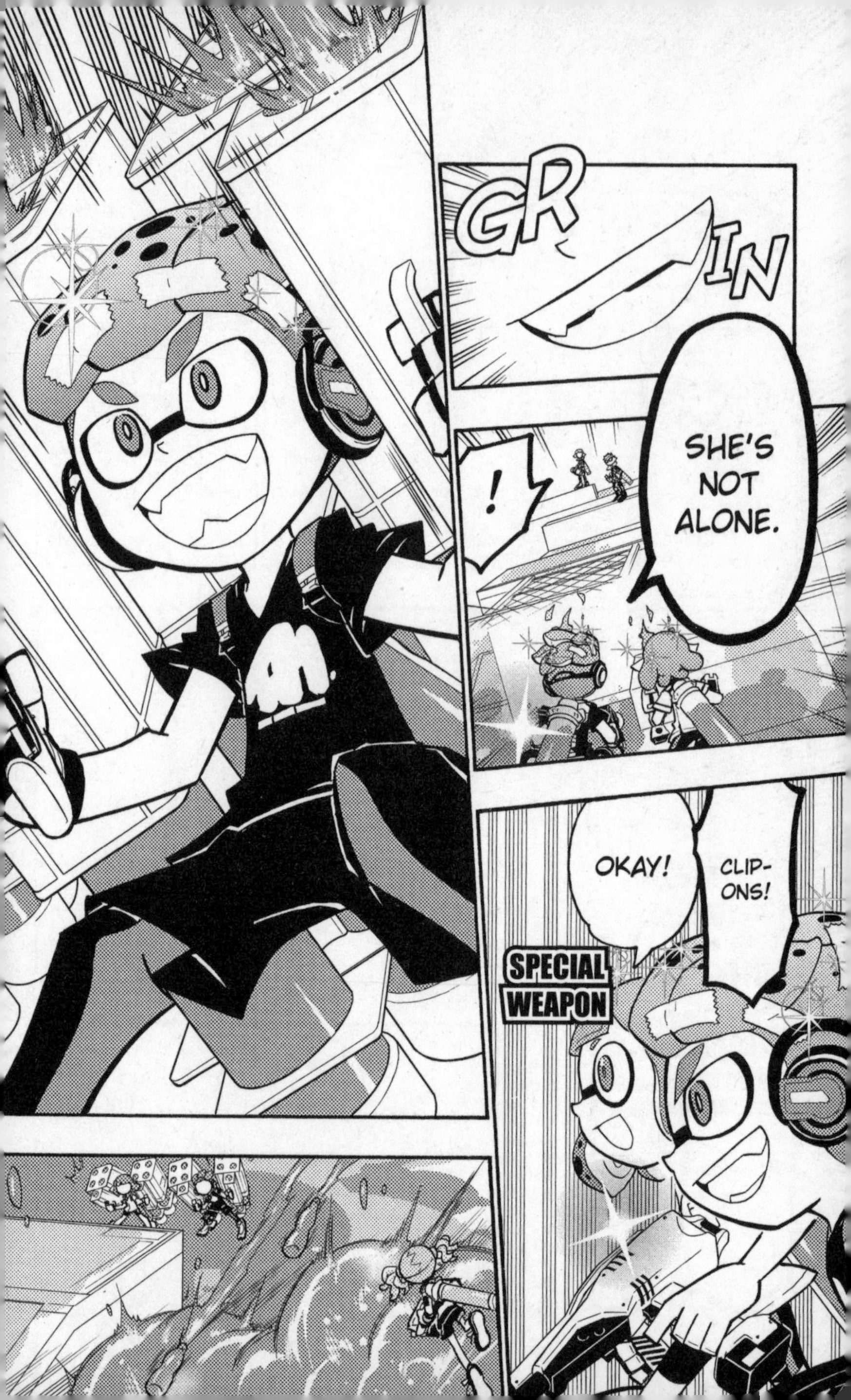
GRIN
SHE'S NOT ALONE.
!
CLIP-ONS!
OKAY!
SPECIAL WEAPON

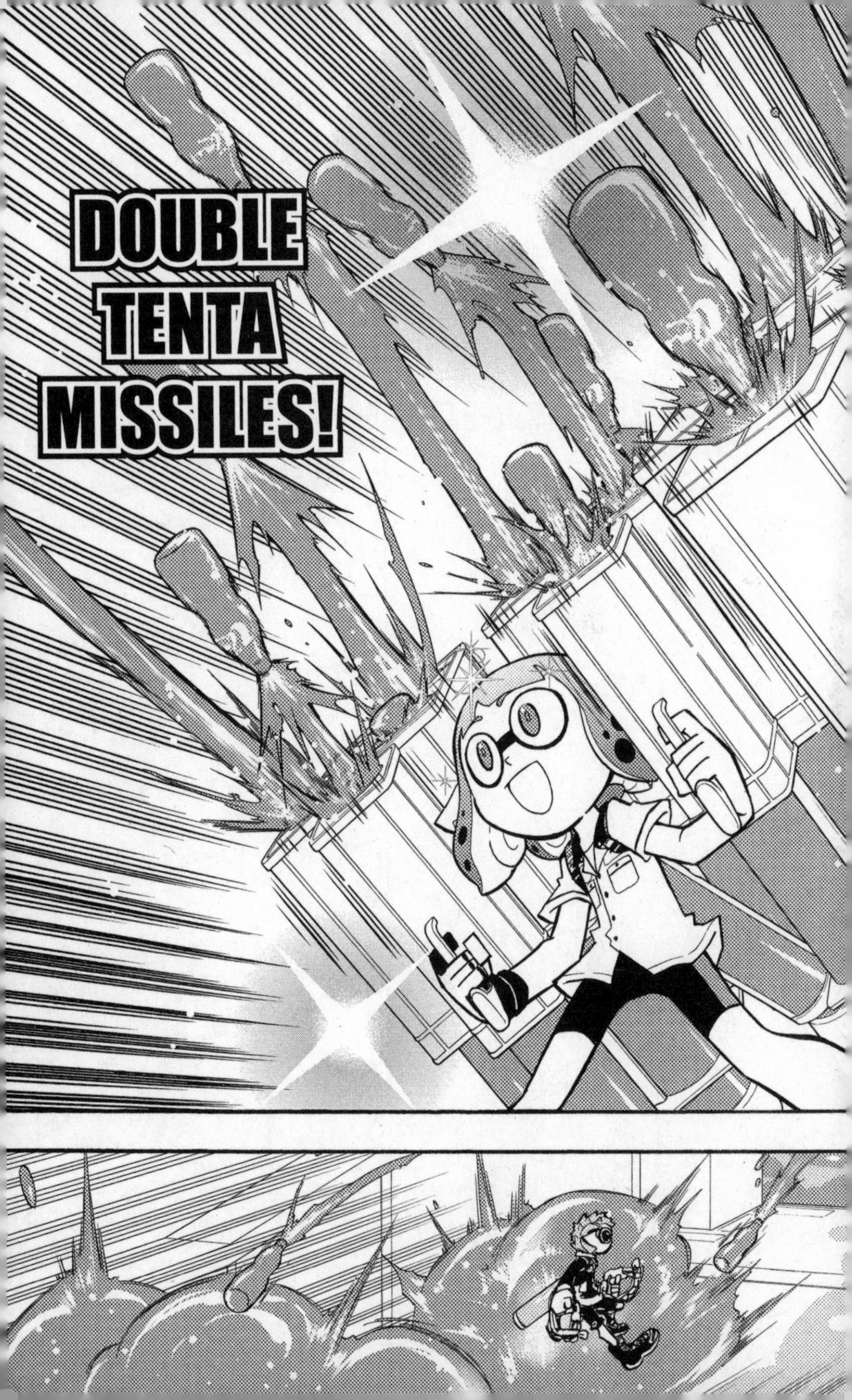
DOUBLE TENTA MISSILES!

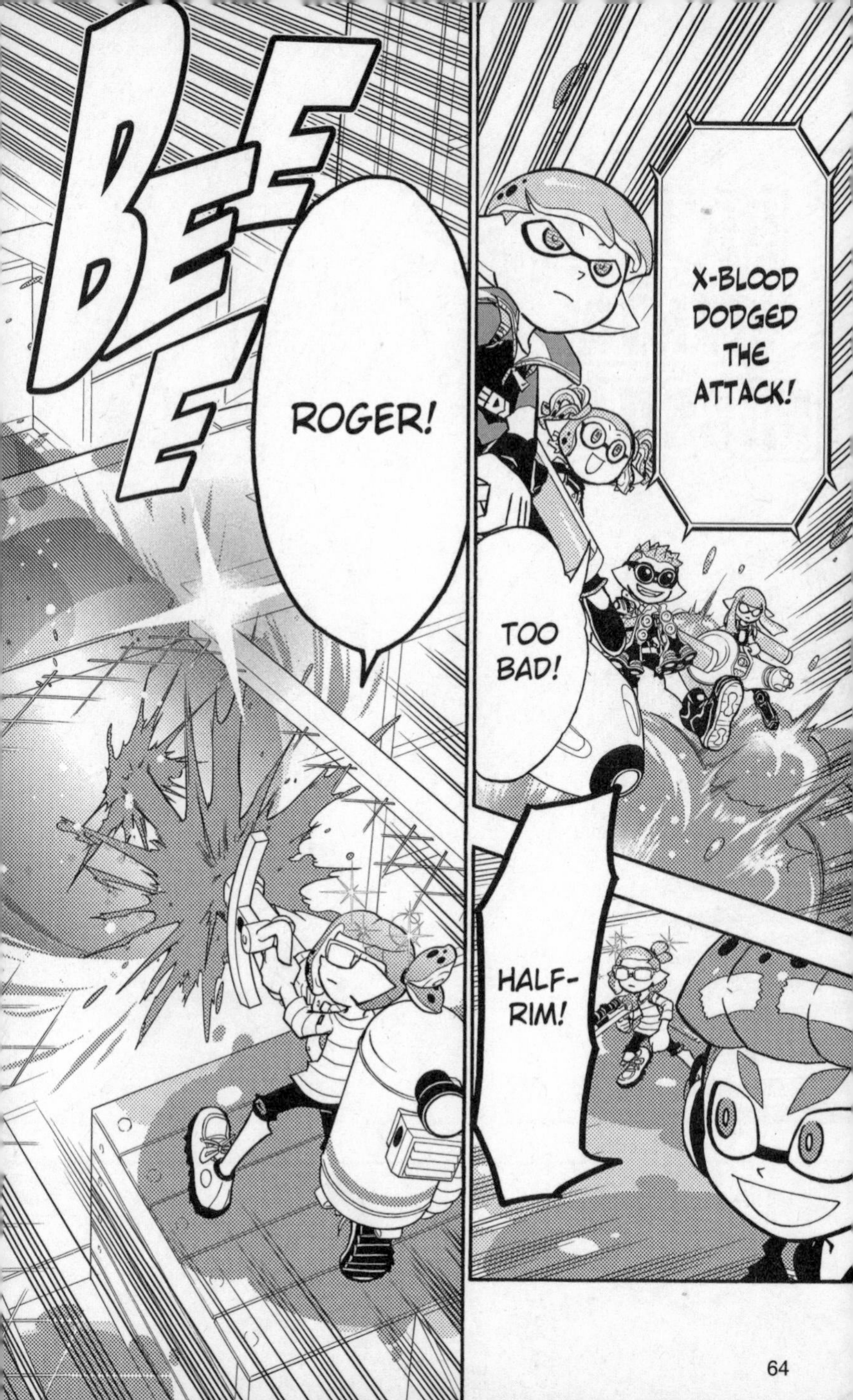
X-BLOOD DODGED THE ATTACK!
TOO BAD!
HALF-RIM!
BEEEE
ROGER!

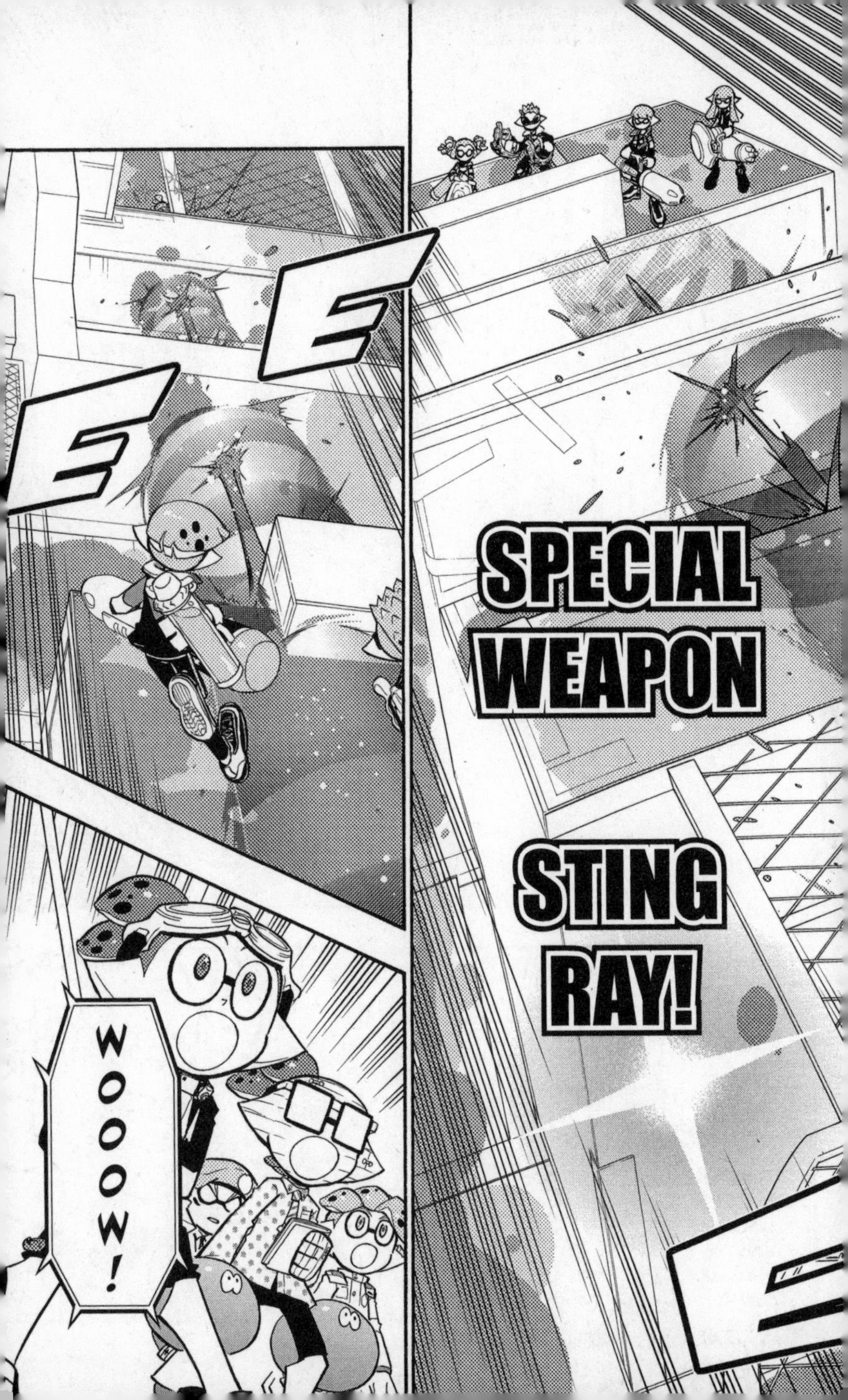
SPECIAL WEAPON
STING RAY!
WOOOW!

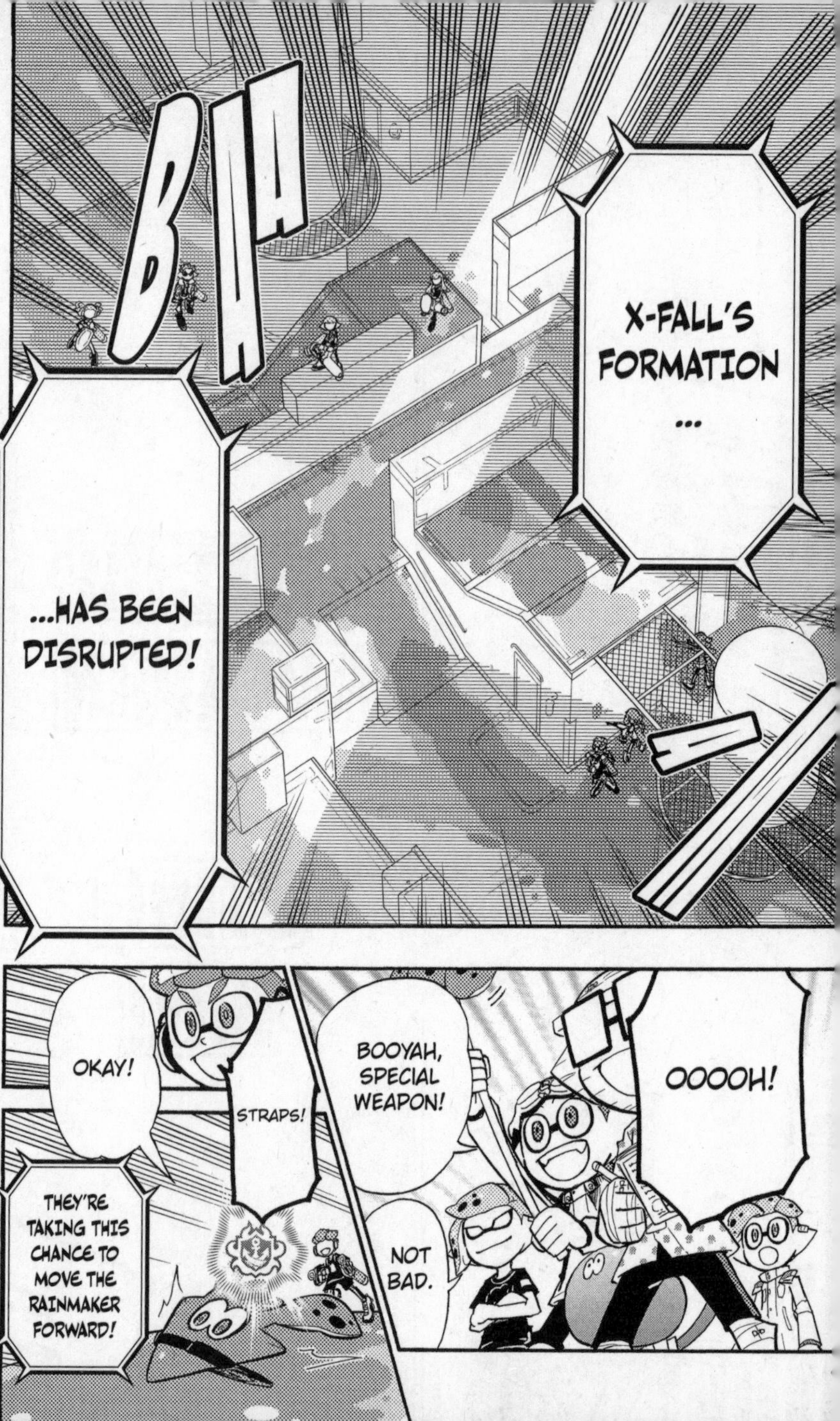
X-FALL'S FORMATION ...
...HAS BEEN DISRUPTED!
OOOOH!
BOOYAH, SPECIAL WEAPON!
NOT BAD.
OKAY!
STRAPS!
THEY'RE TAKING THIS CHANCE TO MOVE THE RAINMAKER FORWARD!

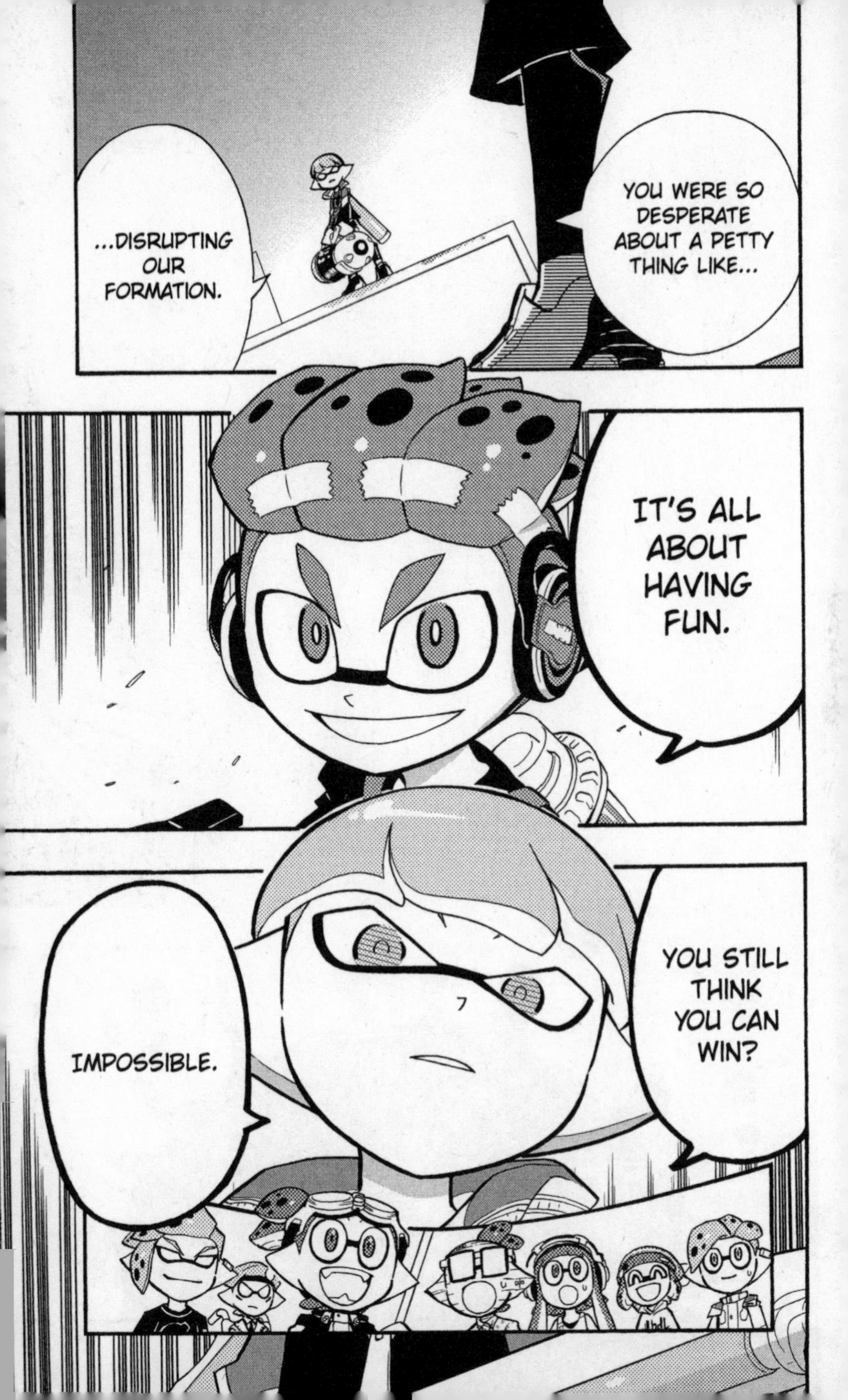
YOU WERE SO DESPERATE ABOUT A PETTY THING LIKE...
...DISRUPTING OUR FORMATION.
IT'S ALL ABOUT HAVING FUN.
YOU STILL THINK YOU CAN WIN?
IMPOSSIBLE.

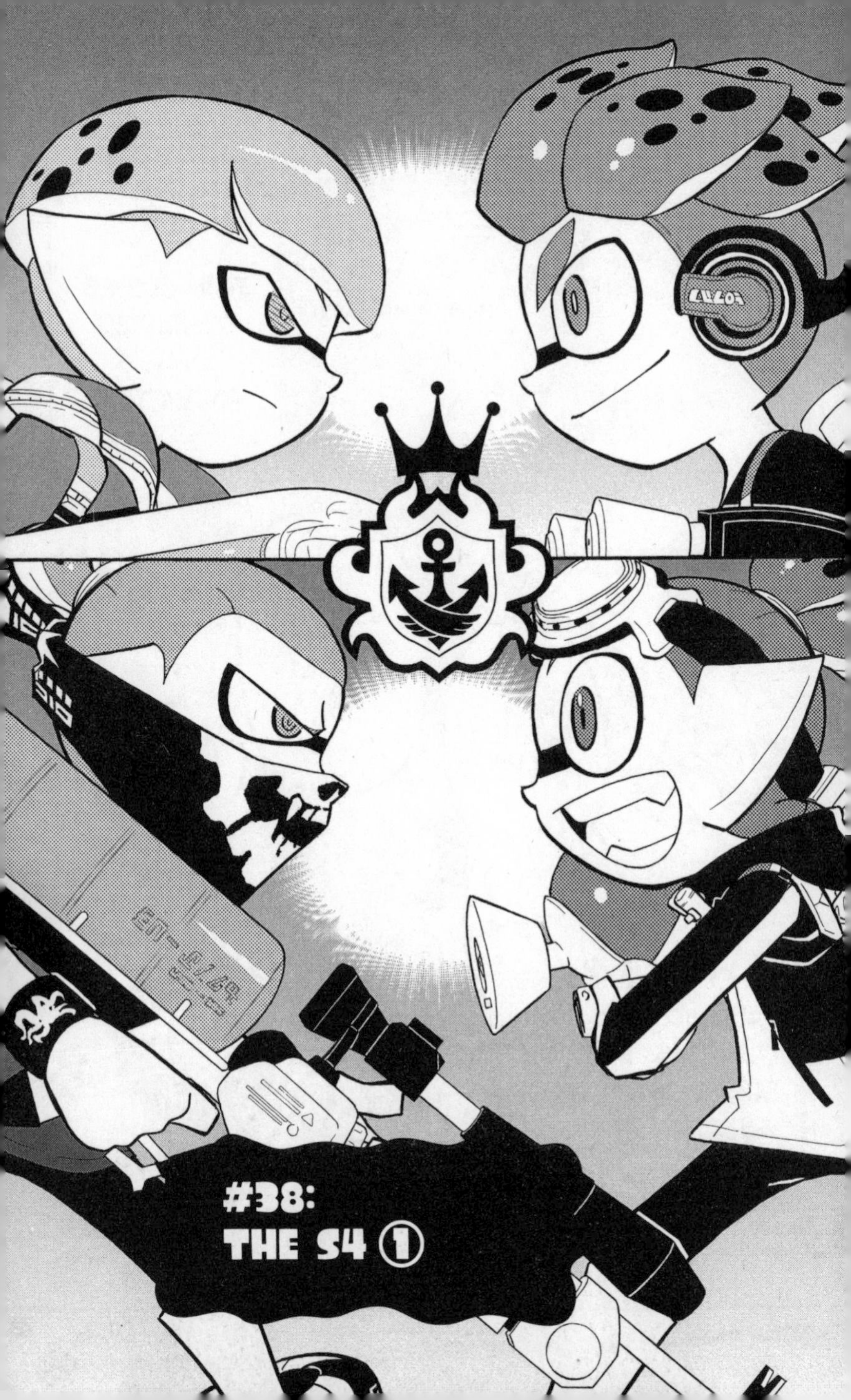

#38:
THE S4 ①

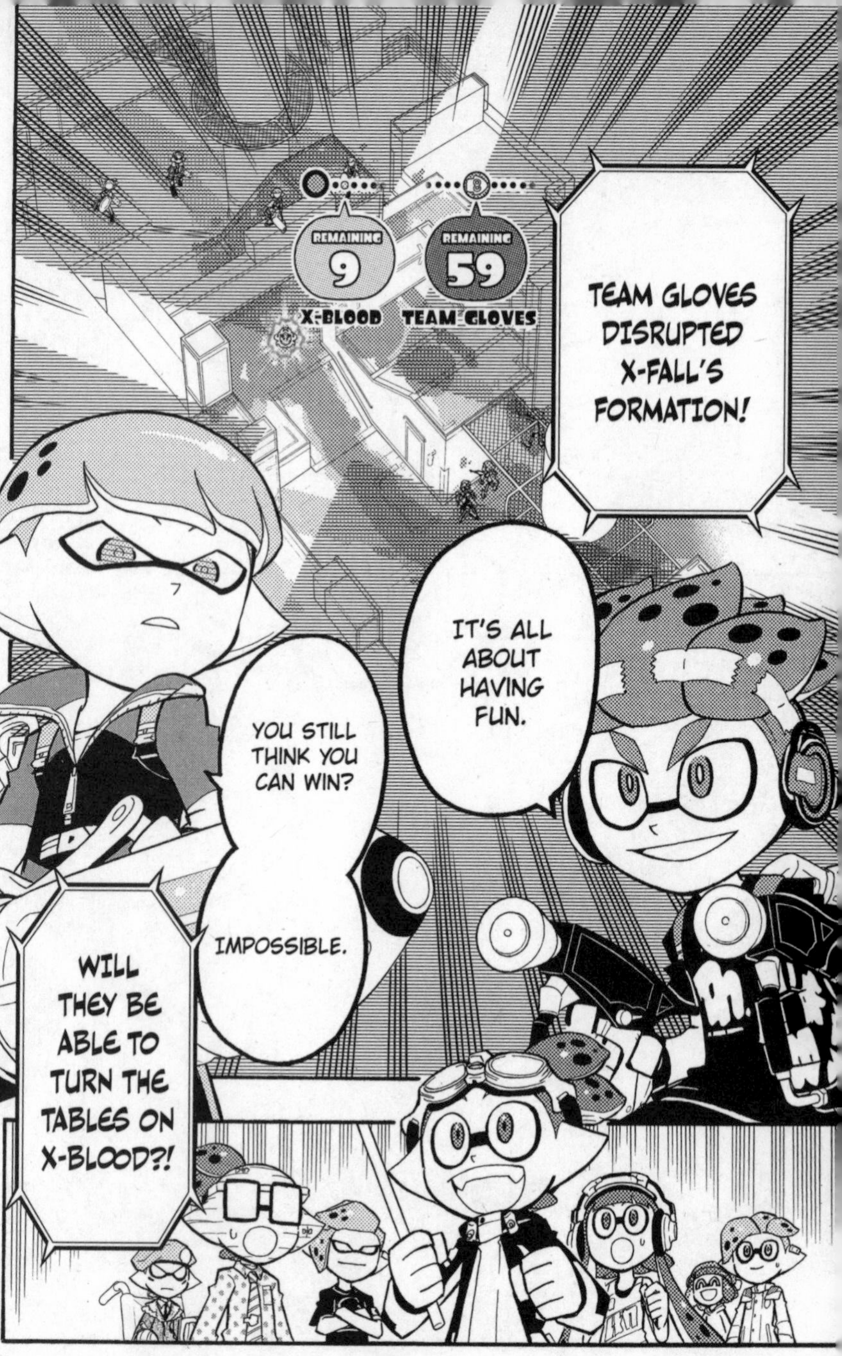
TEAM GLOVES DISRUPTED X-FALL'S FORMATION!
REMAINING 59
TEAM GLOVES
REMAINING 9
X-BLOOD
IT'S ALL ABOUT HAVING FUN.
YOU STILL THINK YOU CAN WIN?
IMPOSSIBLE.
WILL THEY BE ABLE TO TURN THE TABLES ON X-BLOOD?!

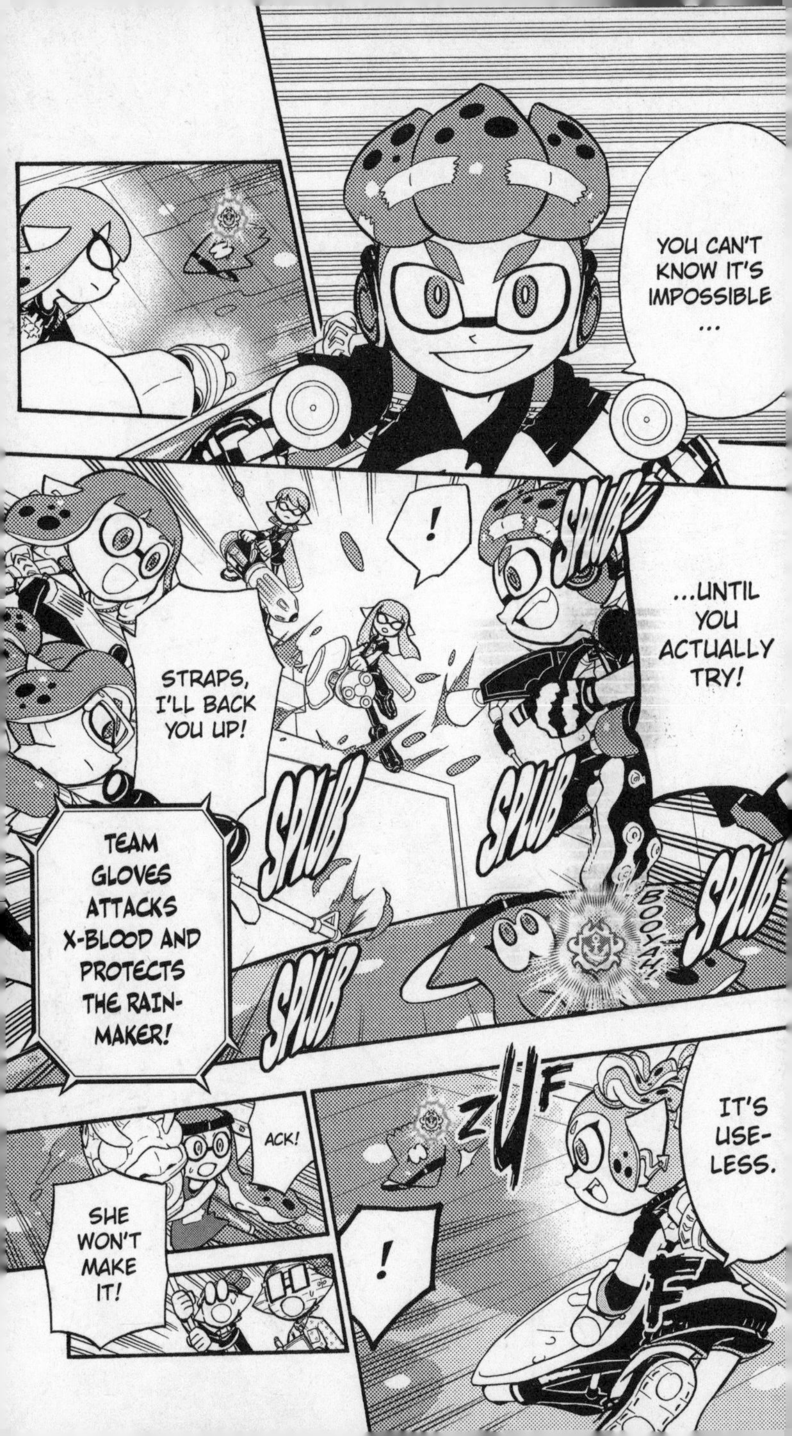

YOU CAN'T KNOW IT'S IMPOSSIBLE ...
...UNTIL YOU ACTUALLY TRY!
SPLUB
!
STRAPS, I'LL BACK YOU UP!
SPLUB
SPLUB
SPLUB
BOOYAH!
SPLUB
TEAM GLOVES ATTACKS X-BLOOD AND PROTECTS THE RAIN-MAKER!
IT'S USE-LESS.
ZUF
!
ACK!
SHE WON'T MAKE IT!

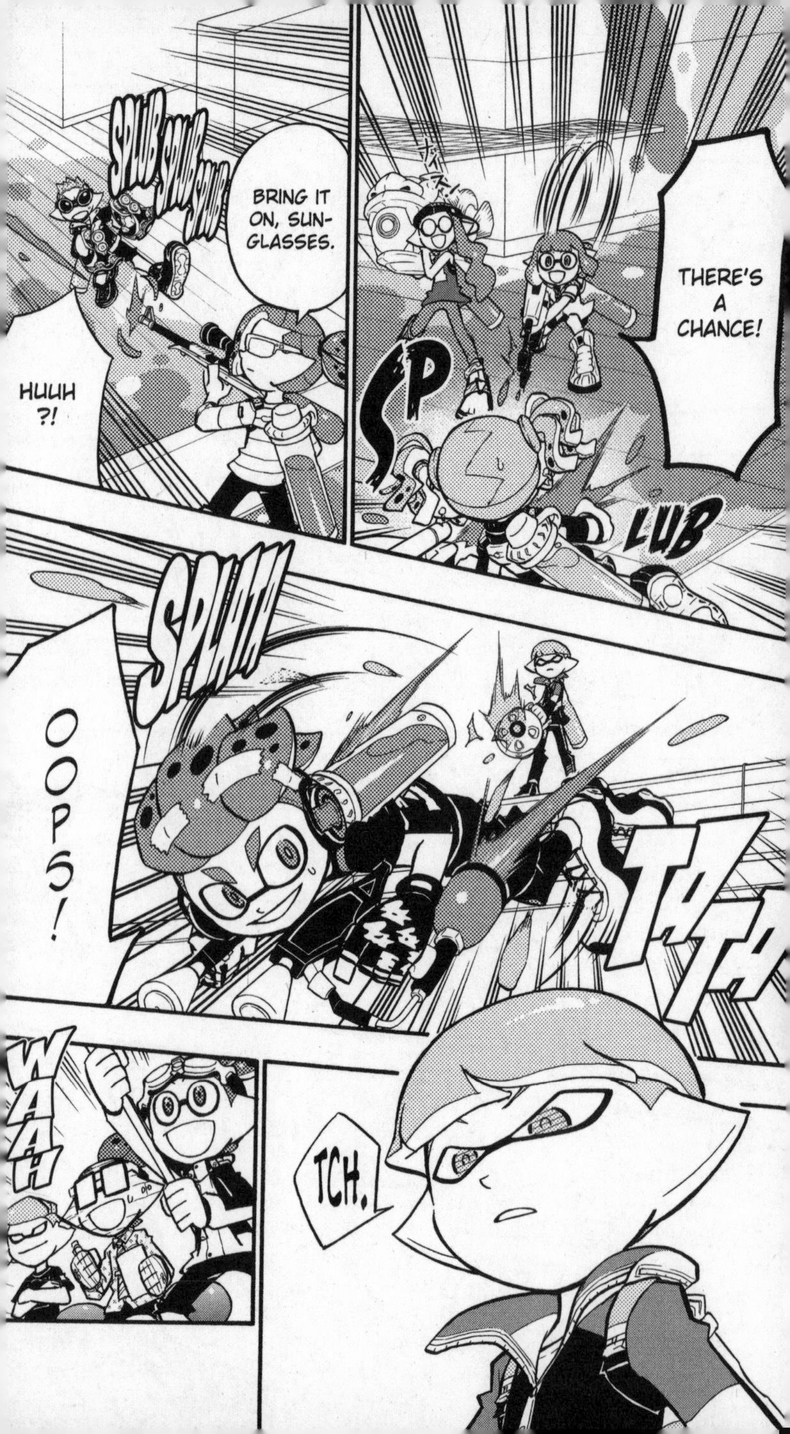

THERE'S A CHANCE!
SP
LUB
SPLUB SPLUB SPLUB
BRING IT ON, SUN-GLASSES.
HUUH ?!
SPLAT
TA TA
OOPS!
TCH.
WAAAH

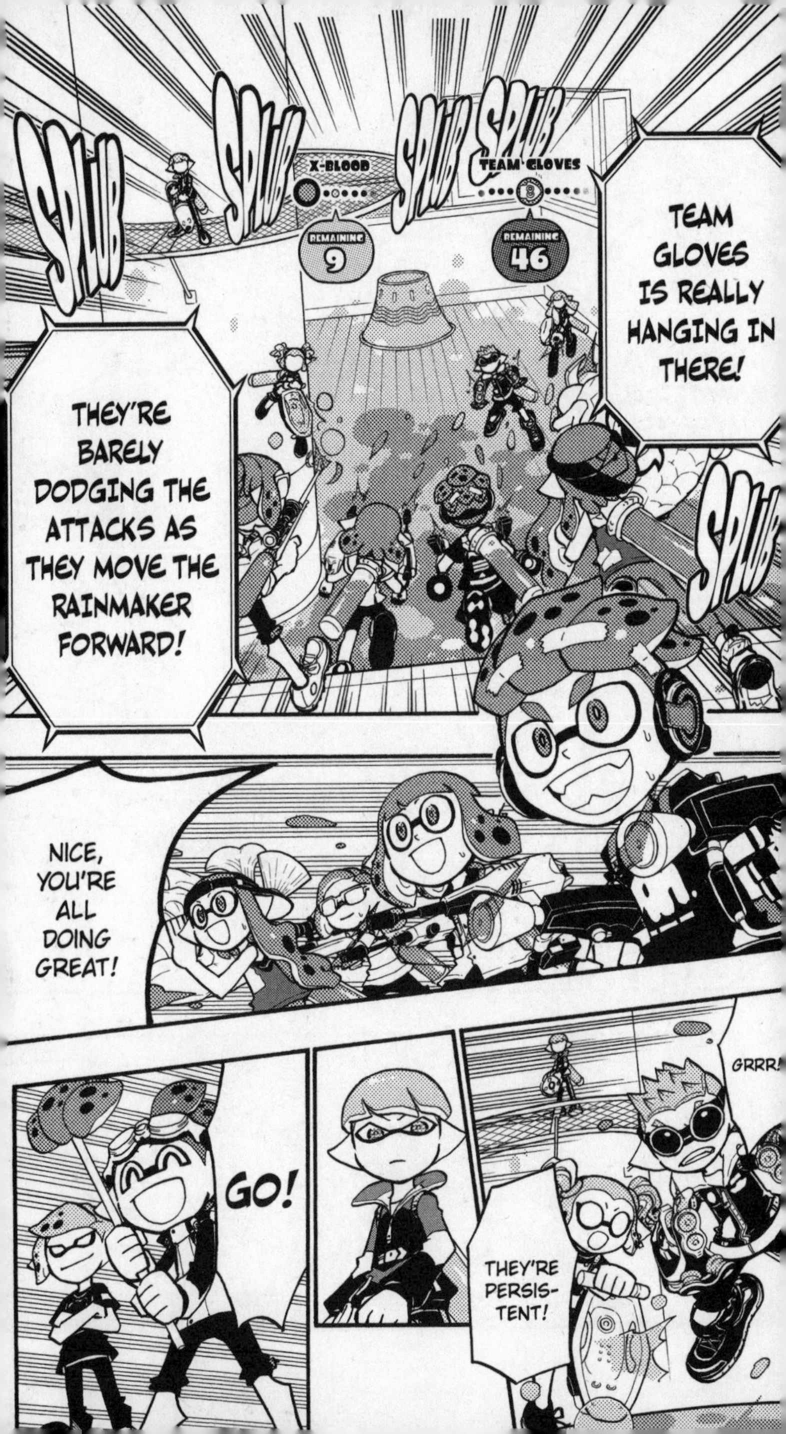
SPLUB
TEAM GLOVES IS REALLY HANGING IN THERE!
TEAM GLOVES
REMAINING 46
SPLUB SPLUB
X-BLOOD
REMAINING 9
SPLUB SPLUB
THEY'RE BARELY DODGING THE ATTACKS AS THEY MOVE THE RAINMAKER FORWARD!
NICE, YOU'RE ALL DOING GREAT!
GRRR!
THEY'RE PERSIS-TENT!
GO!

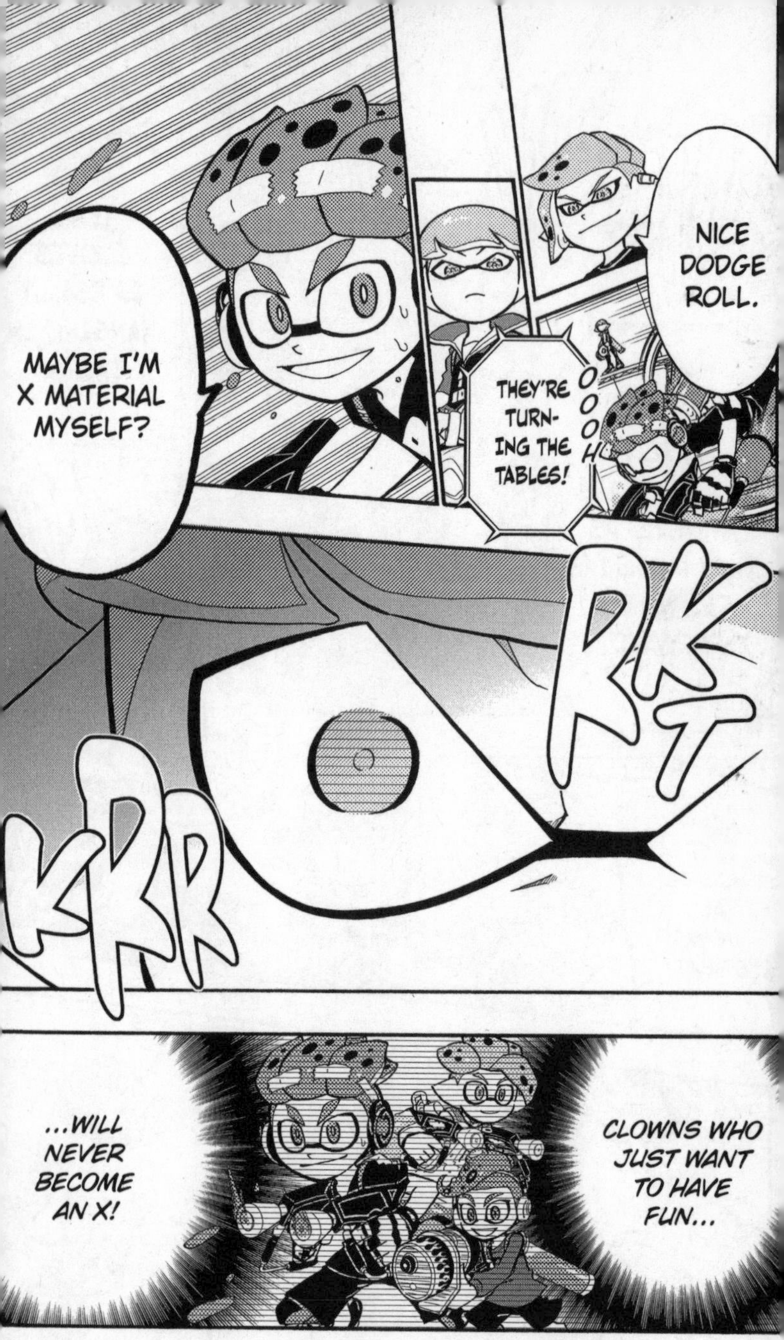
NICE DODGE ROLL.
OOOOH
THEY'RE TURNING THE TABLES!
MAYBE I'M X MATERIAL MYSELF?
KRR
RKT
CLOWNS WHO JUST WANT TO HAVE FUN...
...WILL NEVER BECOME AN X!

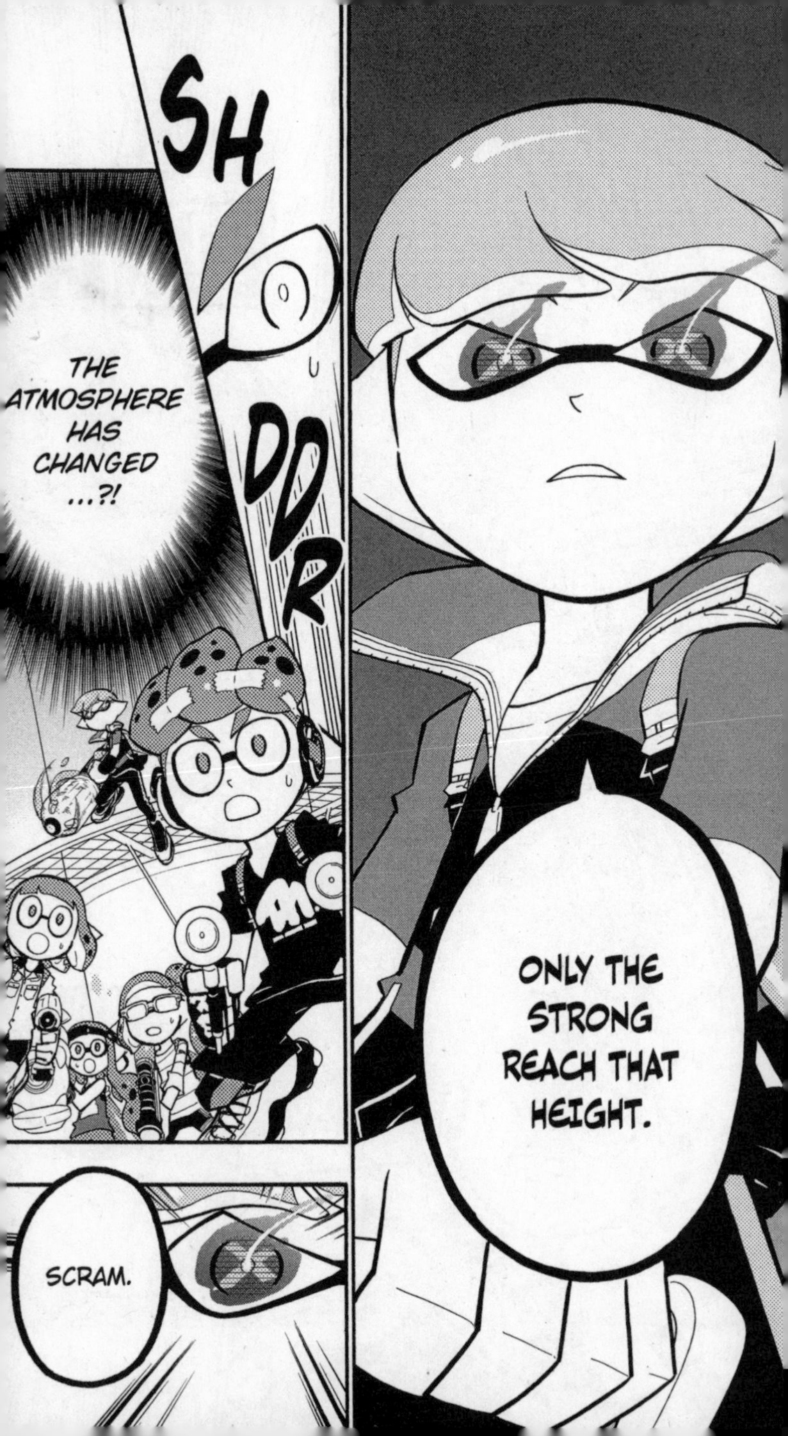
ONLY THE STRONG REACH THAT HEIGHT.
SH
DDR
THE ATMOSPHERE HAS CHANGED ...?!
SCRAM.

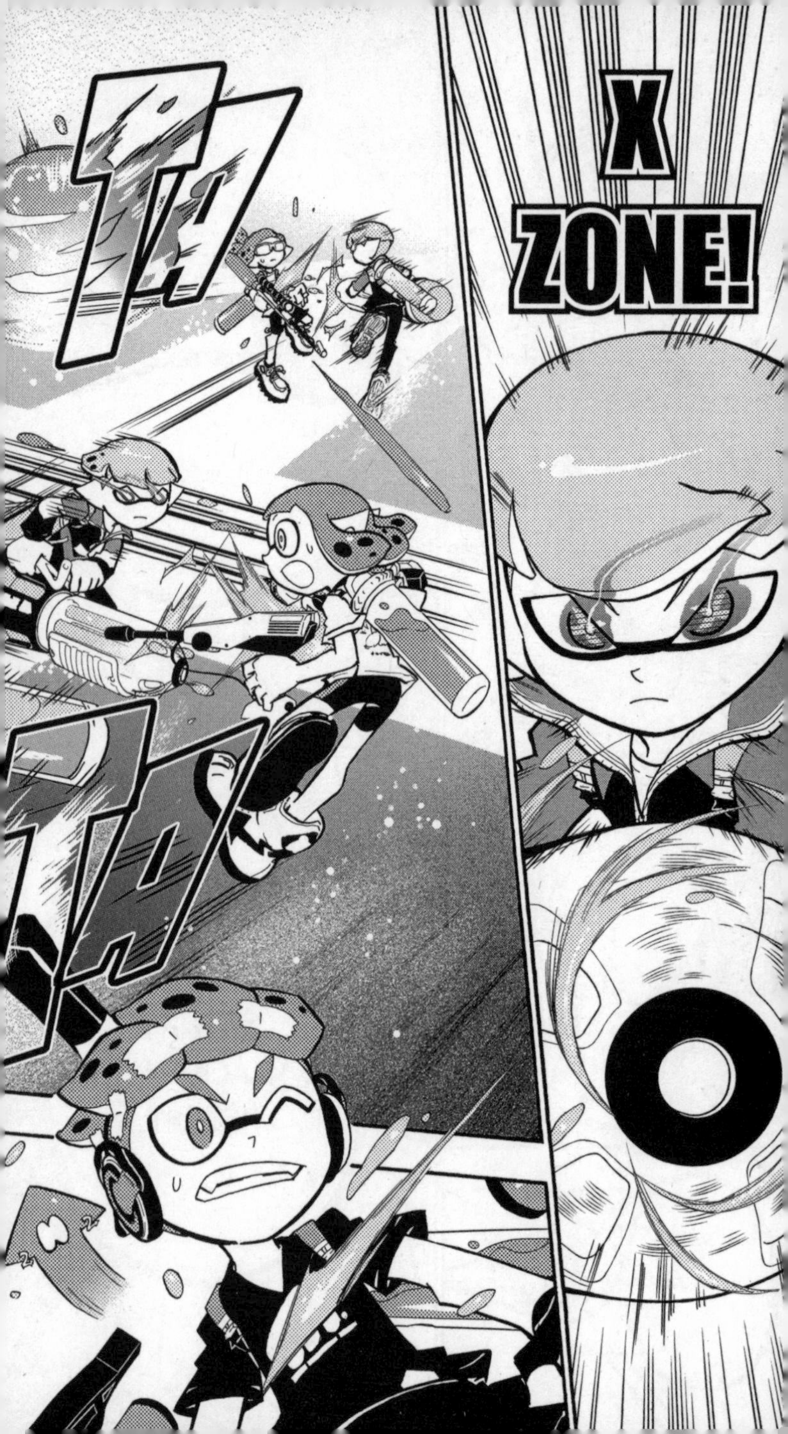
X
ZONE!

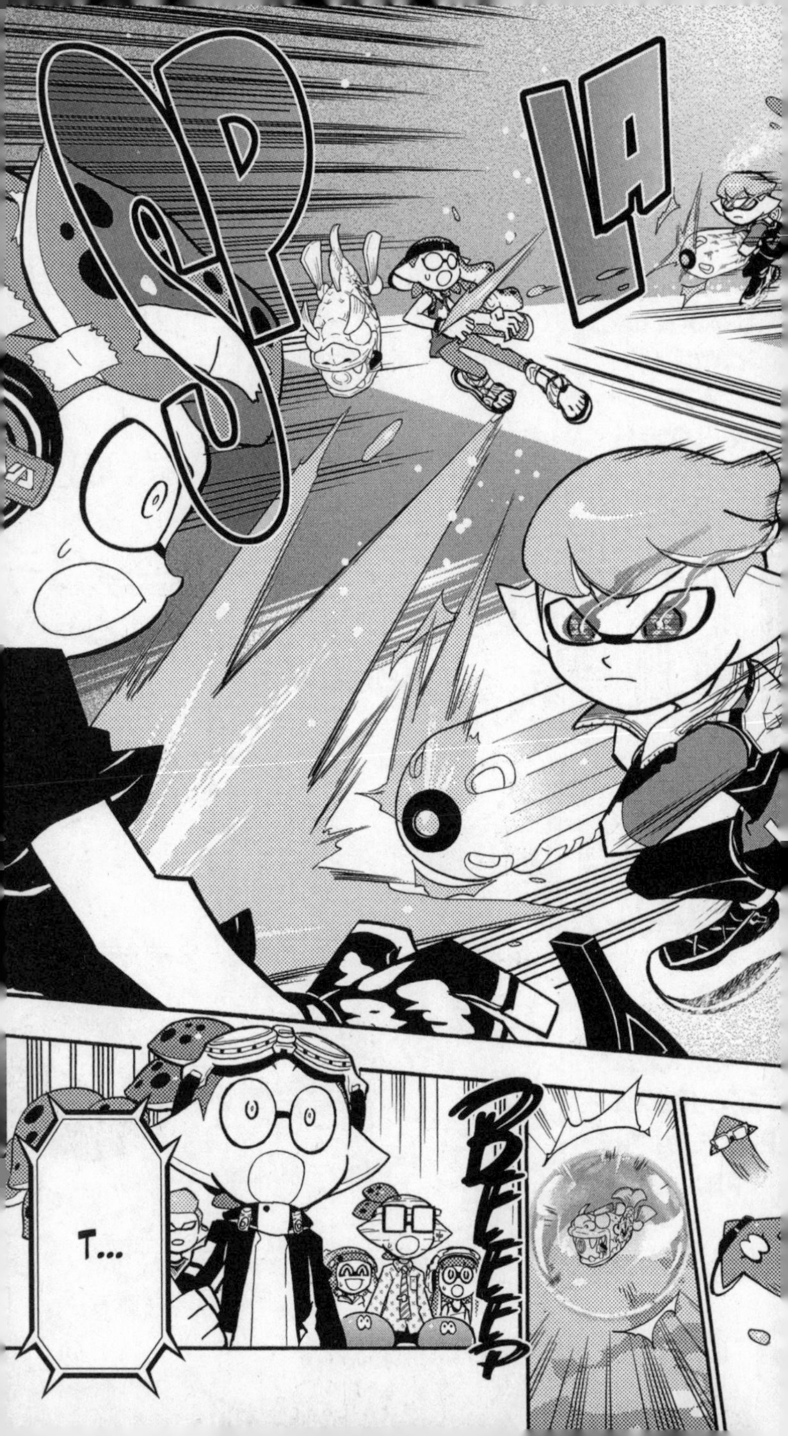
SPLA
BEEEEP
T...

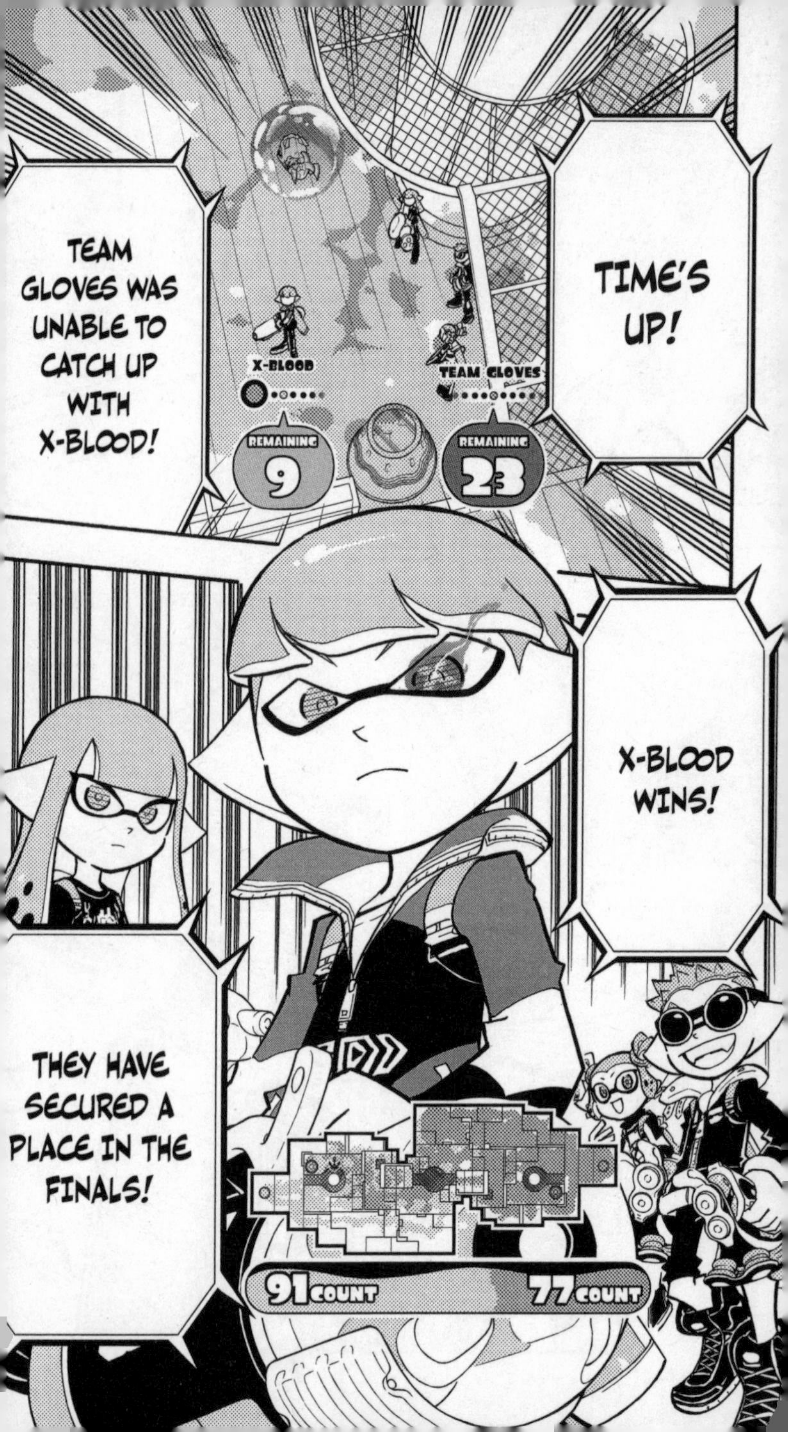

TIME'S UP!
TEAM GLOVES WAS UNABLE TO CATCH UP WITH X-BLOOD!
TEAM GLOVES
REMAINING 23
X-BLOOD
REMAINING 9
X-BLOOD WINS!
THEY HAVE SECURED A PLACE IN THE FINALS!
77 COUNT
91 COUNT

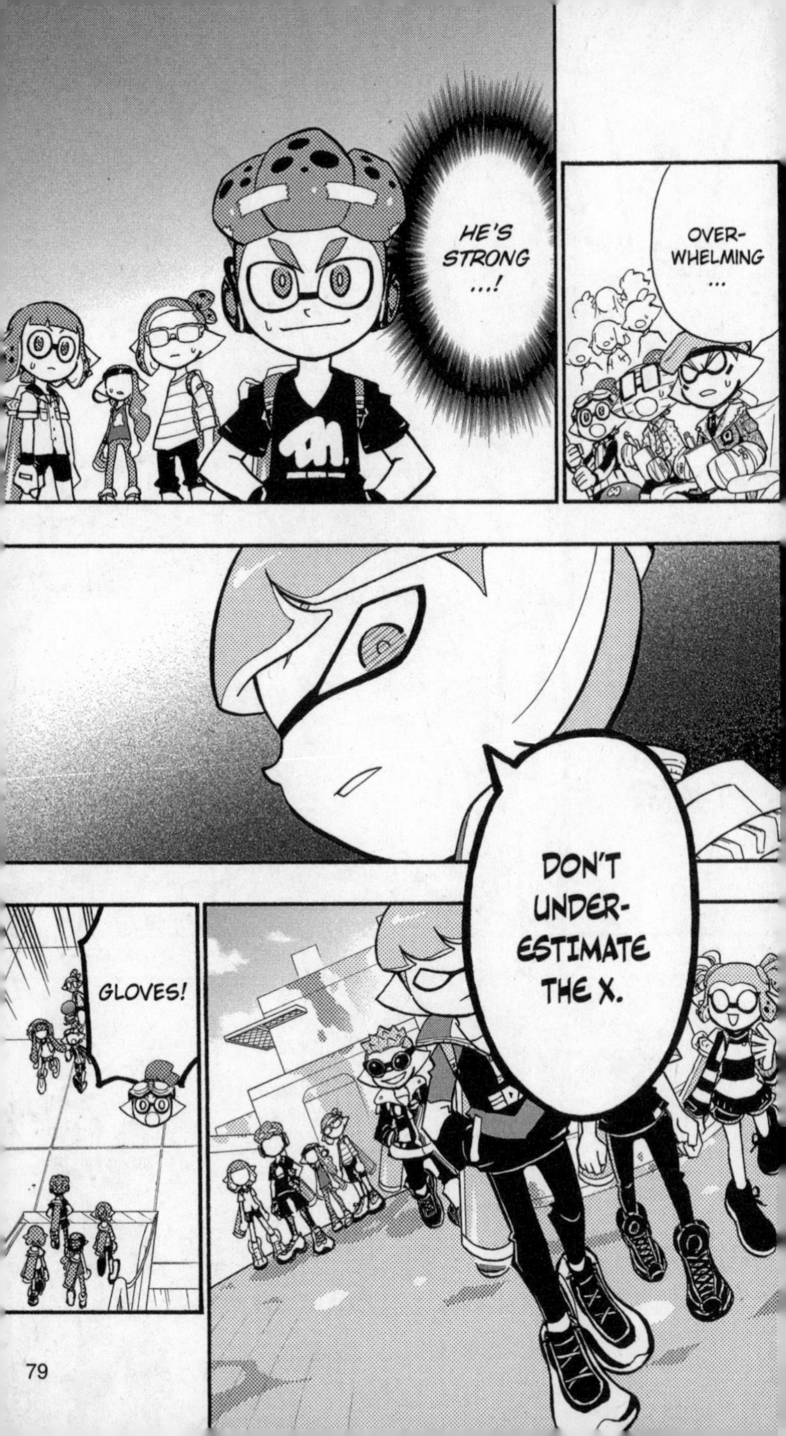
OVER-WHELMING ...
HE'S STRONG ...!
DON'T UNDER-ESTIMATE THE X.
GLOVES!

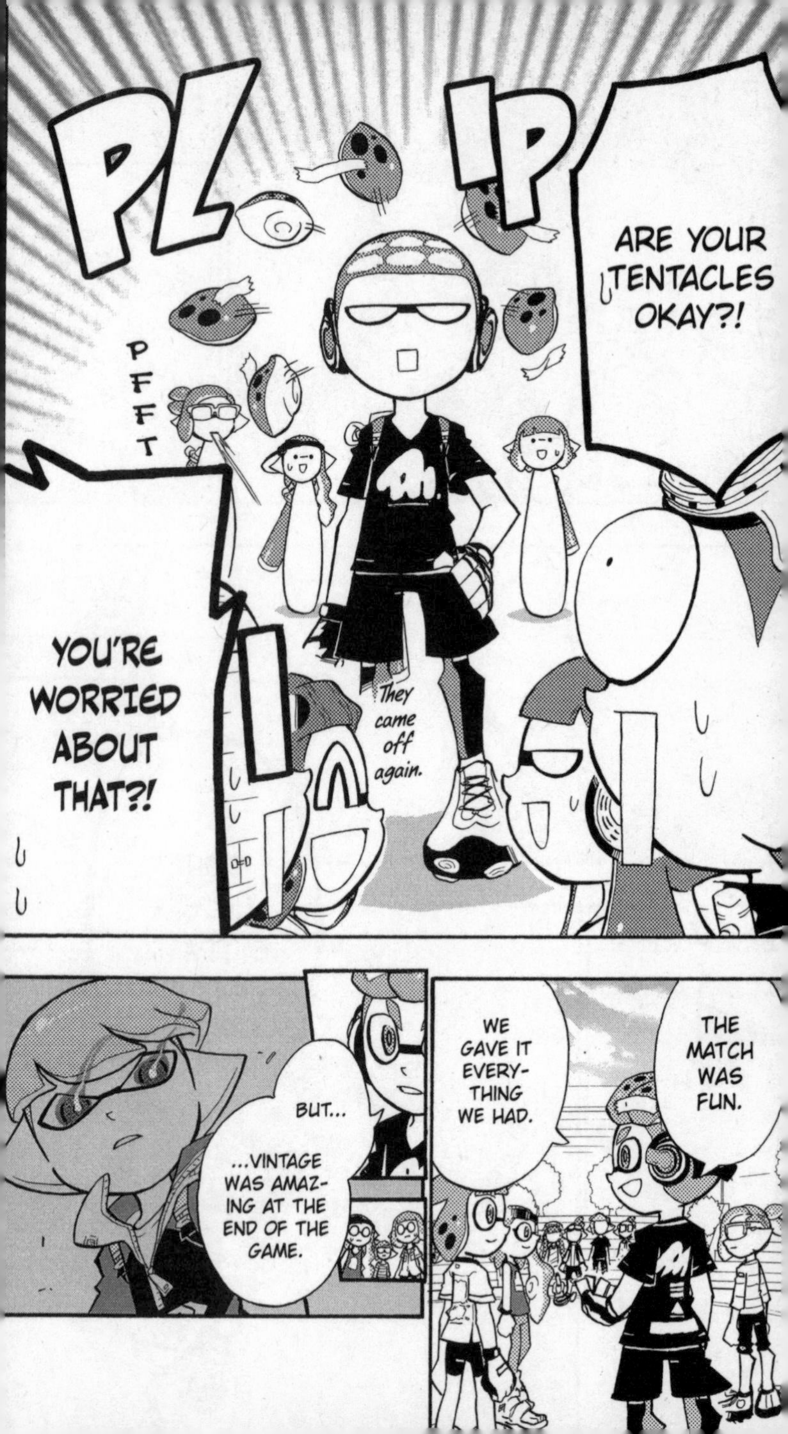
PL IP
ARE YOUR TENTACLES OKAY?!
PFFT
They came off again.
YOU'RE WORRIED ABOUT THAT?!
THE MATCH WAS FUN.
WE GAVE IT EVERYTHING WE HAD.
BUT...
...VINTAGE WAS AMAZING AT THE END OF THE GAME.

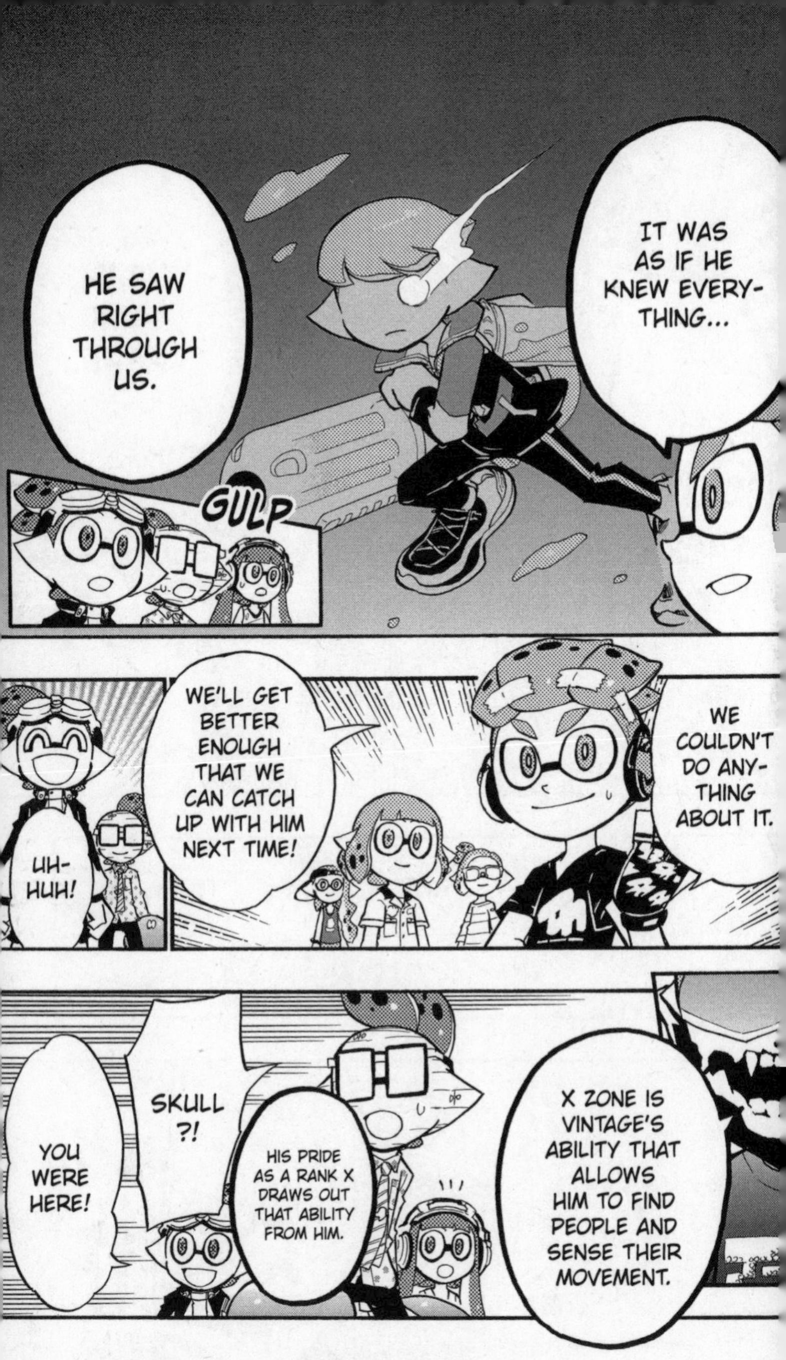
IT WAS AS IF HE KNEW EVERYTHING...
HE SAW RIGHT THROUGH US.
GULP
WE COULDN'T DO ANYTHING ABOUT IT.
WE'LL GET BETTER ENOUGH THAT WE CAN CATCH UP WITH HIM NEXT TIME!
UH-HUH!
X ZONE IS VINTAGE'S ABILITY THAT ALLOWS HIM TO FIND PEOPLE AND SENSE THEIR MOVEMENT.
HIS PRIDE AS A RANK X DRAWS OUT THAT ABILITY FROM HIM.
SKULL?!
YOU WERE HERE!

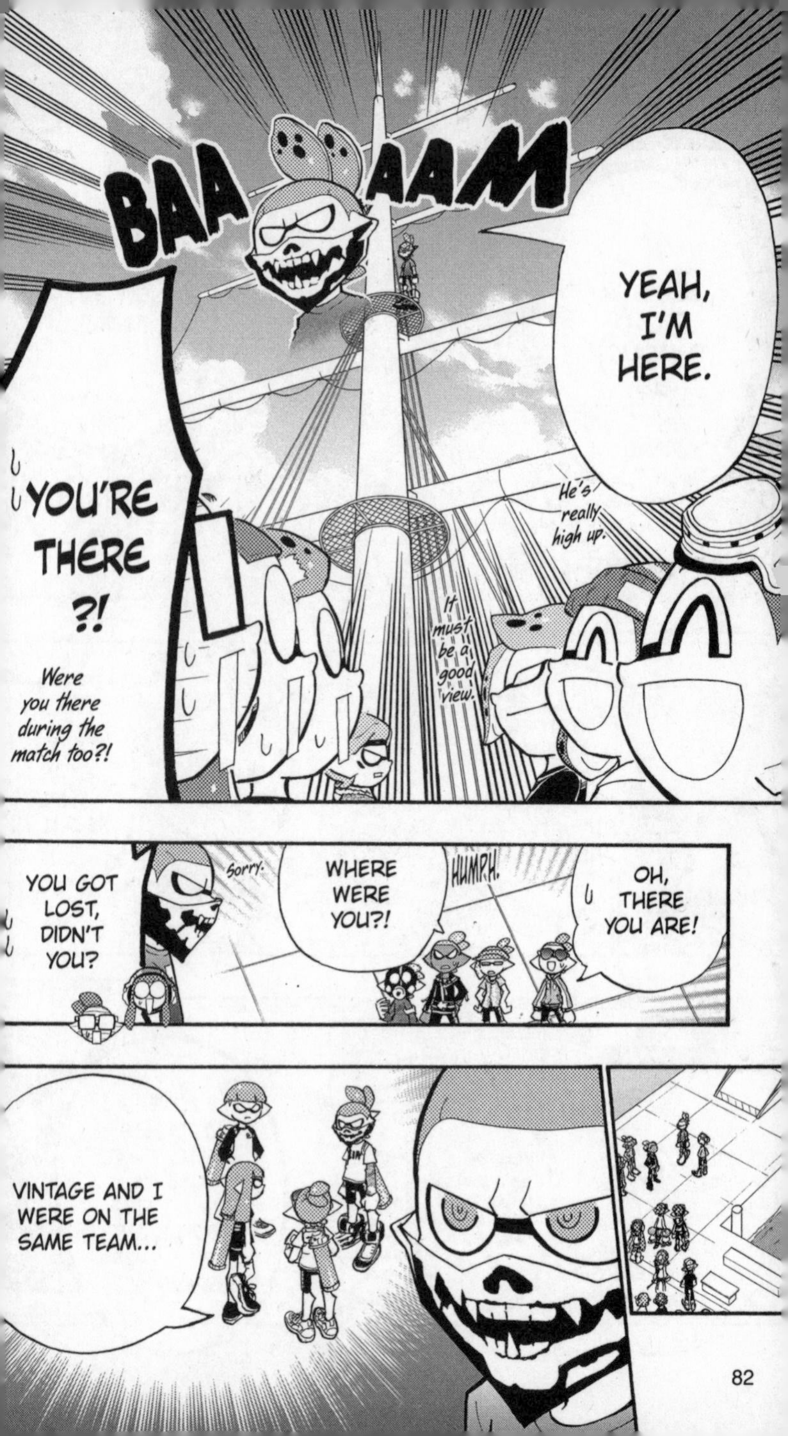
BAAAAM
YEAH, I'M HERE.
He's really high up.
It must be a good view.
YOU'RE THERE?!
Were you there during the match too?!
OH, THERE YOU ARE!
HUMPH.
WHERE WERE YOU?!
Sorry.
YOU GOT LOST, DIDN'T YOU?
VINTAGE AND I WERE ON THE SAME TEAM...

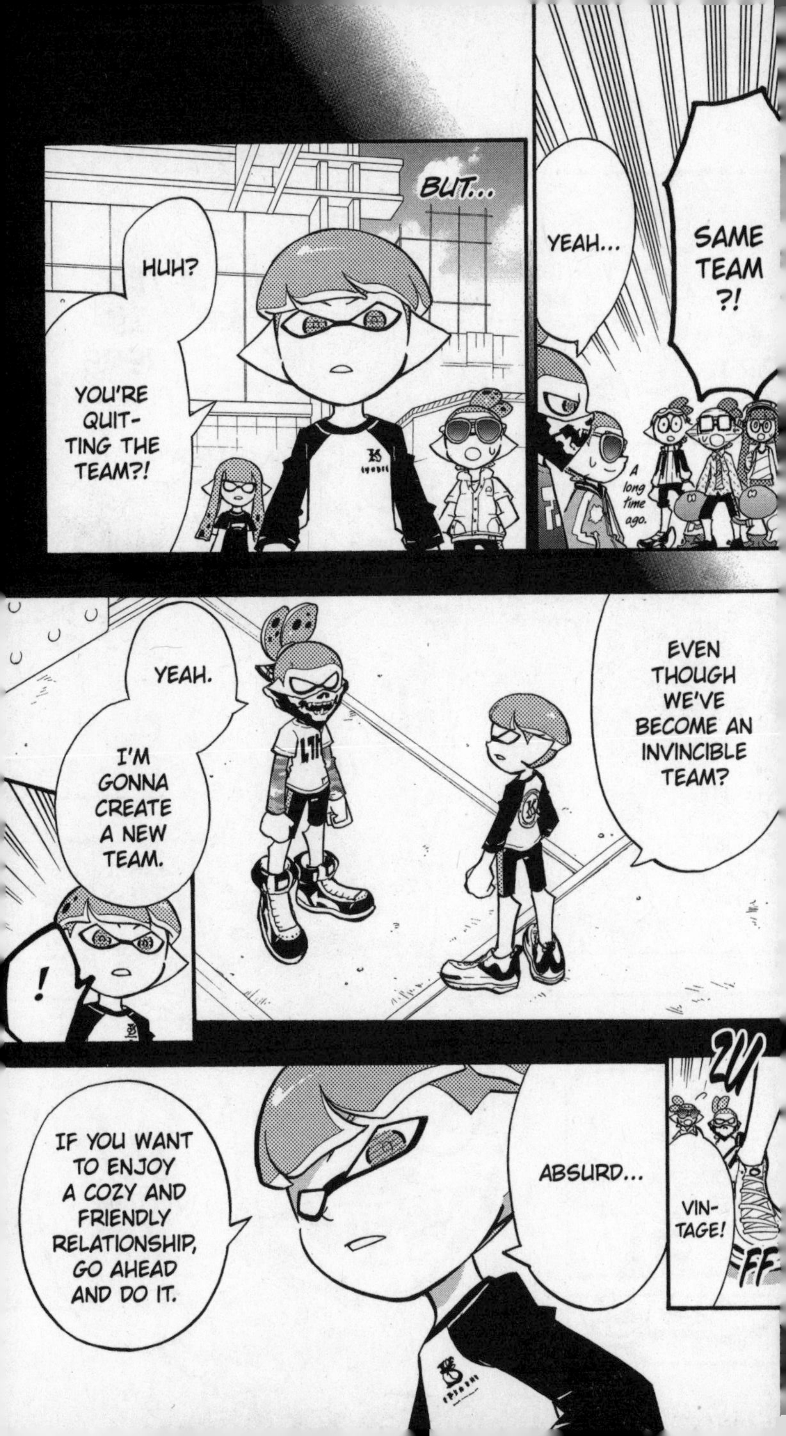
SAME TEAM ?!
YEAH...
A long time ago.
BUT...
HUH?
YOU'RE QUIT-TING THE TEAM?!
EVEN THOUGH WE'VE BECOME AN INVINCIBLE TEAM?
YEAH.
I'M GONNA CREATE A NEW TEAM.
!
ZU
VIN-TAGE!
FF
ABSURD...
IF YOU WANT TO ENJOY A COZY AND FRIENDLY RELATIONSHIP, GO AHEAD AND DO IT.

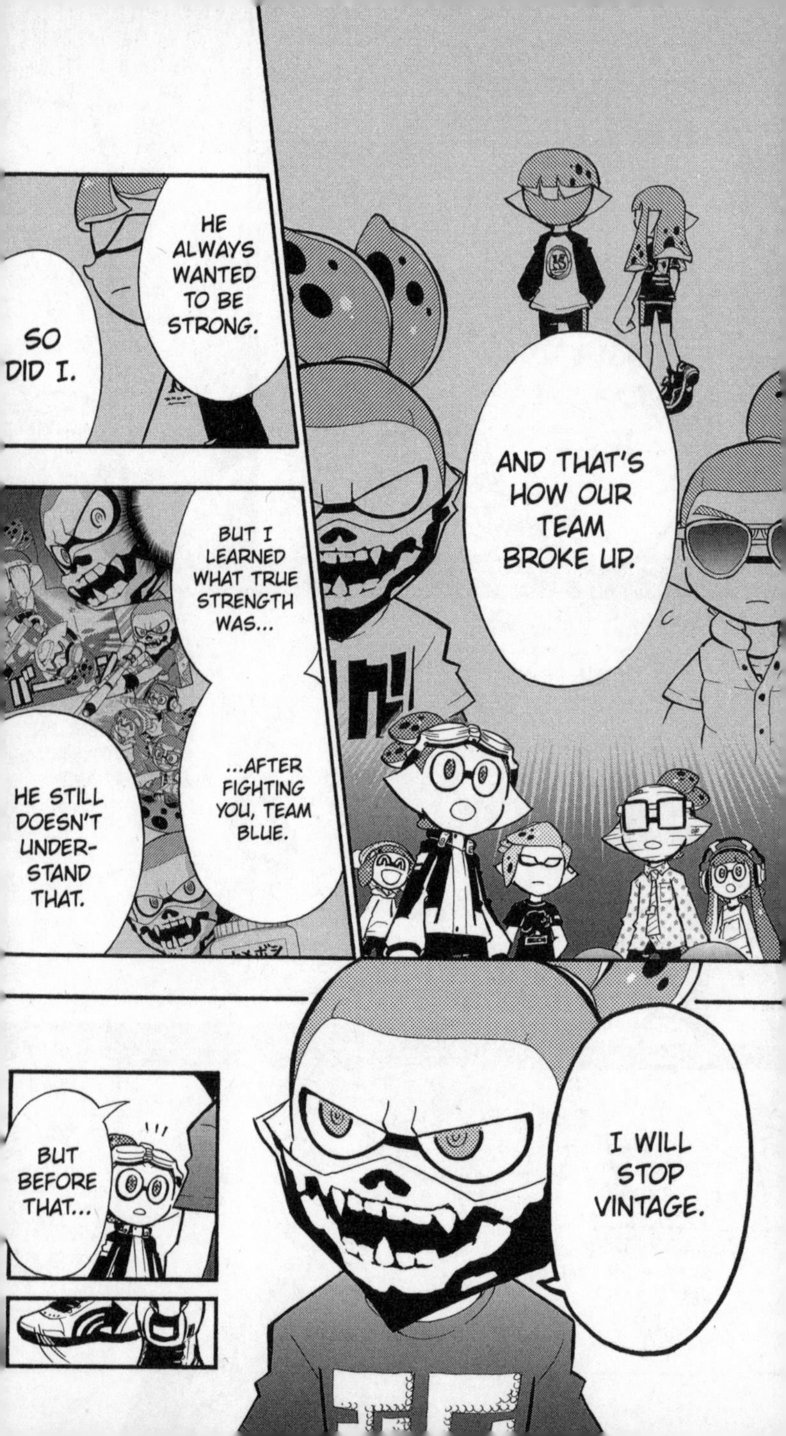
AND THAT'S HOW OUR TEAM BROKE UP.
HE ALWAYS WANTED TO BE STRONG.
SO DID I.
BUT I LEARNED WHAT TRUE STRENGTH WAS...
...AFTER FIGHTING YOU, TEAM BLUE.
HE STILL DOESN'T UNDER-STAND THAT.
I WILL STOP VINTAGE.
BUT BEFORE THAT...

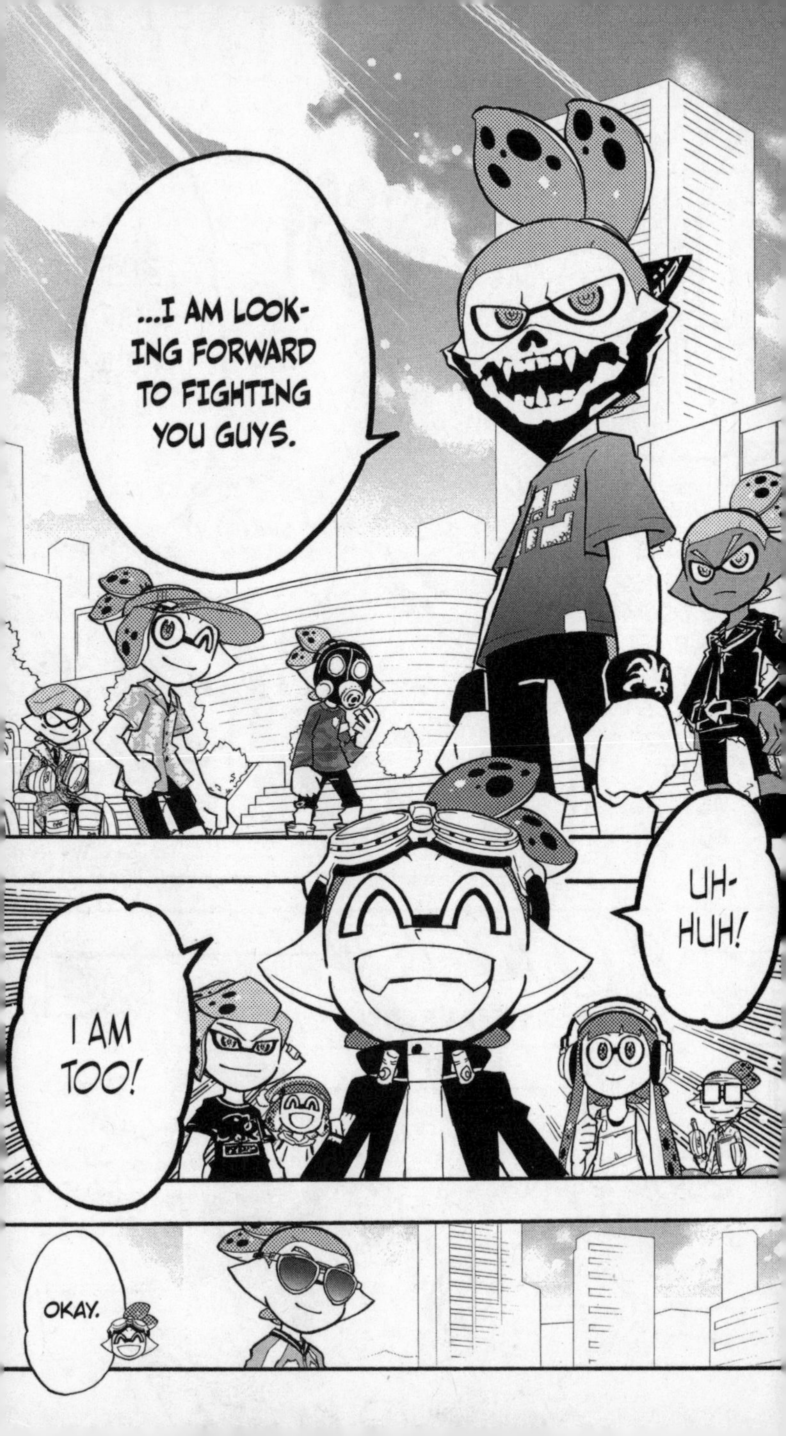
...I AM LOOK-ING FORWARD TO FIGHTING YOU GUYS.
UH-HUH!
I AM TOO!
OKAY.

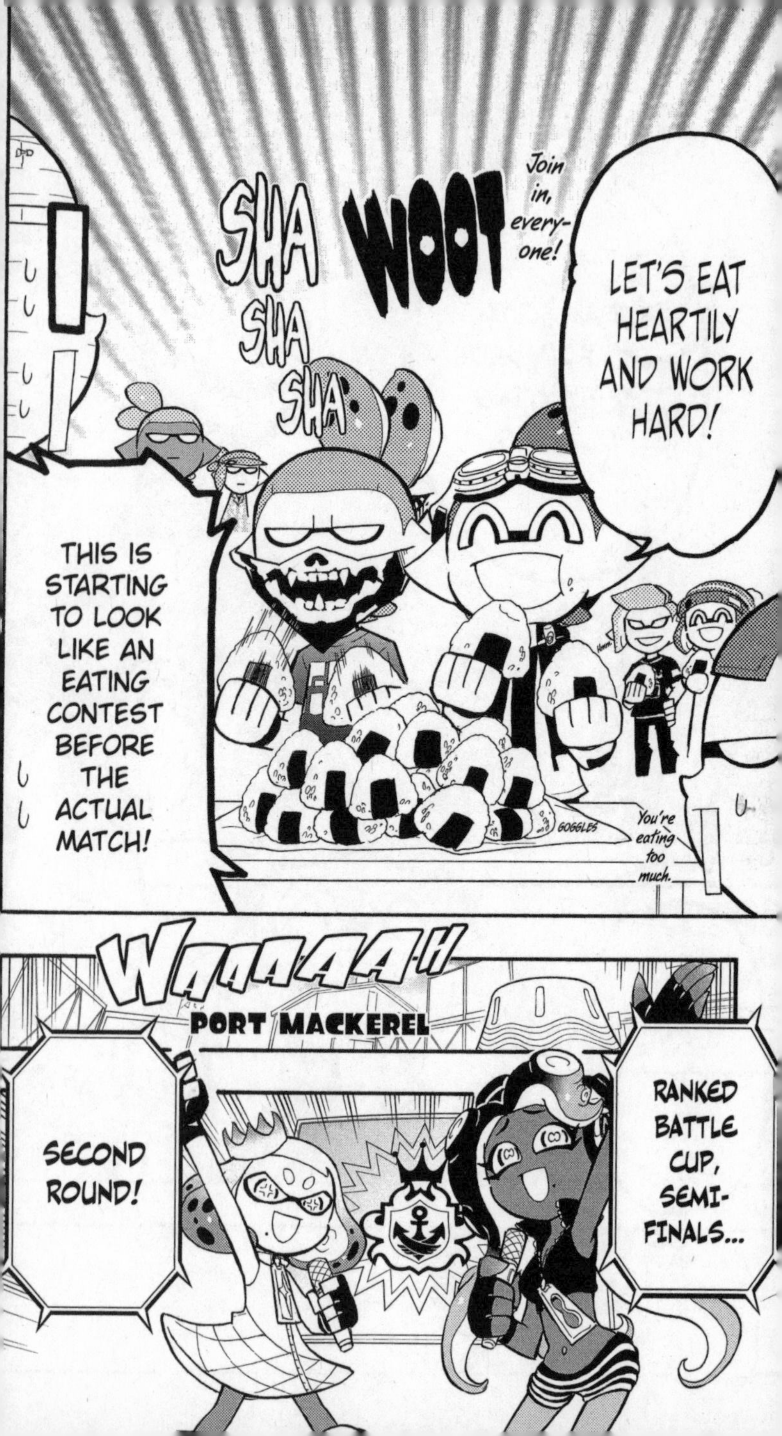
LET'S EAT HEARTILY AND WORK HARD!
Join in, every-one!
WOOT
SHA SHA SHA SHA
GOGGLES
You're eating too much.
THIS IS STARTING TO LOOK LIKE AN EATING CONTEST BEFORE THE ACTUAL MATCH!
WAAAAAAH
PORT MACKEREL
RANKED BATTLE CUP, SEMI-FINALS...
SECOND ROUND!

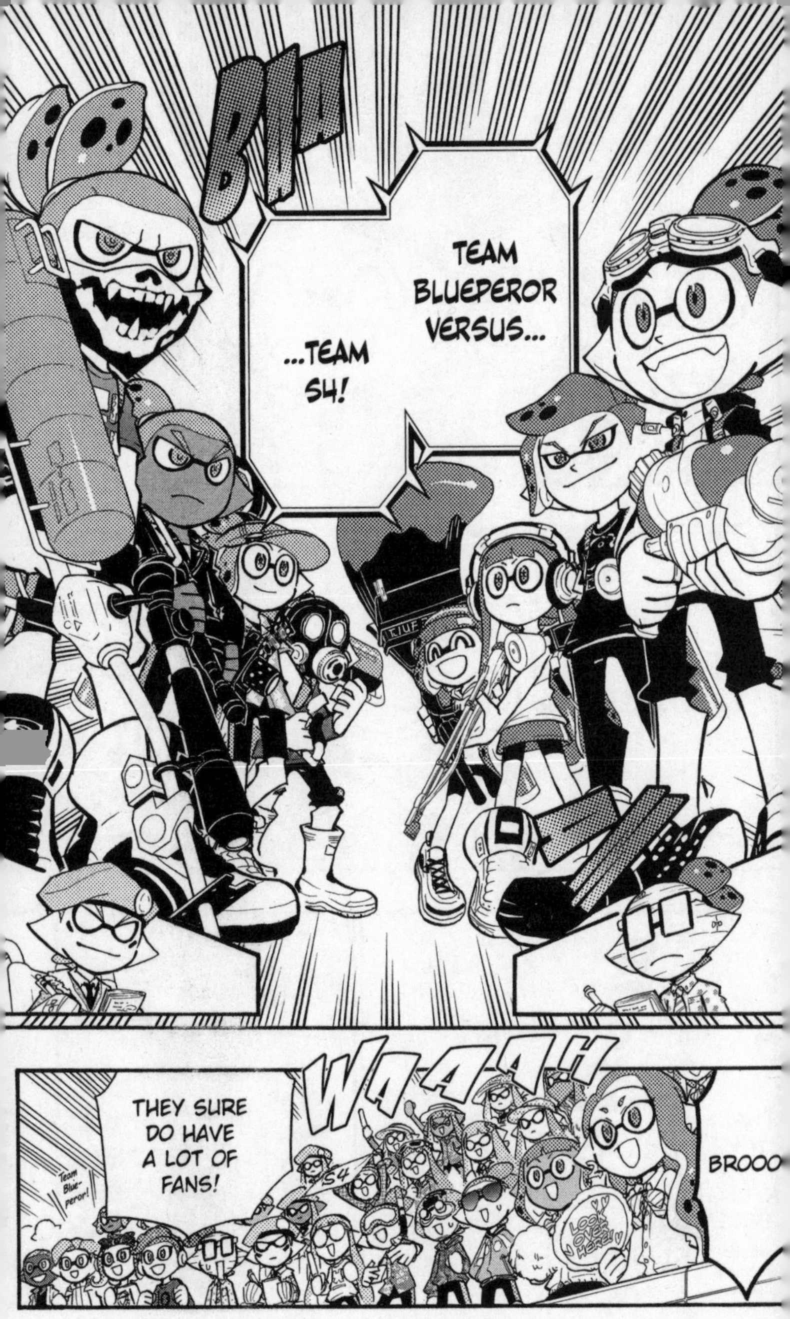
BWA
TEAM BLUEPEROR VERSUS...
...TEAM S4!
BROOO
WAAAH
LOOK OVER HERE!
S4
THEY SURE DO HAVE A LOT OF FANS!
Team Blueperor!

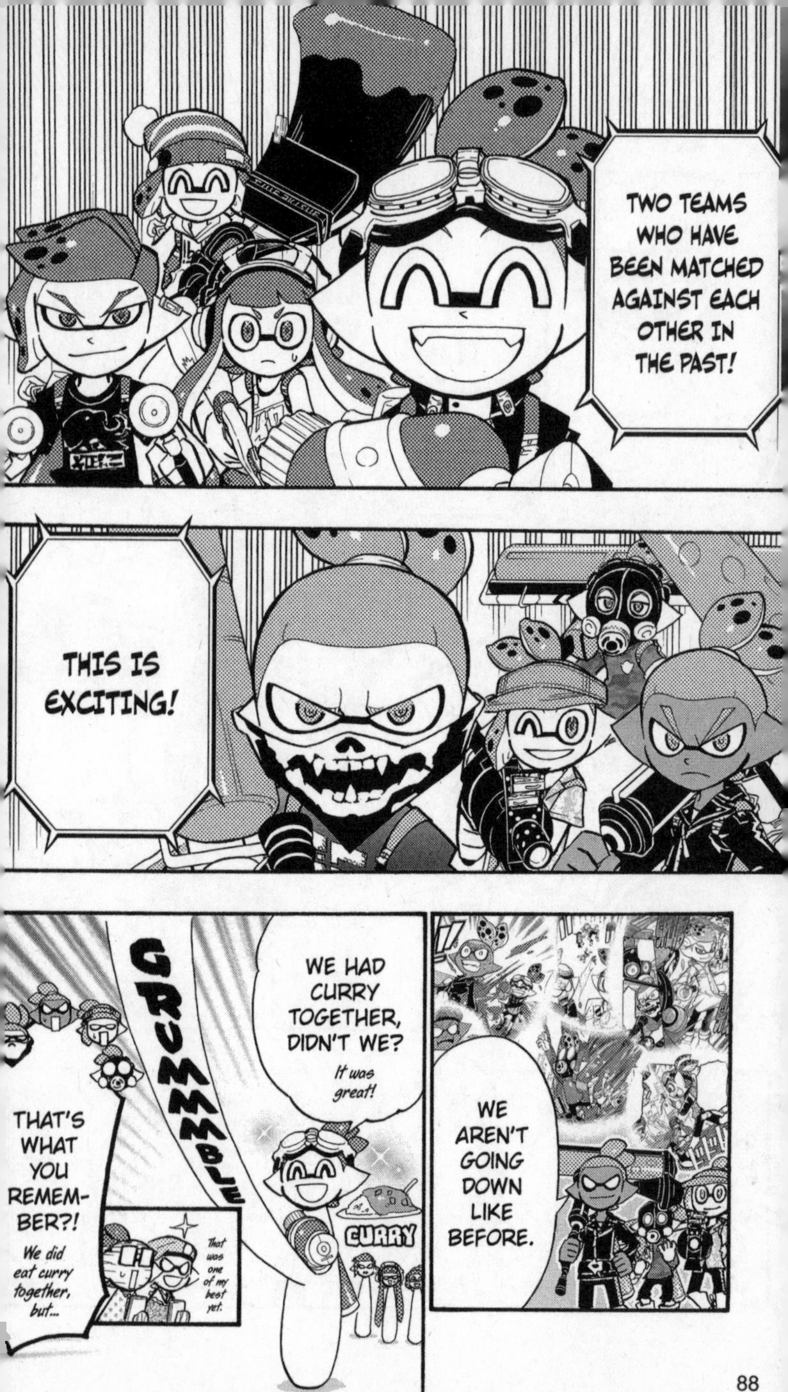
TWO TEAMS WHO HAVE BEEN MATCHED AGAINST EACH OTHER IN THE PAST!
THIS IS EXCITING!
WE AREN'T GOING DOWN LIKE BEFORE.
WE HAD CURRY TOGETHER, DIDN'T WE?
It was great!
GRUMMBLE
CURRY
THAT'S WHAT YOU REMEMBER?!
We did eat curry together, but...
That was one of my best yet.

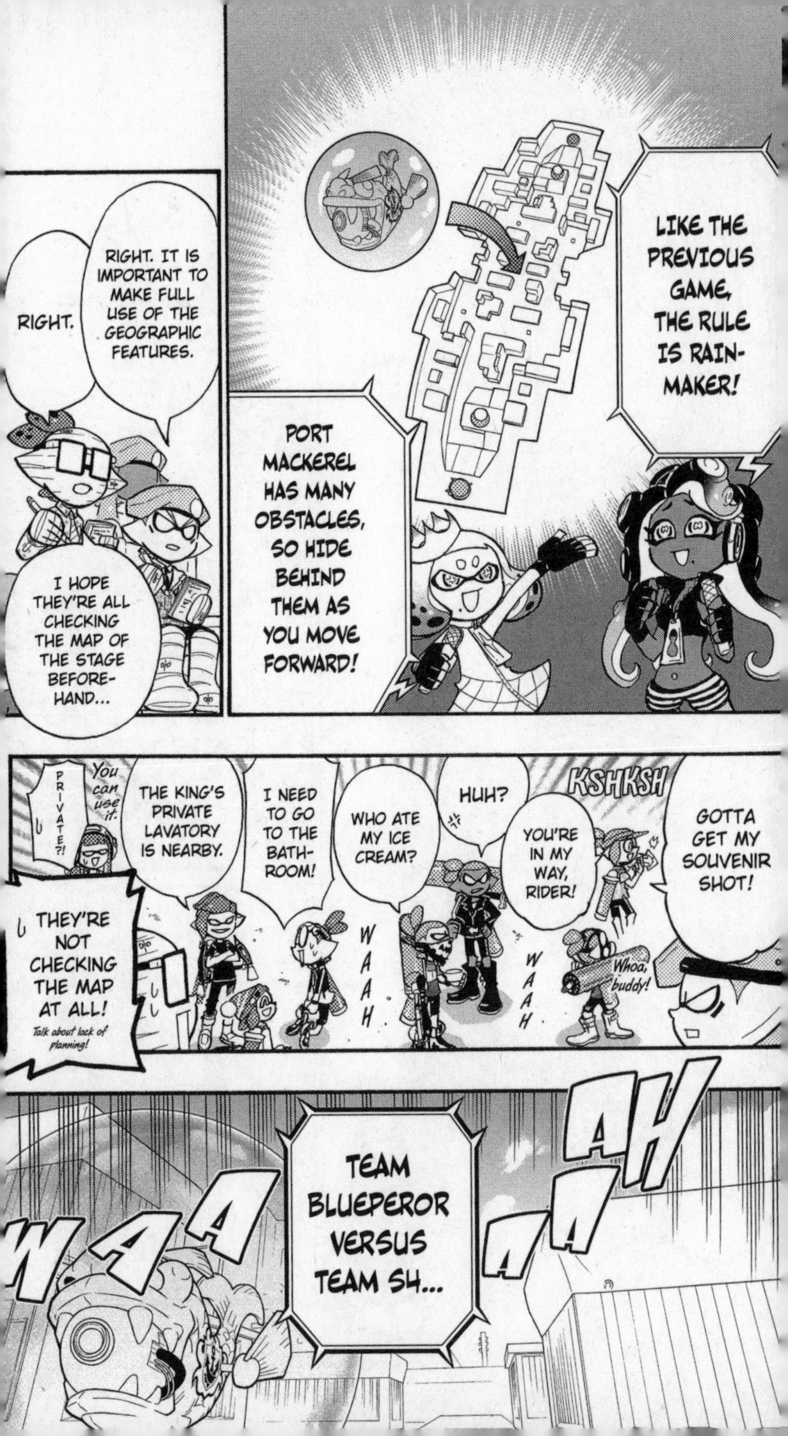
LIKE THE PREVIOUS GAME, THE RULE IS RAIN-MAKER!
PORT MACKEREL HAS MANY OBSTACLES, SO HIDE BEHIND THEM AS YOU MOVE FORWARD!
RIGHT. IT IS IMPORTANT TO MAKE FULL USE OF THE GEOGRAPHIC FEATURES.
RIGHT.
I HOPE THEY'RE ALL CHECKING THE MAP OF THE STAGE BEFORE-HAND...
KSHKSH
GOTTA GET MY SOUVENIR SHOT!
Whoa, buddy!
HUH?
YOU'RE IN MY WAY, RIDER!
WAAH
WHO ATE MY ICE CREAM?
I NEED TO GO TO THE BATH-ROOM!
WAAH
THE KING'S PRIVATE LAVATORY IS NEARBY.
You can use it.
PRIVATE?!
THEY'RE NOT CHECKING THE MAP AT ALL!
Talk about lack of planning!
AAAH
TEAM BLUEPEROR VERSUS TEAM S4...
WAAA

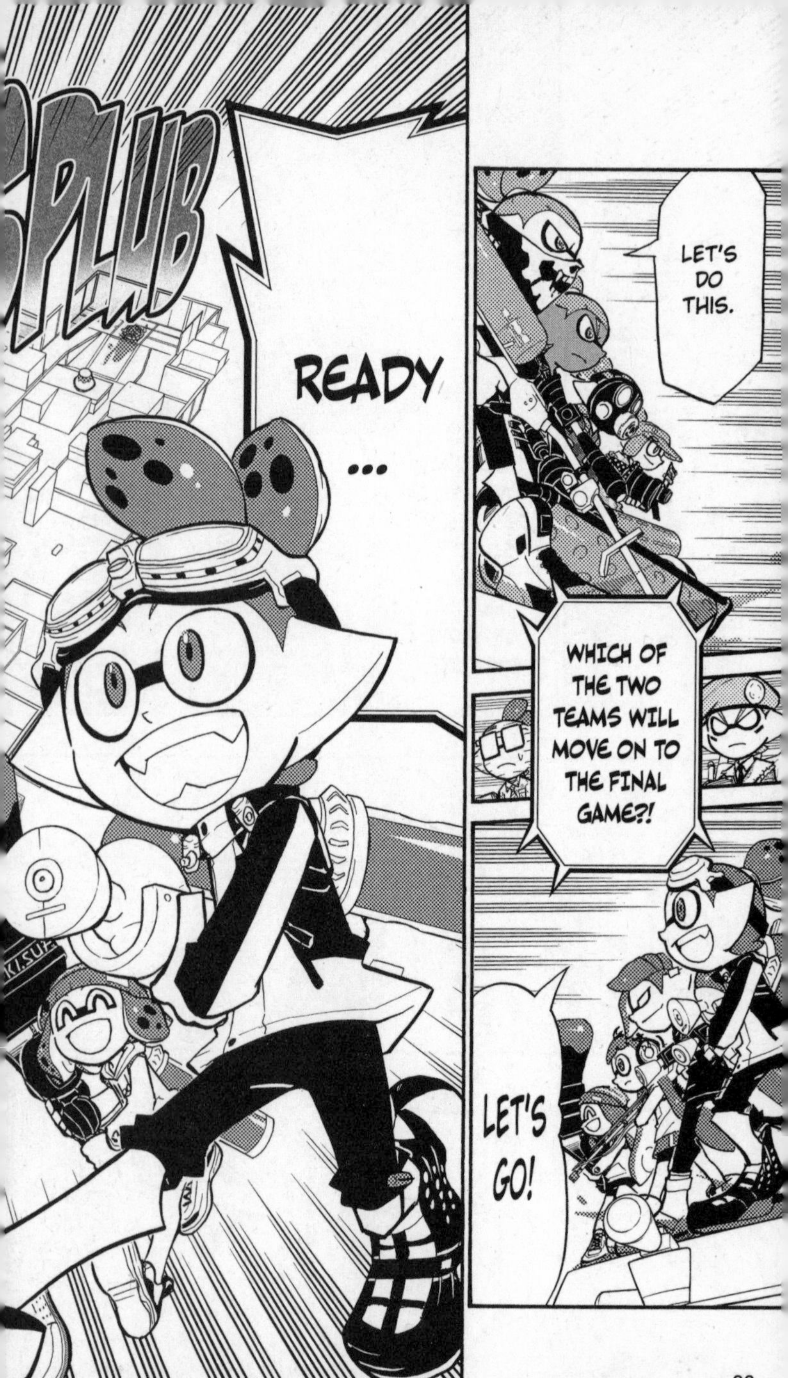
LET'S DO THIS.
WHICH OF THE TWO TEAMS WILL MOVE ON TO THE FINAL GAME?!
LET'S GO!
SPLUB
READY ...

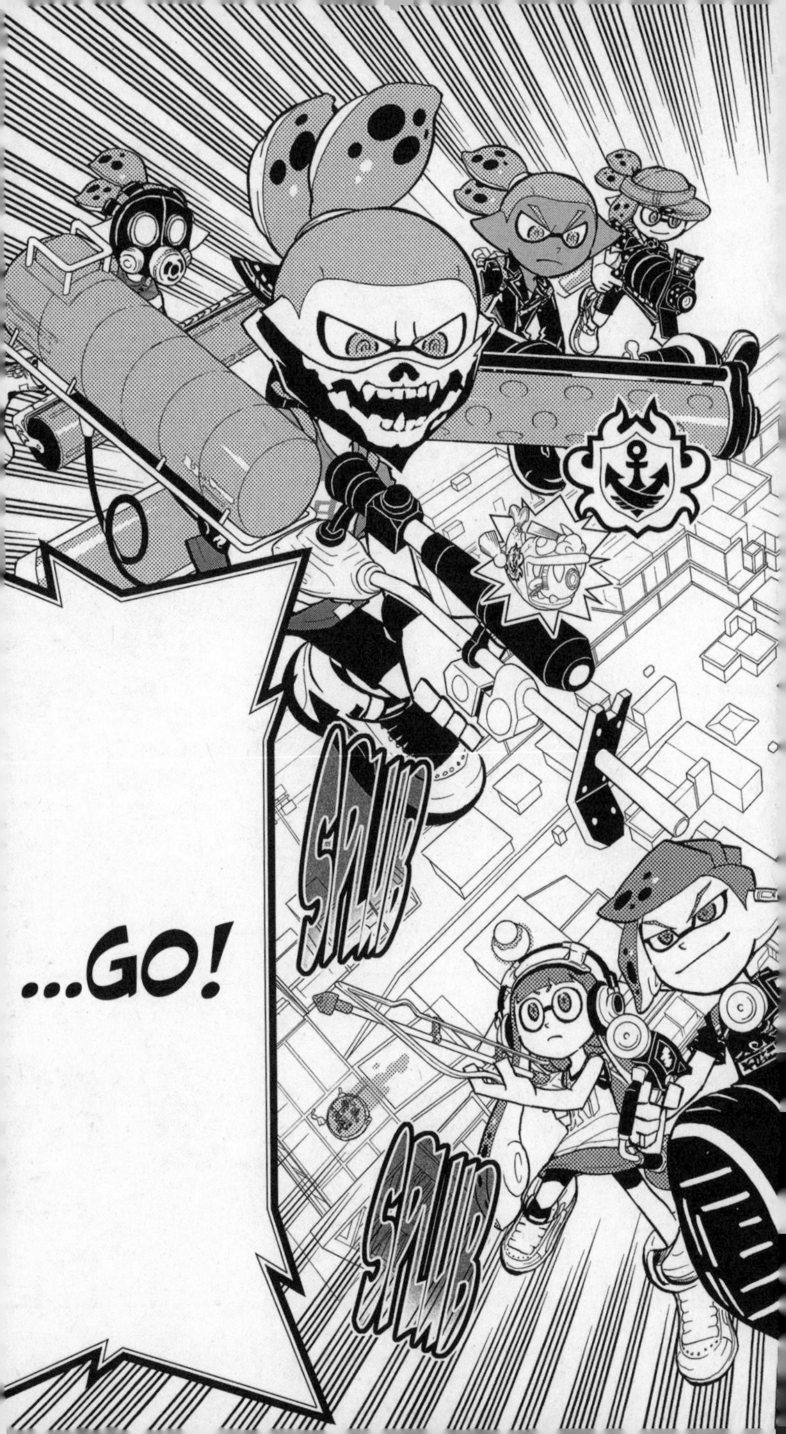
...GO!

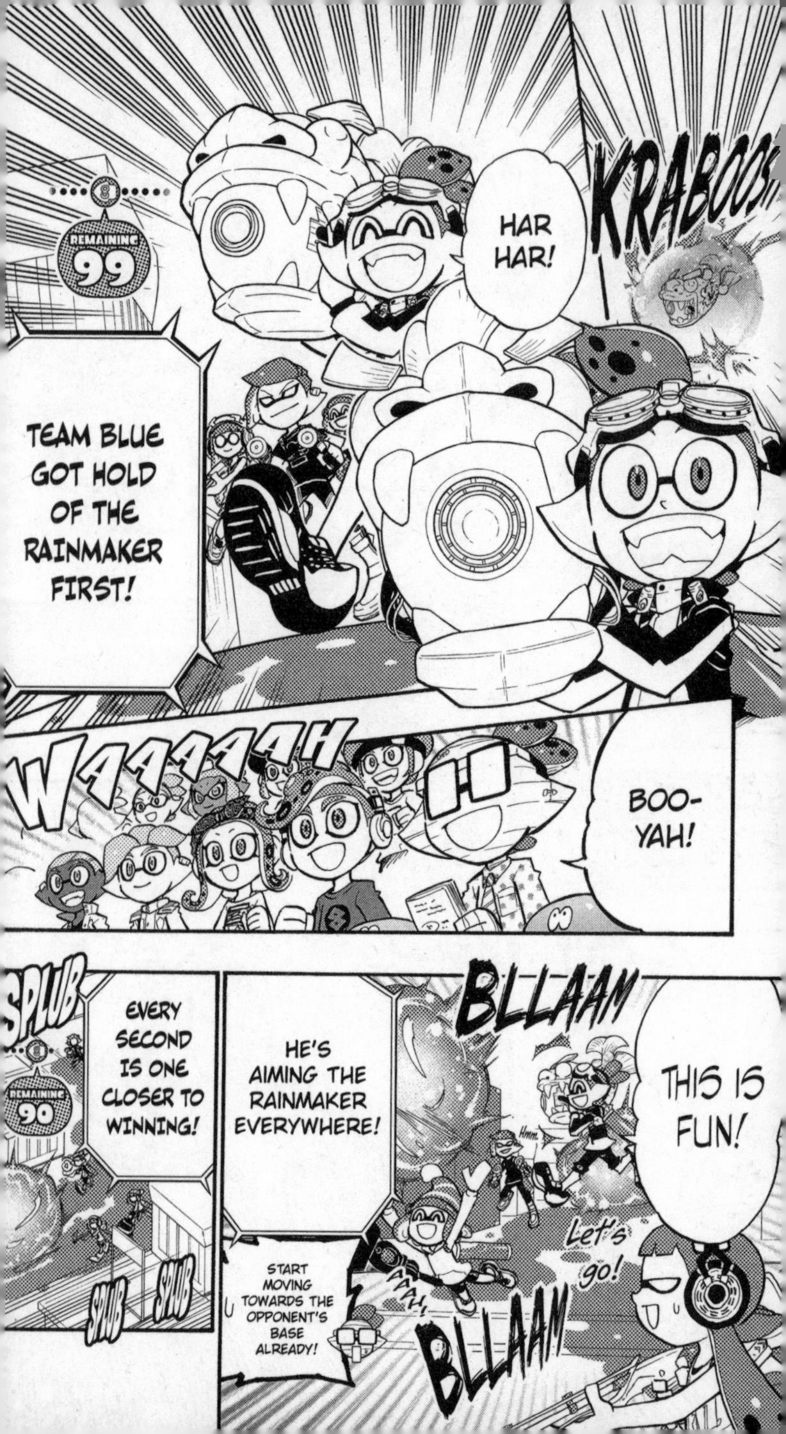
KRABOO
HAR HAR!
REMAINING 99
TEAM BLUE GOT HOLD OF THE RAINMAKER FIRST!
BOO-YAH!
WAAAAAH
THIS IS FUN!
BLLAAM
Let's go!
Hmm.
HE'S AIMING THE RAINMAKER EVERYWHERE!
START MOVING TOWARDS THE OPPONENT'S BASE ALREADY!
AAAH!
BLLAAM
EVERY SECOND IS ONE CLOSER TO WINNING!
REMAINING 90
SPLUB
SPLUB
SPLUB

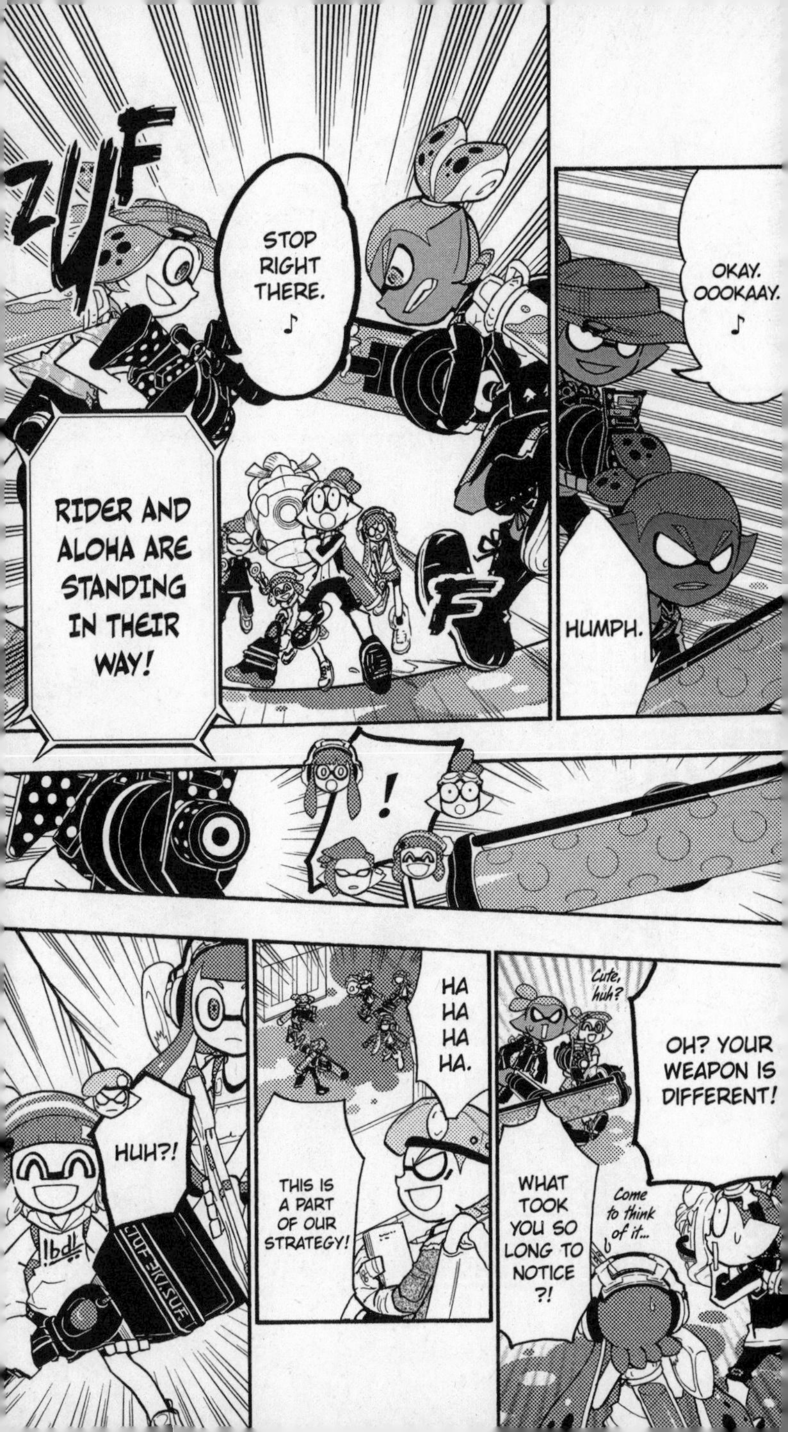
OKAY. OOOKAAY. ♪
HUMPH.
ZUF
STOP RIGHT THERE. ♪
RIDER AND ALOHA ARE STANDING IN THEIR WAY!
!
Cute, huh?
OH? YOUR WEAPON IS DIFFERENT!
Come to think of it...
WHAT TOOK YOU SO LONG TO NOTICE ?!
HA HA HA HA.
THIS IS A PART OF OUR STRATEGY!
HUH?!

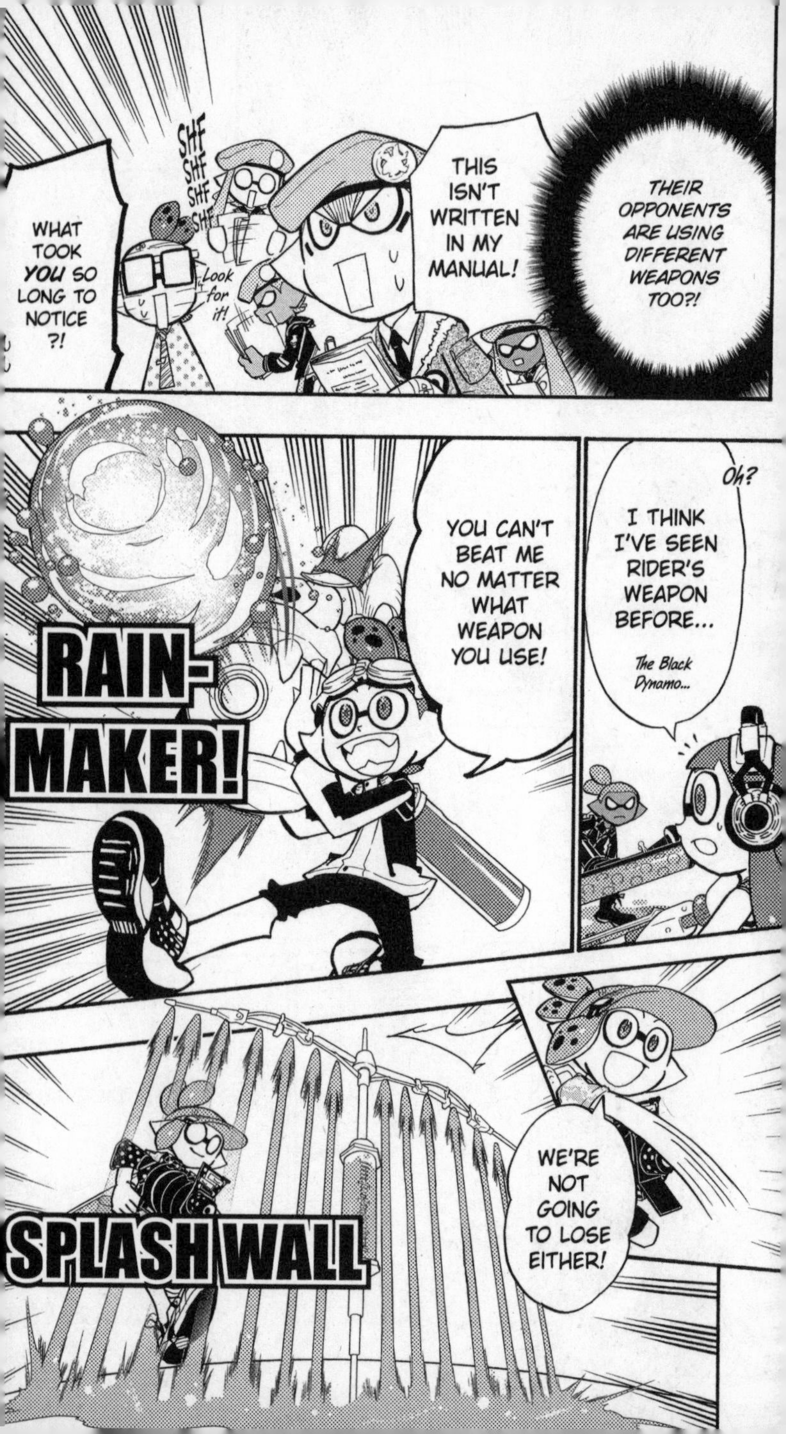
THEIR OPPONENTS ARE USING DIFFERENT WEAPONS TOO?!
THIS ISN'T WRITTEN IN MY MANUAL!
SHF SHF SHF SHF
Look for it!
WHAT TOOK YOU SO LONG TO NOTICE ?!
Oh?
I THINK I'VE SEEN RIDER'S WEAPON BEFORE...
The Black Dynamo...
YOU CAN'T BEAT ME NO MATTER WHAT WEAPON YOU USE!
RAIN-MAKER!
WE'RE NOT GOING TO LOSE EITHER!
SPLASH WALL

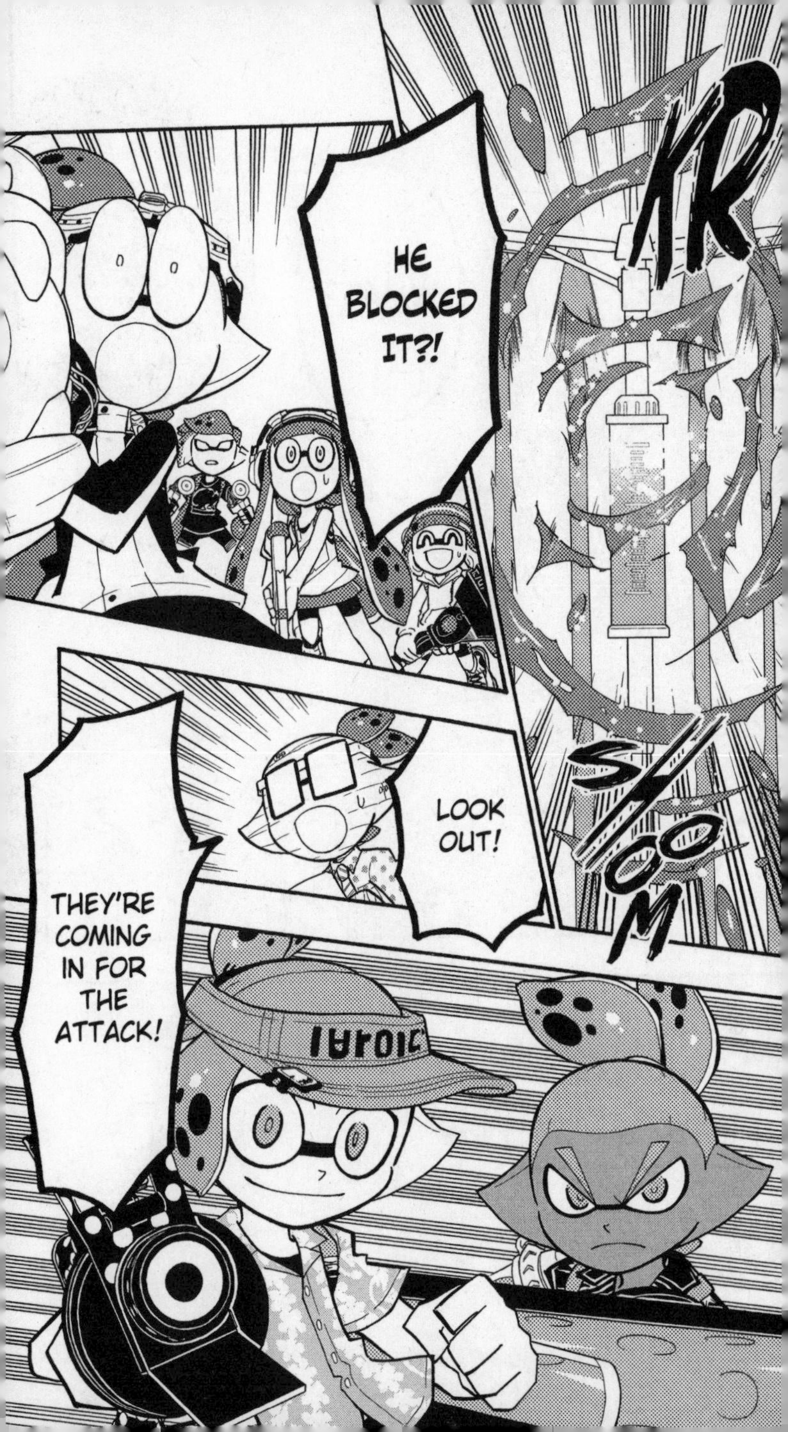
KR
SHOOM
HE BLOCKED IT?!
LOOK OUT!
THEY'RE COMING IN FOR THE ATTACK!

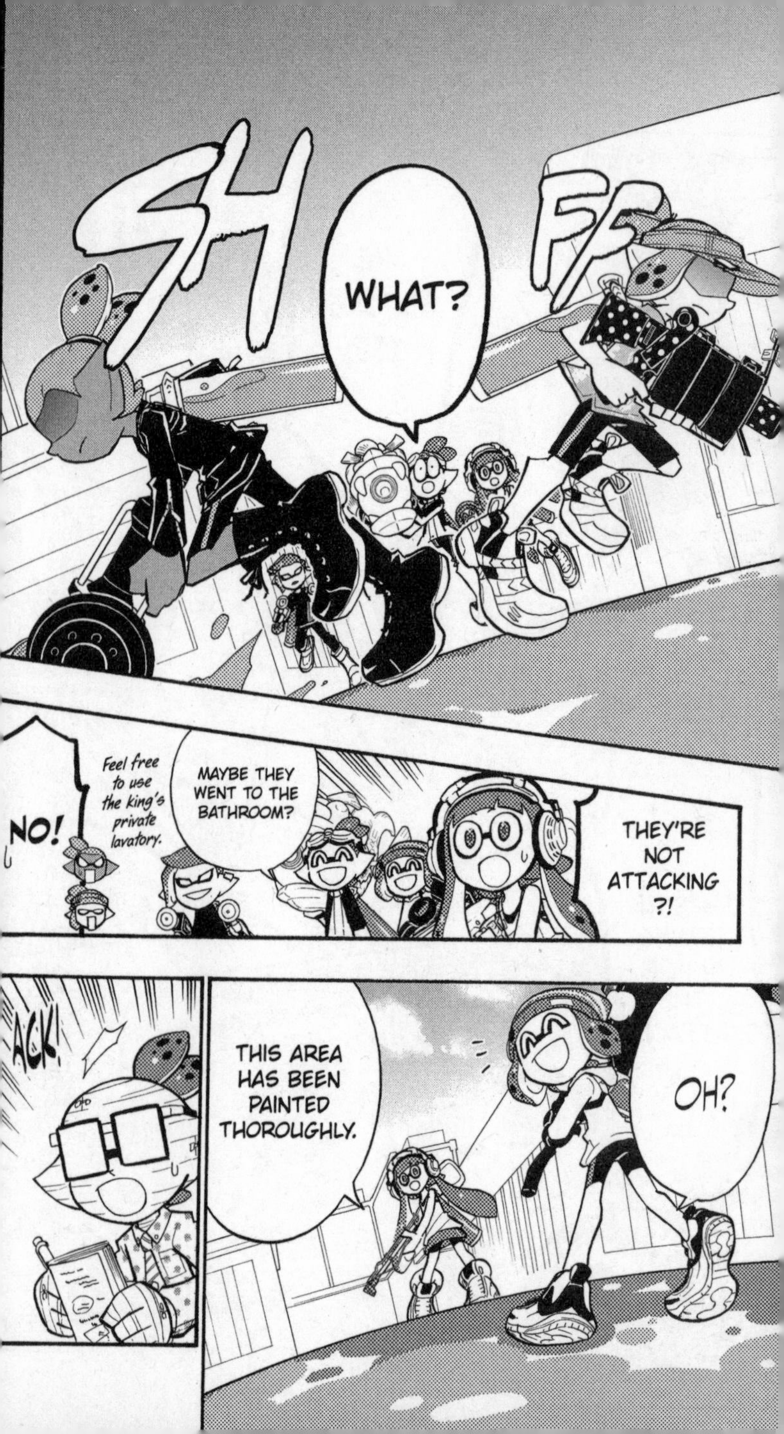
SH FF
WHAT?
THEY'RE NOT ATTACKING ?!
MAYBE THEY WENT TO THE BATHROOM?
Feel free to use the king's private lavatory.
NO!
OH?
THIS AREA HAS BEEN PAINTED THOROUGHLY.
ACK!

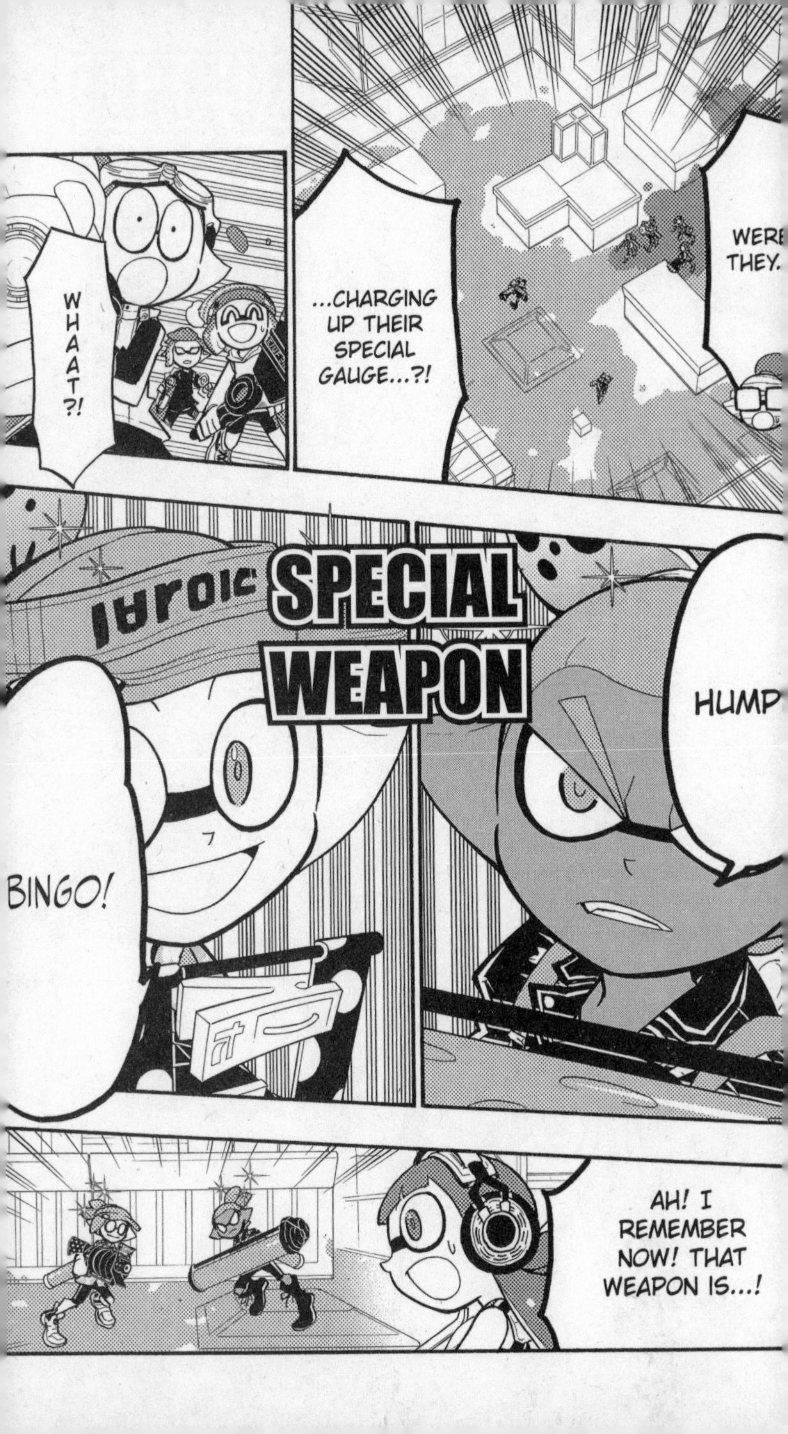

WERE THEY..
...CHARGING UP THEIR SPECIAL GAUGE...?!
WHAAT?!
HUMP
SPECIAL WEAPON
BINGO!
AH! I REMEMBER NOW! THAT WEAPON IS...!

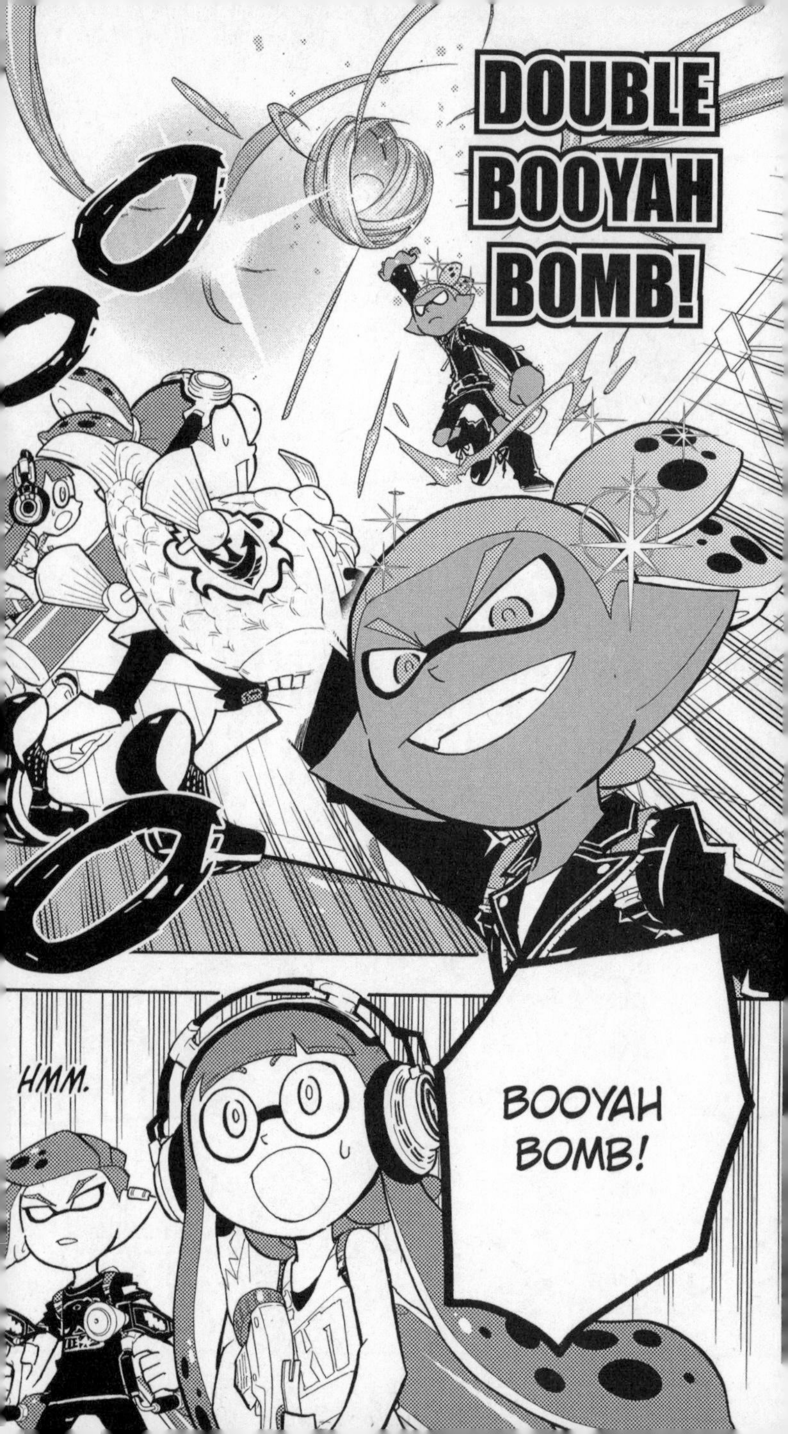
DOUBLE BOOYAH BOMB!
BOOYAH BOMB!
HMM.

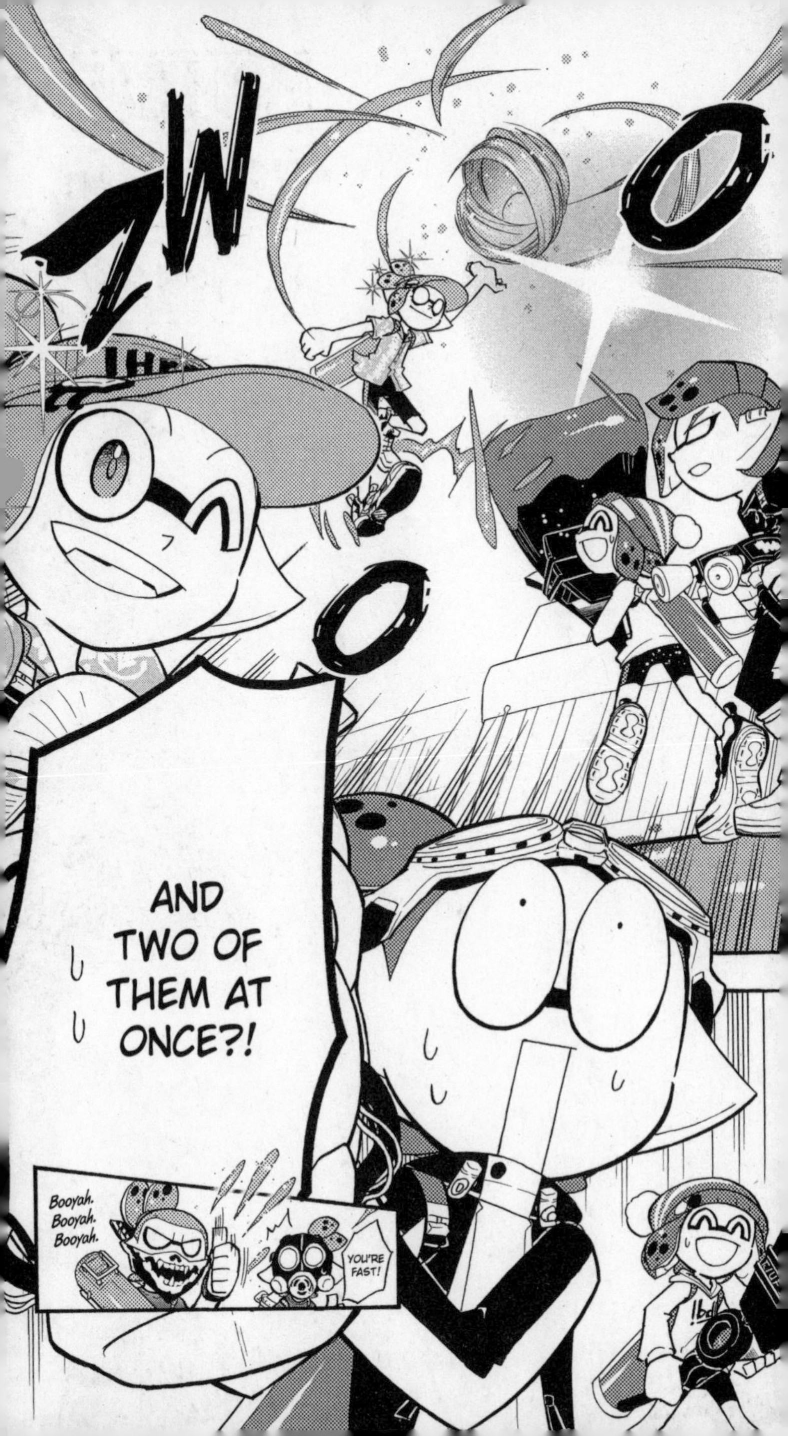
ZWOO
AND TWO OF THEM AT ONCE?!
YOU'RE FAST!
Booyah. Booyah. Booyah.

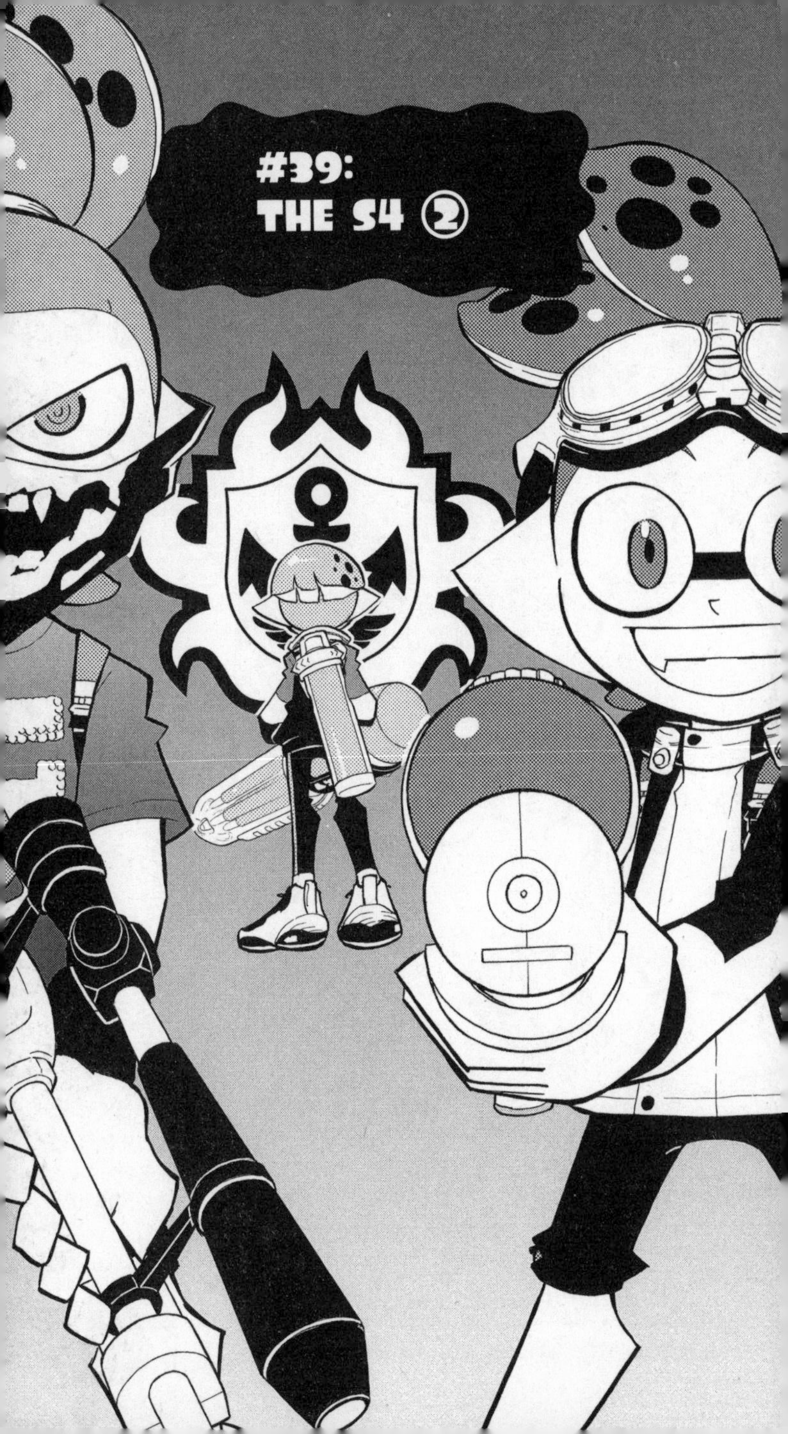
#39:
THE S4 ②

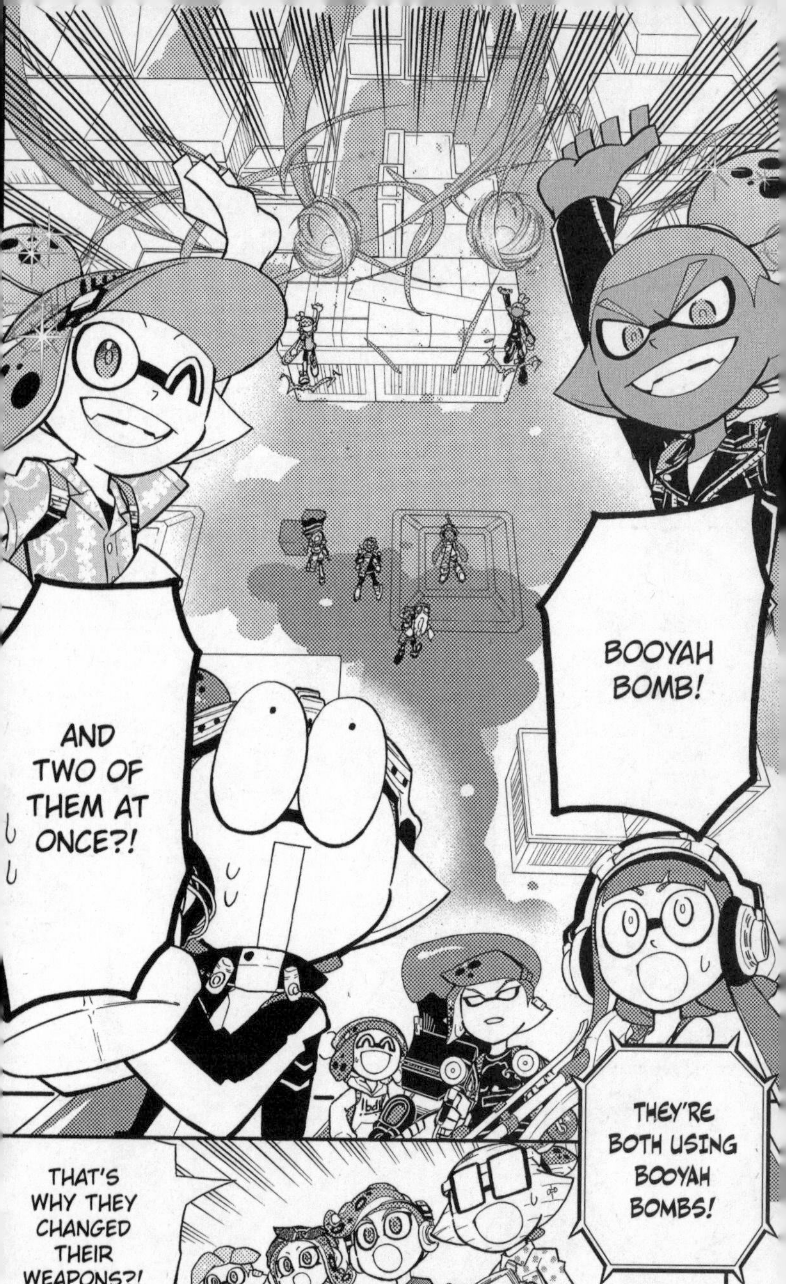
BOOYAH BOMB!
AND TWO OF THEM AT ONCE?!
THEY'RE BOTH USING BOOYAH BOMBS!
THAT'S WHY THEY CHANGED THEIR WEAPONS?!

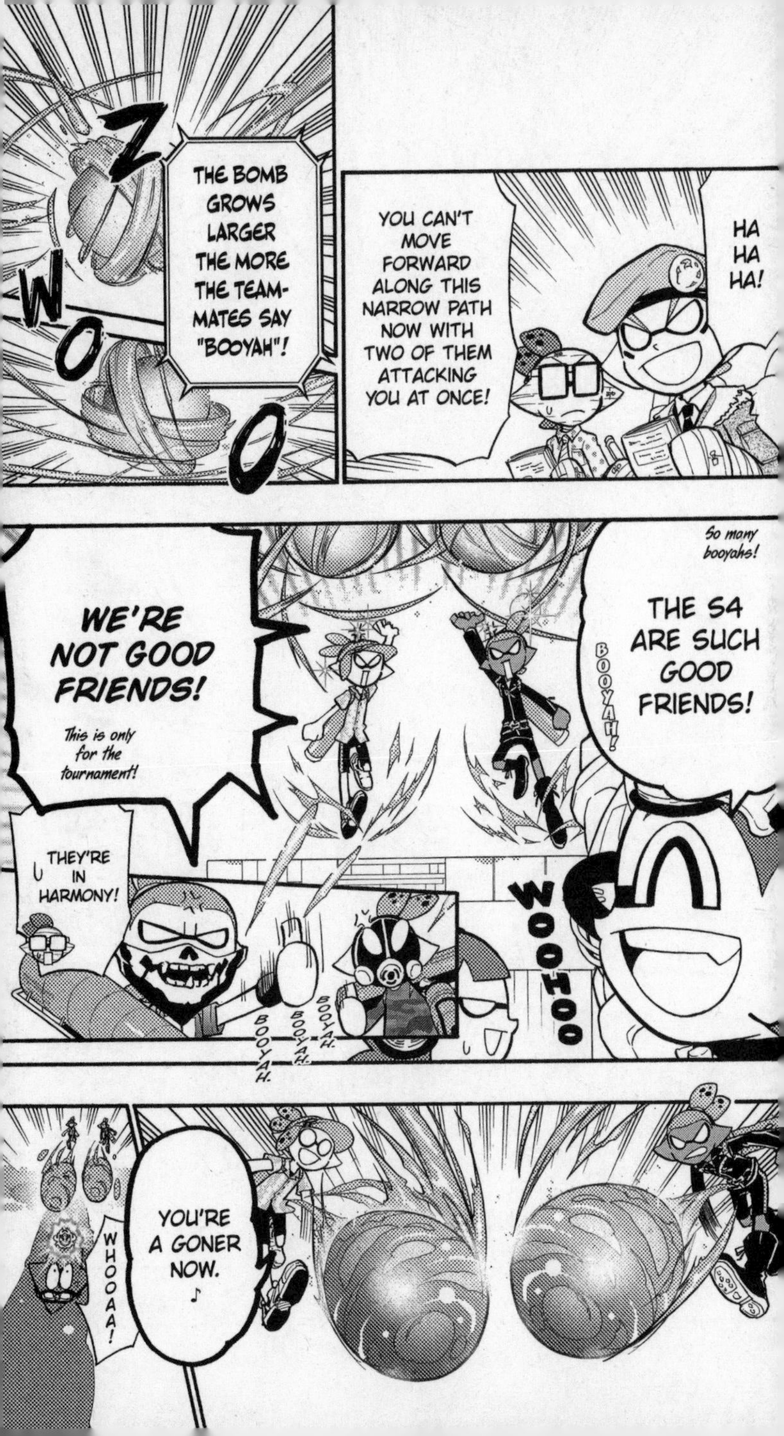
HA HA HA!
YOU CAN'T MOVE FORWARD ALONG THIS NARROW PATH NOW WITH TWO OF THEM ATTACKING YOU AT ONCE!
THE BOMB GROWS LARGER THE MORE THE TEAM-MATES SAY "BOOYAH"!
So many booyahs!
THE S4 ARE SUCH GOOD FRIENDS!
BOOYAH!
WOOHOO
WE'RE NOT GOOD FRIENDS!
This is only for the tournament!
THEY'RE IN HARMONY!
BOOYAH.
BOOYAH.
BOOYAH.
YOU'RE A GONER NOW. ♪
WHOOAA!

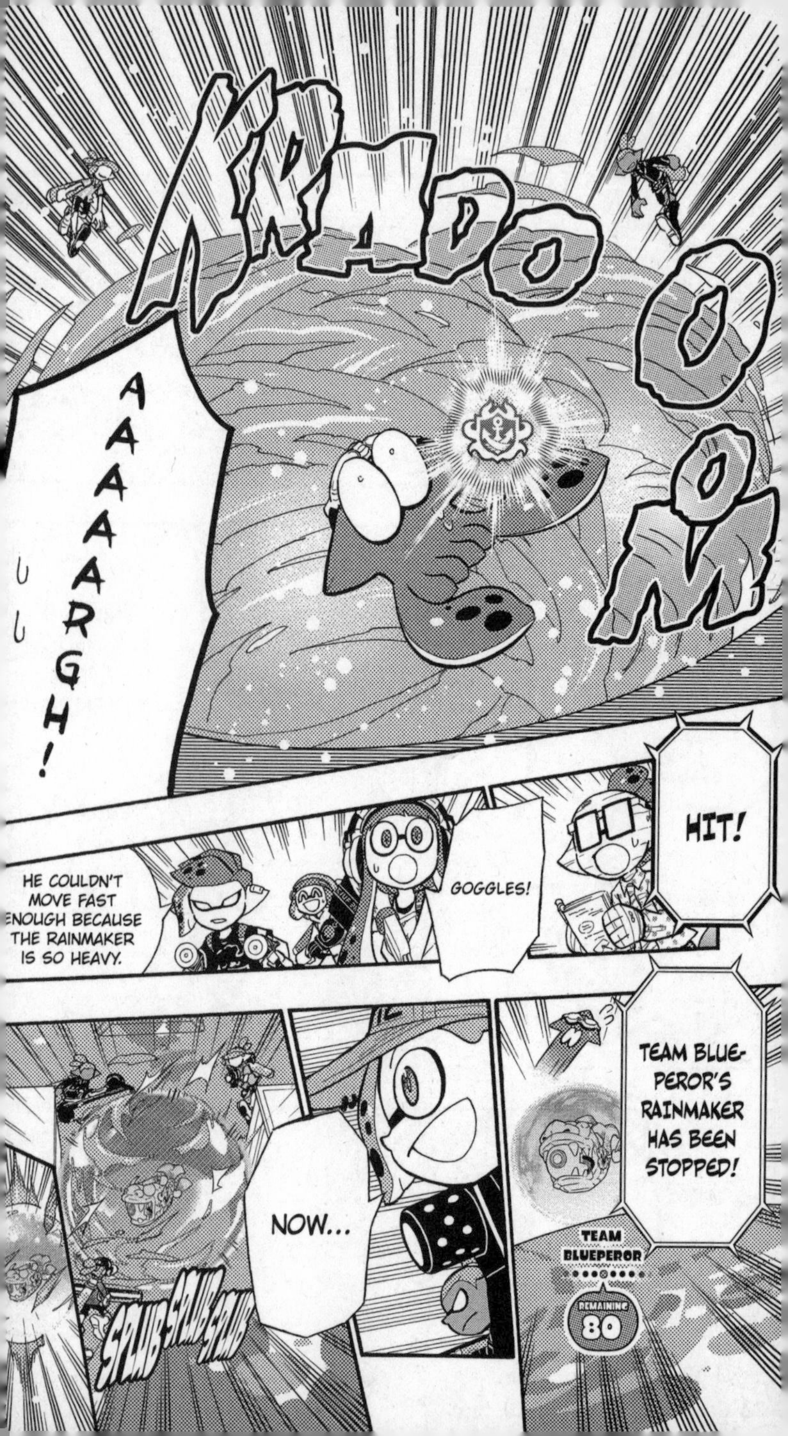
KRADOOOOM
AAAAAARGH!
HIT!
GOGGLES!
HE COULDN'T MOVE FAST ENOUGH BECAUSE THE RAINMAKER IS SO HEAVY.
TEAM BLUE-PEROR'S RAINMAKER HAS BEEN STOPPED!
TEAM BLUEPEROR
REMAINING 80
NOW...
SPLUB-SPLUB-SPLUB

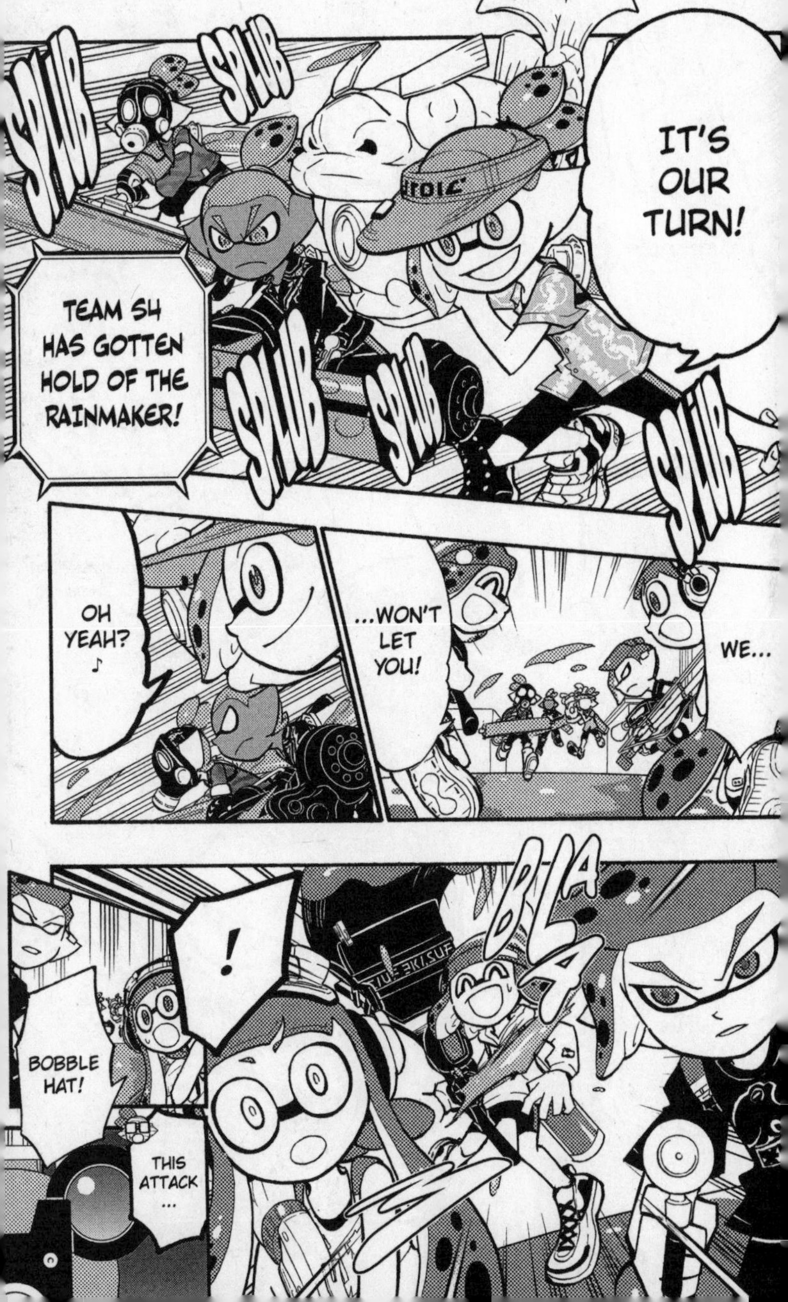
IT'S OUR TURN!
SPLUB
SPLUB
SPLUB
SPLUB
SPLUB
SPLUB
TEAM S4 HAS GOTTEN HOLD OF THE RAINMAKER!
WE...
...WON'T LET YOU!
OH YEAH? ♪
BLA
BLA
!
BOBBLE HAT!
THIS ATTACK...

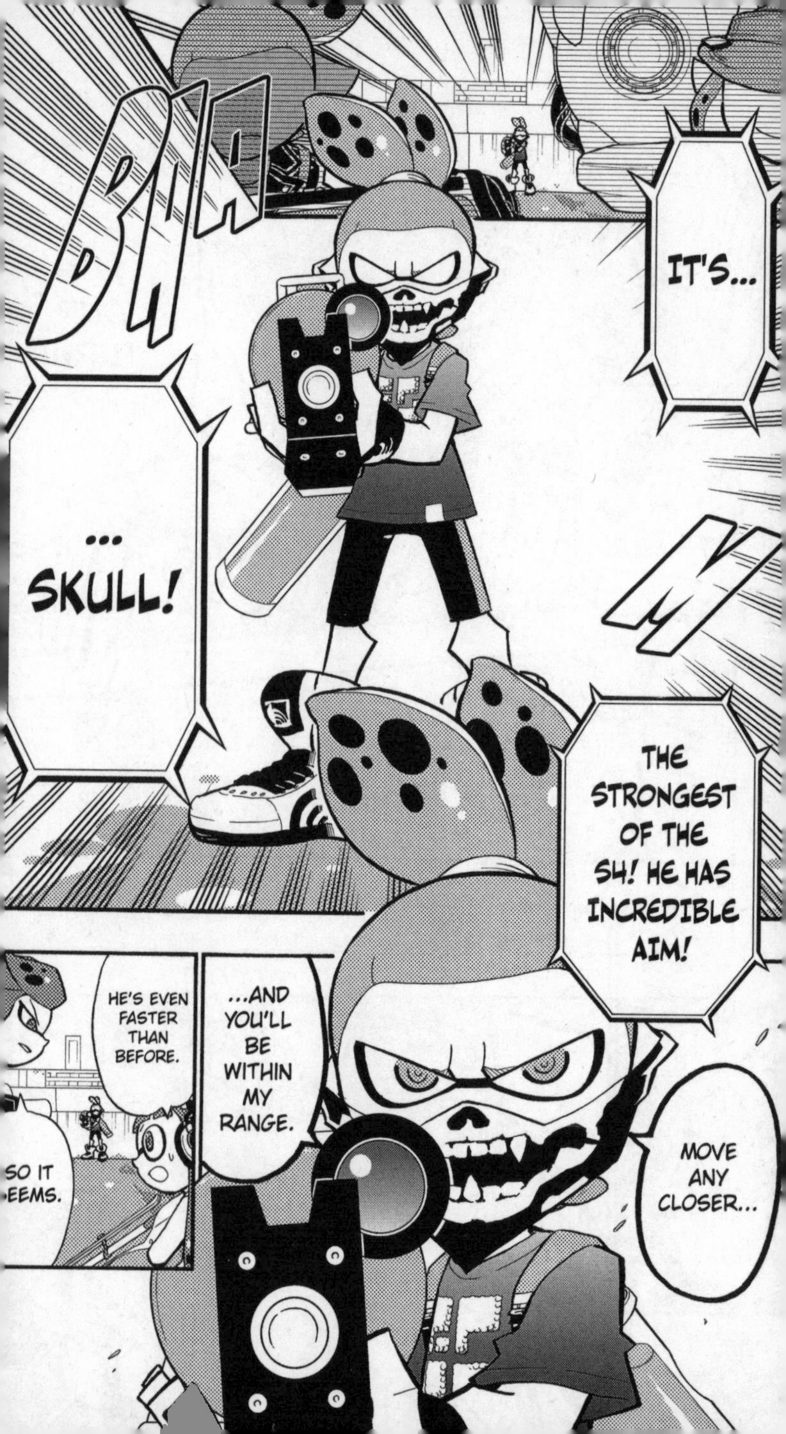
IT'S...
... SKULL!
THE STRONGEST OF THE S4! HE HAS INCREDIBLE AIM!
MOVE ANY CLOSER...
...AND YOU'LL BE WITHIN MY RANGE.
HE'S EVEN FASTER THAN BEFORE.
SO IT
EEMS.

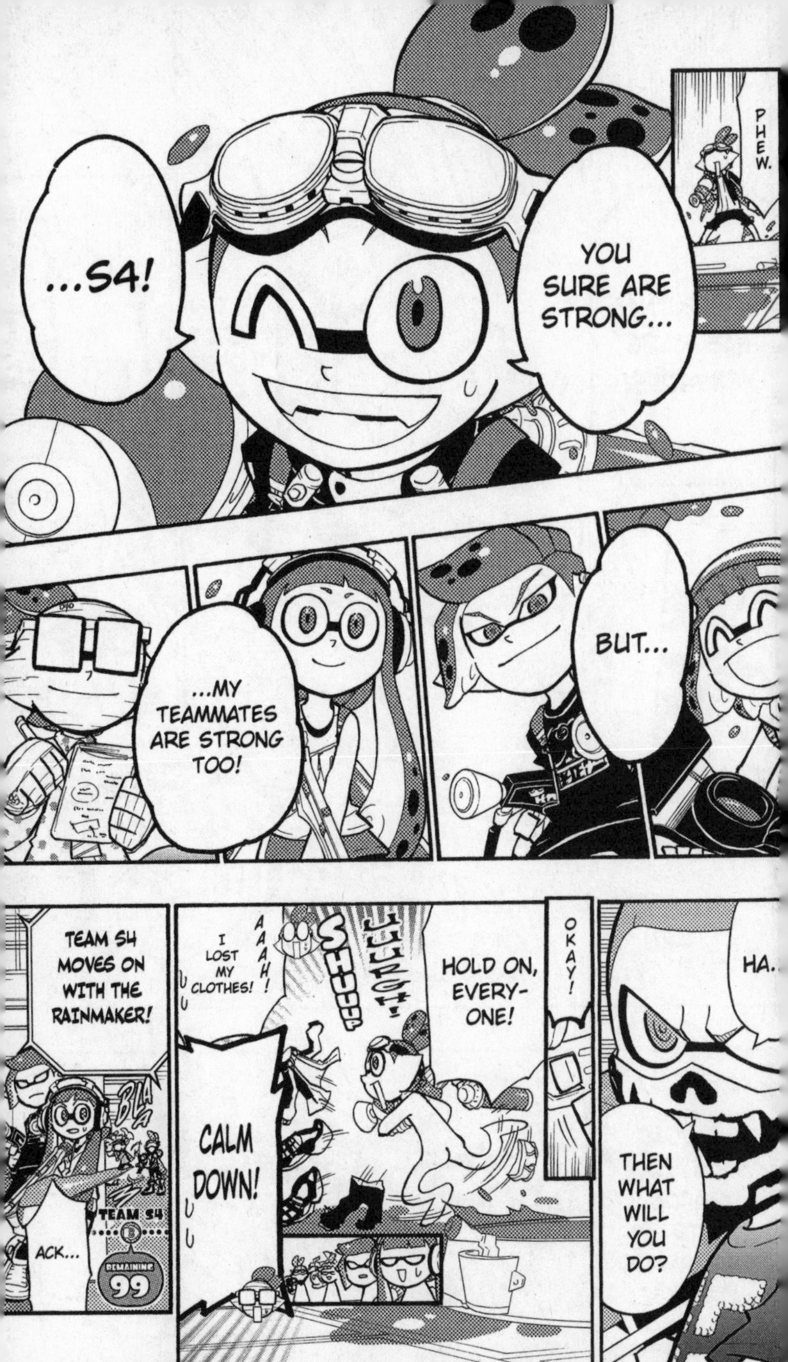
PHEW.
YOU SURE ARE STRONG...
...S4!
BUT...
...MY TEAMMATES ARE STRONG TOO!
HA...
THEN WHAT WILL YOU DO?
OKAY!
HOLD ON, EVERY-ONE!
SHUUUP
JUURGH!
AAAAH!
I LOST MY CLOTHES!
UU
CALM DOWN!
UU
TEAM S4 MOVES ON WITH THE RAINMAKER!
BLAA
TEAM S4
REMAINING
99
ACK...

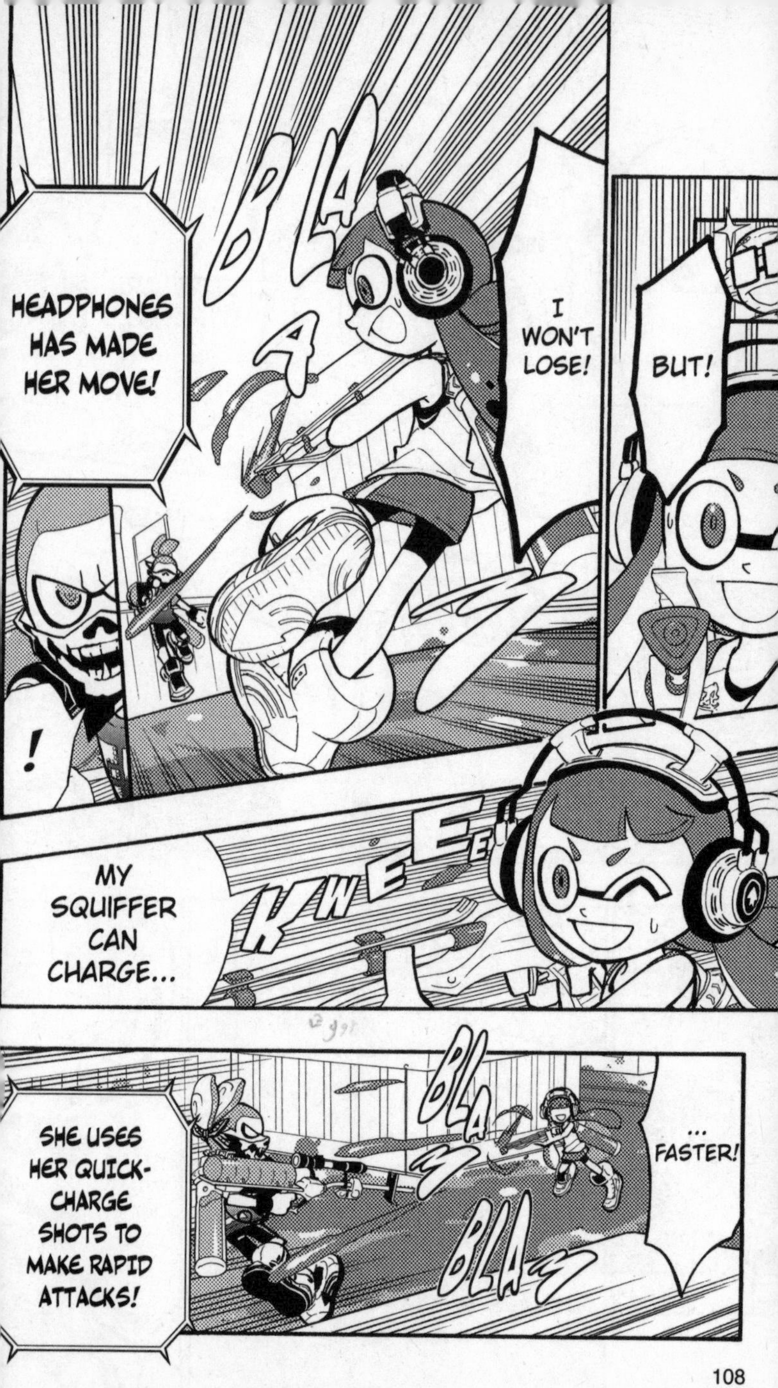
BUT!
I WON'T LOSE!
BLA
A
HEADPHONES HAS MADE HER MOVE!
!
KWEEEe
MY SQUIFFER CAN CHARGE...
... FASTER!
BLAM
BLAM
SHE USES HER QUICK-CHARGE SHOTS TO MAKE RAPID ATTACKS!

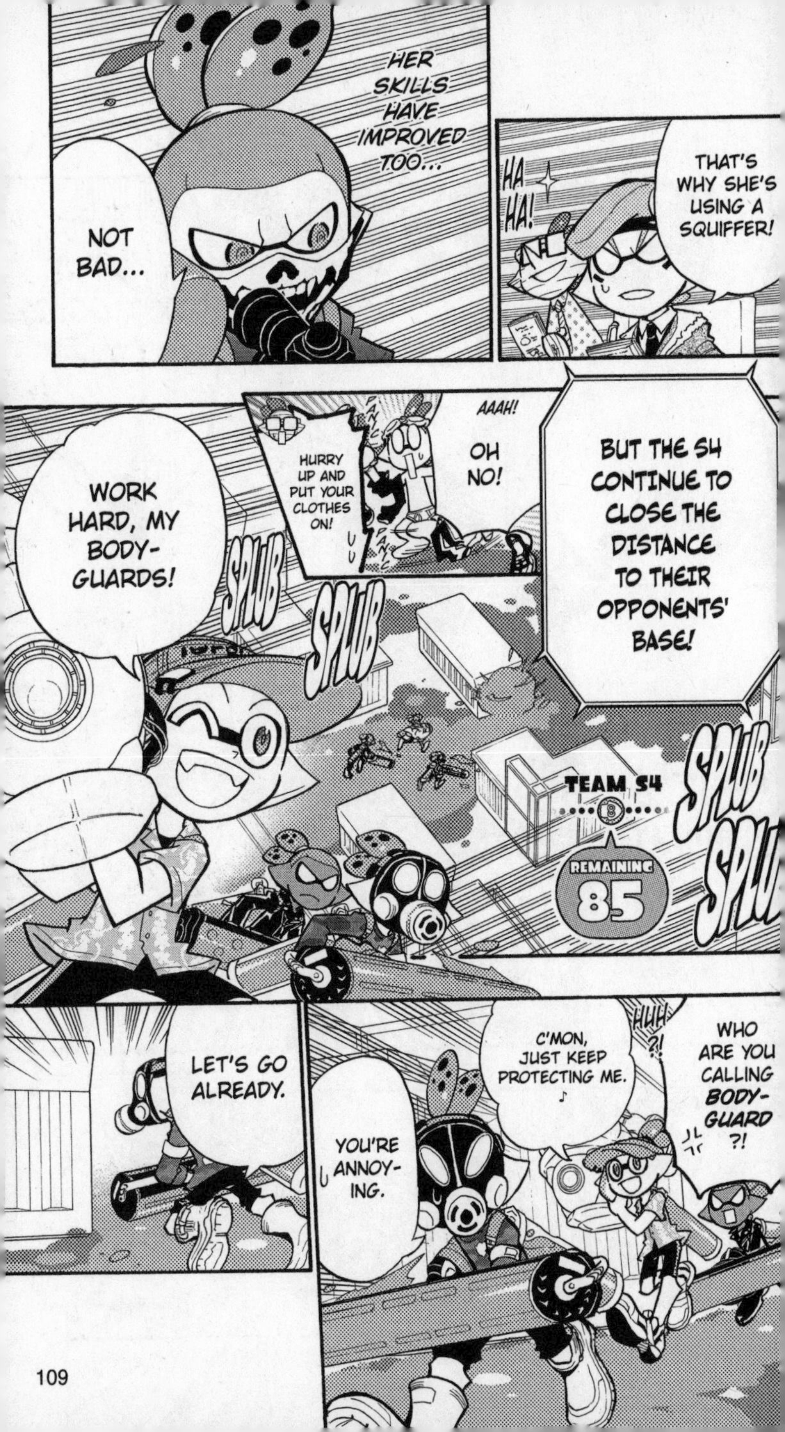
HA HA!
THAT'S WHY SHE'S USING A SQUIFFER!
HER SKILLS HAVE IMPROVED TOO...
NOT BAD...
BUT THE S4 CONTINUE TO CLOSE THE DISTANCE TO THEIR OPPONENTS' BASE!
AAAH!
OH NO!
PANIC PANIC
HURRY UP AND PUT YOUR CLOTHES ON!
WORK HARD, MY BODY-GUARDS!
SPLUB SPLUB
SPLUB SPLUB
TEAM S4
8
REMAINING
85
WHO ARE YOU CALLING BODY-GUARD?!
HUH?!
C'MON, JUST KEEP PROTECTING ME. ♪
YOU'RE ANNOY-ING.
LET'S GO ALREADY.

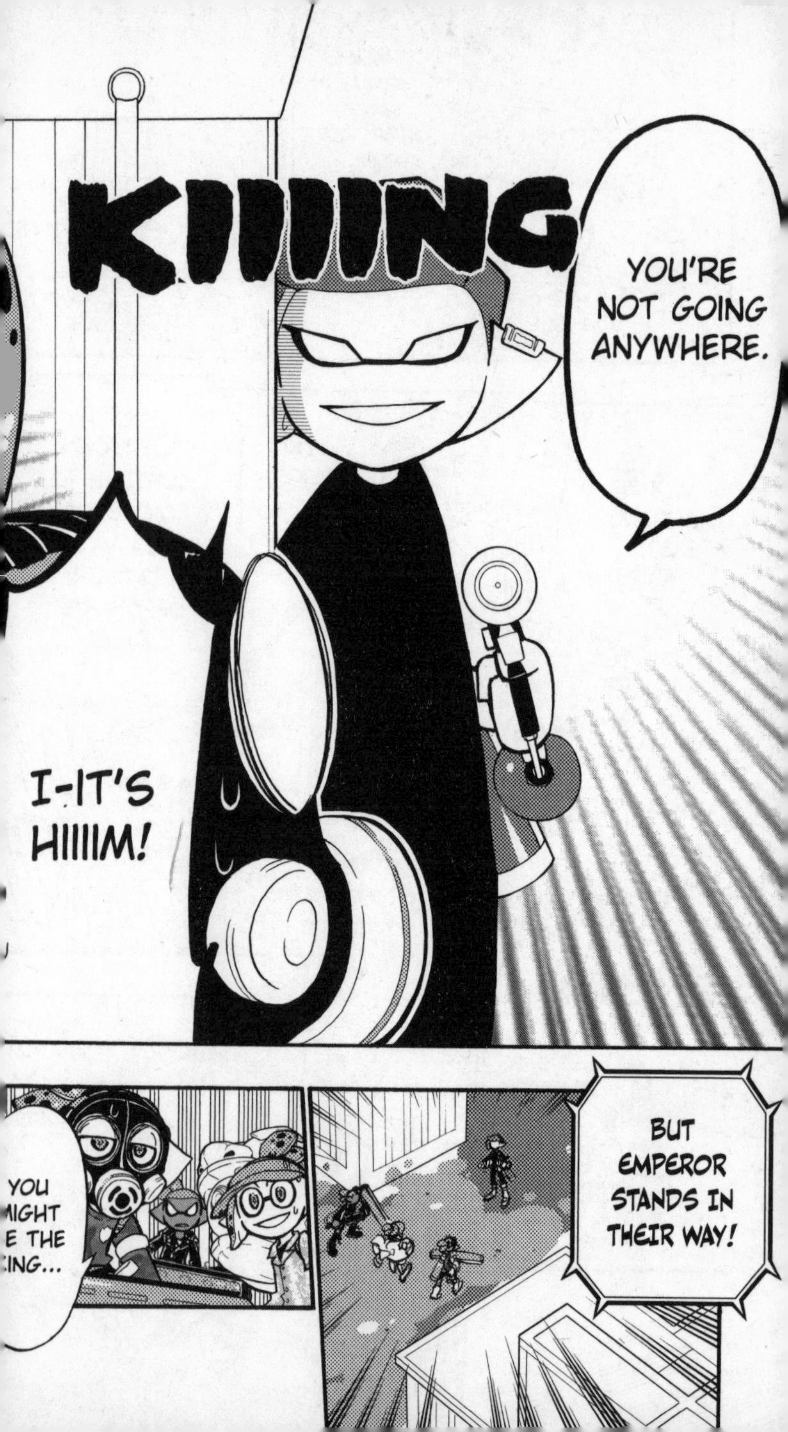
KIIIING
YOU'RE NOT GOING ANYWHERE.
I-IT'S HIIIIM!
BUT EMPEROR STANDS IN THEIR WAY!
YOU MIGHT E THE ING...

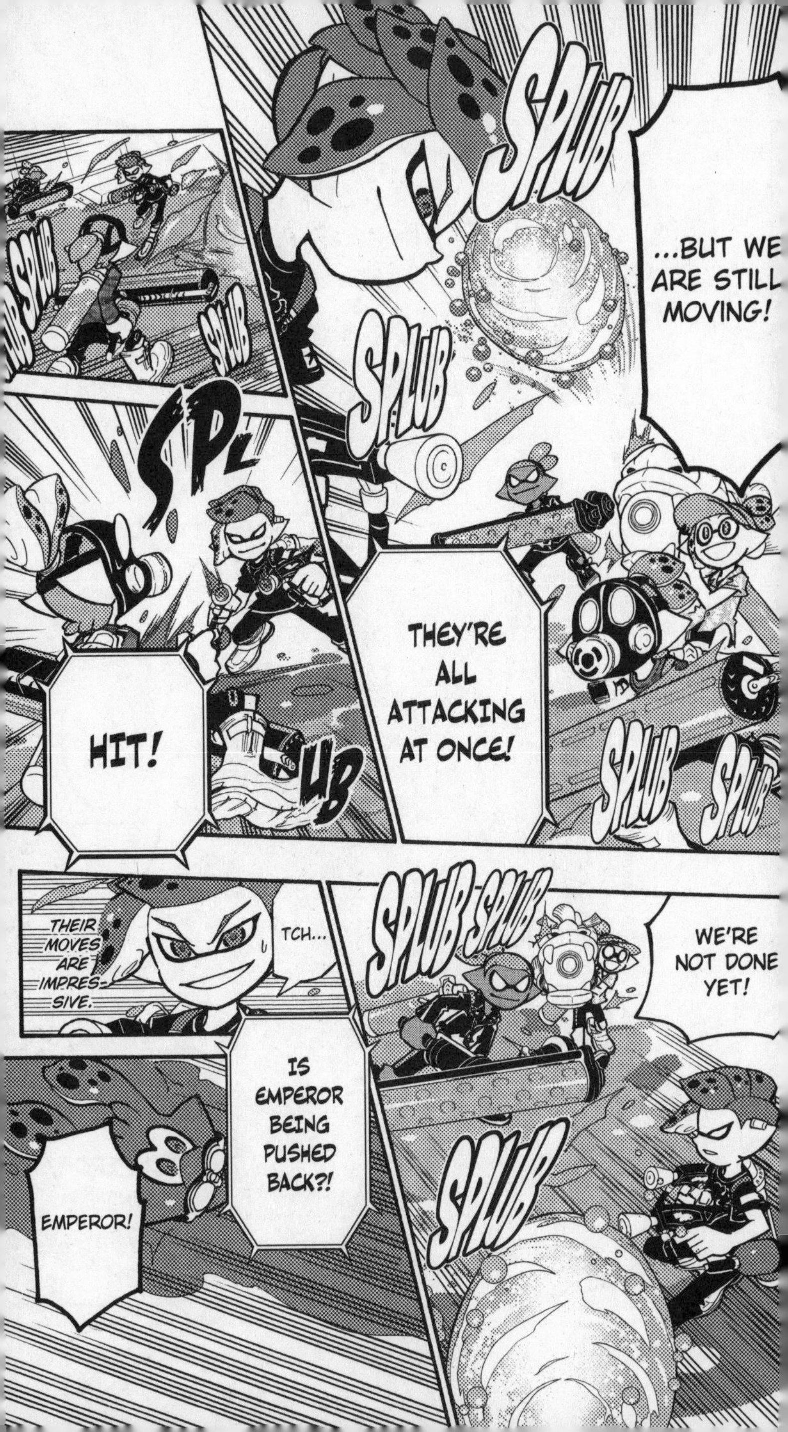
SPLUB
...BUT WE ARE STILL MOVING!
SPLUB
SPLUB
SPLUB
SPLUB
THEY'RE ALL ATTACKING AT ONCE!
SPLUB
SPLUB
SPL
UB
HIT!
WE'RE NOT DONE YET!
SPLUB-SPLUB
SPLUB
TCH...
THEIR MOVES ARE IMPRES-SIVE.
IS EMPEROR BEING PUSHED BACK?!
EMPEROR!

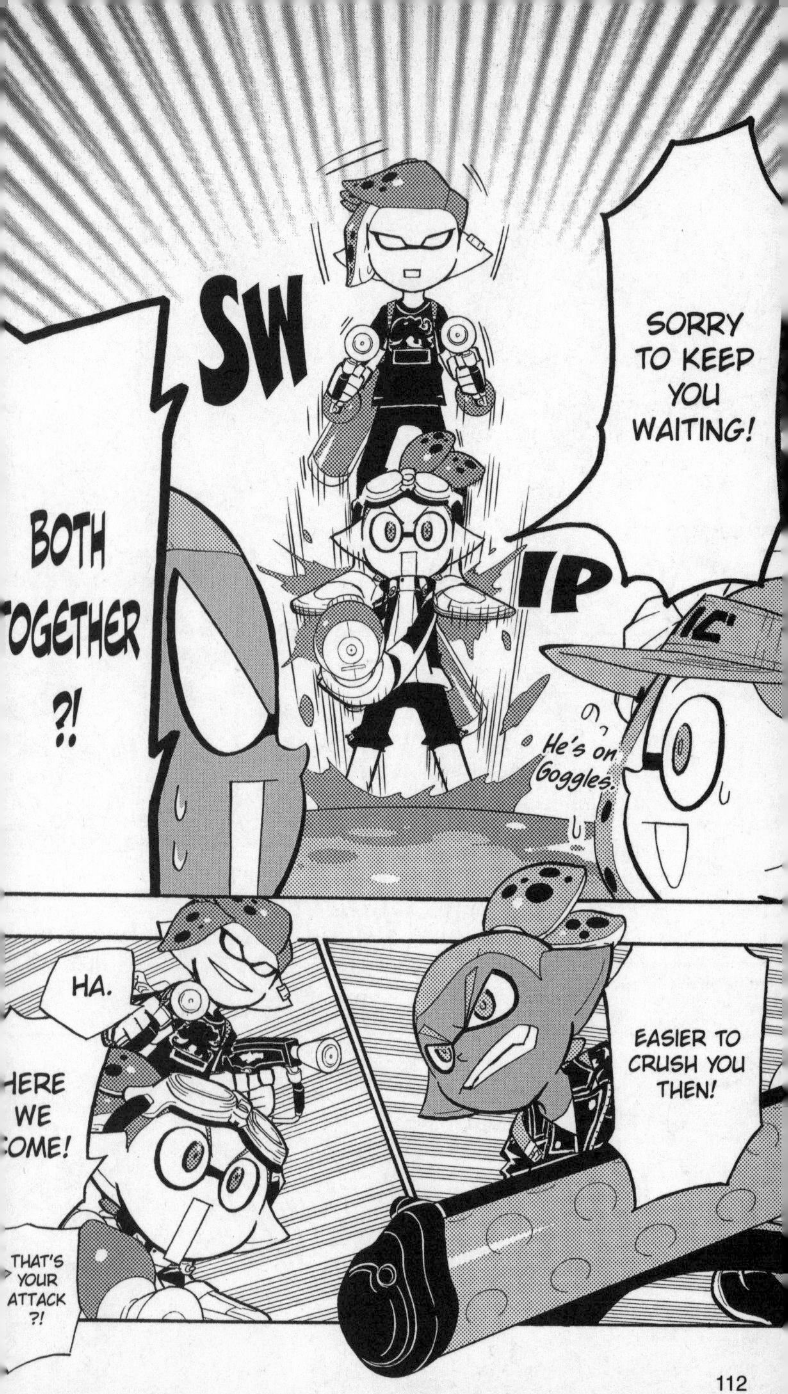

SORRY TO KEEP YOU WAITING!
SW
IP
He's on Goggles.
BOTH TOGETHER ?!
EASIER TO CRUSH YOU THEN!
HA.
HERE WE COME!
THAT'S YOUR ATTACK ?!

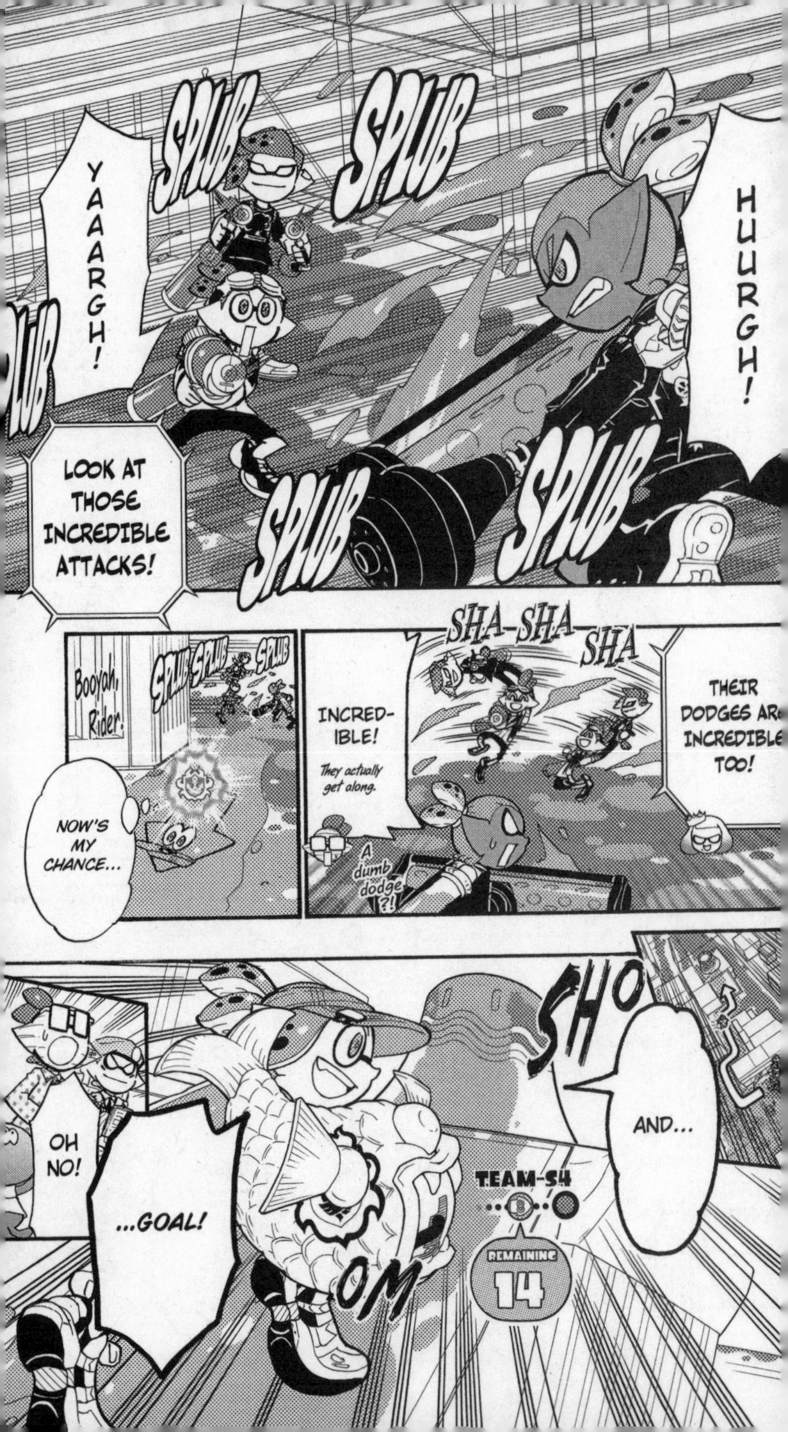
HUURGH!
SPLUB
SPLUB
YAAARGH!
SPLUB
SPLUB
SPLUB
LOOK AT THOSE INCREDIBLE ATTACKS!
SHA-SHA-SHA
THEIR DODGES AR INCREDIBLE TOO!
INCREDIBLE!
They actually get along.
A dumb dodge?!
SPLUB SPLUB SPLUB
Booyah, Rider!
NOW'S MY CHANCE...
SHO
AND...
TEAM-S4
8
REMAINING
14
OM
...GOAL!
OH NO!

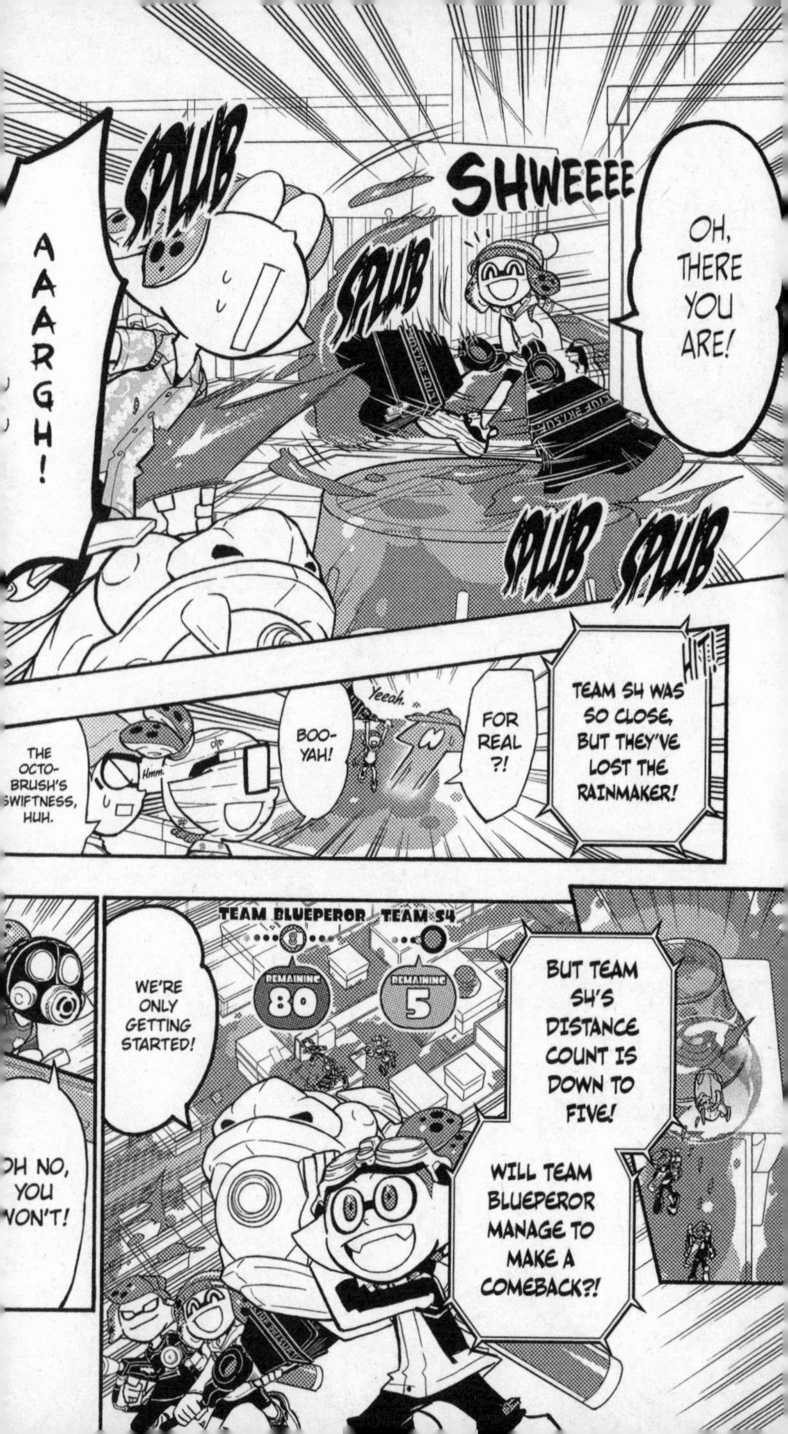
OH, THERE YOU ARE!
SHWEEEE
SPLUB
SPLUB
SPLUB SPLUB
AAARGH!
HIT!
TEAM S4 WAS SO CLOSE, BUT THEY'VE LOST THE RAINMAKER!
FOR REAL?!
Yeeeah.
BOO-YAH!
Hmm.
THE OCTO-BRUSH'S SWIFTNESS, HUH.
BUT TEAM S4'S DISTANCE COUNT IS DOWN TO FIVE!
WILL TEAM BLUEPEROR MANAGE TO MAKE A COMEBACK?!
TEAM BLUEPEROR TEAM S4
REMAINING 80
REMAINING 5
WE'RE ONLY GETTING STARTED!
OH NO, YOU WON'T!

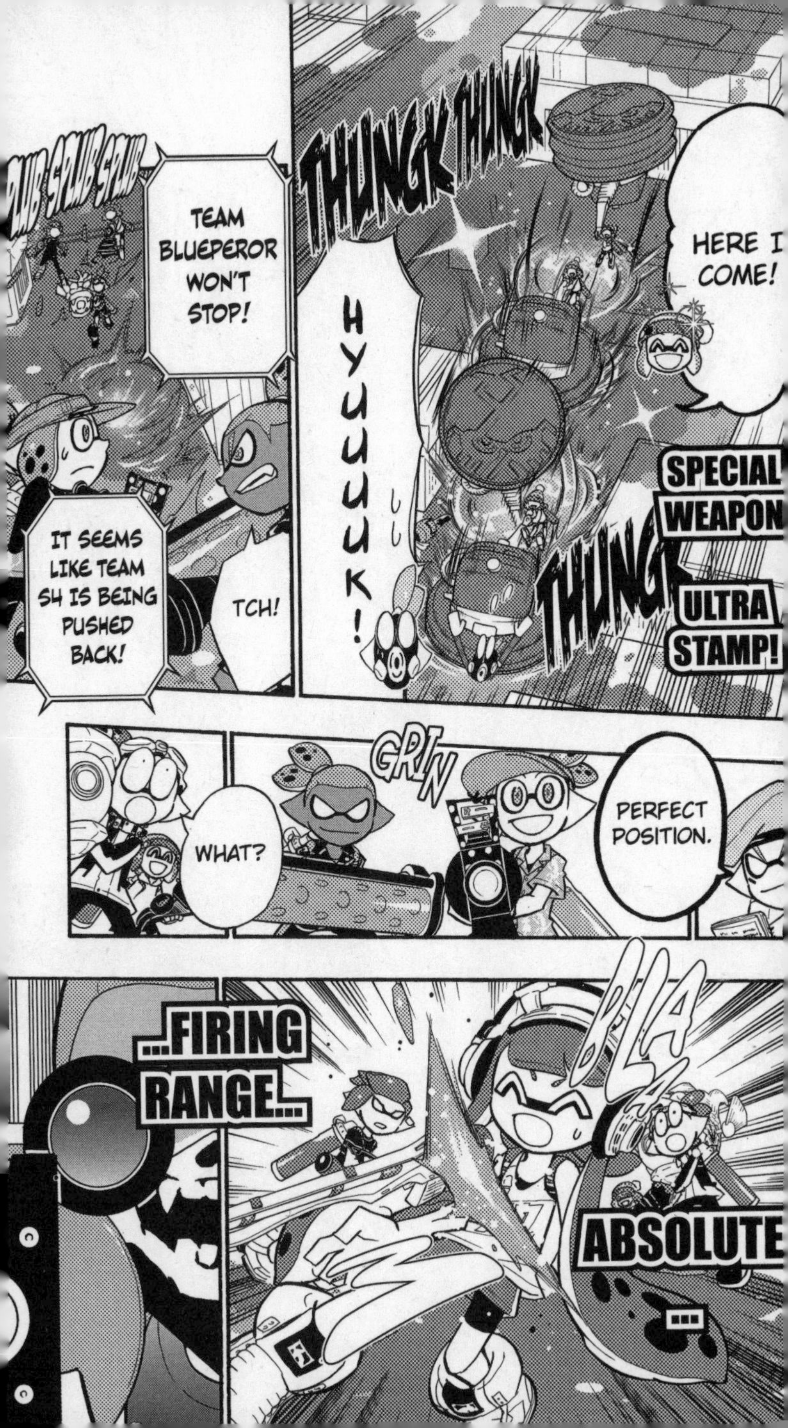
THUNGK THUNGK
HERE I COME!
SPECIAL WEAPON
ULTRA STAMP!
THUNGK
HYUUUUK!
SPLUB SPLUB SPLUB
TEAM BLUEPEROR WON'T STOP!
TCH!
IT SEEMS LIKE TEAM S4 IS BEING PUSHED BACK!
PERFECT POSITION.
GRIN
WHAT?
ABSOLUTE
...
...FIRING RANGE...

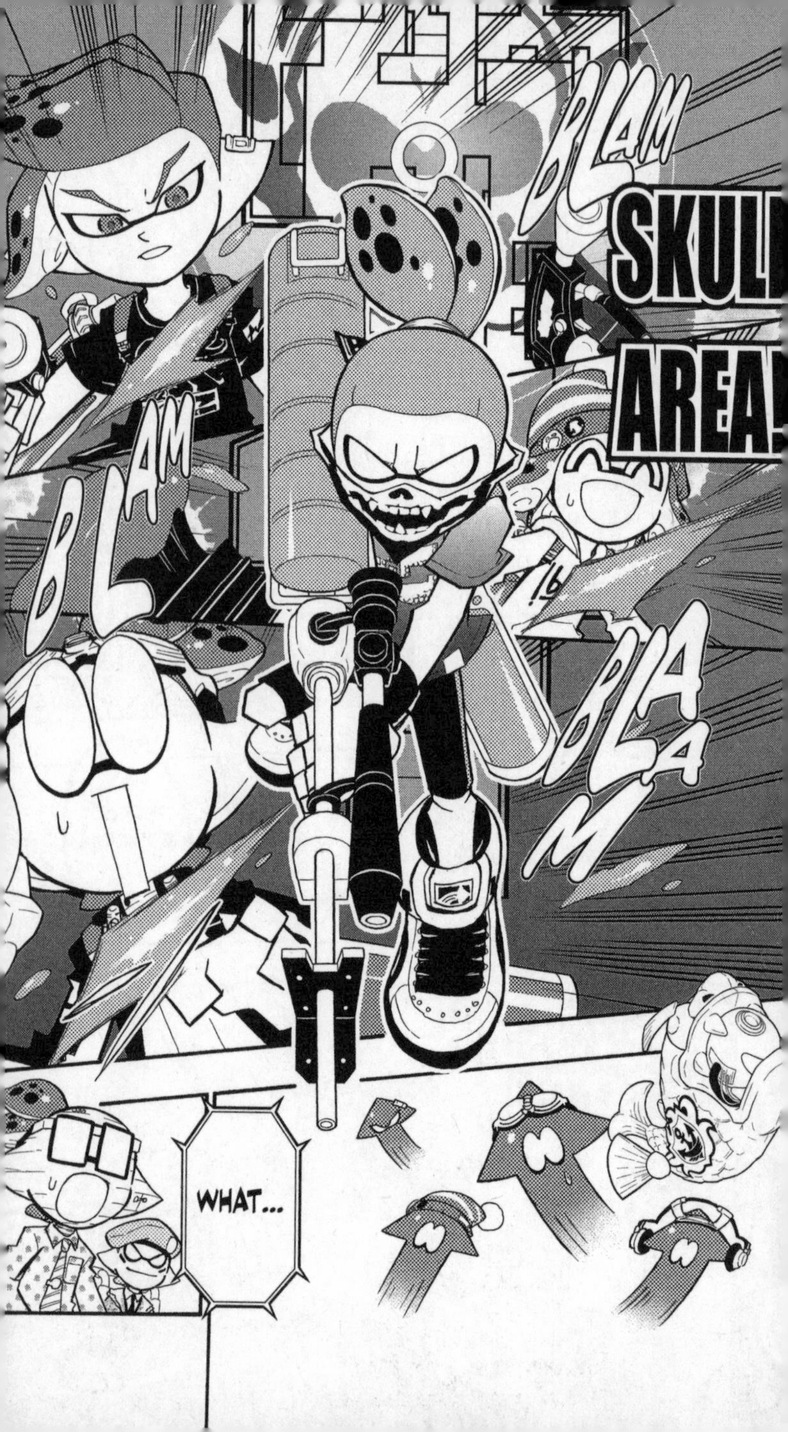
BLAM
SKULL
AREA!
BLAM
!?
BLAM
WHAT...

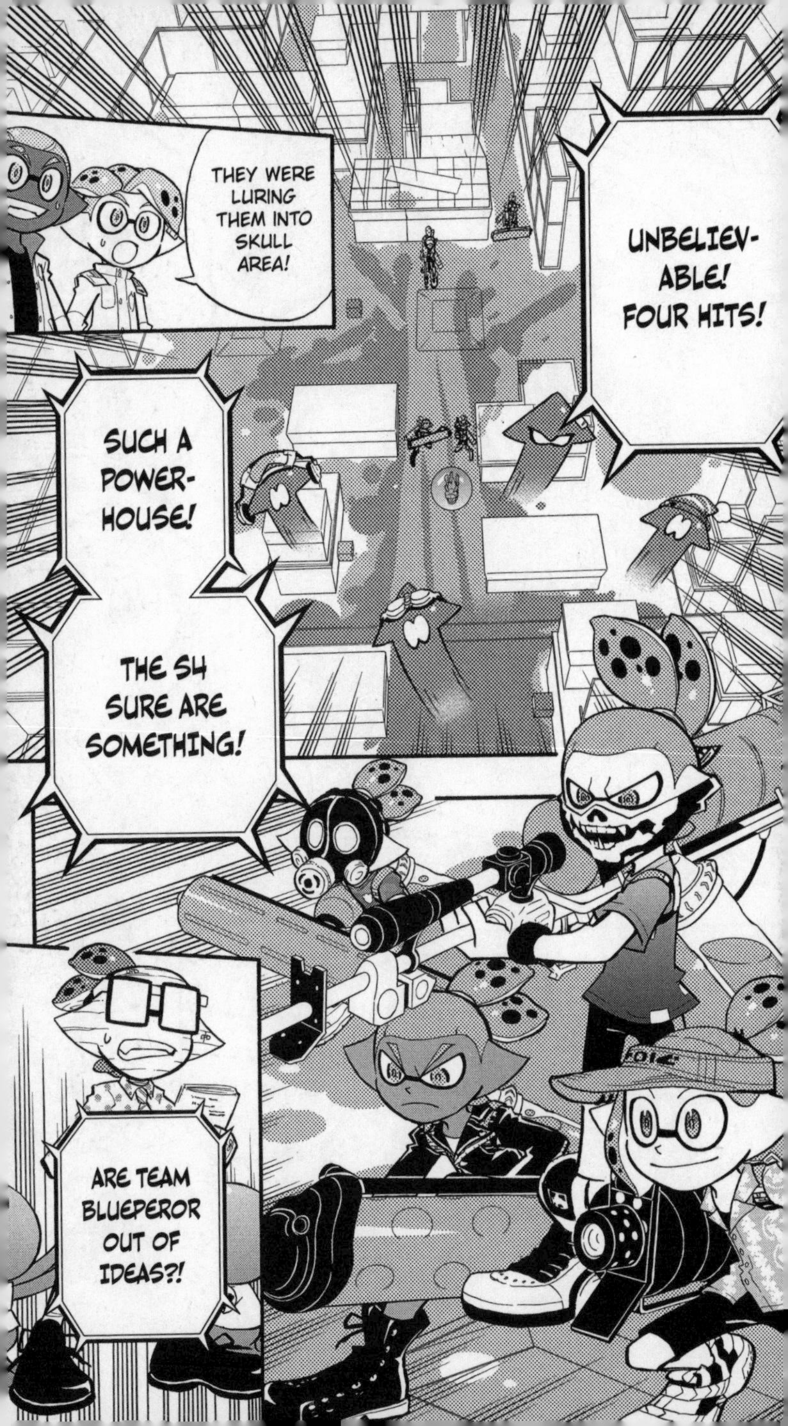
UNBELIEV-ABLE! FOUR HITS!
THEY WERE LURING THEM INTO SKULL AREA!
SUCH A POWER-HOUSE!
THE S4 SURE ARE SOMETHING!
ARE TEAM BLUEPEROR OUT OF IDEAS?!

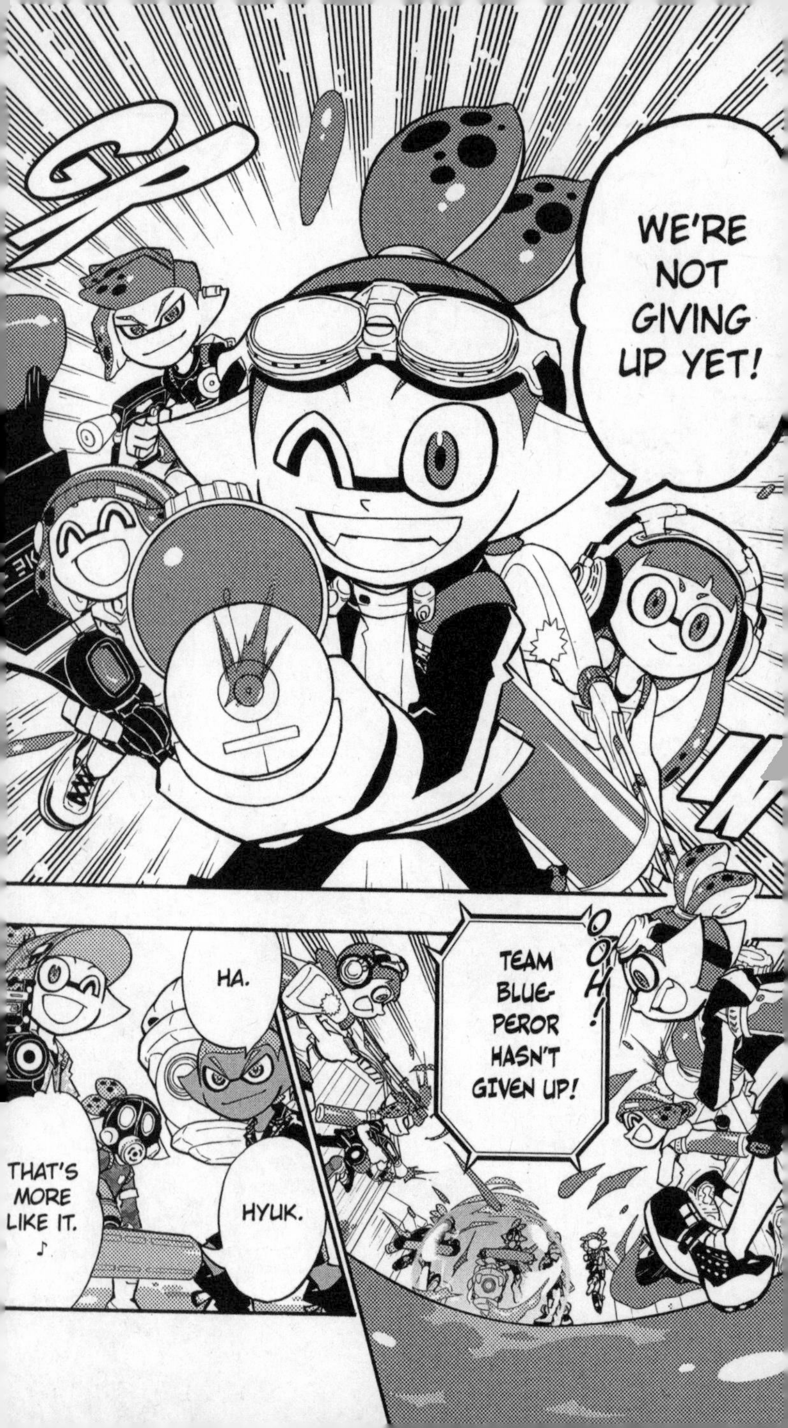
WE'RE NOT GIVING UP YET!
OOOH!
TEAM BLUE-PEROR HASN'T GIVEN UP!
HA.
HYUK.
THAT'S MORE LIKE IT. ♪

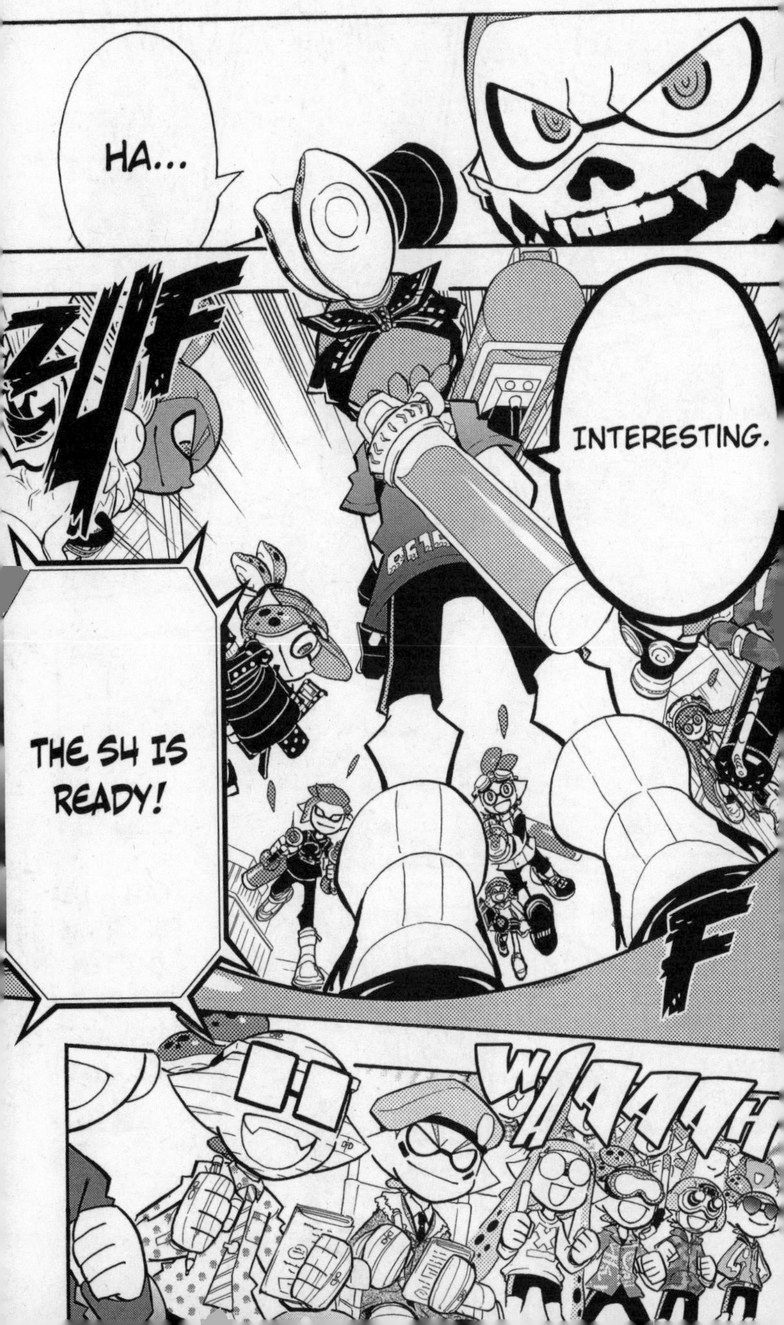
HA...
INTERESTING.
ZIF
THE S4 IS READY!
F
WAAAAH

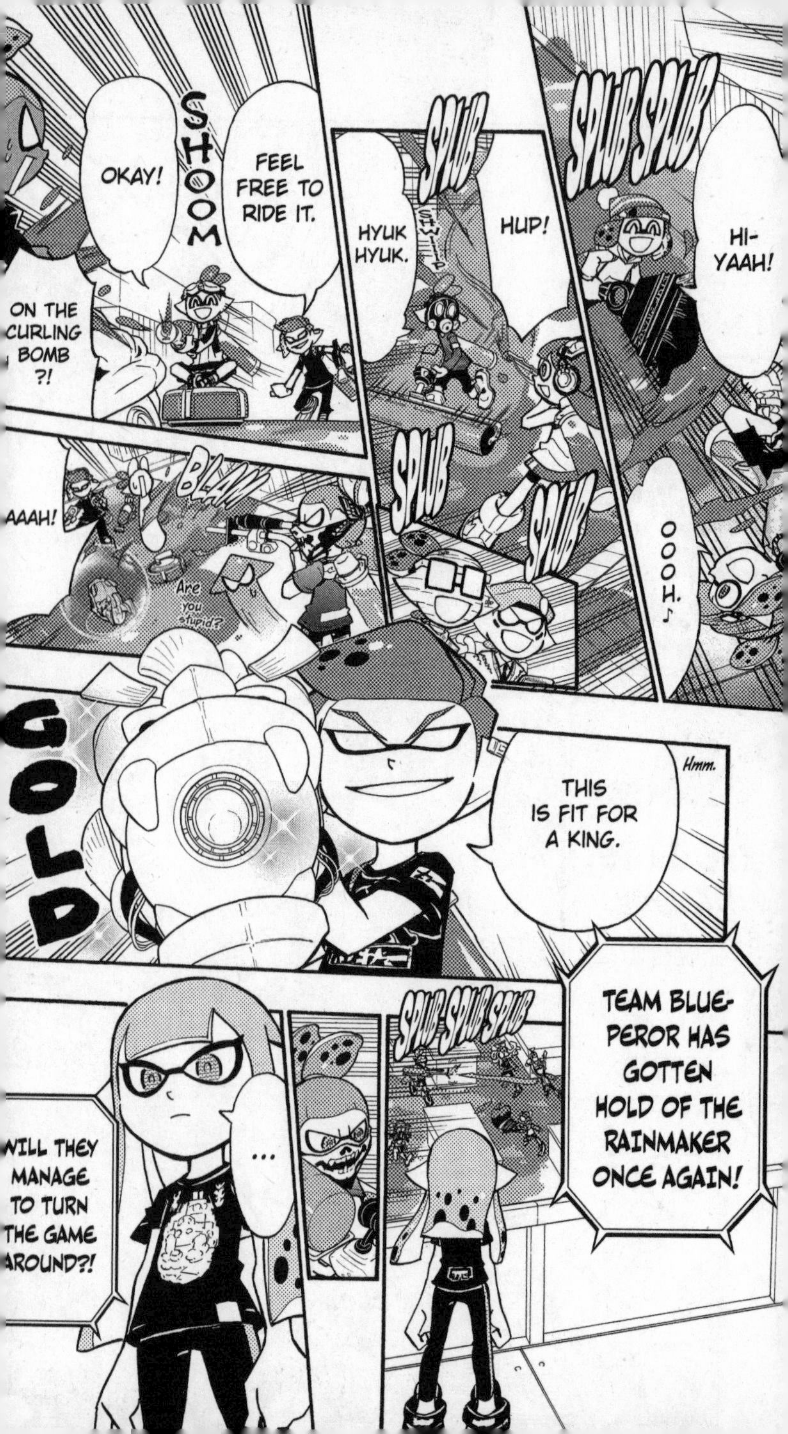
SPLUB SPLUB
HI-YAAH!
OOOH.♪
HUP!
SPLUB
SHWIP
HYUK HYUK.
SPLUB
SPLUB
FEEL FREE TO RIDE IT.
SHOOM
OKAY!
ON THE CURLING BOMB?!
BLAM
AAAH!
Are you stupid?
Hmm.
THIS IS FIT FOR A KING.
GOLD
TEAM BLUE-PEROR HAS GOTTEN HOLD OF THE RAINMAKER ONCE AGAIN!
SPLUB-SPLUB-SPLUB
...
WILL THEY MANAGE TO TURN THE GAME AROUND?!

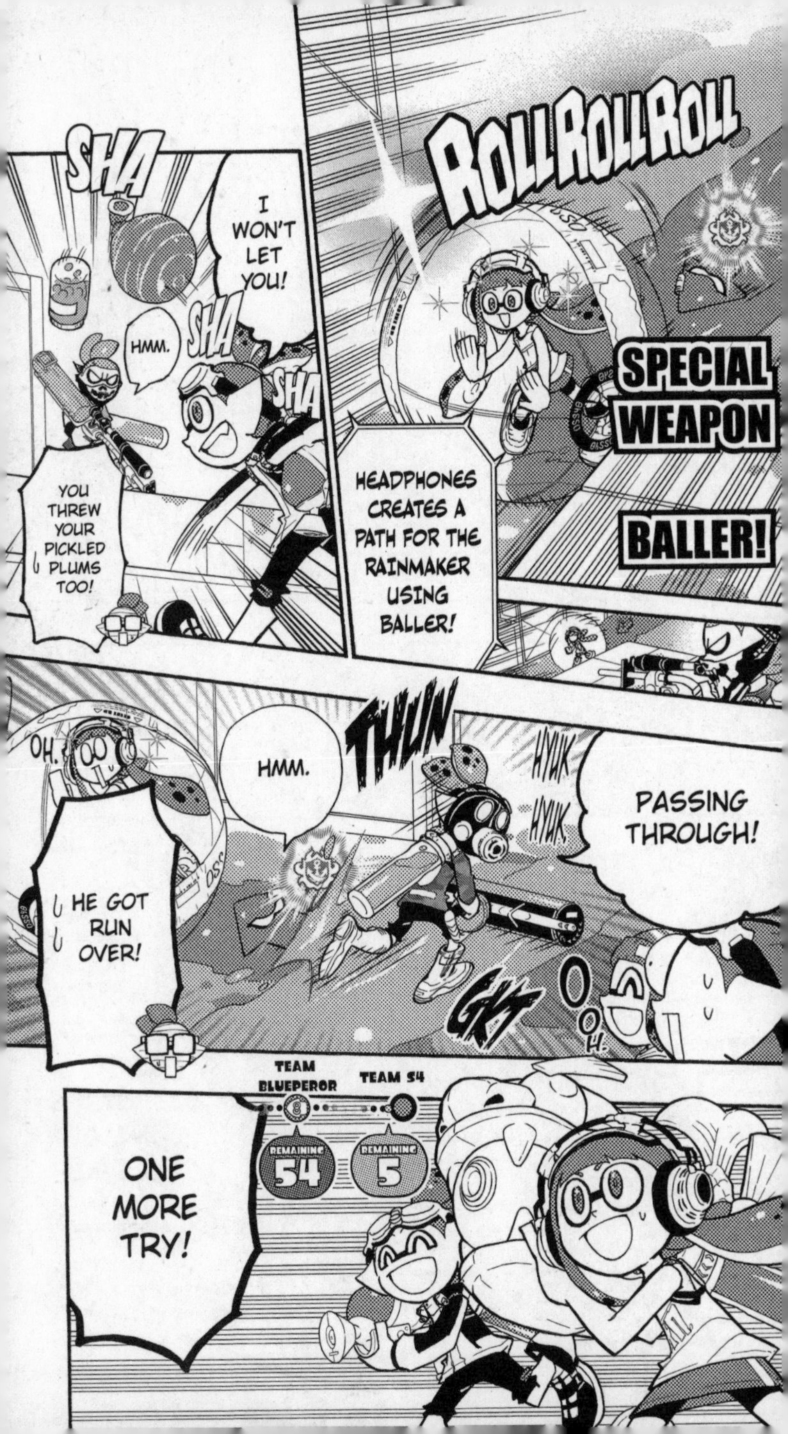
ROLL ROLL ROLL
SPECIAL WEAPON
BALLER!
HEADPHONES CREATES A PATH FOR THE RAINMAKER USING BALLER!
SHA
I WON'T LET YOU!
HMM.
SHA
SHA
YOU THREW YOUR PICKLED PLUMS TOO!
THUN
HYUK HYUK
PASSING THROUGH!
GAK
OOOH.
OH.
HMM.
HE GOT RUN OVER!
TEAM BLUEPEROR
TEAM S4
8
REMAINING 54
REMAINING 5
ONE MORE TRY!

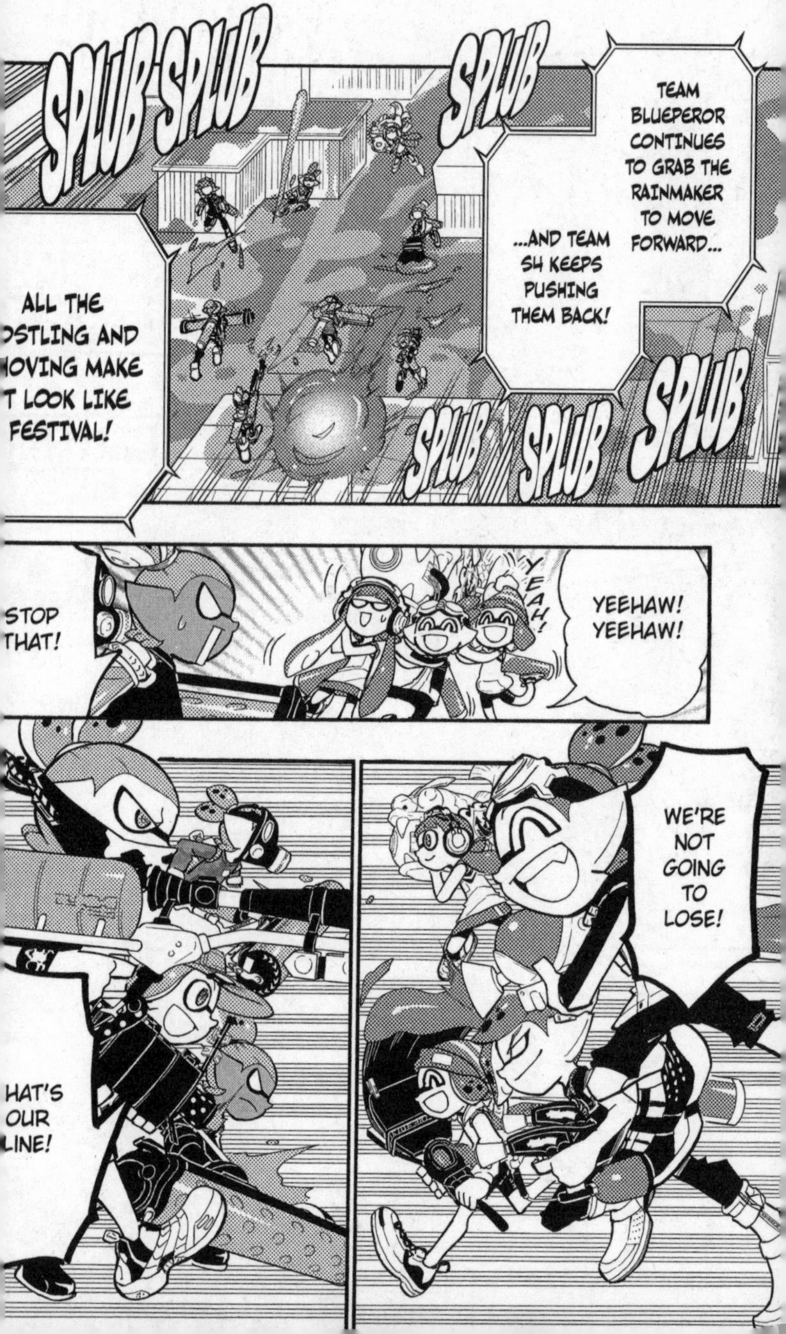
TEAM BLUEPEROR CONTINUES TO GRAB THE RAINMAKER TO MOVE FORWARD...
...AND TEAM S4 KEEPS PUSHING THEM BACK!
SPLUB
SPLUB SPLUB
ALL THE OSTLING AND HOVING MAKE T LOOK LIKE FESTIVAL!
SPLUB SPLUB SPLUB
YEEHAW! YEEHAW!
YEAH!
STOP THAT!
WE'RE NOT GOING TO LOSE!
HAT'S OUR LINE!

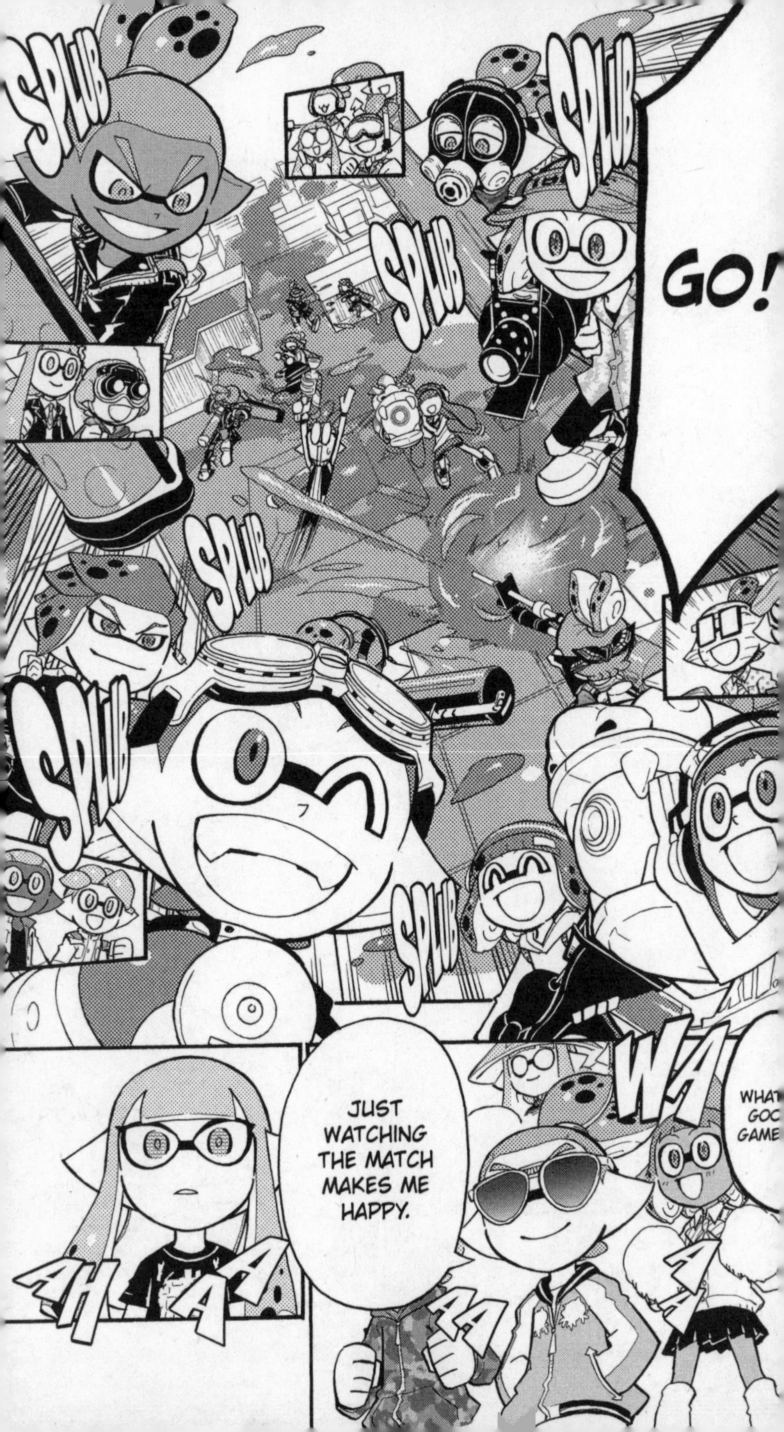
GO!
SPLUB
SPLUB
SPLUB
SPLUB
SPLUB
SPLUB
WHAT GOO GAME
WA
A
A
AA
JUST WATCHING THE MATCH MAKES ME HAPPY.
AH A A

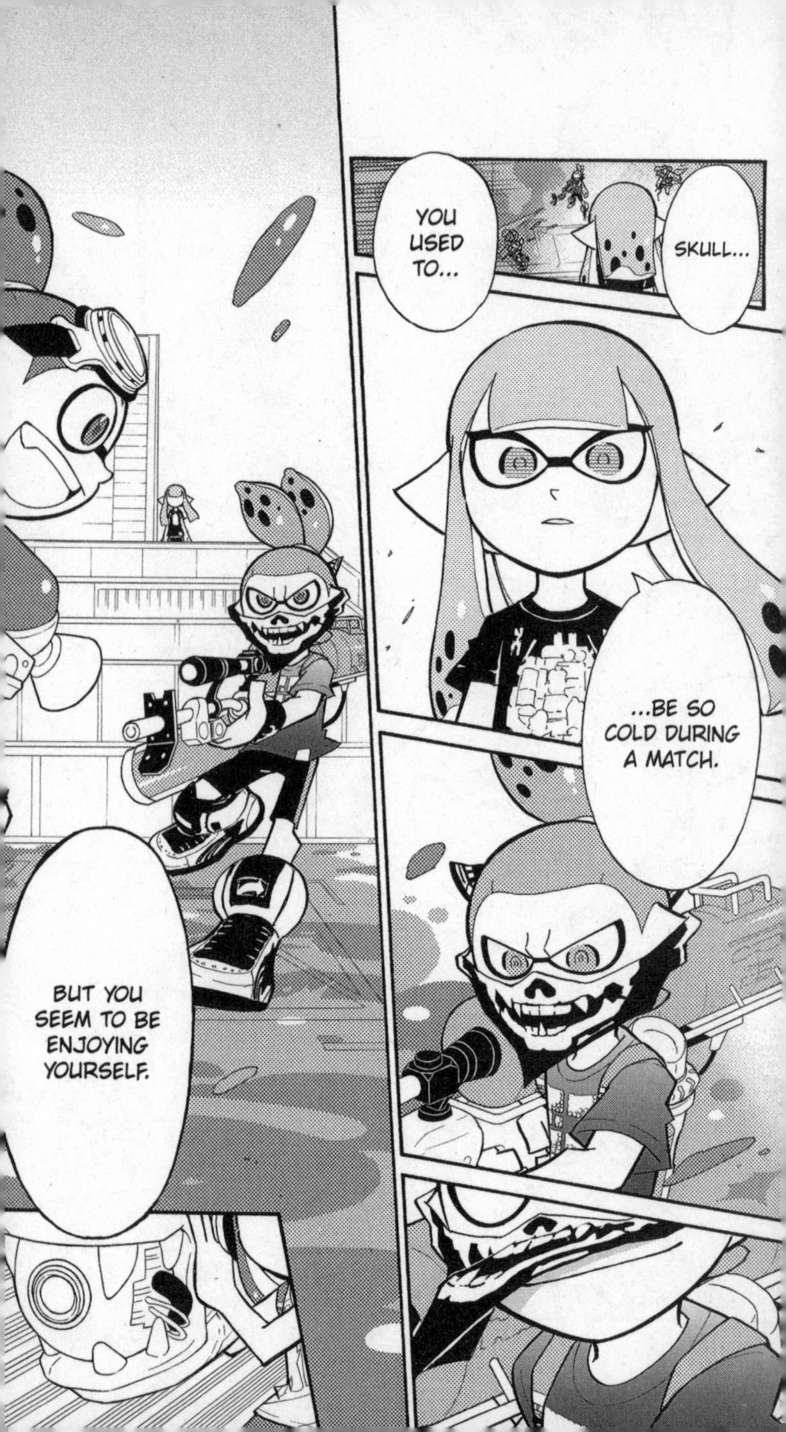
SKULL...
YOU USED TO...
...BE SO COLD DURING A MATCH.
BUT YOU SEEM TO BE ENJOYING YOURSELF.

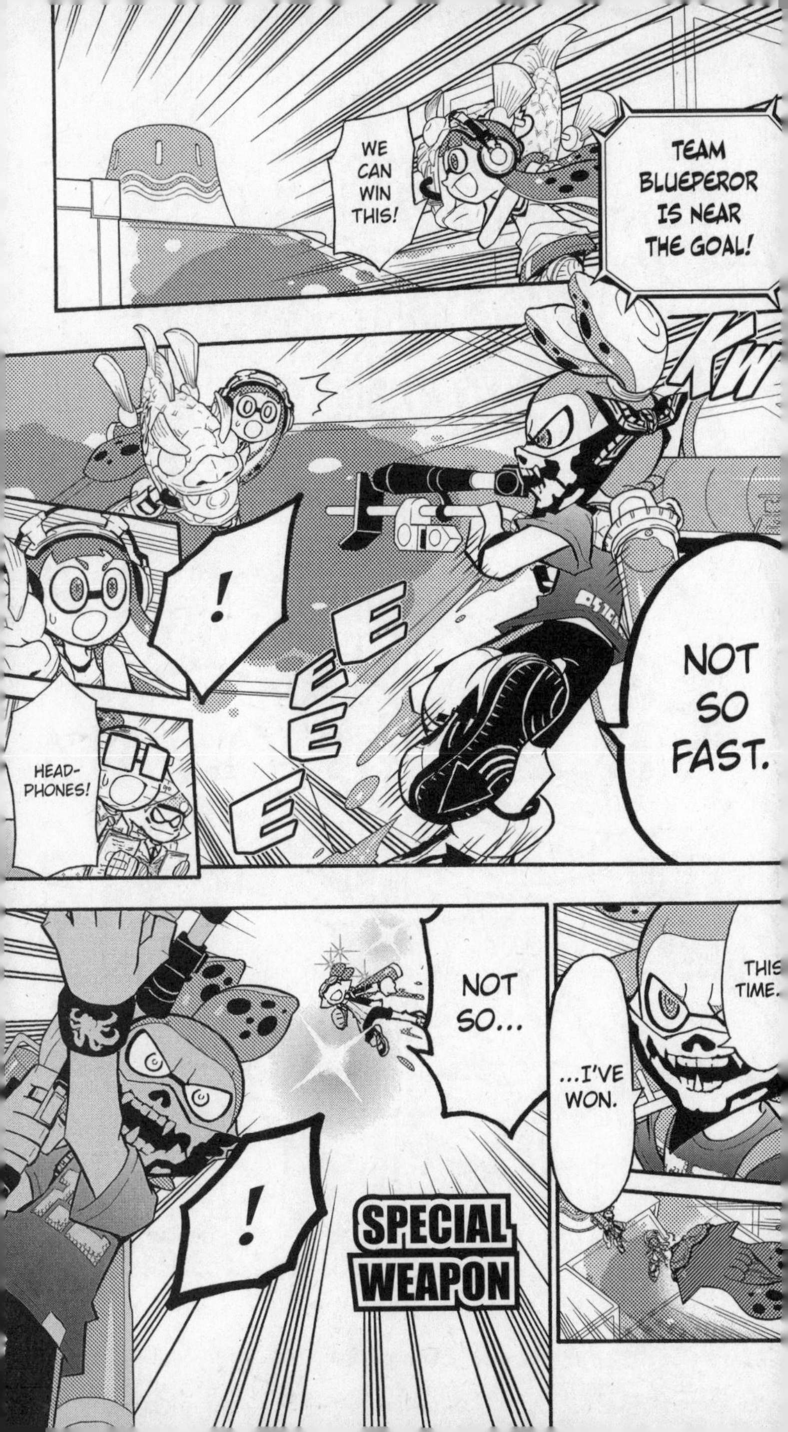

TEAM BLUEPEROR IS NEAR THE GOAL!
WE CAN WIN THIS!
KWEEEE
NOT SO FAST.
!
HEAD-PHONES!
THIS TIME.
...I'VE WON.
NOT SO...
SPECIAL WEAPON
!

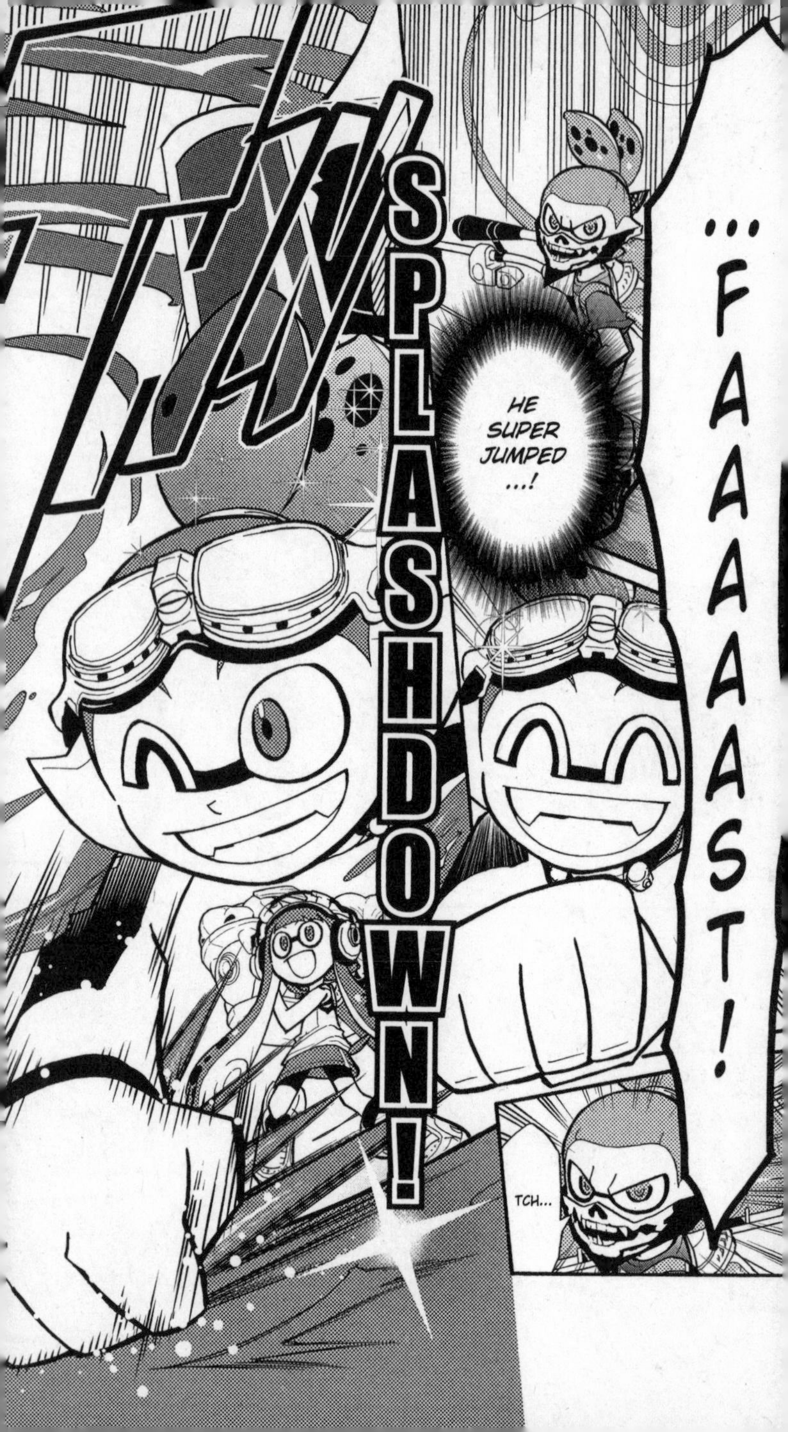
...FAAAAAST!
HE SUPER JUMPED ...!
SPLASHDOWN!
TCH...

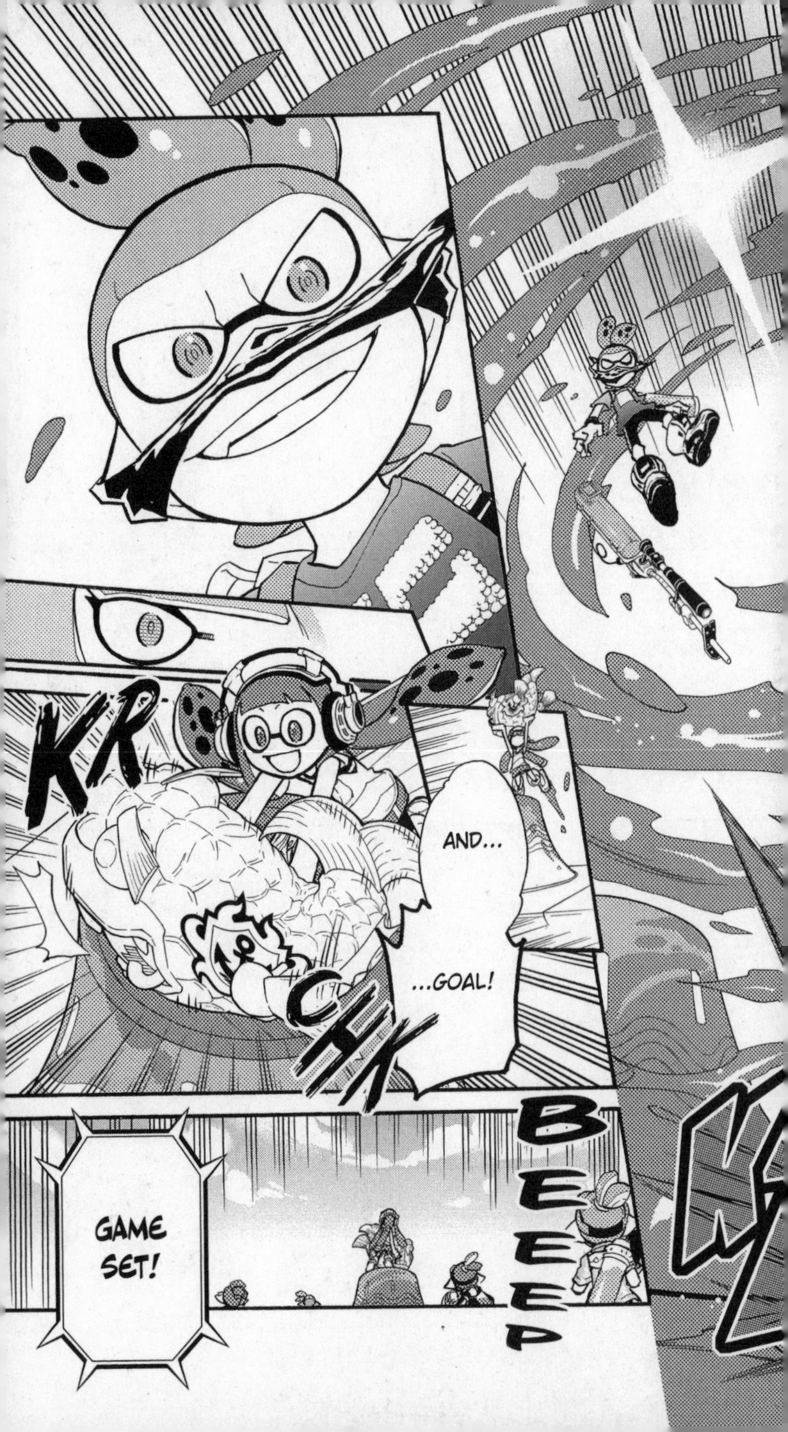
AND...
KR-
...GOAL!
CHK
BEEEP
GAME SET!

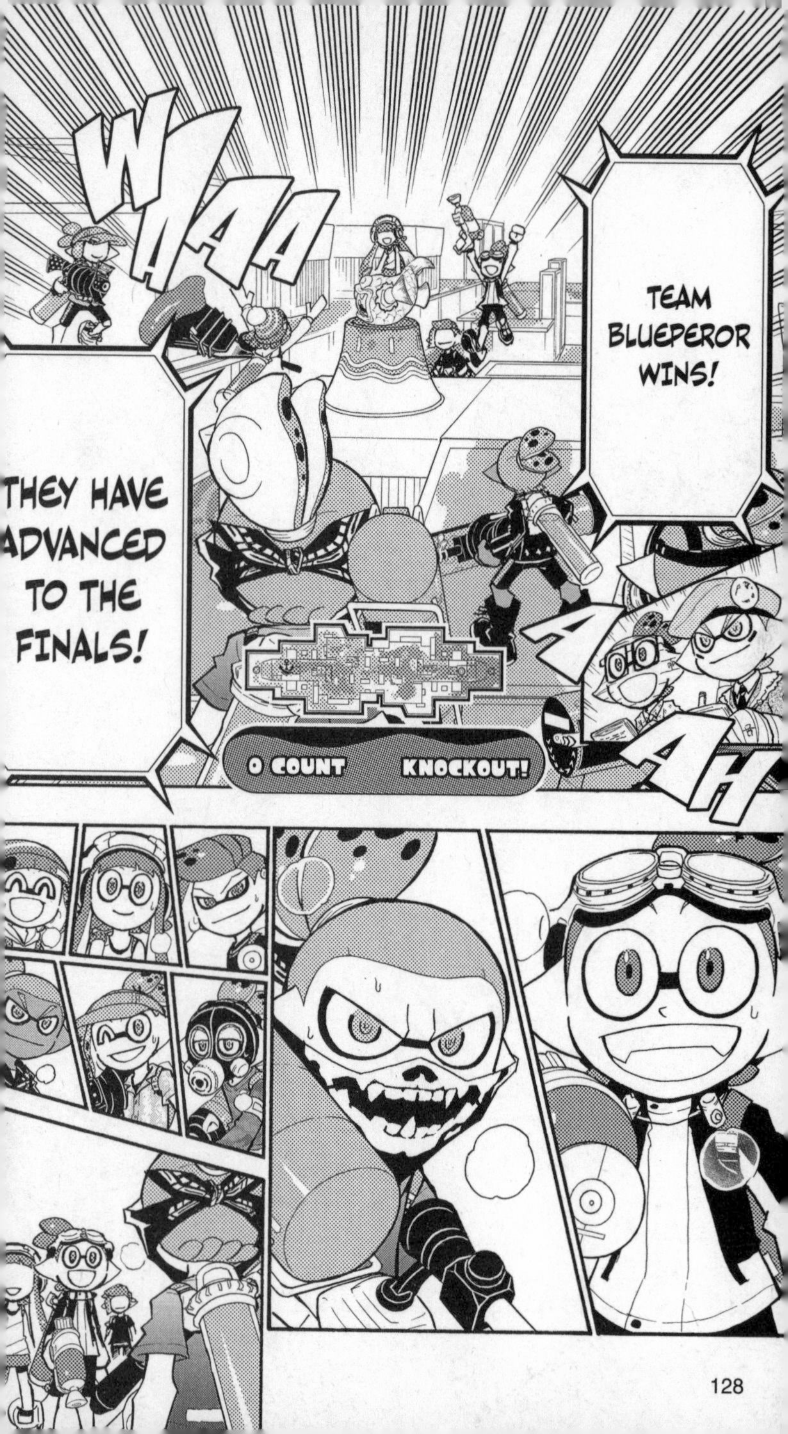

TEAM BLUEPEROR WINS!
WAAA
THEY HAVE ADVANCED TO THE FINALS!
0 COUNT
KNOCKOUT!
A
AH

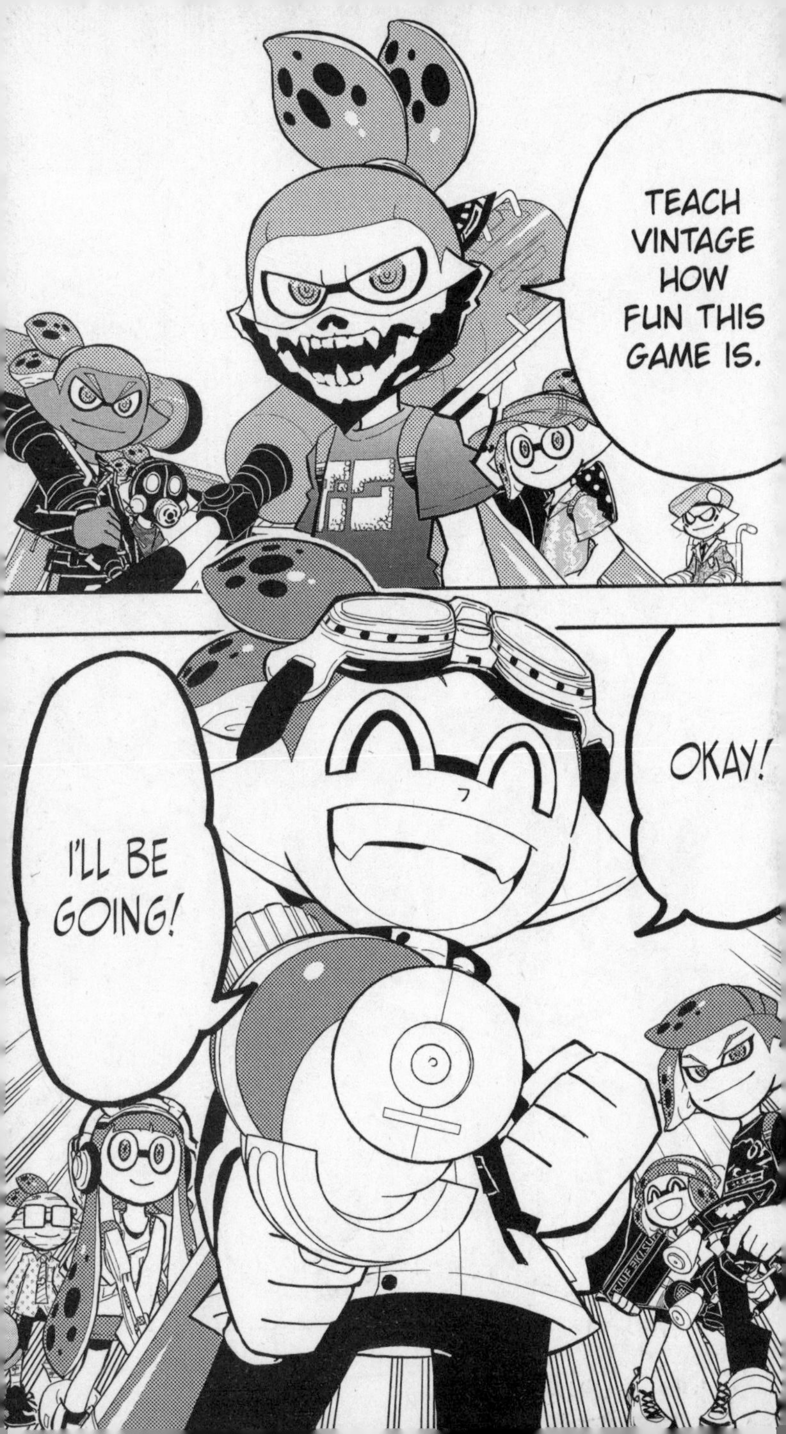
TEACH VINTAGE HOW FUN THIS GAME IS.
OKAY!
I'LL BE GOING!

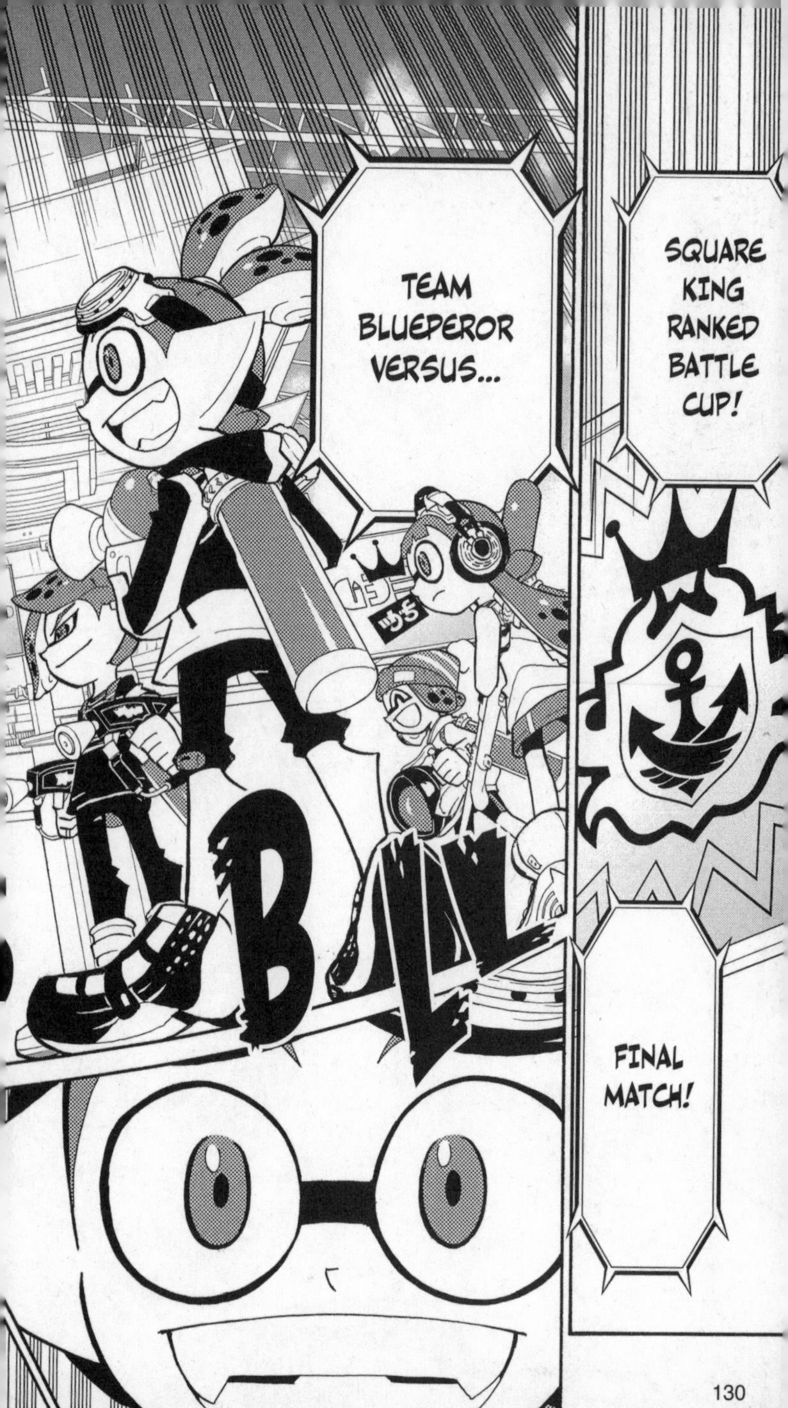
SQUARE KING RANKED BATTLE CUP!
FINAL MATCH!
TEAM BLUEPEROR VERSUS...

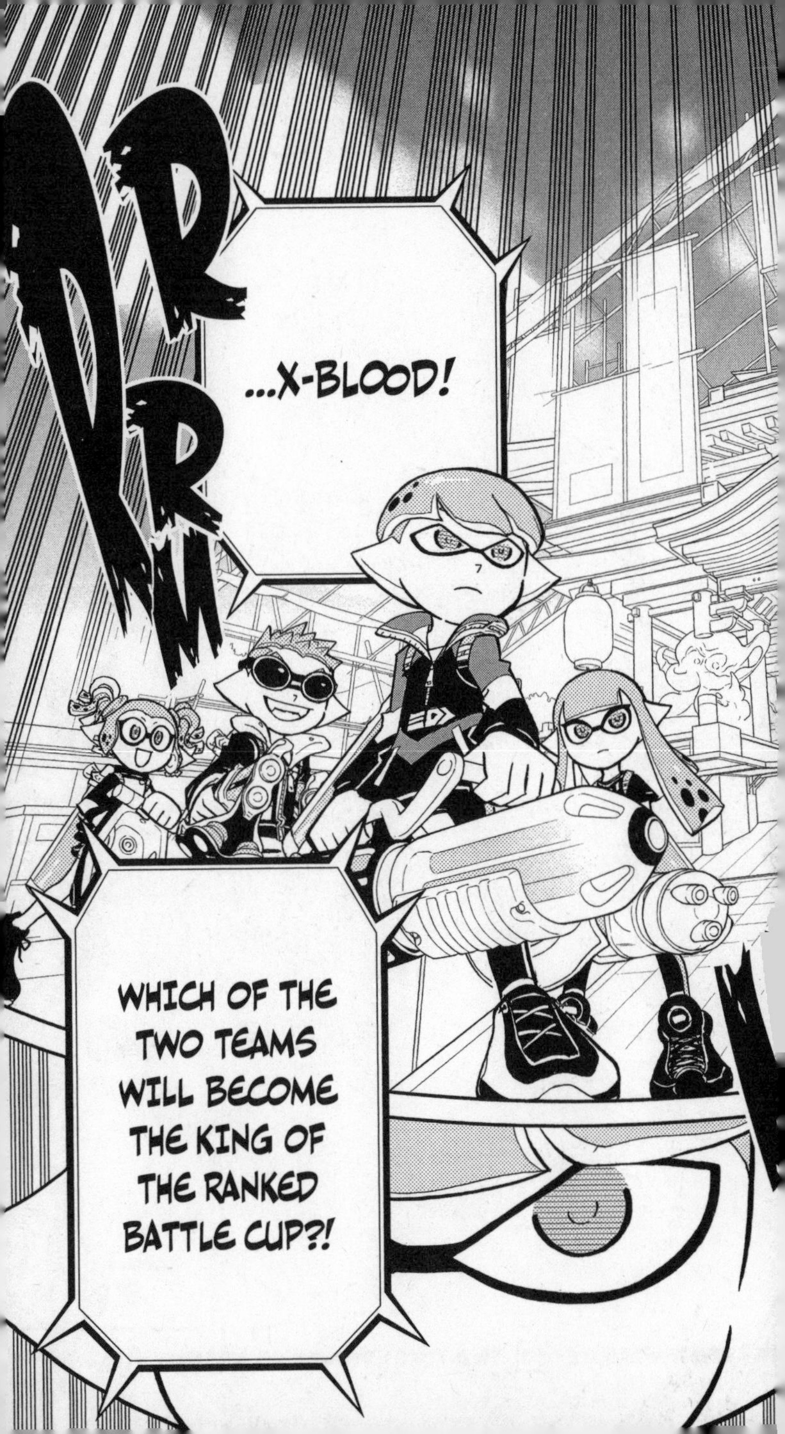
...X-BLOOD!
WHICH OF THE TWO TEAMS WILL BECOME THE KING OF THE RANKED BATTLE CUP?!

PLATOON VOLUME 10 END / CONTINUED IN VOLUME 11

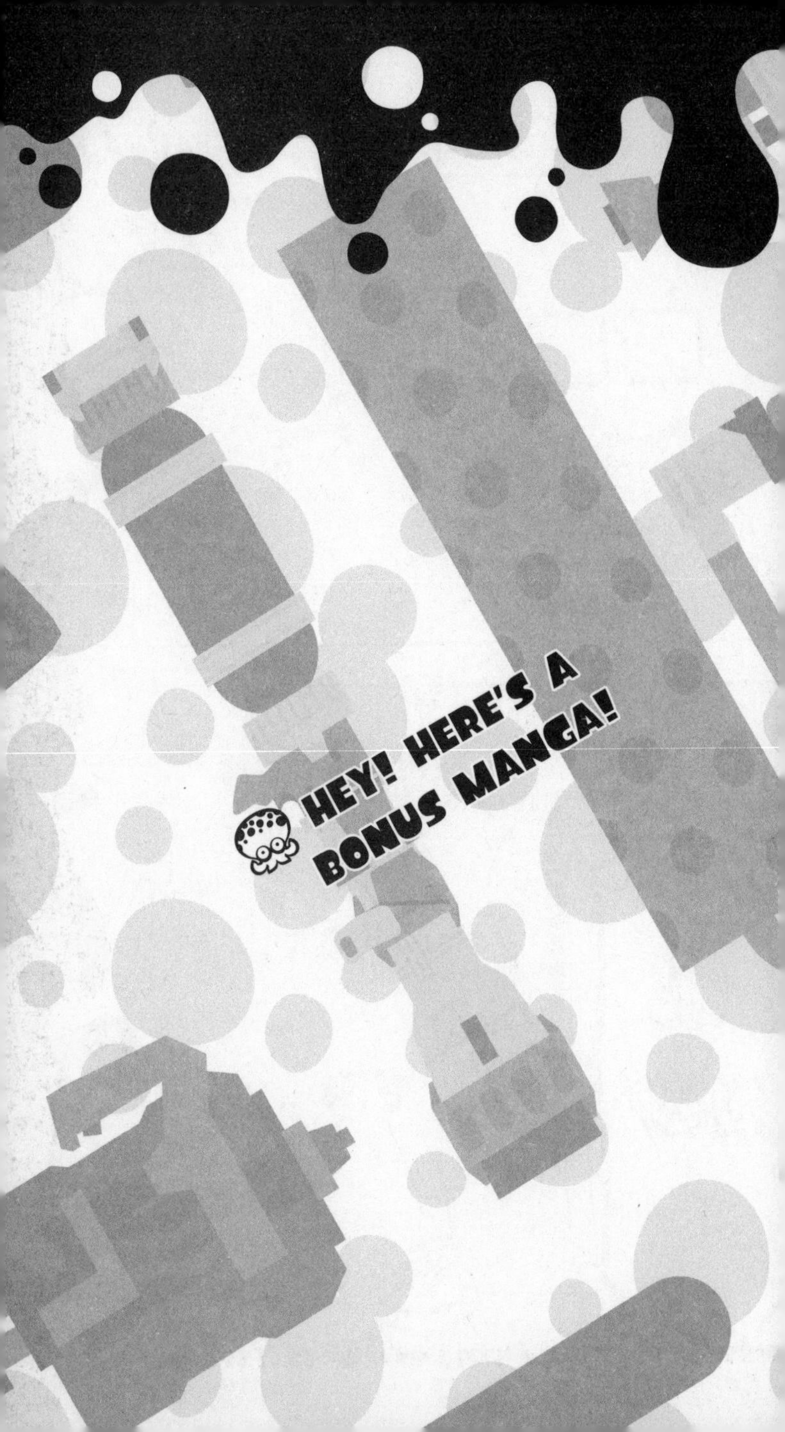
HEY! HERE'S A
BONUS MANGA!

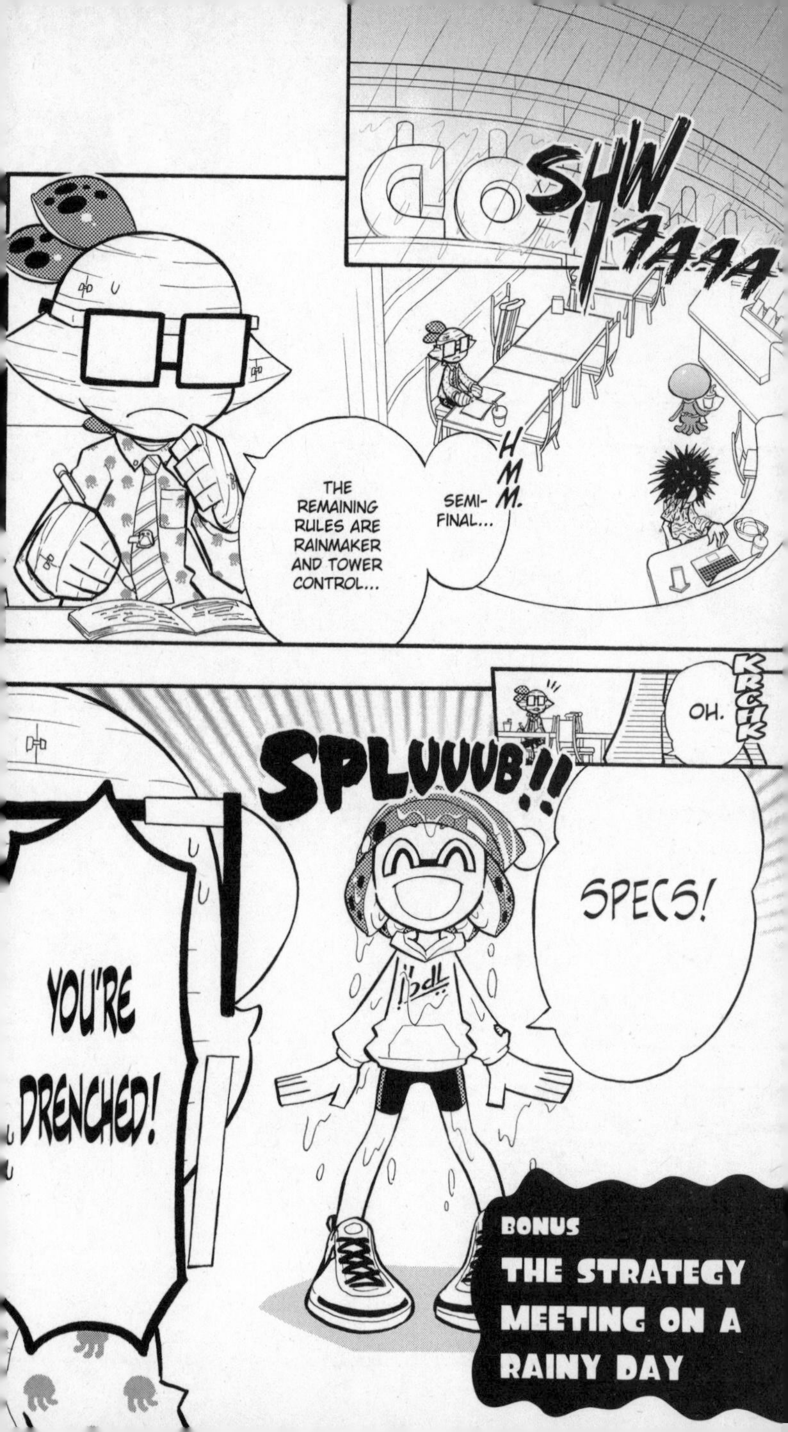

SHWAAAA
HMM.
SEMI-FINAL...
THE REMAINING RULES ARE RAINMAKER AND TOWER CONTROL...
KRCHK
OH.
SPLUUUB!!
SPECS!
YOU'RE DRENCHED!
BONUS
THE STRATEGY MEETING ON A RAINY DAY

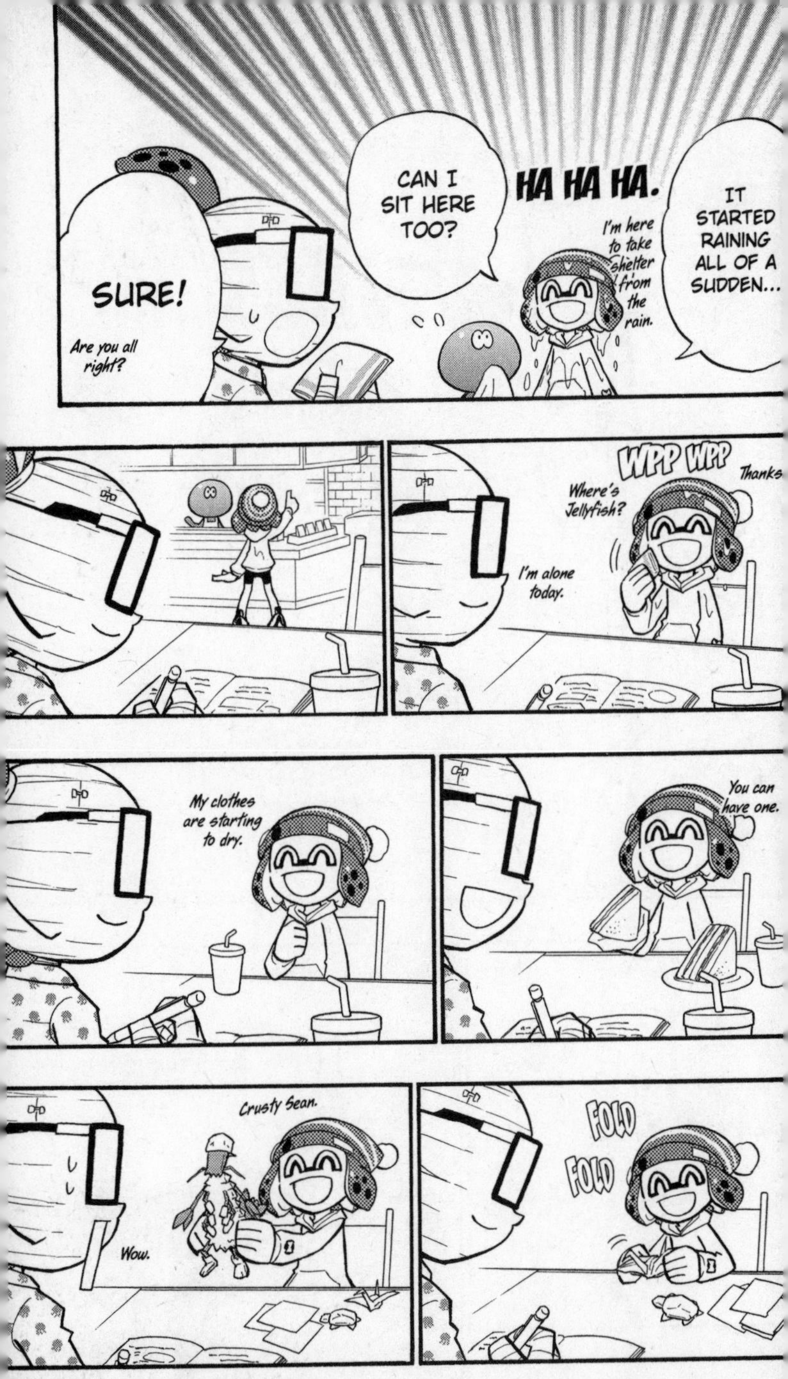
IT STARTED RAINING ALL OF A SUDDEN...
HA HA HA.
I'm here to take shelter from the rain.
CAN I SIT HERE TOO?
SURE!
Are you all right?
WPP WPP
Thanks
Where's Jellyfish?
I'm alone today.
You can have one.
My clothes are starting to dry.
FOLD
FOLD
Crusty Sean.
Wow.

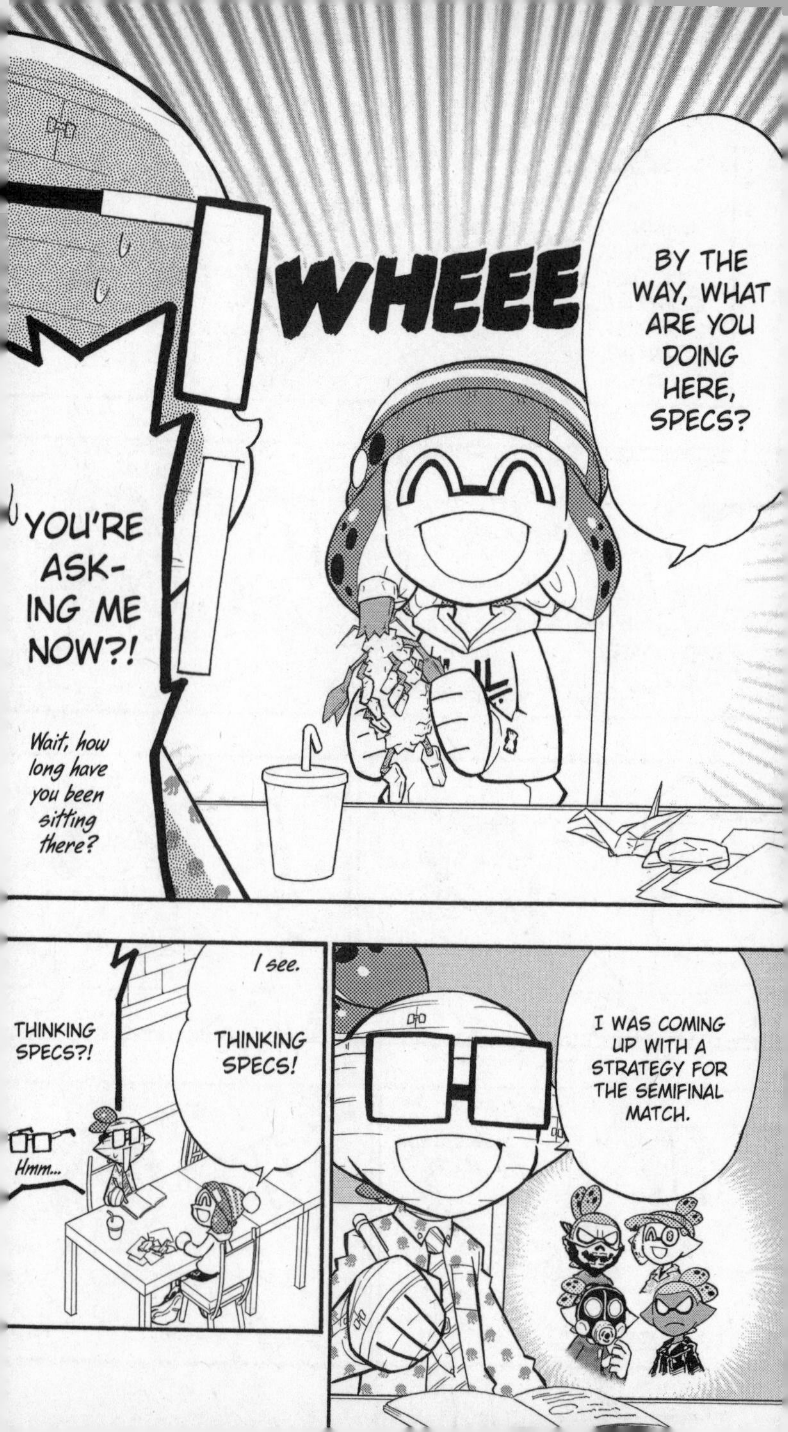
BY THE WAY, WHAT ARE YOU DOING HERE, SPECS?
WHEEE
YOU'RE ASK-ING ME NOW?!
Wait, how long have you been sitting there?
I WAS COMING UP WITH A STRATEGY FOR THE SEMIFINAL MATCH.
I see.
THINKING SPECS!
THINKING SPECS?!
Hmm...

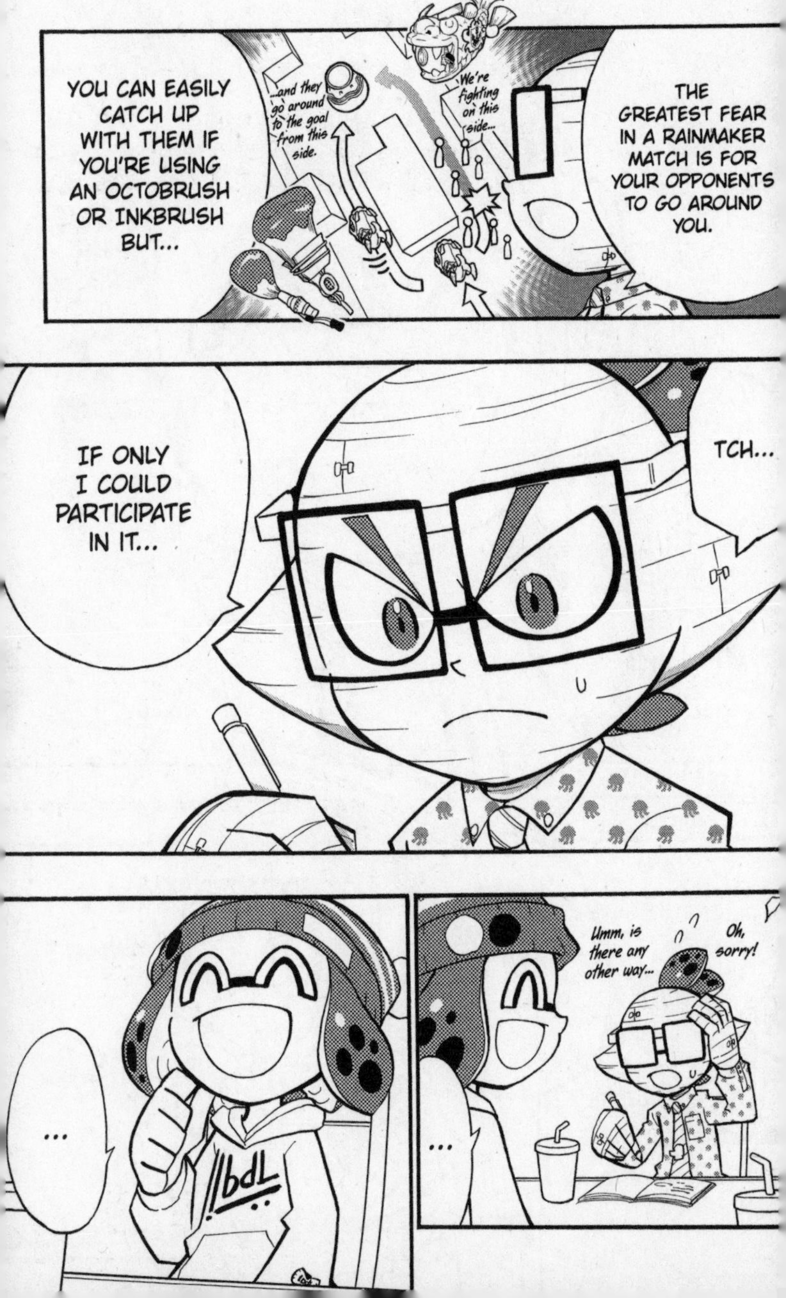
THE GREATEST FEAR IN A RAINMAKER MATCH IS FOR YOUR OPPONENTS TO GO AROUND YOU.
We're fighting on this side...
...and they go around to the goal from this side.
YOU CAN EASILY CATCH UP WITH THEM IF YOU'RE USING AN OCTOBRUSH OR INKBRUSH BUT...
TCH...
IF ONLY I COULD PARTICIPATE IN IT...
Oh, sorry!
Umm, is there any other way...
...
...

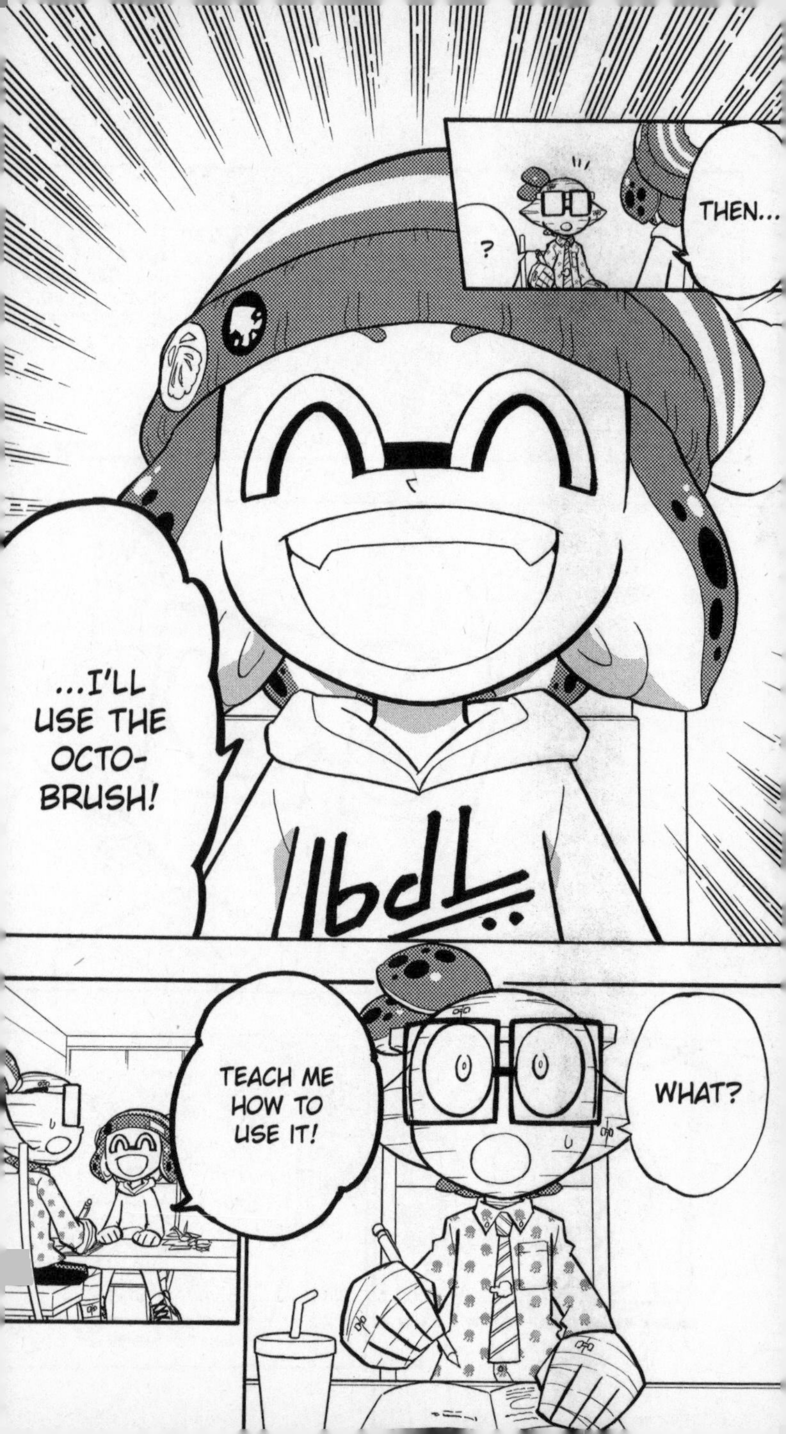
THEN...
?
...I'LL USE THE OCTO-BRUSH!
WHAT?
TEACH ME HOW TO USE IT!

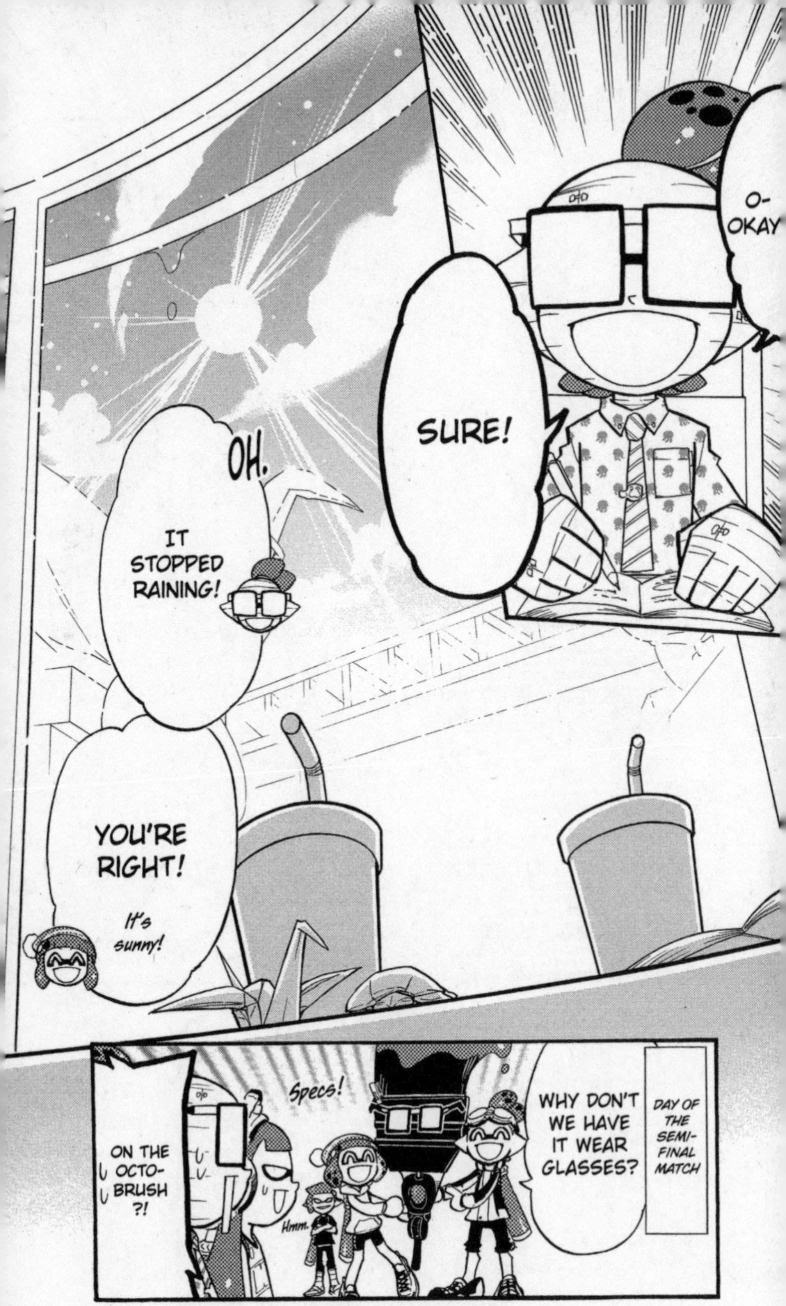
O-OKAY
SURE!
OH.
IT STOPPED RAINING!
YOU'RE RIGHT!
It's sunny!
DAY OF THE SEMI-FINAL MATCH
WHY DON'T WE HAVE IT WEAR GLASSES?
Specs!
Hmm.
ON THE OCTO-BRUSH ?!

(BONUS: THE STRATEGY MEETING ON A RAINY DAY / END)

TAKING A BREAK

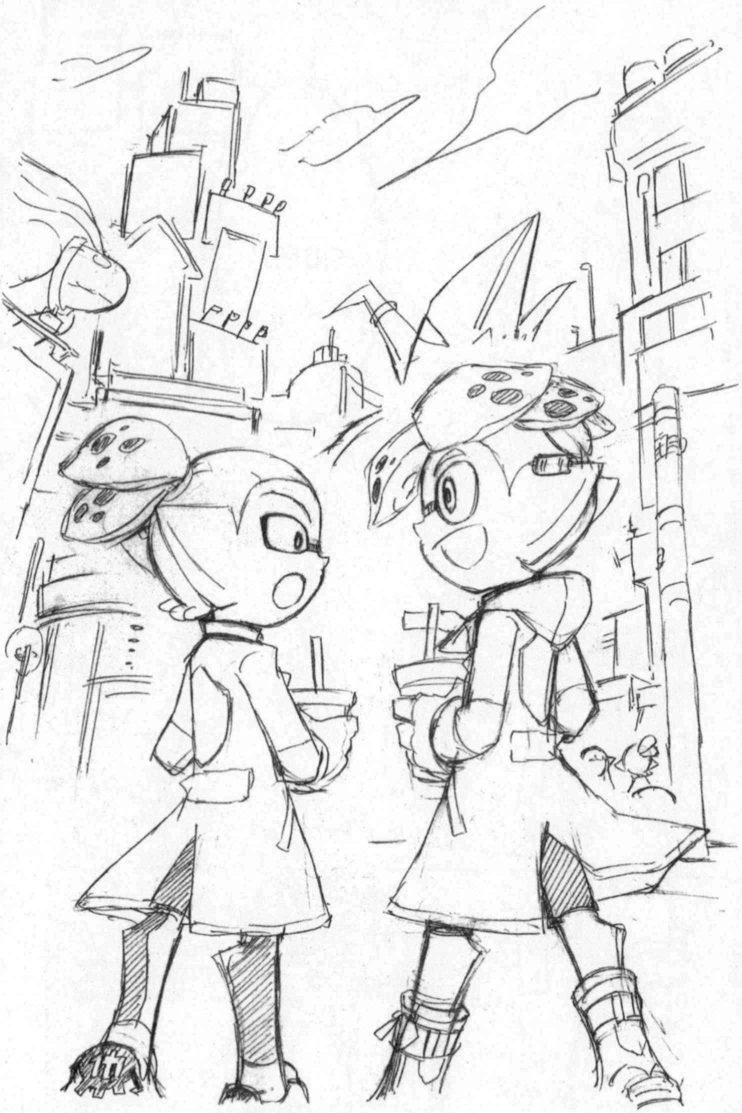

PREPARING TO CHEER

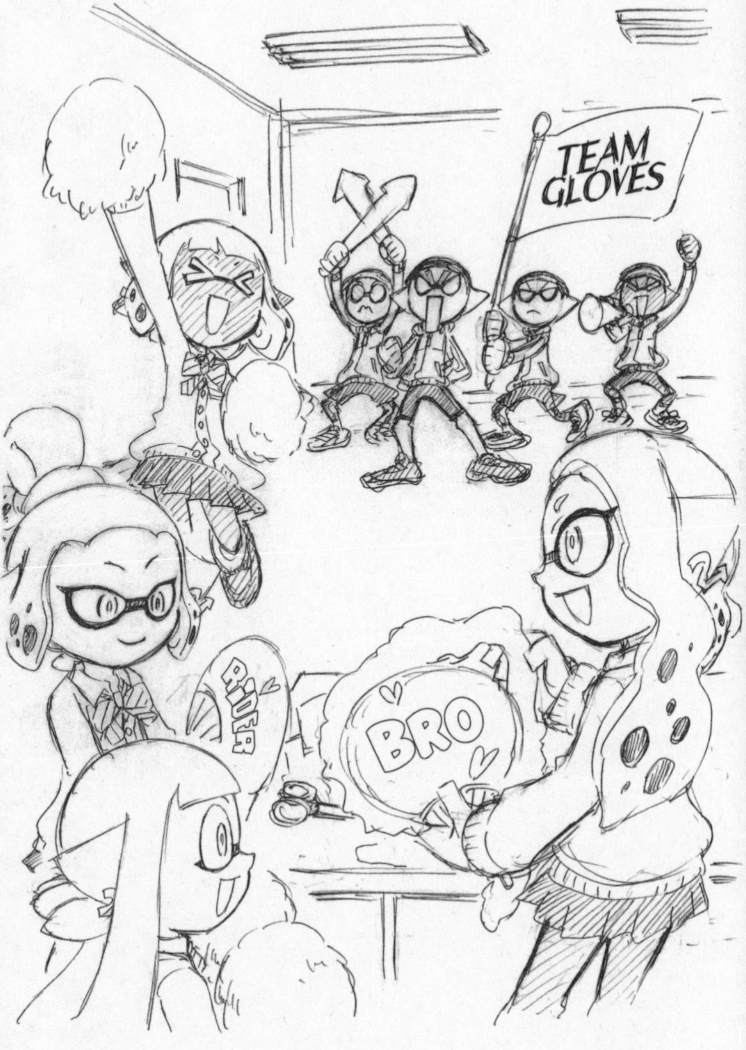
TEAM GLOVES
RIDER
BRO

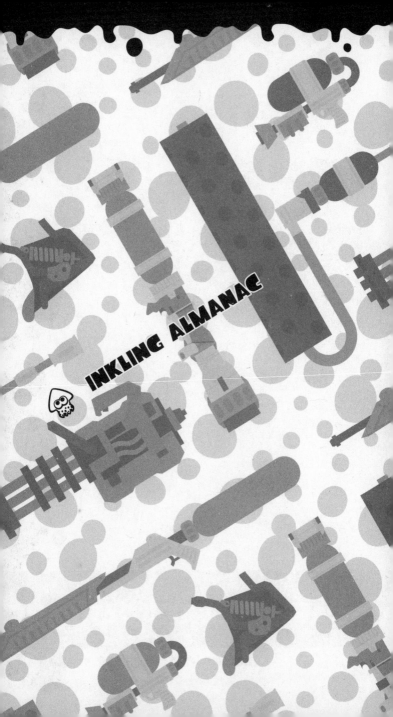

INKLING ALMANAC

RED IROMAKI

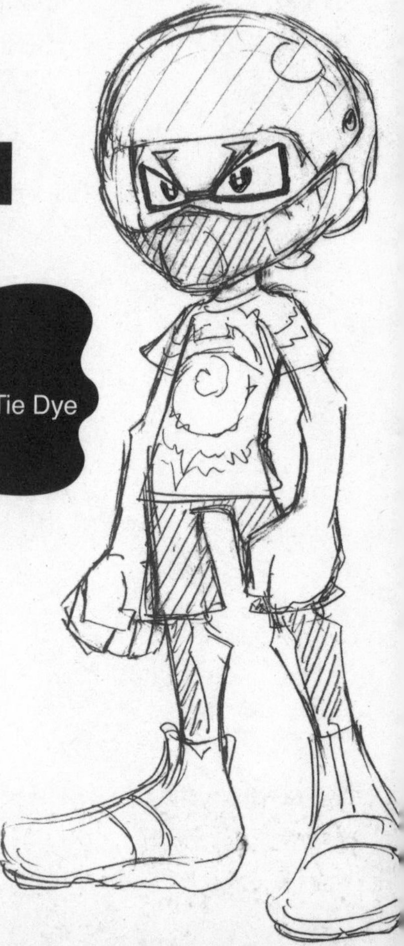

Weapon: Dapple Dualies
Headgear: Null Visor Replica
Clothing: Takoroka Rainbow Tie Dye
Shoes: Red Iromaki 750s

INFO

He works with his teammates
o come up with cool poses for
hem.

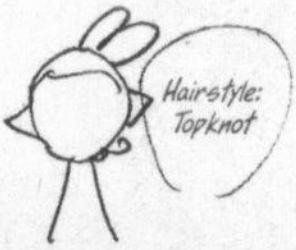
Hairstyle: Topknot

TEAM IROMAKI RANGERS

(INK COLOR: MIDNIGHT PINK)

PURPLE IROMAKI

YELLOW IROMAKI

GREEN IROMAKI

Hairstyle: Buzz cut

Weapon:	Dapple Dualies
Headgear:	Null Visor Replica
Clothing:	Takoroka Rainbow Tie Dye
Shoes:	Purple Iromaki 750s

Weapon:	Dapple Dualies
Headgear:	Null Visor Replica
Clothing:	Takoroka Rainbow Tie Dye
Shoes:	Yellow Iromaki 750s

Weapon:	Dapple Dualie
Headgear:	Null Visor Replica
Clothing:	Takoroka Rainbow Tie Dye
Shoes:	Green Iromal 750s

INFO

• They didn't used to like physical activity, but they grew fond of it after practicing their poses.

Practicing the pose
at Wahoo World

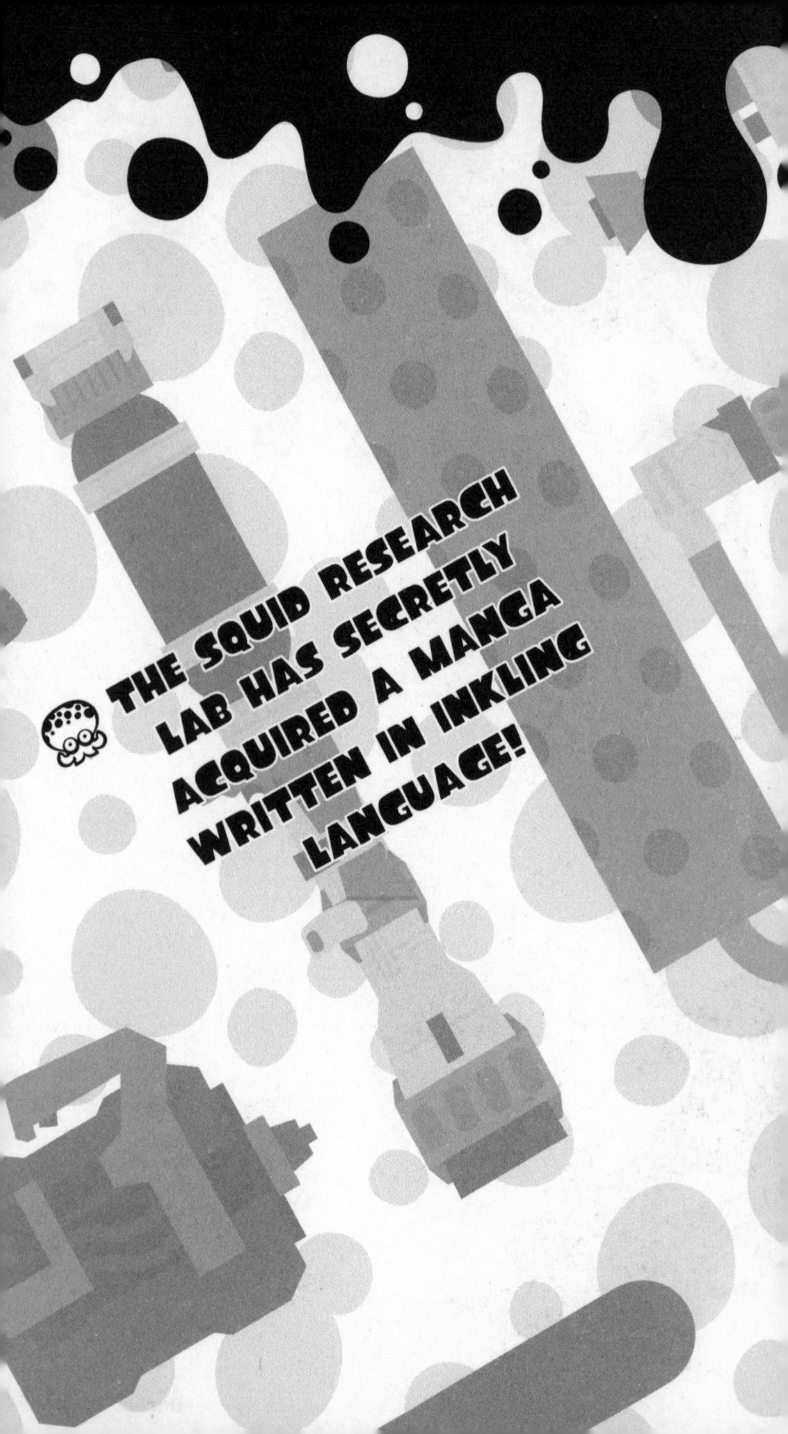
THE SQUID RESEARCH LAB HAS SECRETLY ACQUIRED A MANGA WRITTEN IN INKLING LANGUAGE!

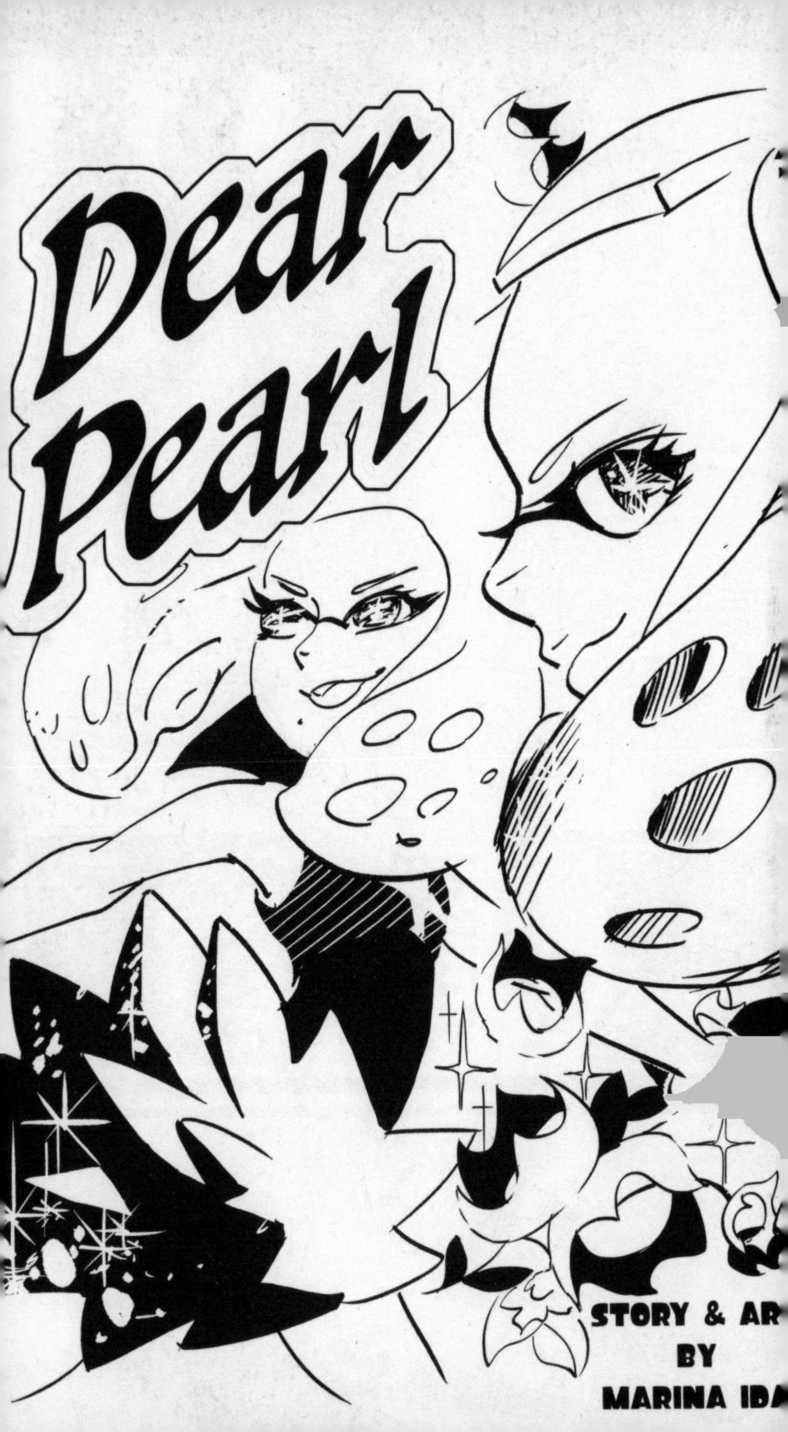
Dear Pearl
STORY & AR
BY
MARINA IDA

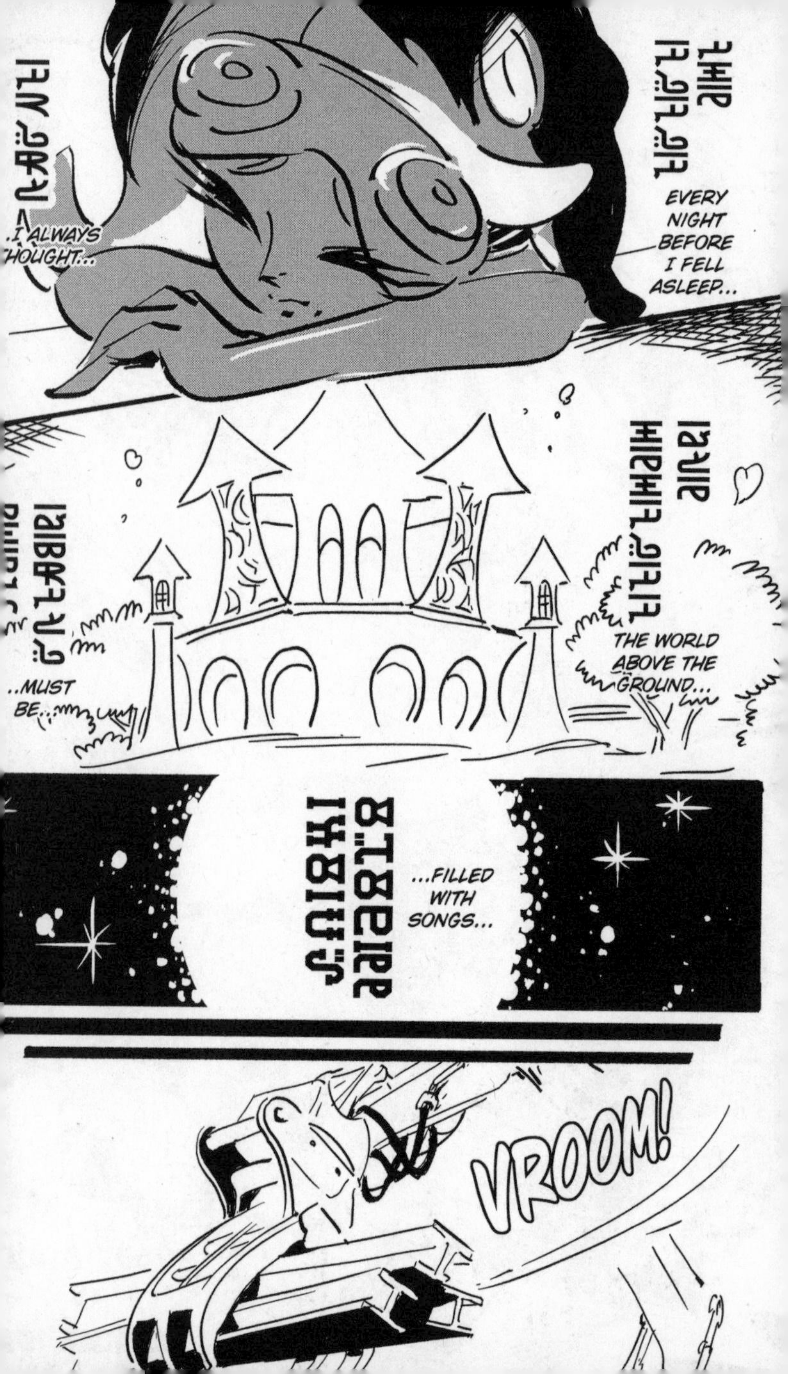
EVERY NIGHT BEFORE I FELL ASLEEP...
...I ALWAYS THOUGHT...
THE WORLD ABOVE THE GROUND...
...MUST BE...
...FILLED WITH SONGS...
VROOM!

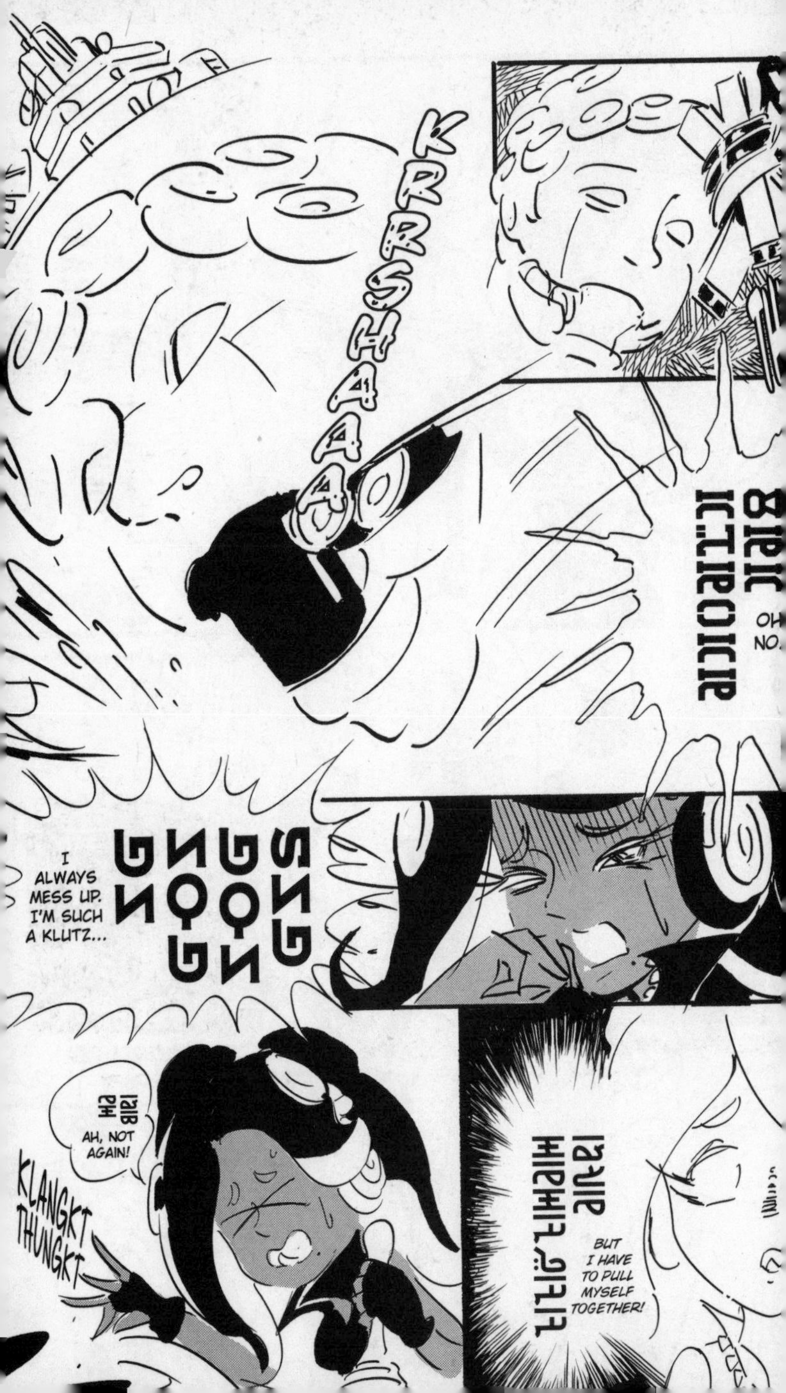
OH NO.
BUT I HAVE TO PULL MYSELF TOGETHER!
KRRSHAAAA
I ALWAYS MESS UP. I'M SUCH A KLUTZ...
AH, NOT AGAIN!
KLANGKT THUNGKT

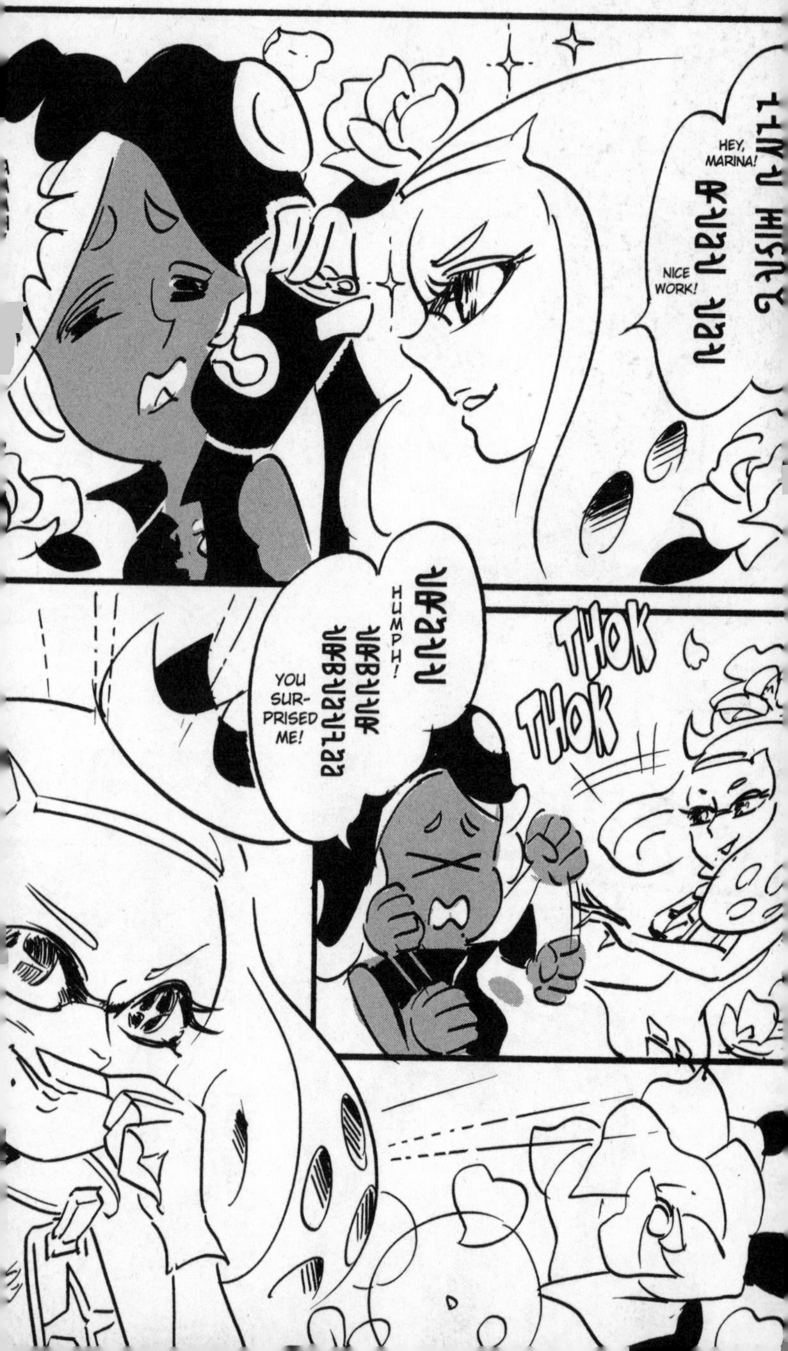
HEY, MARINA!
NICE WORK!
THOK THOK
HUMPH!
YOU SURPRISED ME!

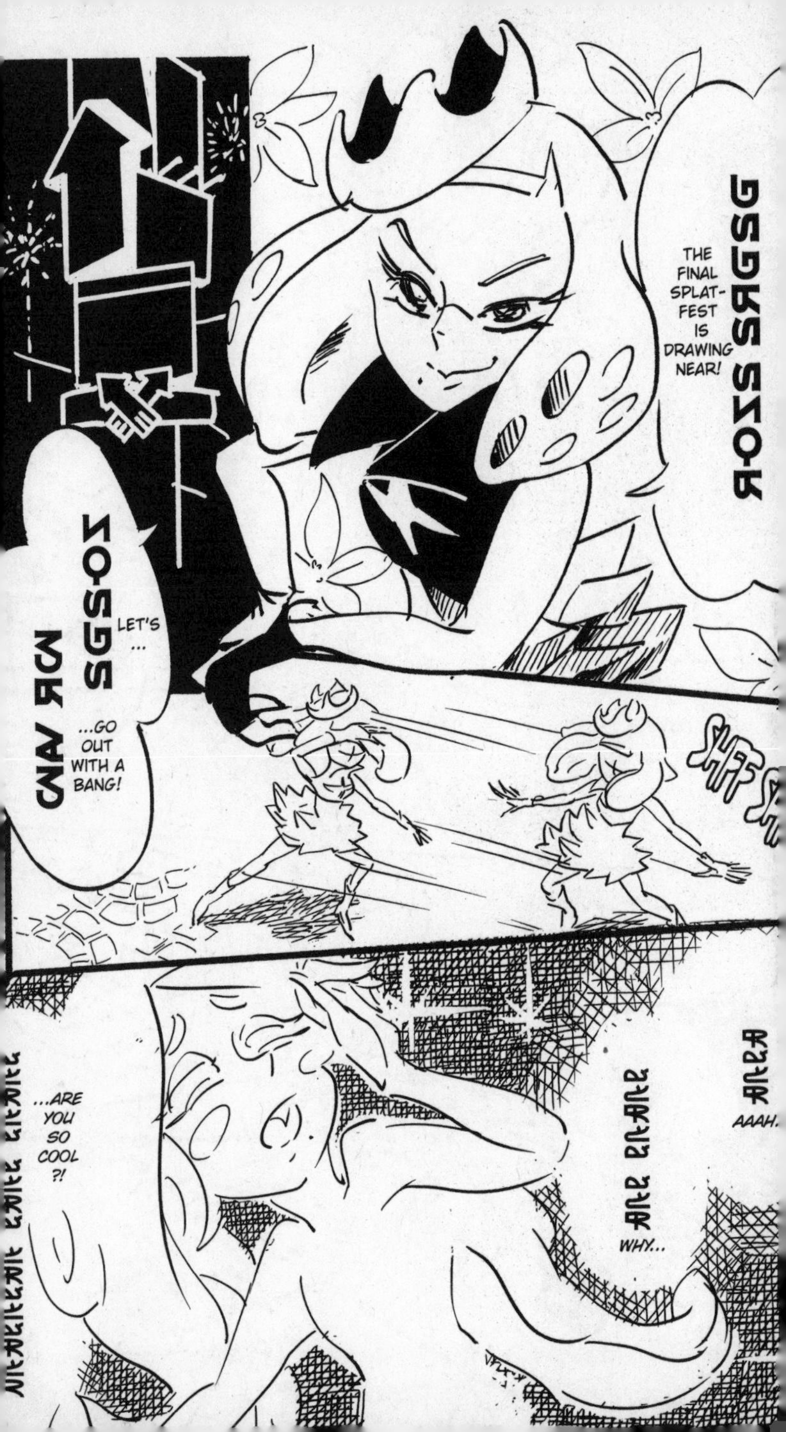
THE FINAL SPLAT-FEST IS DRAWING NEAR!
LET'S ...
...GO OUT WITH A BANG!
AAAH.
WHY...
...ARE YOU SO COOL ?!

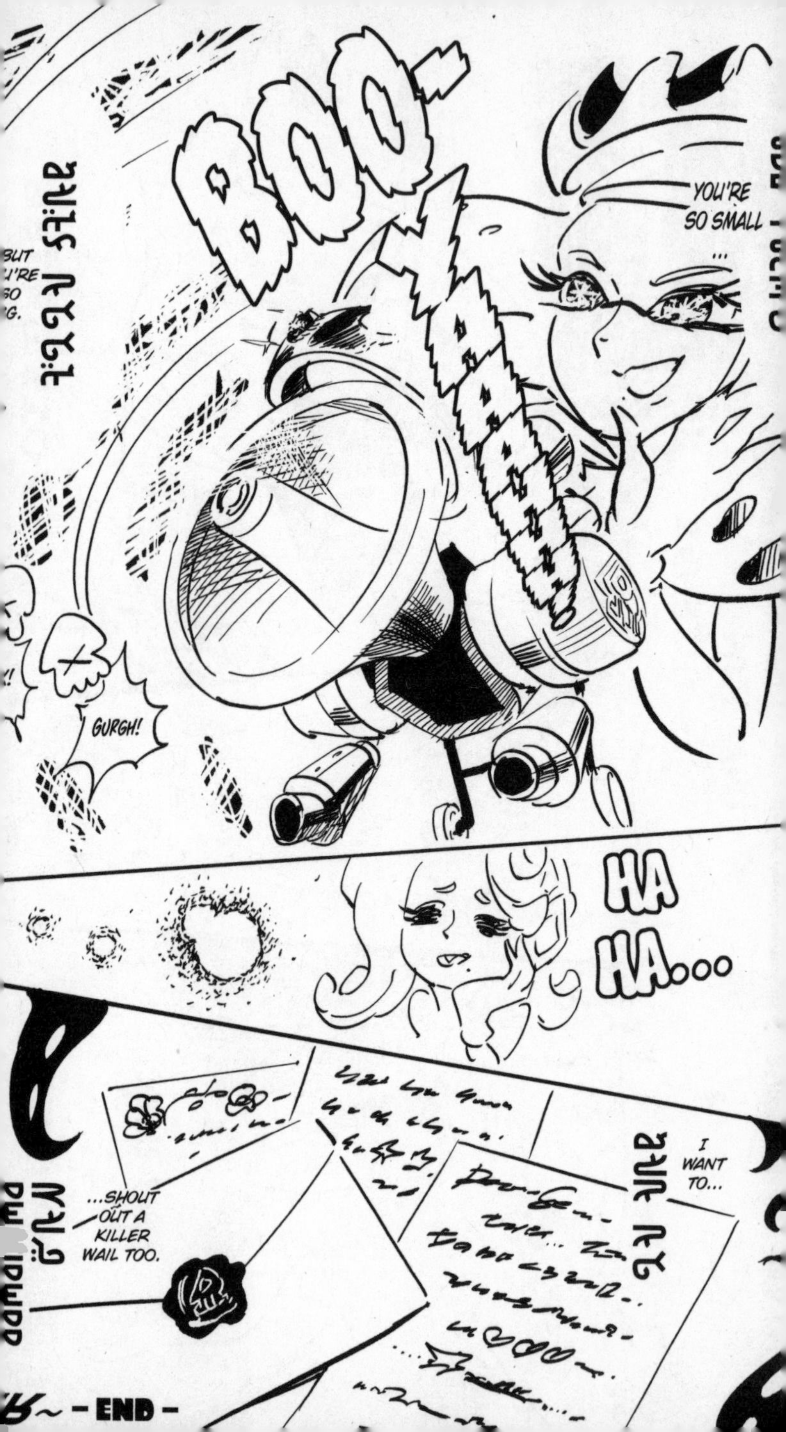

YOU'RE SO SMALL ...
BOO-
GURGH!
HA HA...
I WANT TO...
...SHOUT OUT A KILLER WAIL TOO.
- END -

Squid
Research
Lab, Seita
Inoue, thank
you very
much!

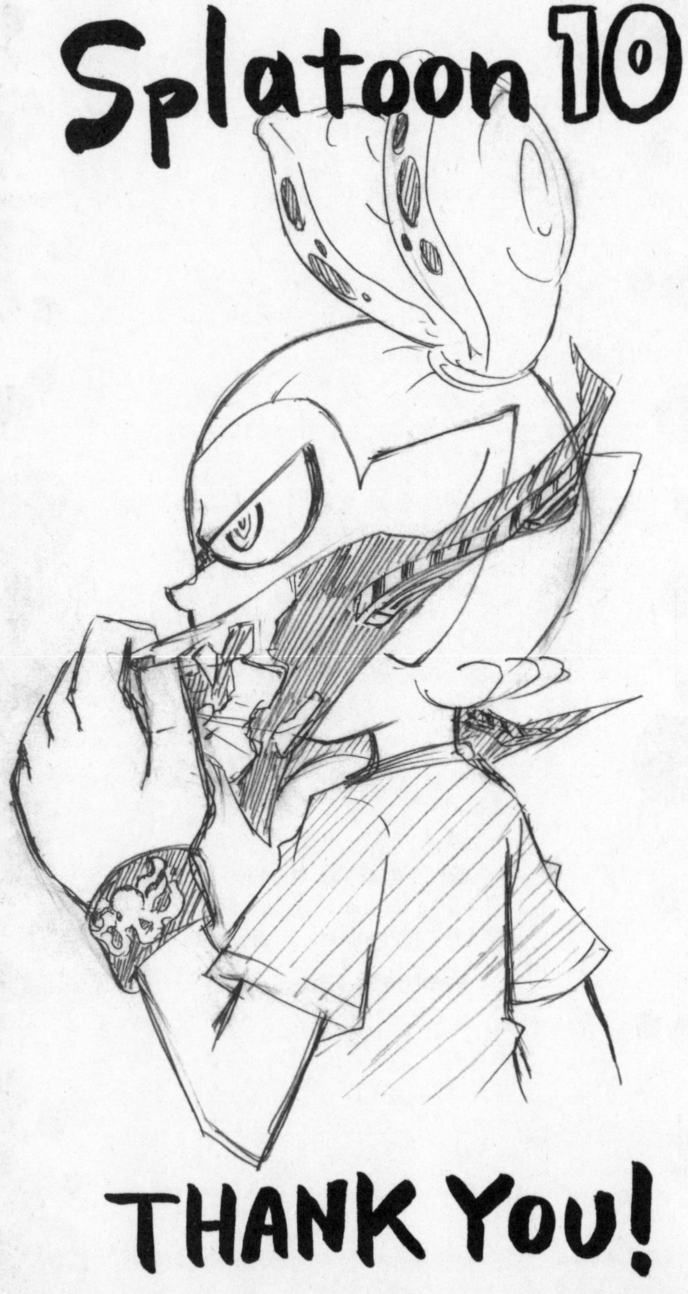
Splatoon 10
THANK YOU!

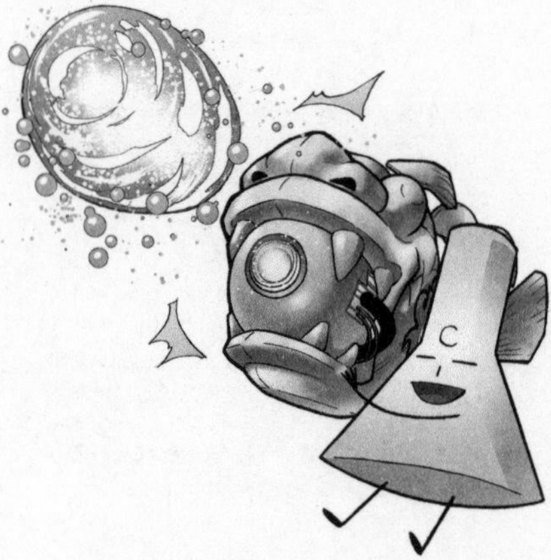

Rainmaker looks like so much fun!!
It's time for the second match
and the tournament semifinals!

Sankichi Hinodeya

Splatoon

Volume 10
VIZ Media Edition

Story and Art by
Sankichi Hinodeya

Translation **Tetsuichiro Miyaki**
English Adaptation **Bryant Turnage**
Lettering **John Hunt**
Design **Kam Li**
Editor **Joel Enos**

SPLATOON Vol. 10 by Sankichi HINODEYA
© 2016 Sankichi HINODEYA
All rights reserved.
Original Japanese edition published by SHOGAKUKAN.
English translation rights in the United States of America,
Canada, the United Kingdom, Ireland, Australia and
New Zealand arranged with SHOGAKUKAN.

The stories, characters and incidents mentioned
in this publication are entirely fictional.

Original Design **100percent**

Printed in the U.S.A.

Published by VIZ Media, LLC
P.O. Box 77010
San Francisco, CA 94107

10 9 8 7 6 5 4 3 2 1
First Printing, September 2020

PARENTAL ADVISORY
SPLATOON is rated A and is suit-
able for readers of all ages.

viz.com

Splatoon reads from right to left!

This is the end of this graphic novel.